THE
CROWN OF
MOONLIGHT

ALSO BY MARTINA BOONE

LOVE FOR TWO LIFETIMES

THE CELTIC LEGENDS COLLECTION

LAKE OF DESTINY
BELL OF ETERNITY
MAGIC OF WINTER
ECHO OF GLORY
HEART OF LEGEND

HEIRS OF WATSON ISLAND SERIES

COMPULSION
PERSUASION
ILLUSION

THE FIVE CROWNS: BOOK ONE

THE
CROWN
OF
MOONLIGHT

MARTINA BOONE

MAYFAIR
PUBLISHING

THE CROWN OF MOONLIGHT is a work of fiction, and the characters, events, and places depicted in it are products of the author's imagination. Where actual events, places, organisations, or persons, living or dead, are included, they are used fictitiously and not intended to be taken otherwise.

MAYFAIR
PUBLISHING
712 H Street NE, Suite 1014
Washington, DC 20002
First Mayfair Publishing edition, November 2025
Copyright © 2025 by Martina Boone
Cover copyright © 2025 by Mayfair Publishing

Jacket design by Arsalan Ali
Map illustration by Irene Adam
Published in the United States of America
Library of Congress Control Number: 2025922040
ISBN 978-1-946773-24-1 (hardback)
ISBN 978-1-946773-26-5 (paperback)
ISBN 978-1-946773-25-8 (e-book)
Enhanced Edition

NEVER LOSE HOPE

FOR A FULL-COLOUR VERSION OF THE MAP, SEE

HTTP://WWW.MARTINABOONE.COM/TCOM-MAP

THIS BOOK IS WRITTEN IN UK ENGLISH IN KEEPING WITH THE SETTING AND SUBJECT MATTER. SOME WORDS AND TERMS WILL BE SPELLED DIFFERENTLY THAN AMERICAN READERS ARE USED TO SEEING.

WARNING: THE STORY TAKES PLACE DURING A BRUTAL PERIOD OF WAR. IT CONTAINS MATURE CONTENT, INCLUDING EXPLICIT LANGUAGE, CONSENSUAL SEX, DEATH, TORTURE, VIOLENCE, SEXUAL THREAT, OFF-PAGE SEXUAL ASSAULT, AND CHILDHOOD TRAUMA AND ABUSE.

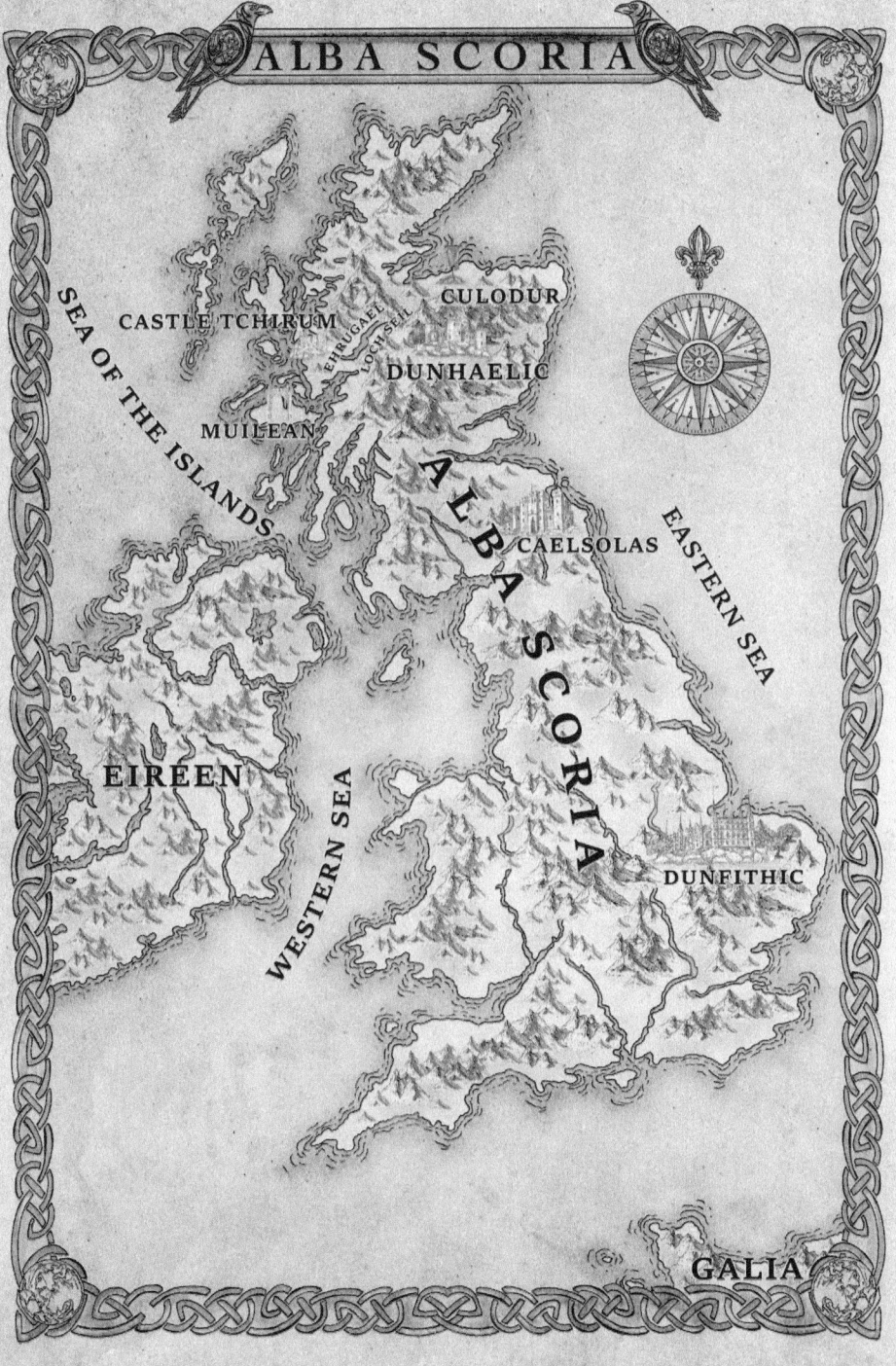

Important Pronunciations

For a full character and location reference list with pronunciations, plus a bonus painting, please see the Glossary, Pronunciations & Terms guide located at the back of this book.

Alba Scoria (AL-buh SKO-ree-uh)
Anvar'thaine (an-var-THAYN)
Cailleach (KAL-yakh)
Chyr (KHEER)
Dunhaelic (doon-HAY-lik)
Flora Domhnall (FLOH-ruh DOH-nuhl)
Siorai (SHEER-ee)
Tirnaeve (tir-NAY-veh)
Vheara (VYAR-uh)

1739 YEARS AGO: Everfolk pass through the Veil from Tirnaeve into Alba Scoria and begin exploiting and kidnapping humans.

1694 YEARS AGO: Human uprisings, resistance, and retaliation begin against the Everfolk.

1642 YEARS AGO: Tirnaeve banishes the powerful runesmith Vheara for crimes against humanity. Queen Nicnevin of Alba Scoria and High King Chulainn Solas of Tirnaeve sign the Compact to end the Human Uprisings, limit immortal and human interaction, and seal the doorways through the Veil.

402 YEARS AGO: Fionn Solas comes through the Veil and murders the last human queen in violation of the Compact. He declares himself the Sun King, murders the queen's potential heirs, outlaws human magic on pain of death, and prohibits women from leading clans.

14 MONTHS AGO: Vheara escapes from her banishment in the Gloaming, murders Fionn, and declares herself the Raven Queen of Alba Scoria.

ONE YEAR AGO: Fionn's son brings the Riders of the Anvar'thaine to Alba Scoria to reclaim the Sun King's throne from Vheara, starting a brutal war between immortals that forces humans to choose sides and pits clans against each other.

PRESENT DAY

CHAPTER 1
STRANGER IN THE WOOD

FLORA

W ar is never glorious. That's a lesson we women learn at our mothers' knees. Apart from those closest to the immortal royals, no human in Alba Scoria will benefit from this battle over the throne they stole from us—the one neither side deserves.

Destruction marches ever closer, and I'm preparing in every way I can: working the horses, storing food for a siege, readying medicines for the injured. The Clan Council may never accept me as Chief, and the Ever laws may forbid it. But none of that changes the fact that I won't let Dunhaelic fall.

Today, the cold bites deep. My fingers are numb on the reins against Ari's steaming neck. The sun spills pink and crimson over the hilltops behind us, yet ahead in the Sacred Wood where the old military road climbs among the ancient trees, frost and gloom still linger beneath the mid-April canopy.

Ordinarily, I'd turn back at the edge of the Wood. Now I give in to a whisper of rebellion instead. Urging the stallion faster, I lose myself in the sensations: the surge of his muscles, the chuff of his breath, the thunder of hooves on hard-packed earth. Crouched low over Ari's mane, the wind whips my face and billows the long skirt I've kilted through my belt for riding.

We're flying, the ground blurring beneath Ari's strides. Then he suddenly snorts and throws his head. His shoulder drops out from under me, and he turns to bolt back the way we came.

I fight to keep my seat and hold him.

"Easy, lad. What is it?" I pull him in a circle, patting his neck as I force him forward again. He watches the slope on our right with his ears pinned back and his eyes rimmed white.

Nothing stirs around us. Nothing rustles. Yet still Ari bucks and fishtails, jolting me against the pommel.

Pain flashes white, and I circle him again, keeping him moving.

Then I realise that I've been slow to understand. It's always hard for me to pinpoint the source of sound. My left ear is deaf—lost to a fever when my father sent for healers who arrived three days too late—but I don't need both ears to hear what *isn't* there.

Silence coils around us. Gone is the usual dawn chorus of thrushes and blackbirds, whose morning calls can seem insistent enough to wake the dead. Gone, too, are the rustlings of squirrel and hunting cat, of marten and deer and capercaillie.

Something large is hiding among the trees.

It's the perfect place for an ambush. Centuries of wagon wheels and iron-shod horses have worn the road away, leaving steep banks of earth and roots on either side that cut off any escape. The thick-trunked trees would give good cover for a highwayman or a deserter to lie in wait, but it could also be some of our own missing men returning.

I whistle the five notes of Dunhaelic's signal call and wait. No one answers.

Still, part of me clings to hope. We've already lost my brothers and father, along with too many warriors, in the battles that came before the recent massacre at Culodur.

If any of our men survived, I need to know. They could be weak, or wounded and unconscious.

Shifting Ari's reins to one hand, I draw the dagger from my belt. My fighting skills are limited, but if all else fails, I have my one trick of outlawed magic to help—my ability to grow the blade into a sword. I have only a remnant of the ancient Cailleach power passed down in my Domhnall blood, though I've spent years coaxing it out in secret, learning to control it despite the death sentence it carries. These days, though, one death is as good as another. I can only pray that if I have to use the magic, the ember of power inside me will be enough.

I kick Ari sharply. He rears in protest, then surges into a gallop. I run him ten yards, wheel him, and use his momentum to scramble up the bank.

Weaving through trees and low-growing brush, I search for intruders and follow a diagonal line towards the ridge to cut off anyone lurking near the road. The haunting stillness follows us, and Ari's footsteps rustling through the leaves and bracken sound impossibly loud. Then twenty yards below the ridge, a gust of wind stirs up a strange, sweet scent.

Fingers of ice crawl along my back.

I've encountered this stench before—only once, but some memories burn themselves into your soul and refuse to fade. The smell hurls me back four months into the landscape of my nightmares.

I'm walking among the bloated dead on the battlefield where I went to retrieve the bodies of my father and oldest brother. Searching each corpse for familiar features, I stumble over the severed head of a

3

Grey—one of the Raven Queen's monstrous enforcers. Its bleached irises stare sightlessly, ash-coloured skin stretched over features twisted by the Queen's corrupted magic.

I back away in horror and fall onto the Grey's headless body. The sweet stench of its blood is everywhere, infused with a dark magic that claws against my skin and makes my own power recoil. Lurching to my feet, I brush at the crust of dried blood that clings to my hands, my skirts, my bodice—wherever I touched the Grey's stained uniform and scarlet cloak.

The memory chokes my lungs. I gulp deep breaths and blink away the tears that blur my eyes.

Today, I will not cry.

My tension, on top of the smell of blood, only adds to Ari's nerves. He plants his legs and refuses to go farther.

"Easy, my handsome," I whisper. "We can both be brave."

If there's a Grey bleeding in the Sacred Wood, I need to know. I can't risk having one of the Raven Queen's abominations follow me back to Dunhaelic Keep.

Ari rears as I kick him forward. His front legs thrash the air. Then his hind legs skid on the incline, and I jump from the saddle to keep him from going over backwards. Clinging to the reins, I pull his head down and wait until he steadies. His heart pounds so hard it thuds against my shoulder.

I coax him forward. Then a dozen yards below the ridge, we edge around a thicket of dog rose blocking our path, and Ari snorts and stops. Head low and ears pricked, he stares fixedly at something on the ground ahead.

The trees have thinned to scattered birches and wind-gnarled pines. Light slants through them to reveal a man lying on his back. A few yards beyond him, a second man lies face down. He's tied across the saddle of a dappled mare who's collapsed onto her side. The mare's ears twitch, but she doesn't raise her head.

Neither man is moving.

They aren't Greys—they don't have the pale skin or deformed limbs of the monsters the Raven Queen uses as enforcers. But they aren't human, either.

The magic of the mortal Cailleach Queens was outlawed four hundred years ago when the Sun King came through the Veil and butchered most of my bloodline. Where the ancient magic survives, we guard the secret closely, but what little remains in my blood doesn't carry nearly the strength that charges the air around these Everfolk.

They've done their best to look ordinary, dressing themselves in coats and breeches like tradesmen from the south instead of their usual finery or the kilted plaids our Highland warriors wear. Still, even if I couldn't sense the magic coming from them, the swords buckled at their belts would give them away as the rebel king's companions.

My pulse kicks into a run as I consider what their presence—and deaths—might mean. Neither side in this cursed war is any better than the other. Not only that, but these men didn't die alone. Their bodies have been arranged. The man on the horse is tied to the saddle, but the other lies like a corpse in a coffin, with his hands folded across his chest.

Someone else was here—may still be here.

The thought brings on an eerie sense of being watched. Gooseskin prickles along my arms, and the sweat-slicked hilt of the dagger digs deeper into my palm.

I turn in a slow, wide circle, searching every shadow that shifts in the wind and each tree trunk thick enough to offer a place to hide. Nothing moves, and Ari's attention stays fixed on the mare and the two dead bodies around her.

Eventually, my heartbeat eases. Inch by inch, I persuade Ari to move upwind until I find a sturdy tree where I can tie him. Then I creep back for a closer look. Ari whickers anxiously, pulling at his reins and pivoting to watch me.

The sweet smell of the Evers' blood and the warmth of magic thicken as I approach the bodies. I can't see where the man on the horse is injured, but he's bled enough to leave a purple-brown crust dried along the withers, belly, and foreleg of his horse, and more blood has stained the coat and shirt front of the man lying stretched out on the ground. Yet if they are truly Everfolk, and if any of the ancient stories are to be believed, then it makes no sense that they would die of wounds like these.

According to the stories our elders tell by firelight, Everfolk can only die if their heads are removed or their hearts are pierced by steel forged with a celestial ore fallen from the heavens. Such a death is instant, leaving no time for their healing magic to do its work.

These men still have their heads, and if their hearts were pierced, then they must have been here in the Sacred Wood when they were killed. That is a problem for many reasons.

In all the generations since the doorways through the Veil were closed, we can name only twelve Evers who crossed here from Tirnaeve: the Sun King who murdered our last true queen, Vheara—the Raven Queen—who killed him last year, and the rebel king and his Riders who arrived shortly after to challenge her for what he considers to be his father's crown.

If these dead Evers were among the rebel king's close companions, the Sun King's so-called heir will demand revenge.

Snakes of fear coil through my heart as I think it over. The king's wrath isn't the only danger. If Vheara discovers Riders here, she'll take it as proof that I've been sheltering her enemies.

Neither side would need to prove any of us at Dunhaelic were guilty of these deaths. Their laws make it a hanging offence to harm an Ever—no questions, no trial, and no reprieve. And I wouldn't face the gallows by myself.

Vengeance, like water, trickles down to those below, and everyone I'm meant to protect would be as good as dead.

My knees shake as I move to the nearest Ever. I crouch beside him, and a hot flush of magic ripples across my skin. More magic than I've ever felt. But that's not the only shock. Although the ancient tales talk about the beauty of the Everfolk, seeing it in front of me makes my breath catch.

The Ever is handsome in a way that explains the warnings in the ancient stories—the blinding, dangerous sort of beauty that's said to make humans lose their will and descend into madness. His features are too eerily perfect, his black hair has the gleam of raven's wings, and the blue eyes that look unseeingly into the sky catch the light like layers of stained glass, revealing more colours the deeper I look.

His sightless stare unnerves me, and I brush my fingers across his lids to close them. The skin is still warm. I flinch from the contact, and my hand grazes a pale-blue crystal set in a ring on his right hand.

A jolt of pure power jars me as I touch it—so hot and bright that it pulls an answering flare from the ember of magic that burns inside me. Snatching my hand away, I wait for the sensation to ebb. But I miss it when it's gone. My magic misses it, which makes no sense since my magic isn't Ever magic. Careful not to touch the ring again, I bend closer to examine the crystal set within it. There's movement inside, gold threads of magic dancing like lightning behind a thin haze of cloud.

The movement is mesmerising, holding me captive a moment too long after Ari snorts and stomps his foot. By the time the thud and the jingling of his bridle finally register, his muscles are braced as he uses his back to pull harder against the reins that tie him to the tree.

Then a twig snaps somewhere close. Behind me? To the left? I spin around, searching. But there's nothing. No one.

Well, I refuse to play this game.

"Who's there? Come out and show yourself instead of hiding like a coward."

The Wood falls unnaturally still. Then shadows stir beneath an oak tree to my left.

"I know you're there," I say, gripping the dagger tighter.

A voice answers me from the shadows. "Careful, little one. Taunt the things you fear, and you might just prove you were right to be afraid."

The voice is male—slow and resonant, pitched between a growl and a cat's deep purr. A predator's voice, claws barely sheathed.

A shiver of awareness ripples down my spine. I draw on the cool, gritty power of the earth and fuse it with the fire that burns inside me. Needles of magic rake through bone and tissue as I force it outward, pouring it into the dagger. The blade groans, lengthening and thickening until it becomes a perfect replica of my father's sword and rests cold, heavy, and steadying within my grasp.

An Ever steps forward, his figure cloaked in gloom, footsteps whispering over the frost-crusted moss. He's larger than the bodies behind me seemed, taller and broader, his features carved in bold strokes beneath gilded hair that's tied half-up in a warrior's knot and reveals a widow's peak. He looks gaunt, worn down, though power and command still radiate from him. He's every bit as beautiful as the others—and devastatingly *male*.

He watches me with a faint, treacherous smile. "You can put that illusion away," he says. "You're lucky I didn't mistake it for a threat."

"The sword is no illusion," I say, "and the threat is no mistake."

His easy dismissal stings more than I'd care to admit. I

spent months mastering even this small feat of magic, pouring all my strength and then waiting days—sometimes weeks—for the ember inside me to grow warm enough to try again.

The Ever's eyes harden, the molten honey colour darkening perilously. "You do know what I am, don't you?"

"An Ever...a Rider," I say, resisting the urge to spit the words and still hoping there's a different explanation.

His jaw tightens visibly. "We are *Siorai*. Not Evers. Not Everfolk. Your mortal epithet is impolite."

"You murder us then lecture me about politeness?" I pause to catch my breath. "Just leave. Go away. No one here has done anything to harm you, and we don't want any trouble." My voice stays steady, but the sword quivers and gives me away.

The Ever moves towards me, one step, then two. I back an equal distance, giving myself time to think.

The width of his shoulders and the way his muscled thighs and arms strain the seams of his clothes leave no doubt about his strength. His hand rests on the hilt of his sword in silent threat. Then he steps even closer, emerging from the shadows into a shaft of broken sunlight, and for the first time, I see the blood that slicks his coat and seeps down one leg of the breeches he wears tucked into leather boots. His skin is pale and beaded with sweat, the silver-gold hair that falls to his shoulders damp at the temples and clinging in darker strands along his jaw.

He's wounded. Weak. That gives me a chance.

My blade won't kill an Ever, but I'd lay odds his is made of celestial steel. Is he weak enough that I can grab it?

His mouth twitches at the corners as if he knows exactly what I'm thinking. "Don't do anything foolish," he says in that deep purr of a voice. "Believe me, if I'd wanted you dead, you would never have seen me coming."

The words should terrify me, but it's the way his jaw

tightens and the bitterness in that quiet promise that sends something sharper through my veins. As if he's more angry at himself than he is at me.

I can't let that deter me. Gripping my own sword tighter, I reach for more magic to feed it. Then I wait for an opening.

CHAPTER 2

BLOODY PALMS

CHYR

The woman must have a death wish. I've no magic left, and I can scarcely lift the sword I've carried nearly all my life, yet I could still crush her as easily as a rose beneath my heel.

If she fears me, she hides it well. She promises nothing and cloaks herself in defiance, which only makes the situation harder. Another soul on my conscience today would be the straw that breaks me, but if she attacks me, I'll have no choice. The cursed oathbands carved into my flesh don't care about innocence or courage. If they judge her a threat to the king's orders, they'll make me their weapon regardless of my wishes.

I need a way to save her from herself. *From me.*

Tuirse and Oran, my brothers in arms these past four centuries, are dead from these strange wounds that do not heal, and I couldn't protect any of the countless mortals who've died trying to help us. Reaching Tirnaeve to demand the army we were promised isn't only required to win the war. It's the one way I can make those deaths count for something. Oaths aside, I can't put that at risk by letting this woman get word back to the Raven witch that we were here.

A hard pulse beats at the hinge of my jaw. "Tell me how your illusion works," I say. "Is Vheara giving out some new sort of amulet to her allies?"

"The Raven Queen has given nothing to anyone but herself." The woman sends me a glare that could eviscerate a man at fifty paces. "Not that your so-called king is any better."

The answer doesn't help me much. It says little about the woman's loyalty, but then I'm not sure what I'm hoping to achieve. The size of the bounty Vheara has placed on our heads would tempt a priest to turn his mother over.

Thinking is getting harder. The wind sweeps down from the crest of the hill, and I clench my teeth to stop them chattering. Without my magic, I'm cold to my marrow, and the early sun brings scant warmth to the moss-strewn earth.

I'm not used to being weak. My power has always been enough, and I've scoffed at the other Riders for paying the High King's runesmiths to carve more damned magic into their skin without knowing what was actually embedded in it. Still, in this moment, I'd give a great deal for a rune or two. A small glyph to bolster my air magic could raise the temperature around me and dry the cold sweat from my skin. A conduit to my fire magic could heat my blood and stop the shivering. Simple tasks, both of them. Tasks I've taken for granted since I was no more than a cub, but now I've no power left, and my body diverts every bit of power I can pull from Tirnaeve through my Veilstone ring directly into keeping me alive.

My hand shakes as I pull it from the hilt of my sword and show the woman my open palms to prove it. I don't want her to fear me. In truth, I am tired of being little more than a weapon. "Threatening each other serves no purpose. Can we call a truce?"

The woman's eyes narrow as she frowns at my hands, which I realise belatedly are slick with blood. That's probably not the soothing gesture I had hoped it would be.

Whether she chooses to believe I don't mean to hurt her, or she simply can't hold the illusion any longer, she finally lets the magic go. The sword shrinks and reshapes itself until only a narrow, ordinary dagger remains.

Black dots dance across my vision. I step towards her, treading with care to keep the wound in my chest from bleeding faster.

"Do you have a house nearby?" I ask. "I need a shovel and a horse that isn't spent. If you'll let me borrow those and pretend you never saw me, I'll ensure you're paid twice the reward that Vheara's offering for information."

"Is that your alternative to killing me and stealing my stallion?" Her chin lifts, and she draws herself up, her shoulders stiff and stubborn. "How do I know you won't do that anyway the moment I let down my guard?"

"Forget the horse, then. I'll be thankful for the shovel and your promise."

"I don't want your money. Not everyone's for sale."

"Please. I'm asking for your help. My magic and the mare are both exhausted, and Oran and Tuirse are—they *were*—my friends. My brothers. I can't leave them like this. Surely everyone deserves dignity in death. Don't they?"

"The same dignity your kind gives us?" she asks with her voice shaking. "Leaving our dead to rot on your battlefields until their own families can scarcely find any familiar features? Slaughtering us in violation of the Compact between our worlds? The fact you're in Alba Scoria at all breaks that accord— stripping us of what little dignity your laws have left us."

Oran or Tuirse would have had her on her knees at swordpoint for her disrespect if they were alive. Others among the Riders would be laying bets on who would bed her first. The thought sits uncomfortably, and I push it away.

I need to focus.

She's defying the Master of the Anvar'thaine, but when she lifts her chin despite the fear in her eyes, what I feel is closer to admiration than irritation. That's its own kind of problem.

Yet she isn't wrong.

I step closer, searching for something to say—an apology, a reassurance. A way for her to see *me* rather than the threat I am.

She backs away instead, stumbling over the hem of the skirt kilted into her belt. The shawl pinned around her shoulders billows in the wind. It's one of those endless Highland plaids, a broad tartan pattern in deep green and blue, shot through with narrow bands of yellow. Her hair whips around her face, the long strands darker near her scalp and streaked everywhere else in shades from moon-pale blonde to red the colour of flame. Her eyes, in stunning contrast, are the sort of cool, deep grey I could sink myself into. They stare back at me, unflinching.

A fresh wave of pain kicks me in the chest. I reach for a stunted birch nearby, clutching the lichen-softened bark to keep from falling.

The woman sighs and turns away.

I expect her to walk uphill to where she left her black beast tied, but she crosses back to Tuirse's dappled mare instead, running practised hands along her legs and withers. Murmuring soothing nonsense, she checks for injuries and pinches the skin on the mare's neck to see how fast it bounces back.

She knows horses, that much is clear. Despite being dehydrated and exhausted, the mare does her best to get up when the woman coaxes her, though Tuirse's weight over the saddle is still too much. Seeing that, the woman rolls Tuirse over, grasps him beneath the arms, and drags him to lie beside Oran on the ground. A feat, given Tuirse's weight.

The woman's chest heaves by the time she's finished. She stands looking down at Tuirse, hesitates, then stoops to cross his hands over his chest in the sign of peace. That's a kindness I don't expect, and somehow it unmans me.

She has nothing to gain from such tenderness, but she gives it despite what she clearly thinks of Siorai and the cruelties we've inflicted on her people.

My chest throbs, and I press my hand against the wound. It's bleeding again. The rough wool of the unfamiliar coat squelches under my fingers, and a wave of dizziness makes the trees spin. The Pit take me, but I'd prefer a blade through the heart over this festering weakness.

It's too much to hope the woman doesn't notice. Of course, she does.

"Sit down before you fall, you bloody idiot," she says. "I'll have enough work burying two bodies without you adding another to the count. Let me get the mare to her feet so she doesn't hurt herself, then I'll see what I can do for you."

It takes a moment to process the words, and I don't dare let go of the birch to lower myself to the ground.

"Thank you," I say. The words come out in a humiliating rasp.

The mare has shifted her weight to get her knees beneath her, but she can't manage the final push to her feet. The woman takes the reins to keep them from tangling and causing the mare to panic. Then a puff of magic surrounds them both—a shimmer and stir of air so faint that if I weren't gifted with magic-sense, I would never notice it. The mare's breath slowly lengthens as she calms.

I didn't see the woman touch an amulet or any rune, and this gentle energy feels nothing like Vheara's corrupted sorcery. The woman is human, I have no doubt, but the native magic of Alba Scoria has been eradicated—the Sun King saw to that—so it's difficult to reconcile what I sense from her with what I know. I'd almost say the woman was using Siorai magic, and that's definitely not possible. The sealed doorways have blocked nearly all of Tirnaeve's power from leaking through. Even the Veilstone rings the runesmiths created to supply us with magic give us far less than we need.

Another cramp of pain squeezes my chest. A crow lands on a nearby branch as if to taunt me, and when the cramp eases, I look up and find the woman staring at me.

A faint pink stains her cheeks when her eyes meet mine. "Do you have a flask?" she asks. "Where are your supplies?"

"We lost them. We've been on the run for days."

Her brows furrow in what looks like disapproval, and I don't know why that bothers me. My uncle taught me early that a traitor's son has no right to anyone's good opinion. Still, I find myself wanting to explain: "We've been evading the queen's hunters since we lost at Culodur three days ago. The battle itself we lived through, but an ambush the next morning left these wounds. We thought nothing of them at the time—they were inflicted by ordinary men with ordinary swords, yet they refuse to heal, and we've had no time to rest. With the three of us injured, we were too slow to outrun a pair of Greys who were closing in. The other Riders took all but Tuirse's mare to draw the Greys away—"

"Greys are close by? *Here*?" The woman's skin has gone pale as if she knows exactly how dangerous that would be.

Every instinct screams at me to say that I'll protect her, but I can't. "If not those two, then others will be coming. The queen will keep searching for us. For anyone who survived the battle. She is out for retribution."

A cough racks my body, and my knees fold out from under me. The bark of the tree grates against my arm as I slide to the ground. The woman runs towards me, but thinking about Vheara and all the destruction she will bring to her enemies makes me remember the danger I'm putting this woman in simply by being here. I can't—I won't—put her at more risk.

"You should leave," I say. My tongue feels stiff, and the woman's face swims in and out of focus. "Save yourself. Pack what you can carry and move your family south. Stay somewhere far from the Highlands until the queen's thirst for revenge is spent. There may be little left here by the time you return, but at least you'll be alive."

Her lips move as she responds, but my ears ring, and I can't hear anything. The ground lurches sideways and rushes up to meet me. Sky and forest and moss-furred earth all blur to black, and my breath escapes when I hit the ground.

The woman's soft hand on my skin is the last thing that I feel. Her touch is warm and kind—and the Father only knows that kindness is more than I deserve. Still, I can't help but crave it.

CHAPTER 3
MERCY IS A WEAPON

FLORA

The Ever crumples to the moss. His pale hair spills around him, and the sharp lines of his jaw go slack in a way that only heightens the shock of seeing all that immortal strength toppled to the ground.

I inhale deeply and try to will myself to stay calm. The scent of birch and pine resin and cool, wet earth serves to ground me. Somewhere a thrush calls and another answers.

I press my hand against the Ever's throat, feeling for his pulse. It's there, faint and thready. He isn't dead. Not yet, anyway, but there's too much blood seeping from his chest.

Why isn't his body healing itself? Evers are meant to be able to survive almost any wound, and this injury must have happened days ago.

Though really, it would make things simpler if he died. Wouldn't it?

He's unconscious, and his sword lies within easy reach. The pommel glimmers in the sunlight, a solid globe of yellow crystal with a heart that glows like fire. I can feel the heat and magic rolling from it, so there's no doubt the weapon is made of celestial steel.

He probably wouldn't even feel it if I drove the blade into his heart. Then I could bury all three Evers deep enough to ensure no one would ever find them.

I stare down at him, trying to work up the courage to take the sword from its scabbard. But even unconscious, there's something about him that is equal parts magnificent and vulnerable. Something almost human in the way his brows draw together, leaving a small crease that speaks of tension, and in the way that pain etches small brackets around his lips.

Like generations of women in my family, both of my grandmothers were healers. The thought of betraying what they taught me makes my heart pound and my stomach sink.

Mercy is a two-edged weapon. I have no doubt it will come back to make me bleed. Yet I can't bring myself to kill the Ever, and I won't let him die. Though his presence here is dangerous, if I kill him while he's defenceless, I'd be no better than the Everfolk are.

Cursing myself, I drop to my knees beside him. Cold damp from the moss seeps through my skirts as I lay him on his back.

He doesn't wake, even when I unfasten the buttons of his coat and drag it from his shoulders. The fabric catches on his arm, and his shirtsleeve slides down to his elbow, revealing a dozen or more rows of runes circling his biceps in tight black bands. They're not tattoos—not merely that. Scored deep into the flesh, they're blackened in a way that's left them angry. Something about them repels me, and I find myself reaching for my dagger to slit his shirt open so that I don't have to touch them as I pull it off.

There's a thick, blood-soaked bandage already wrapped

around his chest and stomach. I slice through that, too, and my nose wrinkles at the sharp, metallic tang of something that isn't the iron found in human blood. This is more like the air after a lightning strike.

The sodden bandage drips with blood as I peel it back to reveal a gash that starts a hairbreadth below whatever passes for the Ever's heart. Bone gleams white between torn flesh crusted with unnatural streaks of black that make my magic roil and flinch away. My hands shake as I sit back on my heels, but that area nearest the heart is the worst of all the damage. The wound grows shallower down the laddered muscles of his abdomen, and by the time it vanishes under the waistband of the breeches that sit low across his hips, it's little more than a thin pink line of healing skin.

The Ever groans beneath my touch, rolling his body towards me, his breath too hot against my wrist.

The blackening worries me more than his fever does. I've only seen this sort of reaction once—when my brothers shot a boar with arrows dipped in wolfsbane. It took the poor, poisoned beast days to die.

Unless I help him, the Ever won't survive. He certainly won't be strong enough to leave. It's a full day's ride to the boundaries of Domhnall land in every direction, and if he collapses again, there's no telling who might find him.

Even if I decide to treat him, I'll need water and supplies, and he's too weak for me to move him. I'll have to work in stages.

With a sigh, I reach beneath my skirt and use my dagger to cut off a section of my chemise to serve as a temporary bandage before I leave to gather moss and pine pitch to slow the bleeding.

I push his coat aside, and something crackles in the left pocket—a folded piece of parchment sealed in wax.

A corner of the document is stained with blood nearly the same red-brown colour as the seal. The wax is warm from the heat of the Ever's body, and it has lifted away from the paper on one side. It practically begs me to read it, but the Ever is still losing blood.

I set the document aside while I take advantage of his unconscious state and bind his chest as tightly as I can. Then I pick the document up again and weigh the potential invasion of privacy if I read it against my responsibilities.

It's well past sunrise now, and Dunhaelic Keep will be in motion. Iain will be feeding the mares, Faolan checking the battlements, Morag baking, and Catriona carrying my mother's breakfast to her solar. Peat smoke and warm yeast will mix with the scent of horses and heather on the wind. These are the scents of my beloved Dunhaelic.

There's so little left of what my home once was, and too few people remaining in my care. Some days, the loneliness of carrying all that weighs heavier than the grief, but I feel guilty even thinking that. Those who remain with me have lost as much in this war as I have, yet they work beside me every day to keep what's left intact. I cannot let them down.

The parchment unfolds with a whispered hush, and I read the first words. My heart kicks into a sprint as I realise the document is a letter addressed to the rebel king.

> *Your Royal Highness,*
>
> *As no one in Alba Scoria has gambled more than I have in supporting your cause, I find myself deeply affected by our loss at Culodur and the difficulty in which Your R.H. finds himself.*
>
> *Sir, I hope you will forgive a few truths upon which all our commanders agree. It was highly wrong of the High King to send you here without the men, gold, and supplies needed to restore you to your crown. If the Raven Queen retains the throne of Alba Scoria, it shall be on that account.*

I must also acquaint Your R.H. that we are all convinced Lord Sean, whom Your R.H. considers the greatest of friends, committed gross blunders on every occasion. By overruling me on the subject of retreat, I must assure you that this man, in whom you have placed so much trust, has either betrayed you or is as unfit to be a general as he is to be a shoemaker. He has disgusted all our army to such a degree that it bred a mutiny in our ranks. In short, you place too much confidence in him and in one or two of your other companions.

Please consider this warning as you plan your return from Eireen with the additional mercenaries needed. I shall await word of your plans to land the reinforcements and stand ready to venture my life in the cause whenever Your R.H. returns. But to be sure, unless Lord Sean and your Riders give greater regard to my opinions, I cannot flatter myself with hopes of success.

I remain, with great zeal, Sir, Your R.H.'s most obedient and humble servant,

Seoras Mora

The letter trembles in my hand. I read it through a second time before folding it closed.

Lord Mora—General Mora—commands the rebel army.

This letter matters. It makes the Ever an even larger target for the Raven Queen, but it does more than that.

If Vheara finds out the rebel king means to land a force of Siorai warriors from Tirnaeve, along with hired soldiers from other mortal realms, she would scorch the earth to stop him. And does the king already know that one or more of his Riders may be a traitor? Is the traitor the reason the two Riders are dead and the third barely clings to life? Why the idea that the

Ever has been betrayed makes me angry, makes me ache for him, I don't dare examine too closely.

General Mora could be wrong, of course. I know too little to make assumptions. But the thought that crosses my mind before I can stop it is ugly and practical at once: this letter is a weapon. In the right hands—or the wrong ones—it could change the outcome of the war.

The main problem remains the same. Whichever side wins the war, there will be an Ever on the throne of Alba Scoria, and I've no right to decide that outcome.

Keeping Clan Domhnall safe grows harder day by day, and the people in my care will pay for my mistakes. Indecision helps no one, though. I need to move.

CHAPTER 4

OUT OF MAGIC

CHYR

My head pounds like war drums, and my chest is on fire. I blink against the sunlight. The wind lifts the scent of pine mixed with blood and resinous smoke.

I'm sitting, and my back is propped against a narrow, lichen-crusted birch. The sun is high, so I must have drifted in and out of consciousness for hours.

Disjointed images shift through my mind: a beautiful face outlined in flame and moonlight, a voice commanding me to drink. Before that, or maybe after, the same voice is coaxing Tuirse's mare to drink.

And Oran's body...

Shivering, I remember his boot heels cutting through leaf-strewn moss as the woman dragged him up the hill and out of sight.

My mouth is as dry as ash and tastes of human whisky, which explains the pounding head. Was it the flame-haired woman who gave me that? But why? At least I couldn't have drunk much of it, or as miserable as I am at the moment, I'd be feeling worse.

I can smell her on me: crushed bog myrtle and rosemary, with a damp undertone of earth. The scent clings to my skin and to a clean bandage that gleams white against the filthy tatters of my bloody shirt and unbuttoned coat.

Earlier, when she was holding the sword illusion, she looked at me as though she hoped the blade was real so she could gut me with it. Yet when she had an opportunity, she tended to my wound instead. I warned her to leave, and she helped me anyway.

There's no sign of her now. The woods are hushed, save for the scrape of leaves in the wind. A murder of crows argues somewhere in their raucous voices. And now that the woman is gone, perversely, I wish she hadn't left. I'd have liked a chance to thank her.

My stomach heaves, and I twist to the side as a wash of bile escapes me. I spit and wipe my mouth, but the taste of iron and acid remains. Sweat glazes my skin.

I set my hand on the ground to steady myself, and it's only then that I feel the absence of the familiar thrum of power at my side.

The sword of my office is more than a weapon. As Master of the Anvar'thaine, I wield it as the conduit of judgement against oathbreakers and the lawless—the key through which I unlock the doorways through the Veil. My blood responds to the sword's resonance, and I know the hum its magic gives off even when it is dormant. Without it, I am nothing.

Spongy lichen sticks to my palm as I force myself to my knees. I'm shaking harder now, teeth clicking like deathwatch beetles. My heart gallops unevenly as I search the moss and ground around me. Every movement sends fresh fire through the wound, but that's the least of my troubles.

Despite the fever that grips me, the cold emptiness inside tells me I'm dangerously out of magic. My body won't stop trying to heal the wound, so I'll deplete myself back into unconsciousness if I don't get ahead of it.

I reach for my Veilstone—the crystal that channels Tirnaeve's magic through the Veil—but nothing comes: no threads of Tirnaeve's golden power, no strength, no warmth to counter this freezing void. Shocked, I look down at my hand and see only a pale line on an empty finger.

The sword's absence might have been innocent enough—the woman could have set that aside somewhere as she dressed my wound. But there's no reason for her to have taken the ring. None apart from greed.

I fumble with the fabric of my coat as I reach into the pocket. That, too, is empty.

Father of Curses, the woman has taken everything from me—my sword, my magic, my very purpose. If that letter falls into Vheara's hands...I'll fail the king and break my oaths.

Even the thought of failure brings pain as the oathbands carved into the skin around my biceps flare, their sentient runes monitoring my thoughts, enforcing my loyalty.

The pain they inflict is nothing new. Centuries of discipline and deprivation have given me the tools to withstand that, and I know the consequences if I fail my mission. I spend every day hating the oaths already, and the only way I live with my orders—and myself—is by focusing on the reason and not the order. On what I can save or salvage, not the task. That's the sole rebellion I'm allowed.

My hands curl into fists at the thought of the thousands of lives Vheara has shattered already. Those will be nothing compared to the carnage if she's allowed to keep the throne of Alba Scoria.

I cannot—I *will* not—let that happen.

A wash of red blurs my vision as I think of the flame-haired witch. The image of her burns bright in my mind so clearly that I can almost feel the touch of her fingers and smell the scent of her. My stomach twists in a way I don't want to acknowledge. But the ice in my veins is more than enough of a reminder. I have to get back everything she took from me. I have no choice in that, even if I bloody well have to kill her to get it.

Using the birch as leverage, I force myself to my feet. Darkness rushes in from every side, and mercifully, I pitch back to the ground.

FLORA

I can't move the Ever until he's lucid enough to walk. He's drifted in and out of consciousness for more than two hours while I cleaned and packed the wound with moss and fir pitch, treated his fever, and wrapped him in fresh bandages that I retrieved from our former steward's house. Now all I can do is tend to the mare and wait.

I manage to coax her across the ridge and down the other side to the stream that runs behind the Sacred Wood. Leaving her and Ari tied to a solitary willow tree growing along the bank, I go in search of something she can eat to regain a bit of strength.

Forage has been slow to return after the lean Highland winter, but spring grass, horsetail, and nettles all grow nearby. I collect two armloads and bring them back.

Ari has missed his breakfast, so he shows no restraint. The mare only sniffs at the offering, and I've yet to see her drink. Mud squelches beneath my boots as I step closer and scoop my cupped hands into the stream to try to tempt her. Her lips twitch, whiskers rasping against my palms. Her breath is warm, but the water is icy cold. She takes a small drink from my hands, then lowers her head to the stream and finally takes a gulp.

I rub my cold palms, then slip them into my pockets. My knuckles brush the three rings I've taken from the Evers. The magic surges as I touch them, as if each has its own stream of power that feels uncomfortably familiar. I pull them from my pocket. They radiate heat, and I can hear them humming faintly. Within the mist-blue crystals, the gold threads coil and dance, reminding me of the Ever's eyes, the way the colours shift down through the layers.

The noose that's been tightening around my neck since this war began feels as if it's getting even tighter. Too many things are making me aware of my inadequacies: the deaths of my father and brothers, the Clan Council, and now the Ever. Things I haven't wanted to face. Even the empty steward's house is proof of that.

I never meant to avoid the place these past few months. Even so, when I went to get supplies to tend the Ever this morning, it was the first time I had crossed the threshold since Padraig and his sons marched off to battle with my father. The dust-covered stillness inside was thick with the ghosts of the hours I've spent there. It was Padraig who taught me to manage the farm accounts, helped me identify the best markets for our horses, and kept the old stories alive for me after the last of our oldest generation died.

Beside me, the mare lifts her head from the stream with her muzzle dripping. Both she and Ari prick their ears and turn to look down the long gully that leads past Padraig's house. Then I hear it, too—the sound of wagon wheels and horses' hooves moving along the military road that cuts between Padraig's and the keep.

The mare whickers softly. I place a hand low over her muzzle, pushing out some calming magic to keep her from calling out any louder. Another soft neigh vibrates beneath my fingers.

Soothing the mare requires only a small amount of magic, but after conjuring the sword earlier, I'm surprised I have any left. Warm streams of it spill out from the three rings in my hand, though, and the gold threads in the crystals dance faster as my body seems to soak their power in. That makes no sense, but the magic doesn't feel foreign or wrong. Still, it reminds me of a story Padraig once told me.

It's a cautionary tale, and it should frighten me now. But there's been too much fear, and it's a relief to be still, to set down the weight of the morning and let my mind take refuge somewhere other than the world in which I'm standing.

"Do you wish you could know the future?" Padraig had asked, his greying hair gleaming in the firelight.

I'd nodded eagerly. "Of course."

This was the year I turned fourteen, not long after I'd started to hear the whisper of magic in my mind. Padraig was one of the few people my father trusted enough to know that.

"Magic has never died," Padraig said, "even if most of the Domhnall women have lost the ability to use it. But the laws aside, our people know better than anyone that power of any kind has a price."

Then he began the story.

There was once a child named Lannraig who lived between loch and forest and between glen and brae, where the Veil between worlds was thin.

One Samhain Eve, when Lannraig wasn't much younger than you are now, a strange, keening wail woke her from sleep and pulled her outside. And there, not far from her mother's cottage, was a shimmering curtain of mist woven through with gold threads of magic as fine as hair.

The threads called to Lannraig: "Come closer, child. Come to us."

The child knew better than to trust the magic, and she stopped halfway between the cottage and the veil of mist. But even that wasn't enough to save her. The magic spun out to meet her, and the threads twined themselves through flesh and bone and Lannraig's young, mortal heart.

Lannraig's breath turned to frost that night, and her blue eyes turned snow-white. From then until the last of her days, she was blind to the sights of the world she had known, but she foresaw deaths and births and loves and heartaches yet to come. And for the price of being held for an hour in a warm human embrace, she would tell anyone whatever they wished to know.

I think it must be a lonely, frightening thing to see the future. But not knowing is lonely, too.

CHYR

The moss is cold against my cheek. That much I know is real.

The rest comes in shards, the way it does when my heart stops and my body begins to fail. I've been here before—not in this wood, not on this hillside carpeted in frost-stiff bracken—but in this place between life and death where there's nothing left but the memory of a heartbeat. There's a difference this time.

I'm not certain I'm coming back.

Would it be a welcome escape?

Punishment is swift at the thought, my oathbands sending ice and fire and pain to deny me any hope of freedom.

They didn't always seem like chains, not in those early weeks when the High King himself would come every morning and every night to watch them being carved into my flesh, his arms folded and his expression carefully emptied of his usual cruelty beneath the twisted spires of the Crown of Justice.

I'd never expected warmth, though, so its absence made no difference. After my mother vanished when I was five, I'd seen no one apart from the servants for a full month or more, and I'd long since learned it was easier when my father was away. But the king's attention… Well, I was young enough then that the idea of oaths still carried echoes of honour and justice and loyalty. Of redemption.

The pain as the runesmiths carved the oaths seemed bearable because of that. It felt like a clean pain, a welcome one.

The bands give a warning pulse, even now—even here in this rotting wood with moss in my mouth and Oran and Tuirse dead not twenty feet away. Is it the wound or the runes that are stopping my heart this time? I'm finding it hard to tell.

Carefully, I push the thought away before it costs me.

Think of something else. Heat. A different sort of pain.

Soothing words and a flame-haired woman wrapping my wound. My mouth forced open and something wet burning its way down my gullet. Gentle fingertips and a soft hum of magic.

I can't remember the last time I felt true kindness.

She's gone now. A clatter of hooves and scree falling farther up the slope.

Her scent lingers: bog myrtle and rosemary, earth and something bright underneath, something that doesn't belong in Alba Scoria and yet feels precisely like something this wild landscape has been keeping safe.

The darkness calls me again. I cling to the scent of her warmth, the spark of her kindness. The memory of her hands is still there, and for reasons I can't explain and would be hard-pressed to defend before the court in Tirnaeve, it refuses to let me go. I haven't let myself want anything beyond my duties, not in a very long time. It surprises me how much I wish that she'd come back.

Then I remember what I need from her, what the oathbands could force me to do to her, and I'm thankful as the innocence of oblivion reclaims me.

CHAPTER 5

THREADS IN THE MIST

FLORA

The sound of wagons from the road has quieted. The mare is calm, and her head hangs low as I untie Ari and step away.

"You stay here, pretty girl," I say. "Eat and keep drinking, and I'll be back to get you as quickly as I can."

I put the rings away, thinking of Lannraig, gold-threaded mist, and General Mora's letter to the rebel king. The letter is a millstone in my other pocket as I mount Ari and turn him up the slope into the Sacred Wood.

The letter might save Dunhaelic if I turn it over to the Raven Queen in exchange for her promise to leave the clan alone. Maybe I could even press her to change the Sun King's law requiring clan chiefs to be male.

That's what my father wanted. He chose to support the queen because he believed she would bring us closer to the way we ruled ourselves before the Evers came. A woman on the throne looked enough like justice that he mistook it for truth.

He was blinded by her lies and easy promises. It's easy to believe someone when they tell you what you want to hear.

If I give the letter to the queen, I'll betray the Ever. And even if doing so lets me save my own people, I would betray the lesser Domhnall branches who broke with my father and sided with the rebel king. They'll be punished if Vheara wins, and if I'm to be High Chief in truth, then they, too, are my responsibility.

It would be an empty title if I built it on betrayal.

Do I even want the Raven Queen to win? That's another question I need to ask myself.

Vheara arrived with pretty speeches, but since the start of this war, she has shown exactly who she is. She's brutal, and she cares nothing for the people she wants to rule. I will always believe actions over words.

I set Ari into a trot as we approach the ridge.

The terrain on this side of the Sacred Wood is less steep than that closer to the road. Narrow deer paths wind through heather, bracken, and tumbled outcrops of ancient stone.

Ari snorts and sidesteps as I guide him around the pile of brush and branches that marks the place where I left the two dead Evers. Shadowed patches of skin and clothing show through gaps in the hasty camouflage, but at least the bodies are out of sight—and scent—from the road until I can come back to bury them more thoroughly.

As though the gods themselves want to laugh at my confidence, an eagle gives a shrill cry as it arcs a slow, majestic circle overhead, its feathers spread wide to test the sky. I wonder if the smell will lure it down. Then it gives another shriek, extends its talons, and plunges towards some prey farther up Glen Colm.

A portent, my grandmother would have called that. Or a warning.

Shivering, I rein Ari in at the top of the ridge, peering through the trees to ensure there's no one on the road below. Torn moss and broken undergrowth mark the trail where I dragged the bodies uphill. But the Ever isn't where I left him.

My stomach twists, and panic burns in my throat. The Ever was unconscious when I left. Even if he had woken, he'd be in no condition to be safe anywhere on his own.

I push Ari forward. The woods are quiet again, and Ari's iron-shod hooves ring too loud when they strike rock. He blows nervously and throws his head.

A blur steps from the shadows beside me, and someone seizes my knee and pulls.

I fall. Pain explodes through my skull. Breath is ripped from me, and my lungs won't draw more in.

Something—*someone*—heavy lands across my hips. The Ever. His weight is a weapon, keeping me from moving. Then he shoves my hands down and pins them beneath his knees.

I kick and buck my hips. Try to summon enough leverage to push him off.

He's weak, I know he is, yet I can't dislodge him.

The wounded chest I treated and wrapped so carefully rises and falls in short, ragged breaths. His jaw clenches as he stares down at me, honey-gold eyes burning feverishly. He braces his hand beside my head. The scent of him cuts through pine and damp earth—sweat and sweet, ironless blood, and that odd spent-lightning smell.

"Where. Are. They?" he growls. The words are torn from somewhere deeper than fury, and he leans down, his mouth inches from my face.

The fear doesn't hit all at once.

It trickles in. Paralyzes.

My head swims from the fall, pain pulsing in time with my heart. But it's the weight of him, the feel of him, close enough to press into the hollow of my pelvis... That's what breaks me open.

Because I'm more than afraid. I'm aware in ways I should not be—and that has nothing to do with what I want. It's my body betraying me in the most brutal way it can.

Awareness turns to terror, and I remember the stories. I remember what they say about the women and men the Evers used to steal. The Ever-touched. I know the nursery rhymes we heard as children.

Don't give them your name,
Don't sup at their table,
They'll feast on your heart,
Escape while you're able.

The stories say Everfolk can muddle your mind until nothing else matters. Until your thoughts aren't your own and your body aches to please them, to serve them. Until you'd steal, lie, and betray everyone you love for one more taste.

They say the craving starts like this: the heat of skin, the pounding blood, that helpless flush of want you do not choose.

This is how it begins. Helplessness. Confusion. Hunger.

Shame for something outside your control.

And now, pinned beneath the Ever, gasping, heart hammering, aware of the way he looks at me, I hate that I'm beginning to understand.

That even now, some part of me wants to trust him.

Given his wound and the danger he poses as a Rider, I'd forgotten that fundamentally the Ever is still an Ever.

The real fear isn't that he'll kill me. It's what's in the stories, the fear that he'll do things that make me want him so much that death would have been a mercy.

The thought renews my strength.

I twist under him and use every muscle to throw him off.

He leans even closer, so close I can taste the sweetness of his breath as it comes in ragged, uneven gusts.

"Where are the things you stole?" he demands again. "My ring and sword. The damned letter from General Mora."

A twig snaps somewhere, and I want to scream for help, but the words won't form in my throat. No one is coming to save me. There's no one left at the keep who's come out to search for me, not yet.

The Ever's forearm shifts to press against my throat. Not to crush it, just enough pressure to make me feel the threat. The choice.

"Don't make me ask again," he says, low and cold. "You will regret it."

The menace is there, but there's also a wavering, desperate note to his voice.

Strands of his silver-gold hair cling to his temples, and his cheeks are flushed with fever. I can use that to my advantage.

A growl somewhere nearby raises the hair on my arms, a low rumble of anger like dogs snarling. I can't see anything, and I've no idea where the sound comes from. Then the Ever's attention flicks over my shoulder, his brow furrowing.

Magic whispers in my mind, and that moment of distraction is all I need. I drive my hips down into the moss, using all my strength. The Ever doesn't budge, but I reach for the power inside me and use it to draw magic from the root-threaded soil and the stone that lies beneath it. I pull the magic into myself the way I do when I call the sword into being.

The three rings flare in my pocket, hot enough that I feel the threads of magic through the fabric of my skirt. They surge towards the ember inside me, and my blood burns as power pours through me, raking with an agony as sharp as nails. Suddenly, I'm flooded with more magic than I've ever dreamed of wielding.

Too much. Far too much.

Power explodes from me in a burst that shakes the ground and pitches me upward, throwing the Ever off. Pain leaves my teeth buzzing and every cell inside me raw.

The Ever lands on the moss while rocks rattle and trees shake around us, scree and pebbles tumbling downhill from the ridge.

Throwing myself on top of him before he can collect himself, I ram my forearm against his wounded chest, using the pain of the existing injury against him. Then I press my dagger to his ear hard enough to make him hesitate.

Leaning in close, I separate each word. "I took your valuables to keep them safe. You were out of your head, and someone on the road below could have heard you or seen you. You're welcome to take them back now that you're awake. The swords are over the ridge, where I left the two Ever bastards you wanted buried. Your mare is tied by the stream. Not that you seem concerned about her, but she'll recover if you handle her carefully."

The Ever's jaw clenches, his eyes wide as he stares at me.

I release his chest and pull the rings and the letter from my pockets. The crystals hum louder in my hand, and they're charged and hot, like lightning coiled within my palm. I throw them down beside the Ever's hand.

"There, now you have everything back. And if you have the strength to attack me, there's nothing to stop you from walking over the ridge, retrieving your horse, and leaving. The military road will take you all the way to the Western Sea if you survive long enough. But if—when—you inevitably collapse, do me the courtesy of waiting until you've gone beyond the next two villages so you're outside Domhnall territory. Your kind has brought enough ruin to our clan already."

I push myself to my feet and stand a moment, looking down at him. He doesn't speak, doesn't move. For one treacherous second, I hope for a word—anything to show he isn't the monster he's proven himself to be.

My hands won't stop trembling. I bite the inside of my cheek until it bleeds. The sting's a welcome anchor. I need something to focus on other than the Ever and the terrifying truth that part of me wants to excuse what he's done, to believe it's pain and fever and fear. Part of me still wants to heal him, to help him—and not just because the gallows loom over us as long as he remains on Domhnall land.

I'm the last to dismiss the way he threatened me, but I do know true shame when I see it. I also know that my own reactions are tempered by the fact that he's shown me there are things I fear more than I fear the gallows. Reacting from fear or anger instead of logic, duty, and mercy is not what I was taught.

I will help him because I choose to, not because he deserves it. That difference matters more than he is likely to understand.

CHAPTER 6

WALK THE SHADOW

CHYR

Moss crackles beneath me, hard with frost where the sun never reaches. Cold seeps through my clothes, and through the shallow breaths I drag into my lungs, pressing into the raw ache across my chest.

Every heartbeat drives guilt and shame deeper into my bones, piling atop the regrets I already carry.

The woman bound my wounds when she had every reason to let me die. She risked herself, risked her people, to help me. I repaid her by pinning her to the earth like an enemy whom I needed—wanted—to punish.

Cruelty is a game in my family, but I swore I would be better.

The three Veilstone rings lie sunken in the moss where she threw them, and General Mora's letter rests against my hand, moisture seeping into a corner of the parchment. Her words echo in my mind: "If you're well enough to attack me..."

Thinking she had stolen from me felt like a personal

betrayal, and I don't particularly want to examine that. Whether it's the fever or something about the woman herself, I've forfeited the last threads of honour I still claimed as mine.

Worse yet, I felt her become aware of me, and a part of me wanted her to respond. Though not with fear. Never fear.

She's back on the horse and riding towards the road. I see her in flashes: the fire of her copper-gold hair, the dark shimmer of her stallion's coat, blacker than the shadows.

My ribs scream, and my vision narrows as I pick up the rings and the letter. I drag myself to my feet.

"Wait!" My voice cracks. "Please."

She doesn't turn.

Two smudges of grey trail behind her, revealed when they block out trees and vanishing again in the open spaces. Long-legged, lean, and forged of twilight, the Shadehounds who growled at me earlier trot like docile pets behind her, ghosting silently through the bracken.

Shadehounds, for Pit's sake. As if they're guarding her.

I've only seen a few glimpses of the magical creatures since we arrived from Tirnaeve.

Like other Shadelings, the magical creatures who occupy the shadows and *in-betweens* of Alba Scoria, Shadehounds have long since hidden themselves from mortals, careful not to draw attention. Yet these answered the woman's fear, ready to leap at me for hurting her. Their snarls exposed their fangs, and the silver-moonlight rings around their eyes turned cold with threat. She paid them no attention, as if they weren't even there.

And that tremor of earth she summoned to throw me off her? Even in Tirnaeve, where the air is thick with magic, only a handful of the strongest Siorai can bend the earth to do their bidding.

Who—*what*—is this woman? Where does such magic come from?

But that's a question for later. It's the apology I owe her that matters more.

With no strength left, I gamble the last dregs of my magical reserves to shadow-walk. Choosing a patch of darkness ahead of her, I fling myself into it across the distance. It's like treading through a bog, my feet mired where I stand, the *here* of my location clutching, sucking, squeezing at me as I try to move my body *there* only to get stuck in between.

Shadow-walking, like most illusion work, is innate to all Siorai. My air magic makes that ability stronger, but now even this smallest pulse of magic threatens to rip me in two pieces.

I tighten my fist around the Veilstone rings and pull hard at the power flowing through them. With the added seals the Raven witch placed on the doorways through the Veil, there's barely a trickle available, and as depleted as I am, I've too little magic left in my blood to attract it to me.

The effort heats the stones, but they never grow hot the way they should. I can only pray the magic they give me will be enough.

I keep pulling, and finally, the resistance rooting me to the ground near the ridge releases with a pop. Landing in the shadows thirty yards above the road, I stagger out into the path of the woman's stallion.

The beast rears and lashes out with his forelegs. The Shadehounds leap forward, their low growls felt as much as heard—vibrations in the air.

I evade the stallion's hooves and turn to stare the Shadehounds down. Their magic is different from mine, but they can sense what I am. Even so, their lips curl back, noses wrinkling as they expose their fangs. Then they back away two steps and sink to their haunches. The coarse grey fur tipped with shadows makes them seem less present, and those uncanny moonlit eyes watch my every motion.

The woman fights to control her horse. "Get out of my way," she says. "And I thought you said you were out of magic. Or was that another lie?"

"Please," I say. "I owe you an apology—many apologies—if you'll spare me a moment."

"I was trying to help you," she says, her voice clipped with anger. "If anyone else had found those things on you, you would never have gotten them back."

"I'm not trying to excuse myself, but when I woke and you were gone—when I discovered what you'd taken—it felt as though you'd stripped me of the only pieces of myself that I had left. But I jumped to conclusions and attacked you without giving you a chance to defend yourself."

"I make my own chances. I don't need you to give me any."

She wants to be angry, but there's something more vulnerable than accusatory in the self-protective set of her shoulders. I hate to think I've played a part in that, and the urge to offer comfort is strong enough to steal my breath. Even that realisation is alarming.

Whenever I think I can't feel more shame, there's always a deeper level.

"I'm sorry. I made you afraid, and that's mine to answer for."

She looks down at me, her eyes wide and still. Neither accepting nor rejecting the apology. Not yet.

I look away for a moment, then force myself to continue, to ask what I need to know. If Vheara learns what General Mora wrote, any chance of getting help from Tirnaeve could vanish.

"Did you read the letter?" I ask.

The woman stiffens in the saddle, and the stallion shifts beneath her. The Shadehounds bristle. "I won't apologise for it," she says. "I have people to protect."

"Of course, but you said this was Domhnall land. If so, we're on the same side, and you can understand how important—"

"I am not on *any* side that includes an Ever. This is *Dunhaelic* land, and my father was High Chief of all the Domhnall. He supported the queen until your side slaughtered him on the battlefield, but the smaller Domhnall branches, including two of my own brothers, broke with him to support your king. Now they and most of our warriors are dead as well. We've lost too much to your war already. Do not think to ask for more."

The Shadehounds rise at her anger, growling low. Breathing hard, the woman glares at me from the stallion's back. Her slender body looks too small to hold such courage and defiance.

I remember her father and brothers. They fought in two different battles, on two different sides, but their characters were much the same. All three had an excess of pride and too little common sense. A flash of memory brings an image of the old chief riding onto the field beside his men, the scarlet flag of the Domhnall Clan flapping in the wind, and the gold script around the crest bearing the ancient title of the Cailleach Queens who were chosen from among Clan Domhnall's strongest women:

Reuhldar un Tisooill
Sovereign of the World

And that's one final piece of the puzzle falling into place.

This small, fierce woman bears the blood of the ancient warriors of the Great Mother goddess.

The Cailleach Queens of Alba Scoria once wielded the power of the elements, sovereign magic gifted to them by the land itself.

To my shame, the shame of all Siorai, Fionn Solas came through the Veil from Tirnaeve, murdered the last Cailleach Queen, and declared himself the Sun King. Then he slaughtered every Domhnall woman the land and the Great Mother might have chosen to reclaim her crown. And as if that wasn't damage enough, he prohibited women from leading clans and outlawed mortal magic altogether.

Yet somehow, remnants of their power linger.

That revelation sparks the first glimmer of satisfaction I've felt in longer than I care to think. It explains, at least in part, why this woman's power feels like Siorai magic but also something wilder and less constrained.

"I'm sorry," I say again, wishing I could tell her more.

If my oaths would let me, I would say that death was too easy a punishment for Fionn and that Vheara has earned far worse. I would admit that no son of Fionn's deserves any sort of throne, much less one bought in betrayal and blood.

The oathbands carved around my biceps snarl at me before the impulse can fully form. Cold sears through the runes and into my blood, freezing me from within. Then comes the flash of heat and the pain that hits like a thousand knives slashing through my veins, reminding me of my reality.

Four centuries of this, and still the injustice stops my breath: to be punished not for cruelty or dishonour, but for the impulse to admit the truth—that by the old laws, her blood carries a claim no Siorai conquest can erase. And *that's* a contradiction that would kill me if the Cailleach Queens were more than ancient history. Right or wrong isn't the question in Tirnaeve. My loyalty is bound to my king by oaths I never wanted, and honour no longer governs.

I can't tell the woman any of that, though she deserves to know it.

My vision narrows again, darkness pressing in. I'm not sure if it's the oathbands or the wound in my chest, but I grip the nearest tree, fighting to keep my legs from buckling.

The woman scowls at me. "You're bleeding again."

Her Shadehounds whine softly, and one inches closer.

I glance down at my chest. Blood blooms red on the white linen, and it is spreading.

"I'll be fine." I shake my head.

"What I did was no more than a stopgap measure. Your wound needs deeper cleaning and many layers of stitching. There's also some sort of infection or poison—" The sentence hangs as though she isn't sure how to end it.

Her scent comes to me as I pull in a deeper breath, and when she tilts her face to look up at me, I wonder how it would feel to touch her. To be held.

I have no right to think such things, but the sting of loneliness is sharper as death approaches. The Riders are the closest thing to a true family I have ever had. Watching Tuirse and Oran die, being left behind in these woods, it feels too much like my childhood spent in beautiful rooms empty of warmth or kindness.

I expect that's what draws me to this woman. Fear of death, a need for connection after all the blood and sorrow of the past twelve months.

She studies the spreading stain of blood on the bandage around my chest. A small dimple forms at the corner of her mouth as she frowns.

"Are you strong enough to ride behind me if I help you into the saddle?" she asks.

I nod, more out of determination than agreement. Her stallion is a magnificent beast, but hardly steady in temper.

"You can lean on me. We won't go far." She steps beside me and slips her arm around my waist.

I suck in a ragged breath.

"Did I hurt you?" she asks.

"Not at all. But we should probably introduce ourselves if we're going to share a saddle."

"It's not that sort of ride," she snaps, then she blushes as she realises what she's said and how it sounds.

I bite back a laugh. "My name is Cóirneach. That's my true name, but to my friends, I'm Chyr."

I can never be what she would call a friend, but she is helping me. If I can't be as honest with her as I would wish, as honest as she deserves, then I can at least be honest with the name I give her. My true name is the one thing I have that's mine alone. A small measure of recompense for all the things I am oath-bound not to say.

Her lips part, and she swallows, a flicker of caution passing through her. She suspects a trap.

"It doesn't have to be your true name," I add more gently. "All I need is something to call you. I swear on my sword, on my honour, and the Father of Light, I won't use it to betray you. Compelling humans violates the Compact. The treaty between Tirnaeve and Alba Scoria prohibits Siorai from exploiting mortals."

Her chin tips up, and her eyes bore into mine. "I know what the Compact was meant to prohibit. That died along with the last true queen when she was murdered by an Ever."

"The Compact isn't dead. Not to the Anvar'thaine. Our oaths still bind us to uphold it, and none of the crimes Fionn or Vheara committed—that Vheara continues to commit every minute she is free to spread her corruption—will change that. We're still bound to stop her."

The woman studies me as though she'd like to pull the truth out through my entrails, but I mean every word I've said. I *will* uphold every clause in the Compact, not because I fear eternal punishment in the Pit, but because I still believe in honour.

Whatever the woman sees in me eventually seems to reassure her. Her shoulders drop a fraction as some of her tension rolls away. "My name is Flora," she says. "And my clan is Domhnall—as you know already."

Among mortals, a name is a seemingly simple thing. Among Siorai, a true name is the most dangerous gift one person can give another: the key to the soul, a thread that can unravel. I gave her mine freely, and I've never done that before. But I owe her, and if I can't give her full honesty, I can at least give her the only truth that's mine to give.

That she returned the gesture—this woman, now—feels like a gift I haven't earned. A small bit of forgiveness I don't deserve.

Flora means flower, but like her flame-coloured hair paired with those cool grey eyes, the name is a contradiction. There's nothing soft or flowery about Flora Domhnall. She's quietly fierce, a rose with daggers disguised as thorns.

I can tell myself that intrigue is all I feel, yet I've lived long enough to recognise that contradictions are often warnings. Flora Domhnall may be willing to help me, but her kindness is likely to cost us both.

The air stills and the temperature drops, as if either my fevered body or the universe wants to argue. Or perhaps the gods themselves have decided to pay attention.

CHAPTER 7
PICKING UP STRAYS

FLORA

The sun is high by the time I have the Ever hidden at Padraig's house. Where the trip there from the woods took me fifteen minutes when I was alone, it took twice that with the Ever in the saddle behind me. Even with his arms around my waist and his weight braced against my back, he could hardly balance himself. I wasn't much help, if I'm honest. My limbs are still as unsteady as a sickly ewe's after that burst of magic earlier.

The Ever claims he doesn't know what sort of poison could be causing his flesh to blacken, so there's only so much I can do. I've packed the wound again to stem the bleeding and applied a fresh, tight bandage and left him resting.

If he stays still, he should be well enough at Padraig's until I return, and I'm glad for the chance to catch my breath. The Ever's presence feels too large for the little house, which still smells of Padraig—peat smoke and old leather—though he and his sons have been gone these many months. The dust and cold ashes in the hearth still break my heart.

Mounted on Ari and leading the dappled mare, I round the corner of Padraig's house, but the distant rumble of wheels and the dull thud of horses' hooves prompts me to turn back and trot the horses out of sight.

Two small wagons laden with young children and household goods approach the keep along the road. A group of older children, women, and elderly men trudge alongside.

They're all too silent, and I recognise that soul-deep tiredness that leaves you unable to think of anything but the need to take another step and then one more. They remind me of the Ever warning me to take my family south, and I wonder where this group is going. On any other day, I'd ride out to offer them food and a night of shelter.

Today, I can't. The Ever aside, the more I consider the situation, the more I wonder whether the choices my brothers made, and those made by the lesser Domhnall chiefs, have already put us in danger from the queen.

I shiver as I wait for the wagons to pass, as if my body's only catching up to everything I've felt. Everything I didn't let myself feel while it was happening.

The Ever who pinned me down and made me want at the same time that he made me afraid was dangerous. When he apologised in that low purr of a voice that slid past my defences and made me crave things I've no business wanting, he became a threat.

Standing here in the shade of Padraig's house, I can still feel the hard planes of the Ever's chest pressed against my back and the warmth of his arms around my waist. With every unconscious flex of his muscles, he made my body feel more alive than I'd ever known it was possible to feel.

I've agreed to help him because he needs to be strong

enough to leave Dunhaelic as fast as possible, and because he admitted his mistakes and his vulnerability. It takes strength to admit weakness to a friend. Confessing it to an enemy requires far more courage. I can admire that the same way I can acknowledge the warmth of his arms and the too-specific way my body recognised his weight pressed against me. But admitting I feel something doesn't make it safe. If the Ever has some admirable qualities, even some that, to my shame, my body seems to want, it changes nothing. I can never trust him.

I peek around the corner of Padraig's house and watch the travellers trudge up the slope towards the Sacred Wood. Then I set the horses into a trot past the fields that lie waiting to be sown, past the larch trees that stand sentry between them, past old furrows that catch the light, and past lambs bleating in the sheep pens. Smoke rises from the cottage by the mill and the smaller ones up the glen, carrying the earthy scent of burning peat and the green bite of April heather.

Seeing Dunhaelic like this, I take a moment to etch every piece of it into my memory. The morning has reminded me of how easily I could lose it, and I love it all so fiercely, every acre from the peat-cutting trench that runs like a scar to the south to the snow-capped crag of Ben Aran in the distance.

I hurry on, hoping the road stays clear, but as I cross the military road, a cloud of dust appears at the far eastern side of Dunhaelic Glen, where it first curves into view. The speed suggests riders without carriages or wagons, and these days that means soldiers. One side or the other.

Urging Ari and the mare into a gallop, I race across the few hundred yards of fields that separate the road from the keep's exterior grounds and buildings. I ride through the gate in the outer wall and wait out of sight of the road. Ari chafes at the bit while I make him stand.

Heart thudding, I listen as the staccato hoofbeats of what

must be a dozen horsemen thunder closer. But they trot past without breaking stride. I wait briefly, then ride back into the open, my breath catching as I see their scarlet uniforms. Scarlet and black—the colours of the Raven Queen.

My heart still beating too fast, I nudge Ari forward again. The soldiers worry me. I wonder where they're going and why, but there's no time to indulge such thoughts.

I bypass the outer stables where we keep the less valuable horses and press on across the bridge over the dry moat. Ari and the mare's hooves ring loud across the wood, louder still on the cobblestones as we pass through the arched main gate. Within the courtyard, dogs begin to bark their greetings.

The portcullis yawns wide, leaving jagged-toothed shadows on the ground beneath, but Faolan, our old armsmaster and last semblance of a household guard, is absent from his post in the guard tower. That's unusual enough to make me frown. Then I spot an unfamiliar pair of horses tied across the courtyard.

Visitors are the last thing I need just now. But on closer examination, the horses tied by the stable door look Highland-bred, and the saddle blankets are tartan plaid in Domhnall variants, not the scarlet-trimmed black that the queen's horses wear. That's good news with the bad, at least, though with the Council still weighing options about my chiefship, Domhnall visitors aren't necessarily welcome either.

The household dogs converge around me, barking too loudly, as if even they sense our world is slipping into chaos. I walk the horses across the courtyard beneath too many windows where visitors, not to mention my mother, might be watching. The dogs sniff at me with a mixed reaction of growls, whines, and sneezes as I dismount beside the stable door.

Even my own deerhound, Rab, who is usually more restrained than the smaller herding dogs, sniffs every inch of my shirt and bodice and goes so far as to lift paws the size of plates onto my shoulders. His tail remains low, and his eyes are watchful beneath the scruff of red hair that matches the deer he's bred to hunt. I scratch him behind his ears.

Ari butts me with his head, pushing me towards the building. I give him a quick scratch on the forehead. "Yes, your majesty. I'm aware your breakfast is long past due."

He snorts his disapproval just as Iain emerges from the stable doorway. Sixty-odd years have robbed the old stableman's eyes of much of their sight, but he's lost none of his good sense. Ignoring Ari for the moment, Iain gives the Ever's mare the same quick, frowning assessment he's given every horse that's arrived at Dunhaelic since long before my father was confirmed as Chief.

"Who's this?" he asks. "Picking up strays, are you now?"

"Who are the visitors?" I counter.

"Stewards for the Domhnalls of Ceapaich and Gleanngaradh to see you. They've been waiting."

"Both of them at once?"

"And right peacocks they are as well. Not interested in speaking to the likes of me, but they weren't best pleased to learn they'd have to cool their heels until you showed your face."

"I assume you took great pleasure in listening as they grumbled, in that case?"

Iain's lips peel back in a smile, revealing the gaps of his missing teeth. "Och, aye, I did at that, and Faolan is listening now." Then Iain's expression sobers. "Seems the old Ceapaich chief died at Culodur, and Gleanngaradh won't last long. It's the new chiefs who've sent their stewards to you."

My chest tightens, and I have to blink away sudden tears. "This bloody war never stops taking from us. They were good men, both of them. And good allies."

"That they were. Men you could count on. Can't say the same for the new Ceapaich chief."

My heart gives a thud of dread. "It'll be Dughall, won't it?"

Ugly memories surface with the name, and my mouth turns sour at the thought of Dughall seated at the Council table. The boy who terrorised me while my younger brothers laughed will be no easier to cope with now that he's fully grown.

"You all right, lass?" Iain peers at me. "Seems to me it won't be good news bringing the stewards to Dunhaelic when there's other business for them back at home."

"Let's wait and see what they want before we assume the worst," I say, more optimistically than I feel.

Iain takes Ari's reins and the mare's to lead them into the stable, and he pauses to rub at the crust of blood on the mare's leg and shoulder. He cocks an eyebrow at me, then gestures at my bloody skirt and bodice.

"Anything else you want to tell me?" he asks.

I school my expression and offer the explanation I've carefully prepared. "The mare lost her rider in the Wood, and he must have been injured quite badly. I spent a while searching for him with no success, and then the mare needed water and rest before I could bring her back."

"Och, aye?" Iain cuts me a look that says he knows better— that he knows *me* better.

CHYR

There's fresh rowan above the door.

I know this before my eyes open. The resinous smell is a

familiar one on the borderlands of Tirnaeve, where the old-growth trees still harken back to a time before Siorai shaped every aspect of nature to our command. Here in Alba Scoria, mortals use it for protection in the false belief that, with its habit of planting itself in the *between* places where the Veil is thin, rowan has the power to ward against us. The logic escapes me. If Siorai are close enough to offer a threat, no power in this realm or any other will offer safety.

My oathbands are unexpectedly quiet. That means I haven't said—or thought—anything forbidden lately. A small reassurance, but I'm glad of it as I look around and take in my surroundings.

I'm inside a human home. Not a large one. It is low-ceilinged and full of peat smoke and the ghosts of hundreds of porridge breakfasts and simple dinners—plain, stubborn, and comforting in the way mundane things tend to be.

Someone has put a second blanket over me since I lost consciousness. The flame-haired woman. It smells like her. Feels like her unexpected kindness.

I try to reconstruct her face from the fever's fragments. Cool grey eyes that didn't look away when I threatened her. Hair the thousand and one colours of wildfire in the moonlight. Hands that move efficiently over a wound she had never seen, treating me as if I'm something worth saving even when her own better judgement must be screaming otherwise. Hands my skin remembers.

She helped me. I attacked her. Then she helped me again.

I don't know what to do with that. That gift. That sort of debt.

I've found friendship, love even, since I took my oaths and joined the Anvar'thaine. The Riders are the nearest thing I have to a true family.

Respect I've always had—or at least fear that passes for respect. It comes with the blood running through my veins. That blood also buys me loyalty of a sort, and courtesy from those who want something from me or are afraid to lose what I can take away.

But this woman put rowan above the door, not to keep me out—to protect me from others who would pose a threat.

A mortal woman. Protecting me. *Choosing* to protect me.

My oathbands are still quiet, and I realise it's because I've taken no oaths that prohibit the gratitude I'm feeling. The oaths Chulainn forced upon me don't account for emotions he has never felt himself.

The laws of Tirnaeve and the Anvar'thaine don't cover this, nor does the Compact or any of the seventeen sub-clauses of the treaty between Tirnaeve and Alba Scoria that I have spent centuries upholding.

This is unregulated territory. Something new.

A surprise.

That's very good.

Not only do I need to live, I think perhaps I want to. And when I'm well enough to be dangerous again, I'll find a way to deserve the gift she's given me.

FLORA

Iain stares at me a little longer. Heat rises in my cheeks because deceiving him feels like I'm shredding my integrity.

Every word I've told him is the truth, yet that doesn't make my explanation true. And Iain, like everyone who's remained at the keep with me, is loyal to a fault. That only makes it more important that I let nothing slip about the Ever. That's my best hope to keep them safe.

If there's a price to be paid for the dangerous choices I'm making, I should be the only one to pay it.

"Fine, then," Iain says finally. "I'll give the mare a warm mash, water, and careful watching. She's well-bred, that's clear. Owned by someone of means, no doubt. I assume you want her brushed and kept somewhere out of sight if any strangers happen by?"

"That might be best," I admit. "And I'm sorry to rush off and leave you with even more work, but I'll have to leave again as soon as I can rid us of these visitors."

"You'll be wanting to change that dress before you show yourself, I'm thinking. Seeing as you're wearing more blood on you than the horses are."

My face grows even warmer, and impulsively, I lean over and kiss his cheek. "Thank you, Iain. Truly. I can't imagine what we'd do without you."

"Well, and off with you now, then." He looks down at the cobblestones and clears his throat. "But you know you've only to ask if there's anything you need. I'll be put out otherwise, whatever. At my age, a spot of trouble makes no matter of difference."

I nod, and not trusting my voice, I turn and leave the stables.

Rab follows me across the courtyard to the kitchens, his presence a silent comfort. Morag is kneading bread dough, but since I'm liable to run into the visitors before I can reach the family quarters, I need her help.

She turns from the table when I enter, and the head-to-toe examination she gives me is every bit as canny as Iain's, but there's a hesitant calculation as well that raises my hackles instantly. But knowing who the visitors are, I can't say I'm surprised. I only wonder how long it will take her to say what's on her mind and whether I'll be able to keep my temper when she does.

I'll have to pretend to at least consider it. The Mother only knows Morag's earned a right to her opinion after all she's been through. Her hair has greyed rapidly these past months, and her arms are thick with muscle from the added work she's taken on for us.

"And where have you been, mistress?" She brushes flour off her hands and wipes them on her apron. "Here we've been wondering if you're lying dead in the Wood somewhere and had no one to send out after you with the visitors here making trouble."

I heave an inward sigh. "What sort of trouble?"

"Thinking themselves too important, to begin with." Morag shakes her head. "I don't suppose you want to tell me why you're covered in blood?"

"Not at the moment." I smile at her, already feeling guilty. "I've kept the visitors waiting long enough as it is, and then I have something urgent I have to tend to. I do need a clean dress first, if you can get one for me."

Morag gives me a disapproving stare, then fetches a cloth and points me sternly towards the wet room. "You might as well give yourself a wash while I'm gone, in that case. You'd frighten children, the state you're in."

She crosses towards the threshold, then pauses in the doorway. "Not to poke my nose where it isn't wanted," she says without turning to face me, "but if either of the visitors has brought a proposal for you, then you should hear them out. You've too much on your shoulders as it is, and it could be a husband would ease the burden."

I draw in a long, uneven breath. "You don't think we can manage here on our own? I know you've all been doing too much…"

"That's not it at all." Now she does look at me, and there's pity in her expression. "Maybe it's time to admit the truth," she says more quietly. "Even if you can persuade the council to accept you as High Chief, there's still the law to consider. A husband could help you, love. A strong man who'd be willing to share the burden until the law is changed. Someone to help you rebuild. And you'll be wanting a family sooner or later, won't you? Listen with an open mind, that's all I'm asking."

She means well, I remind myself. I knew she'd have jumped to the same conclusion about what the visitors want as I have, but instead of being angry, she's telling me to give in. To give up.

The idea of selling myself, marrying someone—especially Dughall—for political convenience literally turns my stomach. Unbidden, my mind turns back to the Ever and the way he's fighting for his life. I think we have more in common than he knows.

Rab settles himself near the warmth of the ovens, his massive head resting on his paws.

I strip out of my clothes and wash. Thinking of the Ever, it's too easy to remember the feel of the Ever's arms around me, the warmth of his breath. The way he held me. The way he apologised when he was wrong.

I doubt Dughall, in all his life, has apologised for anything.

Morag takes longer than I'd hoped, but she returns eventually with a clean skirt, bodice, and a scarf to cover my hair. I'm too hurt and furious to say much to her, and I refuse to marry anyone I don't want. After throwing on the clothes, I hurry to the Great Hall, where the visitors are waiting.

I can't afford to waste time while the Ever is alone and bleeding. A picture of him comes to mind too easily, his skin too pale, his breath too shallow, and that spreading blackness in his chest. Maybe it's imagination rather than intuition, but I can't escape the feeling that every moment I waste with these visitors is time the Ever doesn't have.

CHAPTER 8

BANNERS AND THREATS

FLORA

S eated near the hearth at the far end of the Great Hall, the two men are engrossed in food, ale, and an argument between them. I glance at the door to the small receiving room just beyond their table. As I expected, there's an inch-wide gap between the door and the frame, and I've no doubt Faolan will have much to tell me about what was said before my arrival.

It's still painful to greet guests here by myself, in this echoing stone chamber where my brothers used to chase each other amid the joyful voices and roaring fires of clan gatherings and the great feasts at Yule and Beltane.

These days, my mother sits alone in her solar, her mind muddled by grief. The empty tables stand pushed back against the walls, folded hangings rest in storeroom chests, and the dirty scarlet rugs remind me of the blood crusted on the Ever's bandage.

The two men waiting for me are middle-aged and greying. I haven't met either of them before. One has a cane resting beside him on the bench, and he looks as though he might have been a formidable warrior at one time. The other has the crafty softness of a weasel about him.

They're slow to rise when I cross the long room to meet them, and whatever Rab senses from them doesn't win him over. He growls faintly and presses close beside me.

It doesn't surprise me to learn that the smug one is the steward of the Ceapaich heir. He introduces himself as Fergus and the other man as Tormod, and he sits back down without waiting for an invitation.

"By all means," I suggest, taking the chair at the head of the table, "make yourselves comfortable, gentlemen."

But rather than apologise for his lack of manners, Fergus gives me a tight smile as if he's pleased that I've noticed his disrespect.

"Your armsmaster," he says, "told us none of your father's men have returned as yet after the recent battle, though you still hope for word."

"No doubt everyone hopes for more survivors," I say.

"There aren't likely to be many. The Raven witch has her army scouring the countryside, and all the routes south from Culodur are cut. That leaves Dunhaelic undefended."

"As is every other clan seat in the Highlands. But the Dunhaelic warriors who survived my brother's leadership are more than a match for the queen's Lowlanders and mercenaries—as the chiefs of the smaller Domhnall branches such as yours knew full well when they invited them to continue fighting alongside their own men."

"We're hardly smaller branches now," Tormod, the Gleanngaradh steward, says, leaning forward. "The Clan Council will have to recognise the leadership of Domhnall is past due for change when they can finally meet."

His statement makes no secret of why they've come, but if

it comes to a battle for Dunhaelic, I will meet the enemy on my own terms and no one else's.

"Perhaps I misspoke. Let's not call it smaller, then," I say. "Shall we say *lesser*, instead?"

Tormod's lips tighten, and his jaw twitches. "Dunhaelic Keep is the last symbol of Domhnall strength, but it requires men to hold it. We can't let it fall because the line has died."

"The line and the responsibility rest with me. The direct descendant in our branch of the family has been High Chief since the time of the Cailleach Queens, and everyone knows my father intended for me to continue that leadership."

"Your father siding with the Raven Queen was ill-considered. Your younger brothers knew better," Fergus says.

I think of the Ever and his sense of honour, and I can't help but concede that Fergus could be correct. If we had to choose a side, my father chose wrong. But that's the problem. We should never have joined this fight.

I pause to gather myself before I answer. "My younger brothers, though I loved them dearly, were prideful idiots who would have driven Dunhaelic into the ground. My older brother was too soft for the job, and he and my father knew that. As did the Council. I argued then, as I will argue now, that neither the Raven Queen nor the Sun King's offspring give a damn what's best for Alba Scoria. *For us.* Clan Domhnall as a whole should have made small concessions to both sides and kept our warriors to defend ourselves. Thankfully, I didn't let anyone fight under the Dunhaelic banner at Culodur, so there's still a small chance we can escape the queen's reprisals. I'll do whatever's needed to make certain the keep survives for future generations, and I'll do my best to appease her fury at the rest of you who sided with the king. *You* are the ones in danger."

I rise to my feet, and Rab mirrors my movements with his hackles raised.

Both men remain seated, and for a moment, I indulge in a fantasy of calling my magic and placing my sword against their necks, then physically removing them from the room. A long, soft growl from Rab suggests that he agrees.

Fergus gives Rab a wary glance. Then he turns his attention back to me. "We meant no offence, but it's Dughall who'll be chief of our branch now, and it's in his mind that a marriage between you could solve several problems. He'd find it no great difficulty to manage Dunhaelic as well as Ceapaich."

"Is that so?" I place my fists on the table and lean towards him. "How *kind* of Dughall to think of me. And please assure him I remember him very well from the summers my family visited Ceapaich. Dughall always paid me such *particular* attention."

My throat tightens around the words, but I'm surprised to discover there's no longer fear amid my fury. I'm not eight years old now, and Dughall can't hold my head underwater, over and over, until my lungs burn and I'm half-drowned enough to show him the respect he thinks he's earned.

Fergus opens his mouth to speak again, but there's too much history that he doesn't understand, and I'm done wasting time on idiots and their poisonous ambitions when the Ever has actual poison eating his flesh away.

"Does your master have a similar offer?" I ask, turning to Tormod. "Or did you travel all this distance on some other matter of urgent business?"

Colour stains Tormod's cheeks, and he runs two fingers beneath the collar of his shirt. "No. Well, yes. In a manner of speaking. That is to say, Onghas holds you in high esteem and wished to ask your opinion about a possible match."

"I see." I step back from the table. "Naturally, I understand Dughall and Onghas must be too busy to come to me themselves. But given that the queen will have noted both the Ceapaich and

Gleanngaradh banners at Culodur, it will only endanger Dunhaelic if I accept a proposal from either of your masters. I'm sure no one wants to see that happen. Now, thank you for coming, but I have urgent matters waiting, and I'm sure you're both eager to resume your travels. My armsmaster will see you to your horses."

There's no need to raise my voice. Faolan still has excellent hearing.

The door to the small receiving chamber creaks open, and Faolan steps out, his hand resting casually on the hilt of the sheathed sword at his side. Well over seventy, he's hawk-nosed and clear-eyed, and his grizzled hair and broad build allow him to be mistaken, at first glance, for a man twenty years younger. In truth, both injury and age have damaged his grip, and the sword's an idle threat. But like Iain, Faolan's grown adept at helping me distinguish friend from foe.

I have no doubt he'll have more to tell me once we have a chance to speak. Neither of us will hold out hope that Dughall will accept my rejection and stay away from Dunhaelic. I know less about Tormod's master, Onghas. He's at least two decades older than I am, and I remember him only as a quiet presence by his father's side.

I don't need the added worry or danger from still more directions. It feels as though I'm running across a bog as solid ground vanishes beneath my feet.

Keeping the position as Chief was always going to be difficult, but I imagined the threat would come from the Council or the Sun King's law. I never considered that the new heirs might march against Dunhaelic to seize it for themselves.

Once and for all, I need to find a way to prove myself. Dunhaelic is mine, and no one will take it from me. Not Dughall. Not the Council. Not the queen or the rebel king. And not the wounded Ever whose death would turn *every* side against me. I cannot let him die.

CHAPTER 9
NO BETTER THAN THEM

FLORA

My breath clouds in the cool shadows of the narrow, circular steps as I climb. The hope that I can get in and out of my rooms without having to speak to anyone else fades at the scrape of footsteps on the stone above.

Catriona, who has served the family for more than half a century, must hear me coming because she descends the staircase from the top floor that holds my mother's solar and meets me on the landing. With the height of a warrior and the mass of a woman who likes to eat, she wields a broom and a scowl with equal skill.

Her eye twitches, and her face is flushed. "And where have you been all morning? You've frightened me out of ten years' life."

"I'm sorry. I had a horse problem."

"Did you, now?" Catriona says, one eyebrow rising. "Not that you're obliged to tell me your worries. It's only me who's looked after you since you were a wee girl up to more mischief than all three of your brothers together. But far be it for me to poke my nose where it isn't wanted. Mind, if you're going to see your mam, you'd best do a better job washing the blood off your face. Which is another thing I won't ask you about."

She blocks my path, immovable as a boulder, and I know her well enough to be sure she won't give way until she's gotten answers.

The truth is, I no longer have the luxury of keeping her out of my decision about the Ever. Ceapaich and Gleanngaradh have made losing Dunhaelic an imminent threat, and I'll have to prepare the keep to stand against them as well as make sure our people survive whatever the queen may do. I'm going to need Catriona's help.

"I'll tell you if you'll come with me to my room," I say. "I need to hurry."

Catriona's white brows rise nearly to her hairline, but she follows me to my bedchamber and stands with her arms crossed over her ample bosom while I dig through the trunk where I keep the supplies I use for tending injuries. That includes a pair of my mother's silver embroidery needles, which I've put to more practical use on more than one occasion. Rab stretches out to warm himself in the sliver of sunlight that slants through the narrow window.

"Well? Are you going to tell me what you're up to?" Catriona asks.

I explain—mostly, at least—while I gather a supply of tinctures and potions into a small bag to take with me. I leave out General Mora's letter and the way the Ever attacked me.

When I finish, Catriona steps back and makes the sign of horns in the air to ward off evil. "And here I've believed you were the sensible one in the family."

"That doesn't say much, but you can see why I need your help."

"I can see you've lost your mind." She hands me a fresh cloth to dip into the basin of cold water on the dresser so I can wash my face.

Scowling at my face in the mirror, I wipe away a smudge of blood on my cheek that I can only hope was too small for Tormod and Fergus to notice. Then I pick up the battered leather bag to leave.

Catriona steps in front of me again. "Oh, you'll not be going just yet," she says. "Are you seriously meaning to tend the Ever and leave him at Padraig's until he recovers? With only the two of us to go back and forth to tend him while the queen's nightmares—and who knows what else—could descend on us at a moment's notice? Assuming, of course, your Ever's not already dead or waiting to kill you the moment you go back to help him."

"He's not *my* Ever, and I'll take him up Glen Colm to hide in one of the shieling huts in the summer pastures as soon as his fever's broken. I'm planning to position supplies there anyway, in case we need to send the women and children somewhere safe and out of reach."

"I don't imagine the Ever will take kindly to sleeping in a herdsman's hut."

"He'll survive that better than losing his head to a Grey," I retort.

Catriona gives me a look that makes me squirm, then shakes her head. "You don't like to admit it, but you know as well as I do what must be done. Keeping the Ever alive is as good as a trip to the gallows for the lot of us, and there isn't a single one of the outbuildings that offers a place for him to hide if the Queen's monsters come looking for him. Not to mention that he'll be weak as a lamb and have no chance to save himself. It's kinder to kill him quickly, really. Faolan can help if you're too squeamish."

The thought of killing the Ever—killing anyone like a wounded animal—makes my stomach roil.

"Slaughtering him for our convenience would make us no better than the Everfolk," I snap. "We don't change ourselves because we're threatened. I'll find somewhere safer to hide him. I just need a quiet minute in which to think."

"Your mother's been asking for you, speaking of that," Catriona says.

"Yes, and I'm on my way to see her now."

Catriona's silence follows me to the threshold. I glance back, and she stands looking down at the floor, her hands clasped together and her brows slanted into lines of worry.

My anger washes away, leaving me feeling limp. I turn back and smile with what I hope looks like reassurance. "Catriona, I know it's a risk, believe me. But it's the right thing to do, and we'll survive. I'll do everything I can not to let you down."

"It's not myself I'm worrying over. Aye, well." Catriona gives a small shrug, then shakes her head, and her expression softens. "I'll speak with the others while you're up with your mam, and don't give me any of your arguments about trying to protect them. Any of us would give our lives to keep you safe, same as you would for us. The bodies in the Wood will need burying, and Padraig's house will need cleaning once you're done fixing him up."

"Are you sure?"

"Do you think we don't see that you barely sleep with all the extra work you're doing? I hate to say it, but if you're determined to help the Ever, you'd best bring him here. You won't need to wear yourself out flying back and forth to watch over him, and we'll all be here to do whatever you want done to tend him."

I shake my head because that's not an option. "That's too much risk."

"No more than if he's found at Padraig's or anywhere else on Domhnall land. And don't you dare feel guilty." Catriona follows me out of the room. "You did what you thought was right, my lamb. That's no more than I'd expect from you."

I blink at her and swallow past a tightening in my throat. Catriona's always been more likely to fuss at me than to show affection. I don't know what to do with this version of her, and that says more about how frightened she must be than anything else.

I'd love nothing better than to retreat somewhere out of sight and fall apart, but I can't. Not while people are counting on me.

"I won't let the Ever be our downfall. I swear that on my life," I say.

"Then let us choose which burdens we want to carry and what price we're willing to pay." Catriona reaches down and tucks a damp curl of hair behind my ear.

Rab comes to rub his head against my hip and whines softly in his throat until I scratch him behind the ears. I turn and walk away with guilt clawing at my stomach and the smell of the Ever's blood—spent lightning and that odd, gentle sweetness—still on my hands from when I changed his dressings.

With Rab at my heels, I emerge from the shadowed stairwell and step into the solar that my father renovated for my mother when he first brought her to Dunhaelic. Reluctantly, I have to admit that Catriona's right. The Ever might be an even bigger danger to us at Padraig's house or any of the outbuildings than he would be here.

The keep has no safe place to hide him—every room can be searched. My mother will be the biggest hurdle. These days, there are no constraints upon her tongue.

"There you are," she says, patting the bench beside her as she sits in the silvered light pouring through the window above her head. "But did you need to bring that filthy beast in with you?"

I shoo Rab out to the landing with a murmured apology, and he lies down with his muzzle across the threshold.

My mother sets the embroidery hoop aside. "Come talk with me, child. You know how I hate my own company, and you're always flitting here and there these days."

The idea hits me then, a reckless but possible solution for the Ever. I turn it over in my mind as I listen to one of the stories my mother has told a hundred times. After examining the scheme from every angle, I think it's just foolish enough to work—so ridiculous that no one would suspect it. Provided the Ever will agree to play along.

"How would you like to have a visitor, Mother?" I venture cautiously.

She claps her hands together. "I adore visitors. Who is it?"

I press a finger to my lips and start to lay the groundwork. "That you will have to wait and see. You know how difficult travelling all this distance to Dunhaelic can be."

"Is it your father who's coming?" Her eyes glow at the thought, and her cheeks go pink with hope.

And I could kick myself. I should have seen that coming. "I'm sorry, darling. No. It's not father, and not the boys."

"Your father and Rory should have been home ages ago. Oh, and the twins! I long to see them. I wish they wouldn't take so long coming back."

My heart wants to crack into dust behind my ribs. No matter how often I explain that they're all dead, no matter that she was there when I brought home what remained of the bodies and we laid them to their rest, she can't accept their loss. Her mind refuses to retain the information.

"Your embroidery is beautiful today," I say, changing the subject. "Is this something new you've started?"

"Oh, do you like it?" She beams at me brightly. "It's a cloth for the high table. We'll have such a banquet as has never been seen when your father comes home! Hundreds of our people will want to attend. And we should commission new hangings as well, don't you think? The old ones have become so dreary."

"New hangings would be lovely."

I listen with half an ear while she chatters about parties and embroidered cloths. Meanwhile, I turn the ruse over in my mind until I've found solutions for nearly every potential problem.

After leaving my mother, I search out Catriona and find her in the courtyard speaking to Morag. After I explain what I have in mind, they both laugh until tears pour down their cheeks, but they agree the scheme might work.

They run off to gather the clothes and accessories we'll need if we're to have any hope of pulling it off, and they're back before I've saddled my favourite mare to ride back to Padraig's house. I hate involving the household to this extent. For even more reasons, I hate to involve my mother. Yet whether they're conspirators or innocent bystanders, no one will be safe until I get the Ever off Dunhaelic land.

CHAPTER 10
VEILED TRUTH

I wake beneath rough-hewn rafters in a chamber thick with peat smoke and the scent of herbs. Disoriented, I need a moment to recall that I'm at the empty steward's house at Dunhaelic. The same steward who, as Flora explained with her eyes turned mist-soft, died with his two sons and Flora's father and older brother in the first battle of this cursed war. Them and too many others.

I'm a Rider, the Master of the Anvar'thaine. I've taken lives when I must. Most oathbreakers and criminals choose to fight the Hunt when we come for them, hoping for a clean death instead of facing an eternity of torture in the Pit. But even for me, this war—the cost of these battles and the lives snuffed out—is impossible to comprehend.

Immortality leaves little vocabulary for the death of those we love. I still can't fathom the loss of Tuirse and Oran, but death is different on this side of the Veil.

Here, the dead lie on the battlefields by the hundreds,

leaving broken families behind them and holes that will never fill. Wrongs that can't be righted.

Pain scrapes like a knife through my chest as I try to sit up. My body trembles like a cub's, sweat beading on my skin.

"Easy." Flora bends over me, strands of her flame-bright hair escaping from a braid as thick as her wrist that falls across her shoulder. "You need to conserve your strength. You looked half-dead when I left."

"I was half-convinced you weren't coming back," I say without thinking.

It's no more than the truth, but admitting it aloud makes me sound like one of the useless boot-lickers at court. The other Riders would pound me into pulp for letting myself sound so weak.

Flora pulls a chair close to the bed, alongside a table she must have placed there while I slept. The table holds a mug, a lamp, a small but lethal-looking knife, and a variety of bandages, cloths, herbs, salves, needles, and threads—all scrubbed clean and laid out on a crisp white cloth.

With a hand beneath my bare shoulders, Flora steadies me. Her touch is cool against my fevered skin, and our eyes meet as I slowly swing my legs around to face her.

She ducks her head and gives me the steaming cup. "Drink this for me. It's tea brewed with willow bark, yarrow, and meadowsweet. Nothing more, I promise, but it will bring down your fever and help with pain."

My hands shake, and drops of pungent tea spill onto my breeches. Flora places her hands over mine, helping me raise the cup to my lips.

The tea is bitter and scalds my throat, but the warmth of her hands on mine makes me shiver. I'd already accepted that I would die here alone, and her kindness cuts that away, leaving me too vulnerable. She's sheared away all of my defences.

She pulls back too soon, and I drain the cup. Then she replaces that with a bottle of amber liquid. "Now this. Drink as much as you can manage. The cleaning and stitching I need to do to the wound will not be pleasant."

It smells like spirits, so I push it aside and turn my head away. "I can't drink that."

"It's only whisky."

"Only, she says. Are you trying to finish me off?" I push the bottle back at her.

"You don't drink?"

I shouldn't be surprised that she doesn't know. Our weaknesses tend to be closely guarded secrets.

"Human spirits don't agree with us," I say, leaving out most of the truth.

She stares at me, and a blush seeps into her cheeks. "They don't agree with you in the same way that your Ever wine makes us unable to control ourselves?"

I must be feverish, because seeing her blush like that makes me think of the way her body felt beneath mine, and the warmth and scent of her in my arms as she kept me from falling off the horse.

"If you're asking if your spirits make us lose our inhibitions and long for sex, then no. That's a human reaction to the magic contained in anything grown in Tirnaeve. Drinking your spirits merely sickens us enough so we *wish* that we were dead. But before you feel guilty for the whisky you poured down me earlier, I doubt the drink made much difference. I had all the same symptoms earlier."

She turns and crosses the room, her back and shoulders betraying tension that accentuates the sway of her hips. I don't know why she's helping me. Apology or not, she can't have forgiven the way I attacked her. Despite that, she brought me here, and though I'm grateful, I can't understand her kindness.

She ladles steaming water into a basin from the pot heating on the fire and carefully carries the basin back. Setting it down on the table beside her herbs and implements, she stands a moment, frowning at me.

"Where did you learn your healing skills?" I ask her.

Her lips tighten. "My grandmothers taught me. The art has been passed down in my family for generations."

"Yet another reason to be grateful that you found me." I smile, wishing I could make her more comfortable. "I'm aware that I haven't thanked you adequately—or apologised enough for my behaviour earlier."

She pauses a moment, then gives a stiff nod. "I thought 'thank you' was one of the things Everfolk never said."

"You shouldn't believe all the stories."

Her eyes widen. "How do I know which to believe?"

"You could ask."

"You could lie." She lifts one eyebrow in challenge. "Or could you?"

I find myself smiling back. Any other time, I'd give an easy answer, but given what she's doing for me, I owe her more.

"We can't lie, but that's not the same as telling the truth," I say. "Siorai are masters at walking a blade's edge. We always have been."

The oathbands around my biceps give a twinge, more of a warning nudge than outright pain. I feel the runes slithering as they search the various oaths for the words to catch me out.

I've been faithful to every promise I've made for centuries. Before learning what I recently uncovered about the High King and these oaths he forced upon me, I never tried to work around any of them. Even now, I'm still testing the limits, seeing how hard I can push my deeds and thoughts.

Flora tips her head slightly, studying me and uncertain how to respond. Then her manner turns brisk.

"Take your boots and breeches off," she says. "Can you manage that, or would you rather I cut them off?"

"I can undress myself, and I've no particular desire to walk around barefoot and naked when you're done."

"I won't risk having any of your old clothing found if someone searches. I've brought other things for you. Unless you can use magic to disguise yourself?"

"Even if I could summon the power to create an illusion, I couldn't hold it long. And there are some Greys with magic-sense. I wouldn't be strong enough to keep the magic from being felt. Though that would be a problem anyway."

She studies me, then bites her lip and looks away. "All right, so no magic then. But we can work around that."

Something in the determined thrust of her chin makes me hesitant to ask what she means, and I don't have the strength to argue.

I bend to remove my boot, and grit my teeth through a wave of pain. It's not as bad as earlier—whatever Flora has done to the wound, even thus far, has helped. Pain itself isn't unwelcome. A hard-fought battle, sparring with the Riders, the hardships of a Hunt—they're all proof I'm still alive. After centuries of mostly feeling numb, the more pain the better. It's something I can throw myself against, something I can fight.

This is different. This is the sort of pain akin to the first sharp slice of a celestial blade that takes too long to fade. Rethinking the wisdom of contorting myself to remove the boot, I snatch up the knife Flora left lying on the table.

She catches my hand and pries the knife from my fingers with surprising strength. "Don't be stubborn. Twisting and straining will only make the bleeding worse."

There's something maddeningly vulnerable about not being able to undress myself. I bite back my frustration and remind myself that she doesn't have to help me at all.

And she is helping. I'm still feverish, but I don't feel as depleted of magic. That may have less to do with whatever Flora has done to my chest than to the additional power I'm able to pull through Tuirse and Oran's Veilstones. Indirectly, I have to give Flora credit for that as well. If she hadn't taken the rings for safekeeping, I would never have thought to try and use them. That's another debt I owe her.

After she slices my boot from calf to heel, she removes it with one deft pull, then moves to cut the other. Her head is bent, leaving the nape of her neck exposed, and though I've never considered a nape particularly interesting, hers is as strong and graceful as the rest of her.

Throwing the remnants of the second boot on the floor, she straightens. "There, and the breeches next."

She grows more interesting by the moment, but I'm wearing nothing under the breeches, so I protest. "I can do this part."

"Don't worry. I grew up with three brothers. You don't have anything I haven't seen." She leans closer, and her fingers graze my skin as she reaches for the buckle of my belt.

My breath stutters, and I still her hands. I'm injured, but I'm not dead, and the evidence of my body's natural response is too close to Flora's fingers to hope that she won't notice. I doubt *that's* something her brothers ever showed her, and I feel a sting of shame as colour floods her cheeks.

She pushes back her chair and crosses to a chest across the room to remove one of those endlessly long plaids the Highlanders wear like a skirt wrapped around their waists. Unfolding the woollen cloth partway, she drapes it across my lap. Only then does she reach underneath to undo the remaining buttons.

Whether that's kindness or self-preservation, it feels like mercy. A low pop from the fire breaks the silence—sap spitting as the log settles. Flora's enormous deerhound raises his head and growls.

"Raise your hips," Flora says, her voice husky in a way that only makes my problem worse.

She's blushing still, and I try to think of something to defuse the moment, to make her feel safer with me. I'm half afraid anything I say will only make the situation more embarrassing for her, and I stare at the beams on the ceiling instead to calm my body's traitorous response.

Her hands brush my hips again and then my thighs as she pulls the breeches off. I pretend not to notice, but telling myself not to react only makes me unable to think of anything other than the touch of her fingers on my skin.

Clearly, there's something to be said for forbidden fruit. I'm a Rider—there's been no shortage of women happy to undress me and share my bed. Even here in Alba Scoria, more than a few mortal women have offered. I've had little interest, but that's not the same as denying myself. The more I try to ignore Flora, the more I feel each small touch, every heated breath, every scrape of her skin on mine.

She finishes removing my clothes and slices through the bandage around my chest. The linen sticks to the wound, but she pries the fabric off with cautious fingers.

"There, now you can lie down for the rest of it," she says.

Holding the plaid in place across my hips, she helps me shift back around so she can reach the full length of the wound. I lie back as she picks out the moss and melted fir pitch she used earlier to draw out the poison and stem the bleeding. Fresh blood trickles down my chest.

Her hands are gentle, and I'm careful to show no sign of pain.

"You're good at this," I say, partly to break the silence, and partly because it's true.

"Between here and the two Dunhaelic villages farther

along the road, there's rarely a week when someone isn't sick or injured."

I raise my head to study her, unable to tell what I'm hearing in her voice. She's hard to read, though I can't decide whether that's because she's human and the small clues that reveal emotion are less familiar to me or because she is trying not to react to what she's seeing.

"How bad does it look?" I ask. "Be honest."

She darts a glance at me, then quickly looks away. "The blackening—the dead flesh—is too extensive to remove it all. Without knowing what kind of poison this is, cleaning and stopping the bleeding can only do so much."

Light and shadow from the lamp play across her skin. In the hearth, the low flames hiss softly. Catching an odd flicker of movement, I glance over and see the long, lithe form of a Twilight Weaver pull itself from a dark corner. The creature studies me, then turns away and sets a fresh log on the fire before fading into the shadows again in the magical way of Shadelings. They like to make themselves useful, but they're wary of humans and terrified of Siorai. After how Vheara has corrupted them and forced them to turn on each other, I can't begin to blame them.

Flora hasn't paid the Weaver any attention, and I'm starting to wonder if she can see the Shadelings at all. They've spent so long in hiding that humans can only see them if they wish to reveal themselves.

"Did you understand what I said?" Flora asks. Her face is pale, and a drop of pinkish water falls from the cloth she's holding.

"Did I understand that I'm going to die?" I respond more sharply than I intended. "Yes. You were clear. What makes you think it's poison and not an infection?"

"I can't be sure—I don't know how different your bodies are from ours—but areas that were healthy tissue this morning have already turned black and died. And the odour... Your blood doesn't smell of iron, but there's a metallic stench to the wounds I can't account for."

"Thank you for being honest with me," I say.

She opens her mouth as if she's going to protest, then closes it. Her lips are tight as she pries away another clump of sap. The piece is large enough that I notice the gold-black sheen of something embedded in the amber resin as it catches the light.

If I hadn't been thinking of poison and iron, I doubt I would have noticed the resemblance. But I've spent centuries watching the sun play on the gold-black whorls of celestial iron forged into my sword.

"Can I see what you just took out?"

"Why?" She picks up the clump from the table and hands it to me.

I bring it to my nose. The odour is faint but unmistakable, a smell like metal burned out of the stars.

Since the moment Tuirse stopped breathing, I've known I was going to die. But until this conversation, until this moment, I'd clung to a gleam of hope. Having that snatched away again is painful.

My death will not come with honour on a battlefield, nor as part of a hunt with the other Riders. Nor even as an oathbreaker for resisting the promises I will eventually have to break. I will die with my duty undone and my tasks unfinished. Well, I suppose that's better than being banished to the Pit.

"Is the pain worse?" Flora asks, searching my expression.

I toss the lump of fir sap back to the table and wipe my hands. "The powder trapped on the surface of the resin looks and smells like pure celestial iron. The swords that gave us these wounds must have been coated in it."

Flora rinses the cloth again. "What's the point of that in the middle of a battle?"

"This didn't happen on the battlefield. Ordinary men with ordinary swords set an ambush for us the next day. At the time, the attack seemed pointless. But the wounds refused to heal."

"So someone made certain you would die, even if they couldn't kill you outright? In a cruel way, that makes sense. It's surprisingly daunting to know you have to cut off a head or stab someone through the heart to kill them."

"Cruel is Vheara's stock in trade, but that won't be her only reason. She'd never trust an ordinary human with a blade of celestial steel. Not when it could be turned against her or her Greys."

"Can you be sure the queen was behind the ambush?"

"Without a doubt. Anything involving celestial iron points straight to her." I almost smile at the grim irony of it. "It's hard to fathom. More than sixteen hundred years of banishment in the Gloaming—the magicless world between worlds—and she goes straight back to mining ore the moment she escapes."

"Sixteen hundred years?" Flora's hand goes still. "Are you saying the Raven Queen is the same Vheara who enslaved us and brought on the Human Uprisings, the Compact, and the sealing of the doorways between the worlds? But *why*? What does she want with the ore? It's worthless except for weapons, and no one even knows how to make those any more."

I scrub a hand over the stubble on my chin. The skin feels hot and damp. My brain is spinning, and it's hard to pull out any single thought, to know where or how to explain ambition as warped as Vheara's without triggering my oathbands.

"Immortality can be a torment as much as it's a gift." I

pause to take a breath. "It's why Siorai call the Father of Light, who gave us eternal life, the Father of Curses as well. The years take a toll, and Siorai can lose their way. Once he realised that, the Great Father created the Anvar'thaine to keep the peace, and he cast a section of his celestial throne down from the heavens to give the Riders power over life and death."

"Celestial iron," Flora says.

"That's the story as our priests tell it, at least." I study Flora, though I'm not sure what reaction I'm looking for. Horror? Fear?

She turns to the basin and rinses out the bloody cloth.

"Do you know about the Anvar'thaine, what we are?" I ask.

"The Great Hunt." There's nothing in her voice. None of the condemnation she must feel.

"We're the enforcers of oaths and laws, and the gatekeepers of the doorways through the Veil, including those that go to the Gloaming. These days, we're the king's fists, errand boys, and glorified messengers, essentially—but in the beginning, we were meant to be something more."

A pain worse than the wound in my chest flashes through my veins as the oathbands flare. The individual runes glow and shift on my arm, and my back arches as the muscles contract.

"Lie back," Flora says, dropping the cloth back into the basin as she turns back to me. "Breathe through it."

"I'm fine."

"Of course, you are." She pauses, blanching as she sees the runes flaring on my oathbands, then she visibly catches herself and pushes gently against the top of my chest until I sink back onto the bed. Finally, the oathbands settle.

There's a moment of silence between us, and with my head flat, I can't fully see her or what she's doing. There's only the sound of our breathing, the rasp of linen against flesh, and the swish and drip of the water in the basin as she rinses the cloth over and over. Occasionally, I catch glimpses of her pale face or that hair that's like living flame at the limits of my vision, but even without seeing those deep grey eyes, I can almost feel her thinking.

I study the way her shadow shifts along the wall, looking for a hint of what she feels. She has every right to hate us. Treachery can't be forgotten, and all Siorai, everything that is Tirnaeve, must be tainted by what Fionn did to her family when he seized power and made himself the Sun King. What he did to stay in power.

I feel the shame of it on his behalf.

"You still haven't said why Vheara wants the celestial iron," Flora says. "What makes it worth all this destruction and death?"

"I was getting to that. All the celestial iron the Father gave us was forged into the celestial steel swords for the Anvar'thaine and the ceremonial daggers our priests use in the Temple. There's nothing left of it. But there are Siorai who would give everything they own to be allowed to die, and others who would pay anything, betray anyone, to escape the justice of the Anvar'thaine. Some—a more cunning few like Vheara—simply want the power a weapon capable of killing Siorai will give them. The power to offer a merciful death or to threaten someone who doesn't want to die."

Flora's face turns ashen. "The Raven Queen sells death for money?"

"For power. For favours or influence. When she discovered there were deposits of celestial iron in Alba Scoria, she enslaved humans to mine it for her. But that's only the means to an end. She's here to build an army, and ultimately, she'll march into Tirnaeve to capture the throne she really wants."

The cloth stills against my chest, water trickling down the wound in a rivulet as Flora's hand squeezes into a fist.

"Then the war—all this misery and death—none of it's about Alba Scoria at all?" Her voice is soft, every word enunciated carefully.

Water splashes in the basin, and the chair scrapes against the oak planking of the floor. I raise myself to one elbow, and her right hand grips the back of the chair so tight that pale moons surround her knuckles.

She has every right to fury.

"The war is about survival. Yours *and* ours," I say. "Make no mistake, Vheara's end goal doesn't mean she won't destroy this realm, and every other mortal realm, before she ever sets foot in Tirnaeve again. She'll feed on the destruction, grow fat and bloated with it. That's what she does. Who she is."

Flora's expression is haunted, and the colour has bled from her cheeks. "Then that's why the Anvar'thaine and the rebel king have come. You're fighting here so the war doesn't come to Tirnaeve."

"Evil grows the longer it's left to fester." I catch her eyes, and I hope she can see the truth in mine. I need her to believe me. "We have to find a way to stop her. Flora, if there's celestial iron in the wound, it's likely that I'm dead already, even if my body hasn't caught up yet. A clean slice with a celestial blade can take weeks of recuperation in Tirnaeve with magic all around us. I don't have that here for my body to draw on, and I can't afford to stay this weak. Much less get any weaker. What I need is time. You said you can't cut all the poison out. But will you try? I know this is more than I've a right to ask, but I need you to cut out every bit that's been infected."

Her left hand hangs near the edge of the bed, a few scant inches from mine. I reach for it, needing to make her understand the urgency.

"Can you do that?" I ask her. "Is it possible?"

Her hand lies stiff within my palm. Then slowly, she turns

it, flattening her palm against mine, threading our fingers together, as if she realises how much I need the connection to another person. She probably does understand it. Mortals die.

"How fast can your body heal?" she asks. "If you were human, you wouldn't survive if I removed half the flesh that's gone black."

"Try. Give me a chance."

Her hand feels cool and soft and alive against mine.

"The blood loss might kill you. Or shock. Fever," she says.

"It might not. Either way, it wouldn't be your fault."

I don't know her at all, but I can see that my death would weigh on her if she does what I ask. I'm asking her to do something that might kill me, and that's an unfair burden. She has every right to reject it. Every right to hate me for what I am, and what we've done. For what I'm asking.

"I won't promise anything," she says, "but I will do what I can."

CHAPTER 11
ROWAN FOR PROTECTION

FLORA

The fire crackles around the last remnants of the Ever's bloody bandages and clothing, acrid smoke curling into the shadows. I blink away exhaustion as dawn approaches. Chyr teeters beside the bed, one hand white-knuckled on the chair for balance while I lace him into the bodice of Catriona's dress. The wool stretches over bandaging and bare skin, his fevered heat seeping into my fingers.

Given that I've practically carved him apart like a joint of beef and stitched him back together, only his willpower and stubborn strength keep him upright. If I can get him back to the keep alive, let alone pass him off as a believable companion for my mother, it will be a miracle.

On the bright side, being half-dead has made him accept the indignity of the disguise with less argument than expected.

For a warrior, it must be a true humiliation. The sheep's fleece rolled over the bandaging gives him a bosom nearly as large as Catriona's, and elsewhere, he fills the dress out by being wide and hard where she is softly padded. Overall, the fit isn't as bad as I feared, apart from being a foot too short. As a final touch, I arrange the shawl low over his forehead in the way pious old women wear them to church.

"There." I tuck the ends of the shawl under the bodice. "Now stay seated, hunched over, and quiet, and you'll be drab enough to pass as a giant's spinster aunt."

He shoots me a look that promises retribution. "If this is subtle revenge for all that Siorai have done to you, your mind is devious."

"My idea of revenge would be more painful, trust me. This is self-preservation. Dunhaelic has no men left of fighting age. You'd stand out a mile if anyone saw you."

"Then I'll hide so no one sees me."

"There's nowhere safe in your condition. Dressed as a lady's companion, you'll be invisible in plain sight. No one would imagine a Rider stooping to disguise himself in a dress."

"Why would they?" the Ever asks. "Wearing a skirt would make it damned difficult to intimidate, much less kill, someone. And that's literally half my job."

"You're welcome to change back into trousers as soon as you're strong enough to kill again. Or whenever your magic is back and you can do better."

"A dress won't fool anyone. Look at me."

I let myself look. His stained-glass eyes shift from honey to gold to brown and green as I look deeper. They glitter with fever, and the soft drape of the shawl only highlights the strength of the jaw and the straight, sure nose, the harsh perfection of his features.

Even half-dead and wearing a dress, Chyr is more treacherously male than any warrior I've ever met. Every movement hums with coiled strength, tempered by intelligence and command. He's a predator, a hunter. Every sensible part of me wants to run.

"What's wrong?" he asks.

"Nothing. You'll be fine. Your face is pretty enough," I say too honestly.

"Pretty?" he repeats. Then he smiles—a slow, wide grin made slightly crooked by a thin silver scar at the corner of his mouth. The imperfection only makes the rest of his face more dangerously beautiful. His eyes light with amusement, and a wicked spark hooks low and deep inside me. I turn away with an unfamiliar ache drying out my throat.

The smile is trouble. It's the first unguarded expression he's given me, and I don't know what to do with the part of me that wants him to give me more.

Bloody stupid Evers.

"Try not to look so pleased with yourself," I say. "Keep the shawl low and your head bent so no one can see you clearly. With luck, the queen won't send anyone here until you've gone."

The remnants of his smile fade, and he shakes his head. "Don't give in to wishful thinking. Vheara and her Butcher will send someone soon—soldiers, at least, and probably Greys. It really isn't fair of me to put you or your family in danger. My friends and I hid in a cave not far from here. I can rest there for a day. With the poison gone, the magic from the Veilstones should let me heal well enough to leave by then."

This is the part of the conversation I'd hoped to put off until he was stronger. But hiding the truth won't make it easier for either of us.

"I wasn't able to get all the celestial iron out," I admit. "Some of it was sunk too deep. You asked for time, though, and you should have that—as long as you let me help you through the fever, shock, and blood loss."

"How long?" he asks.

The question cuts through me, and I swallow hard. "I can't be sure, Chyr. I'm sorry."

A battle wages across his face. His jaw clenches and unclenches before he sinks onto the edge of the bed, finally acknowledging that he doesn't have the strength to hold himself upright.

"I still think it's too dangerous for you to have me at the keep."

"Probably." I nod. "But I can't risk having you collapse where Vheara's soldiers might find you. There aren't any other healers who would stitch you as I have. You'd risk condemning everyone in my Clan to the hangman's noose. And in case that isn't clear enough, let me make it clearer. You're welcome to leave as soon as you're able to dig up your sword, saddle your horse, mount without help, and ride away without falling off. Until then, you stay where I can watch you without shirking my other responsibilities. Now, stop wasting my time with arguments."

Thankfully, he seems to accept that.

I'm tired to my bones and don't have the strength to keep explaining. Too much is flying at me at once: the Ever and the queen and even bloody Dughall and the Council, all of them pulling me in directions beyond my control.

I cross to the fire and add more wood, then toss the remnants of the Ever's boots into the flames. Leaving the wrung-out cloths on the hearth to dry, I carry the last of the dirty water outside and dump it on the midden heap.

Rab doesn't bother to get up. He gives me a resentful look, yawns, and lays his chin back on his paws, growling now and then at the shifting shadows. Having promised to wake Catriona so she can finish the cleaning, I leave the fire burning.

Getting Chyr onto the horse is almost too much for him. Bramble, the most sensible of our mares, stands patiently until

I manage to get him into the saddle. He shivers, sagging heavily against me. By the time we're halfway back to the keep, I'm supporting so much of his weight it's a struggle to keep both of us upright.

The stars are fading as we approach the military road. I listen for voices or hooves other than our own, but there's nothing—only our breathing and the soft creak of saddle leather. Clouds drift across the descending moon, swift and pale in the pre-dawn sky.

"Your mother will want a name to call me," he says as we approach the keep. "What should I answer to?"

"How about Rowan? For protection and a bit of luck. We can say you're our housekeeper's niece. Her family is from the far north, which will explain your fair hair and some of your height. But you'll give yourself away if you speak, so you'll need to pretend you're mute. My mother will be delighted to have the company regardless."

The Ever's breath fans across my scalp, warm against the cool night air and far too intimate.

"Anything else I should remember?" he asks.

I should try to explain my mother, but her condition is too tangled with blame and guilt. For all our sakes, the fact that the Ever will be too weak to move around for a while might be a blessing. On the other hand, having him bedridden could make him seem more suspicious if anyone comes to the keep searching for injured men.

"Just concentrate on healing," I say.

He shivers against my back, and my heart twists. Maybe it's that image of a wounded animal being put down that Catriona planted in my head, but something about the Ever feels broken in the same way wild things do when you try to help them.

CHAPTER 12
UNEQUAL POWER

FLORA

The sound of urgent footsteps drags me from a fitful sleep. My neck aches, and my head rests at an awkward angle against the back of the chair beside the bed in my brother's room, where Chyr is sleeping. The Ever has kicked the covers off again, his legs tangled in the skirts we were too tired to wrestle off him when we arrived.

I can't have slept for long. The sun slants low through the window, laying bars of light across the wooden floor. Rab lifts his head from his paws and yawns.

"Flora, wake up," Catriona whispers. "Come here."

Her face is pale, tension bunching her shoulders. I follow her out into the corridor, my mind spinning through possible disasters.

"Your uncle's sent a letter for your mother," she explains. "The messenger says he barely made it through the pass ahead of a company of the queen's Greys and soldiers. They're marching, not riding, but they're no more than a day behind."

The news jolts the last remnants of sleep from my brain.

"That's sooner than we'd hoped," I say, "but not unexpected. Did Morag and Faolan get the Evers buried?"

"Aye, and I've seen to Padraig's house and burned the herbs you told me to use. There's no smell of blood, no sign the Ever was there."

"Thank you." I pause, thinking fast. "We'll get the women and children to safety. Iain can move the best horses up Ben Aran—it's hours of riding and a hard climb, but the soldiers won't waste time going there with easier targets closer at hand. I'll take most of the sheep and cattle up to the summer pastures and leave enough here so it doesn't look suspicious."

Catriona presses her lips together. "I hate to say so, seeing as I'm the one who suggested you should bring the Ever here, but having him here is a mistake now that the soldiers are coming. You need to see reason, lamb. He's got one foot in the grave already, that one. And if they're looking for injured men, they'll look extra hard at anyone who's bed-bound. We'd be better off burying him in the midden heap before they come."

"He isn't dead, and he won't be if I can help it."

"I'm not asking you to stab him with a knife, but in the state he's in, he'll die soon enough without medicine and water. You know the Evers would leave us all to die."

"All the more reason for us to do better."

"Being righteous doesn't curry favour with the gods. Haven't you learned that yet?" Catriona crosses her arms as if I've exhausted her patience. "I'd rather sink low and keep breathing. This is what comes of your mam always pretending your shiftless, selfish brothers were better than you, isn't it? You set impossible standards for yourself."

The words hurt more than I expect. Catriona is always happy to share her opinions, but not this harshly. The war coming to Dunhaelic scares her, and knowing she is frightened cuts me to my soul. She's the strongest woman I know.

I wish I could explain why I need to save the Ever—but he's given me no details. That's the curse of unequal power. He wants to keep his people safe, the same as I do. Still, it chafes that he holds knowledge he refuses to share, and I must content myself with crumbs.

Smiling at Catriona with as much confidence as I can muster, I draw her farther from the bed where Chyr is sleeping.

"Is my mother awake yet?" I ask.

Catriona nods. "She's about to have her breakfast in the solar."

"In that case, I'll take the letter up myself. I'll need to start preparing her. In the meantime, will you see if the messenger has anything else to tell us? Feed him, and pay him enough to ride on to warn the villages. There's gold at the bottom of the trunk in my chamber."

"I know where you keep it." Catriona casts a wary glance at the Ever and lowers her voice. "I also know there's little left."

"I won't pinch pennies when it comes to saving lives. Ask him to ride as far as Camhrain, Raghnall, and Gleanngaradh. Their chiefs can send him further to warn the other clans."

"And him?" Catriona nods towards Chyr.

"Can you lend him an old nightdress and cap and help him change into them when you have a moment? Since we don't know when the soldiers might arrive, he needs to be ready at a moment's notice. I'll change his dressings myself when I get back."

Catriona's lips tighten, but she gives a small nod. Then she presses my uncle's letter into my hands and strides back down the corridor.

The Ever stirs restlessly on the bed. Heat radiates off him like a forge.

Either Catriona or Morag must have come in while I slept. They've emptied the washbasin, refilled the water, and left a fresh pitcher of willow-bark tea. It hasn't fully cooled, but sediment swirls from the bottom as I pour a dose into a cup.

I gently shake the Ever. He jerks and tries to sit up, only to fall back as his strength fails.

"Steady. Let me help." I ease a hand behind his shoulders.

He stares as though he's not certain who I am at first. Then he blinks, and the frown line disappears from between his brows.

"Flora." He licks his lips. "Is everything all right?"

"Shh. Nothing to worry about for the moment. I need you to take some medicine."

His mouth twists—resistance, pride, or pain, I can't tell which—but he drinks what I give him. I press a damp cloth to his forehead; he exhales slow, shuddering breaths and reaches for my hand. His pulse is thready and uneven, but he drifts into a restless sleep with his fingers still wrapped around mine.

I linger, studying the rise and fall of his chest, his parted lips, the dark lashes against fever-flushed cheeks. And for all that I want to dismiss Catriona's fears, I can't.

Seated in a darkened corner when the soldiers come, with a shawl drawn low over his face and us nearby to create distractions, the Ever might pass as a woman. But here, in my brother's bed, with sunlight falling across his face, he is every cautionary tale mothers have told their daughters. Too clearly an Ever.

I've long since stopped praying to gods who abandoned us.

Still, I send a silent plea to the Great Mother to spare us and let the queen's soldiers pass by Dunhaelic to wreak their havoc elsewhere.

That sort of selfishness makes me feel guilty, but that's a hard truth I'm discovering about survival. Most people matter to someone, yet not every death matters equally. Some weigh heavier on the scales of fate.

Dunhaelic remains a symbol of hope for many in the Highlands, but the more I consider what Chyr has told me, the more I'm certain the Raven Queen must be stopped. If Chyr can help make that happen, we need him to survive.

I'm more convinced than ever that this war between immortals wasn't ours to fight. But we have made our choices, and I'm not blameless, either.

In hindsight, I should have ordered our remaining Dunhaelic men to come home after the twins were killed in the third battle of the war.

If I had, some might be here to defend their families now. But I wasn't willing to test my authority before the Council met. I brought the crimson banner of Clan Domhnall home to Dunhaelic instead, and I gave the warriors the choice to continue fighting to avenge the dead, as long as they fought under the banners of the lesser Domhnall chiefs.

If I'd found the courage to be a true leader, I might have saved them. I can't change that, but I can ensure I do not fail their families now.

Leaving Chyr to sleep, I climb to the solar with Rab at my heels, taking the letter for my mother with me. Rab waits outside when I enter the room, as though he remembers that he's not welcome.

My mother's head is bent over her embroidery beneath the circular window. The sun streams through the thick diamond-shaped panes of glass, casting prisms along her skin. She looks peaceful, unbothered. Innocent. That's the advantage of escaping into a kinder reality beyond the reach of pain.

I don't know how to prepare her for what's coming.

My footsteps ring hollow as I cross the room, and I put on a smile that I hope looks more authentic than it feels. "I've brought a letter from your brother. With all that's happening, I doubt it's good news, but would you like me to read it to you?"

"That would be lovely. I long to hear news of him and the girls. It's so unfair of your father never to take me to Caelsolas any more. It's been an age since I've last been shopping or heard a scrap of gossip."

The wax snaps as I break the seal, and the parchment trembles in my hand.

My dearest sister,

If you haven't heard yet, know that the queen's armies have cut through the king's forces at Culodur, sending all who survived to hide as best they may. It's said the rebel king has taken ship for Eireen, there to remain until he can assemble enough gold and men to return. The queen sends her Butcher out with Greys and soldiers to punish all who might support the rebels on their return. Even here in the city, her soldiers go house-to-house, but the Highland clans like yours will feel her punishment most. She means to break them all.

Be warned, dear Sister. It can be only a matter of days before they reach you at Dunhaelic. We have narrowly escaped ourselves and mean to go south to find refuge. I urge you to let Flora help you do likewise. We shall pray for you both and hope to see you when we can, though I do not know when that might be.

I remain your loving brother, Eachann

A shiver runs through me as I finish reading. It isn't merely punishment that Vheara seeks; it's annihilation. She means to ensure the clans can never rise against her in the future.

But I can't let the letter turn me into a simpering miss. There's too much to do.

A small sound, almost like a choked sob, draws my attention back to my mother. Her embroidery hoop has fallen, forgotten, into her lap. Tears shine in her eyes, but when I go to her, she looks up and smiles with perfect calm.

"I do hope they will have a pleasant journey," she says. "Do you suppose they shall go as far as the queen's palace at Dunfithic? There will be such celebrations there. Could we not go with them, dearest? We must ask your father. He should be back soon, don't you think so?"

I used to wonder how much of her refusal to live in the present was a deliberate choice, and now the doubt comes roaring back. I've tried to be enough for her, but I was never one of them: the four men who were her pride and joy.

My breath leaves me in a long, trembling sigh.

Does she know? I want to believe she doesn't.

"It's likely to be a long time before you see Father again," I say, my throat squeezing around the words. "I did bring you some good news. Do you remember the visitor I mentioned? Rowan, Catriona's niece, has finally arrived to be your companion."

"She has?" For an instant, my mother stares at me, her expression inscrutable enough to be unsettling. "Where is she? It's unkind of her to keep me waiting, I must say."

"She caught a fever on the journey, but she's eager to see you."

My mother's lips set in a determined line as she discards her embroidery on the bench. "Then I should go to her immediately."

"Not yet, darling." I touch a hand to her shoulder. "Rowan

is sleeping and shouldn't be disturbed until the fever breaks. Do you remember that she's mute? Imagine what a strain it must have been for her to travel this far."

"Oh, the poor girl." My mother peers at me, then her smile brightens, and she pats the seat beside her. "In that case, you must stay and entertain me after getting my hopes up like that. What other news do you have to share? It's so dull here, day after day, with nothing and no one new."

I stoop to kiss the top of her head and let her down as gently as I can. "There's no time for a visit today, I'm afraid. But I'll make it up to you soon, and Catriona and Morag will stop to see you whenever they can."

She makes a show of pouting and doesn't answer, but as I begin to turn away, she clasps the hand I placed on her shoulder and squeezes hard before letting go. I turn back and fling my arms around her, as I haven't done since I was a child.

Her bones are sharp and fragile beneath the fine wool of her dress and the shawl she wears against the morning chill. I whisper that I love her, because the important things can never be said too often.

As bleak as things seem, I'll cling to any small ray of hope. That's what happens when hope and luck are all that's left.

CHAPTER 13

DRAW THE FEVER

I stop to check on the Ever and find that the willow-bark tea isn't doing enough. Sweat runs off him in rivulets, and the linens and his clothes are soaked.

With an ordinary infection, I'd let the fever run its course. But it seems that even the small amount of celestial iron I couldn't remove from the wound is enough to keep the poison spreading. Any strain could overwhelm him.

The cloth cools my own hot fingers as I wring it out. I have to leave with the livestock, but that means I'll be gone late into the night. He could be dead before I return.

Trying to think what else I can do for him, I dip the cloth back into the basin and place it across his forehead.

His eyes open, and his fingers close around my wrist. "Flora—"

Whatever he was going to say, he doesn't continue. Still, the way he says my name—his voice a dry, velvet whisper—and the way he looks at me…

My pulse quickens. I should pull away, but I don't.

"Why are you frowning?" he asks.

"I need to leave, but your fever is too high. Is there any sort of remedy specific to Siorai that could help us break it?"

"Where do you have to go? The truth, please," he rasps, as though he's read my mind. His grip tightens—not enough to hurt, but enough to make me look at him.

"Tell me about the Butcher. What do you know about him?"

Chyr struggles to sit up, and I press my hands into his shoulders. "Stay still unless you want to undo all the hard work I put into stitching you together."

"Why are you asking about the Butcher?"

"My uncle warned us he was moving against the Highland clans."

"General Cumarann." Chyr spits the name like poison, his fever-bright eyes hardening. "The Black Knife of Alba. Did your uncle say he was coming here?"

"Nothing more than speculation. Is he as bad as they say?"

"Worse. He's human, but he thrives on Vheara's cruelty. After we lost at Culodur, he wasted no time destroying nearby towns and villages. He locked women and children in a church and burned it down while forcing the men to watch."

Tears sting my eyes, and I taste blood from biting my cheek. I'm not naïve. Cruelty isn't confined to one species. But the evil Chyr describes? Knowing someone like that walks the earth in human skin is chilling.

Chyr releases my wrist and slides his hand down to lace his fingers into mine. His eyes are sharp with anguish.

"This is why Vheara must be stopped," he says. "She has a gift for evil. She finds the smallest seed of wickedness in others and makes it bloom."

I nod, my stomach churning. "I need to move most of our stock away from the keep, which means I'll be gone late into the night. But how can I leave if there's a chance the Butcher himself is coming?"

"Your instinct to save what you can is right. Whoever comes will leave hunger behind. They'll steal your horses for Vheara's army, kill the sheep and cattle, and foul the fields to keep them from being planted. And if you're worried about leaving me here with a little fever, don't be."

His eyes glow even brighter, the honey colour picking up more brown and amber from the deeper layers. There's such pain and defeat in him as he tries to push himself out of bed that I feel an answering echo in my chest.

Both of my grandmothers were healers, but only one had the gift of laying hands. She always said none of the Cailleach's magic could be taught—that magic is less a skill than a pact between the land, the Great Mother, and the one who receives it. It's a willingness to take on suffering that another cannot bear.

I'm not sure where the Cailleach's magic ends and the power flowing through the Veilstones begins. Now that I've felt that power answer mine, I suspect my trick with the sword is not as simple as I once believed.

Even the magic of the earth feels sharper, clearer. And then it's as if my grandmother is here beside me, whispering in my ear.

Try now.

I cup Chyr's face in my hands. His breath hitches, and he shudders, but he doesn't pull away.

Our breaths mingle, and for one mad moment, I wonder what his lips would feel like against my own. Drawing a deep breath, I push the thought aside and store it firmly with all the other things that are true, and reckless, and far too dangerous to contemplate.

I know how it feels to pull magic from the earth and push it back out into my dagger, shaping it into what I need. Sending calming energy out is similar.

Closing my eyes, I reach deep through timber and stone to search out the power that coils amid the thawing soil. The earth is ancient and waiting—eager. Barbed tendrils of magic rise to meet me, uncurling to fill the hollow spaces inside my body with sharp thorns of power. I use my own magic to shape it, but this isn't a dagger in my hands, waiting to grow. It's Chyr's living flesh, and I need to pull the fever out instead of pushing and building.

Carefully, I sift through what I sense in Chyr: the heat of his fever, the angry wound that wracks his body, the blood that moves slowly beneath his skin, carrying magic that lights up like sparks as my own brushes against it. There's a deeper pool of magic that waits like a reservoir within him. I could take it if I wanted—it's a shimmering temptation, but taking it would be wrong on every level.

But there's something else inside Chyr. Something that rejects my magic and clings to Chyr's flesh, starving it of blood and life.

That poisonous darkness makes my magic angry. Everything in me strains against it, wanting to escape. My heart drums in my ears. Control shatters, and all the power that I had sent into Chyr snaps back at me, pulling Chyr's fever with it. Pain hits me like shards of glass raking through my skin.

Heat throbs in my palms and spreads from my hands to my arms, shoulders, and chest. It burns until I can't breathe, until my lungs are drawing in fire instead of air.

"Flora!" Chyr yells.

I open my eyes and find him staring at me in shock and fear.

Dazed, weak, I wrench my hands away and give myself a mental shake. Chyr's skin feels cooler, but my whole body aches, and my limbs drag as though they're made of stone.

"What in the Pit was that?" Chyr rasps, throat bobbing as

he swallows. "Didn't you hear me calling? I couldn't pull your hands away. I'm weak, but not that weak—it was as though they'd fused into my flesh."

I try to focus. Rab presses against me, his body trembling. He whines softly, and I pat his head.

"Flora," Chyr says. "Look at me."

I drag my eyes back to his. "How do you feel now?"

"Better," he says. "But also terrified for you. Whatever that power was, it was dangerous. I've never seen magic raise smoke from someone's skin."

He looks as though I've scared him. *Him.*

He's the Ever. And *I'm* the thing he fears.

"I need to leave," I say, and my voice is hoarse.

"Don't run. Don't ever run. Talk to me." Chyr tries to grasp my hand, but I pull away.

"Catriona will check on you while I'm gone," I say, "and I'll come back as soon as I can. Stay in the disguise. We don't know when the soldiers may come."

He calls after me, but I don't stop.

I stumble out into the corridor. My hands still ache, and my body is strung so taut it feels as though I could shatter at the slightest tap. The corridor is silent, dust motes dancing like threads of magic in the air. I stop and lean against the wall, gulping breaths to calm myself.

If I can make an Ever afraid, then what am I becoming?

Evers are the monsters our children are taught to fear.

Worse yet, I don't know if what I did helped Chyr at all.

Pulling myself away from the wall, I nearly turn back to demand that he tell me exactly how he's feeling.

Then I think of the fear in his eyes, and I can't.

He's alive—for now. I feel deflated and cold inside from using so much magic, but I have other responsibilities that cannot wait.

By the time the last of the herds are scattered and I've seen the women and children from Dunhaelic away to safety, the moon sails high overhead.

The keep looks even more beautiful than usual as I cross the bridge. Moonlight silvers the towers and battlements and catches on the furrows of the unsown fields. For now, it's still safe and undisturbed.

Faolan opens the gate, and I dismount beside him. I've always thought him young for his age, but now he shows every one of the years he's lived.

"All right, lass?" he asks.

"I hope it will be," I say.

He nods slowly. "And Iain and the horses will be fine, whatever comes, especially with your Rab for company. That's one worry you can put out of your head."

I squeeze his arm and leave him standing at the gate, watching the darkness along the road. I doubt he'll sleep much before tomorrow.

It feels strange not to have Rab come bounding up to greet me as I cross the empty courtyard, Bramble's hoofbeats echoing off the stone, but that's how it's been since this terrible war began.

Our losses pile up, one after another, a series of good-byes that never get easier.

I've so few of my family left to love. How could I bear to lose anyone else? Especially if the deaths come because of my own decisions. My own failures.

Chapter 14

Embroidery and Smoke

CHYR

I'm slow to come awake, and aside from pain, my first thoughts are of disaster: Flora's mother screaming, the thud of her body on the cobblestones, are sounds I'll never unhear.

Flora asked one thing of me, and I failed. I let the import of that sink in before I take inventory of the rest. Then damp clothing—bloody embarrassing clothing—makes itself known, and with it awareness of the change in circumstances. Father of Curses, the Riders would never let me hear the end of it if they saw me like this. The thought brings sharp pain, a reminder that Oran and Tuirse are gone, and the Riders are forever changed without them.

The smoke is a sour bite of damp turf and thatch mingled with the bitterness of green vegetation and the fatty metallic stench of slaughtered animals burning. It seeps in through the windows and small fissures in the walls, leaving a raw ache in my throat.

Vheara's soldiers are moving closer.

I'd hoped to stop them. Hoped to keep Vheara and her Butcher from exacting more revenge. Instead, I'm useless and—may the Pit take me—wearing a woman's nightdress.

I push myself upright and stumble to the window. A greasy smudge hangs over the horizon, a soot-tinged shroud dragging across the eastward hills.

Waiting for the inevitable dizziness that comes when I move, I realise that my fever has broken, or just about. Even my chest feels less as if Flora had filled it with hot coals before she stitched it closed.

Whatever healing magic she worked yesterday has wrought a miracle—I feel a thousand times better than I did before her help. Better even than I did last night when she changed the bandages after she returned to the keep. For the first time in days, the familiar warmth of magic simmers in my veins again, faint but present, now that what little the Veilstones draw to me through Vheara's seals isn't all being siphoned away for healing.

I'll take it, but I don't understand it.

A small skill for healing isn't uncommon among Siorai. But this? Any priest at the High Temple would be proud of such a gift. I saw her confusion, though, as if what she achieved surprised her as much as it astonished me. As if it scared her.

Surprisingly, my oathbands are quiet on the subject. There are references to illicit magic in the Compact, but the meaning isn't clear, and I have no mandate to enforce the mortal laws that Fionn created here.

Hunched like an old woman, I pick up the borrowed dress laid across the chair. It's a cage made of fabric, and I loathe it with the light of a hundred suns. But with Vheara's soldiers approaching, Flora shouldn't need to worry about my disguise.

If Flora can face the possible destruction of her home and family, surely I can be strong enough to wear a dress. That said, trying to fasten the bodice laces without dislodging the sheep fleece "bosom" proves harder than it seems.

Flora arrives while I'm still fumbling with the task. The door is partially open, and she pauses on the threshold, carrying a tray with a pitcher and various medicinal flasks and jars.

"You're up." She sounds surprised.

"Awake and wishing I could do more to help you. Judging by the smoke, we don't have long to wait."

"How can you tell?" She crosses the room to set the tray down on a small table beneath the window.

"The type of smoke, the sorts of things they've burned. There's a pattern to it."

A crease forms between her brows, but she doesn't ask the obvious questions. Blue bruises of exhaustion shadow her eyes and bow her shoulders, and a small bit of straw clings to the heavy, flame-gold braid that tumbles across her shoulder. My hand itches to pull it out.

I hate that she's in danger. The smell of smoke reminds me of the way the Butcher destroyed the last family who sheltered us, and I despise my weakness even more.

"I think we're nearly as ready for the soldiers as we can be," she says. "There's still a part of me that's tempted to shut the gate and lower the portcullis and deny them entry."

"Vheara would take that as an invitation."

"I assumed so." She steps closer and lays the back of her hand across my forehead to test for fever, then insists on checking the wound beneath the bandage.

I stand still while she pulls the dress aside. She's so close, it's impossible not to be aware of her, but I want to avoid doing anything that will make her feel vulnerable. And I remember the feeling of her magic as she healed me, the sheer force of it, the smoke roiling off her skin. The power of the Cailleach Queens has burrowed deeper than anyone suspects.

The silence between us is swollen with unspoken things, and we both look away as the fabric slips from my shoulders to my waist. Flora reaches out to hold the fleece in place over the bandaging around my chest. Her knuckles skim my skin, and a shudder ripples through me.

She stills, her fingers hovering above the section of fleece where I've tucked the three Veilstones. "Is this where you put the rings?"

"You can feel them?"

"There's a vibration. A hum. But would a Grey sense them?"

"Not without a rune or a gift for magic-sense leftover from when they were Siorai. In that case, they'd sense that both you and I have magic anyway. If we have no other choice, I can create an illusion of stillness to dampen all the magic around us, but we would need to stay close together, and I don't know how long I could hold it."

There's no point in saying more. Too much can go wrong. Flora knows that already.

She removes the fleece from the ribbons that bind it in place and catches the rings in her palm. Behind those cloud-grey eyes, her mind is spinning, and she bites down on one side of her lower lip.

"How do the rings work?" she asks. "They're pulling magic here from Tirnaeve, that's obvious. But how? It shouldn't be possible."

"A seal can never be perfect. Even after the doorways were shut at the time of the Compact, there were thousands of tiny fissures around each door where the magic could trickle through. But the flow was reduced when Vheara seized control of the doorways after she escaped the Gloaming. She added a second seal on top of the first, which allows even less magic to seep in and limits how much our Veilstones draw."

Flora seems unaware that her hands have gone still. They rest lightly on the bandages across my chest. Her warmth sinks into me, and I'm afraid to move, afraid to call attention to the contact, the kindness I'm beginning to crave.

I want to stay in this moment, to forget the death marching ever closer. I suspect she feels the same impulse. It's natural to seek escape, even if that's only an illusion.

But then she clears her throat and briskly rolls the fleece back into place, retying it with the strands of ribbon.

"There's no blood on the bandage," she says, "so at least the bleeding has stopped. Try not to tear it open, and I'll clean it again when I get back."

I try not to think about what could go wrong for her out alone with Vheara's soldiers and Greys out hunting, but the knowledge hangs between us like an axe. She looks away, and I clench my hands to keep from reaching for her.

"Finish dressing, and I'll take you up to sit with my mother," she says, her voice quiet in a way that says more than she wants to reveal.

She's about to step away, then her eyes catch on the rows of oathbands carved around the biceps of my left arm. Until the magic activates, they look like nothing more than black ink scored deep into my skin, but they light up and slither away when she reaches out to touch them, reflecting gold in her eyes as the individual runes glow with cold fire, then wink out again.

Flora jerks her fingers back. "Those aren't decorative, are they? We have ancient runes that look similar, but I've never seen any that move. Are they like letters lighting up to make a word?"

"You're not far off. They represent the oaths I've taken to the king and the Anvar'thaine. The layers of magic poured into them run so deep that the runes are sentient."

"So they're thinking when they move like that?" she asks.

"Considering whether I'm keeping my oaths, yes."

There's shame in that these days, instead of the pride I used to feel. I hear the resentment in my voice, and the runes deliver a sharp lash of punishment.

Flora brushes a fingertip over the bands, lightly enough to send a shiver through me. The oathbands spin faster around my arm.

"Do they hurt? And why do they move when I touch them?"

"I'm not sure. They're probably assessing whether you're a threat—whether you're likely to make me break my oaths."

Everything about Flora treads in dangerous waters.

She frowns at the runes, then lays her palm briefly against my cheek. I'm afraid to move, to scare her away. I lose count of the time, but it's too brief, and before I can formulate a coherent question, she breaks the contact and helps me put the final touches on the disguise.

Her head tips down at an angle as she works, exposing the hollow above her spine. I wonder how she'd react if I ran the pad of my thumb along that tender ridge, tracing the curve of her neck. Would she lean into the touch?

She retrieves the thin shawl from the back of the chair and drapes it around my head, pulling it low over my brows and tying it beneath my chin.

Any impulse I had to touch her vanishes. If there has ever been an invention in the history of the world that could emasculate a man more thoroughly than having a scarf tied beneath his chin, I haven't found it yet.

Completing the humiliation, she tucks the ends back inside the bodice.

A gust of wind rattles the window, and beyond it, a raven glides on the current, darker against the thick smoke still rising in the distance.

"There, now," Flora says. "You're back to being a respectable lady's companion as long as you don't make yourself too noticeable when the soldiers are around."

The word punches into me like a fist.

We've been focused on me, but the vile smoke outside is a portent of what's coming to Dunhaelic. And if I can't help but have thoughts of Flora in my arms, how will she fare with soldiers who've been ordered to punish the Highlanders in the most brutal ways possible? Her household consists of women and old men, and I am weak and useless.

Once again, I regret my refusal to pay the exorbitant prices the other Riders paid for the risk of having yet more runes etched into their skin. I can think of dozens that might help us now.

Under the veneer of courage Flora wears, I can see that she is scared. That makes two of us—because I'm terrified for her. For all of them.

Flora leads the way as we climb the round stone staircase to her mother's solar, and I pretend—if only for Flora's sake—that each step isn't heavier than the last. By the time we reach the top, it's all I can do not to brace myself against the wall.

The chamber that opens off the stairway runs the length of the Lord's Tower. Windows flank the hearth, and a large round window dominates the wall at the far end. The room should feel light and airy, but today, rain weeps from clouds the colour of smoke. Still, the windows on one side offer a broad view of the road that crosses the glen, and the opposite windows overlook the courtyard within the keep, providing a good vantage point for everything except the area nearest to the gate.

Flora's mother sits on a high-backed bench across from the crackling fire, a heavy shawl of fine wool draped around her shoulders. She looks up from her embroidery as we step inside.

She's younger than I expected. Her eyes are a similar grey to Flora's, and her hair might once have been a similar colour, though the brightness is dimmed by grey. I'm curious about the woman who sits and chats and embroiders while her daughter struggles to do the work of many.

"There you are, Flora," she says brightly. "And who is this you've brought with you?"

"Don't you remember Rowan? Catriona's niece from the north." Flora casts me a faint, pleading smile. "She's been your companion for ages, since well before Father left."

"She has? How lovely." Her gaze sweeps over me, and I struggle to hide my surprise.

"She can't speak, but she loves to hear your stories," Flora adds gently, folding the lie around her mother with an air of guilt she can't disguise.

"I do love stories, don't I? And company—it's so dull with your father and the boys away. Come and entertain me, Rowan, dear." She sets her embroidery aside and pats the bench beside her. "Or perhaps you'd like to eat a bit of something first? Morag brought far too much food this morning, and I don't know what she was thinking. None of it is to my taste."

"Morag is rushed this morning," Flora says smoothly. "But she brought food up for Rowan as well. Perhaps that's what has you confused. Rowan, you should eat while you can."

She waves me towards a table where a plate holds oatcakes, a slab of yellow cheese, and a generous portion of smoked fish. A crock of butter and a jar of honey sit nearby. My stomach growls, and I catch Flora's small smile.

"Should I fill a plate for you, Rowan?" she asks.

I shake my head, point to myself, gesture with two fingers walking, and indicate the table.

Our eyes meet, and there's so much I haven't told her. So many warnings I haven't given her.

She turns back to her mother. "I'd better go. I still have stalls to muck, among other things."

"Must you rush off again?" her mother asks. "You've only just arrived."

"Yes, but you and Rowan have catching up to do." Flora steps towards the door, then freezes as something outside the window catches her attention. I move to stand beside her, close enough to feel the way every fibre in her slender body stiffens with tension. Mine mirrors hers at the sight of soldiers marching along the road that cuts through the glen.

"Twelve men walking, and only two riders," she whispers. "Wouldn't there be more if the Butcher were with them?"

"What's that, Flora?" her mother asks.

"Nothing, darling. I'm reminding myself of everything I need to do," Flora replies.

Almost unconsciously, her hand reaches for mine. I close my fingers around it. I'd love nothing more than to hide her somewhere safe, but she's not the sort of woman to run from danger. And I am the furthest thing from safety.

"Greys." I mouth the words.

Her face pale, Flora nods. Then she lets go of my hand, deftly removes the dagger from her belt, and presses it into my palm. "Take this. You can do more with it than I can in the circumstances, I don't doubt. Keep my mother safe," she says. "And yourself."

I can't find words to answer her. What could I say? I don't deserve her trust, and she's giving it to me anyway. All I can do is nod, while in my heart, I swear I will not let her down.

Her face has gone so pale that a light smattering of freckles I've never noticed before appears across her nose. But her stride is firm as she crosses back to her mother and crouches to take both her hands into her own. "I need you to promise me something, Mother. Will you promise not to leave the solar until I come back to get you? There are soldiers coming—"

"Your father?" Flora's mother springs to her feet. "Oh, and your brothers. It must be. How wonderful! We should all go down to meet them."

Flora's lip trembles, and I feel her heart crack open in her chest almost as though it's my own heart breaking. She sends me a pleading look.

I can understand why she couldn't send her mother away. The woman's too volatile and unpredictable. As dangerous as she would have been with the other women and children, though, she's doubly dangerous now.

Flora's plan is both shrewd and bold, and it can all spin out of control unless I can keep her mother safe—and safely contained. The problem is that I'm still too low on magic, and mortals are bloody stubborn.

CHAPTER 15
GREY DEATH

CHYR

The smoke-tinged clouds of early morning break into a clammy rain that's over almost as quickly as it starts. The sun emerges as the soldiers march ever closer. Raging at my uselessness—and trapped by this absurd dress—I can only stand at the window in the solar while Flora waits below to meet them.

There are fourteen: a dozen foot soldiers wearing Vheara's uniforms of red and black, escorted by two Greys mounted on well-bred horses. The Greys' red cloaks billow behind them, and light gleams on swords undoubtedly wrought of celestial steel.

The Butcher isn't with them. That's a reprieve, for now.

Oblivious to the stakes, Flora's mother sits embroidering on the bench behind me. It cost valuable time to convince her that the soldiers coming had nothing to do with Flora's father or brothers, but now the woman drones on happily about parties she attended in Caelsolas during Fionn's reign as though nothing at all had happened.

I try to remember to nod at her occasionally as if I'm listening to her with rapt attention. That's difficult when I need to watch what's happening beyond the windows.

The soldiers halt where the military road intersects the track that runs between the keep and the steward's house before continuing to the mill and the cottages farther up the glen. The two Greys confer together, and as always when I see them, I'm horrified by what Vheara has done to them, horrified that they were once Siorai. They speak briefly, then the female Grey takes six of the uniformed men and marches them north towards Padraig's house and the mill. The other Grey turns the remaining soldiers towards the keep.

Flora hopes to remind the Greys that the Dunhaelic banner didn't fly at Culodur, and that—her younger brothers aside—the head of Clan Domhnall has been loyal to the queen. The goal is to convince them that *she* is loyal.

But the fact that the Greys have split up means Flora has little chance of changing the outcome. No matter what happens at the keep, the rest of Dunhaelic is lost already. If the Greys stick to their usual pattern, the group led by the female Grey will search the outbuildings for people. Finding none, she'll have the soldiers loot the dwellings and slaughter the sheep and cattle. Then they'll burn the structures, carcasses, and fields.

If Flora hadn't already gotten her people to safety, the Grey would bring them back to the keep to torture and use as leverage. I'm worried about what will happen when the Greys discover the buildings are empty and most of the livestock is gone.

Vheara's Greys don't use torture to achieve a goal. Vheara consumed the last of their Siorai magic before she turned them in the Gloaming. Now suffering fuels their corrupted power. They feed on agony. On terror. On rage. Their appetite has no limit, and with fewer people available, that simply means they'll draw the torture out as long as possible before they kill.

That's the one faint thread of hope to which I cling.

I pull Tirnaeve's magic through the Veilstone rings as quickly as I can and spool it inside myself to build a reserve of power. It won't be enough for a fight with the Greys, especially since I have no way of knowing what abilities they might have retained from their former lives as Siorai. But power is never about strength alone. It's about knowing how and when to wield it.

The second Grey arrives at the open gate in the outer curtain wall, his six soldiers close behind him. Instead of crossing the bridge into the keep, he has the men fan out to search the buildings outside the moat. The stables seem to draw his particular interest. He approaches them himself, dismounts, and strides inside.

Long minutes tick by before he comes back out. He crosses to a small field where a half-dozen mares are grazing, their bellies too swollen in pregnancy for the hard trek to Ben Aran. These, along with several older mares and a few of the less valuable horses, as Flora explained last night when she returned, are decoys meant to make it less obvious that most of the stock is gone.

The Grey doesn't look convinced. His gestures are abrupt. He's angry.

The mares lift their heads at his approach, then pin their ears and race towards the opposite end of the field.

Magic-sense isn't one of my stronger gifts, not like the power of air or fire, but even from here, I can feel the Grey's corrupted magic rasping like thorns against my skin.

I wonder who he was before the Gloaming and Vheara's corrupted magic twisted him into this abomination. Was he convicted and punished before my time? Or did I banish him to the Gloaming myself?

The Riders and I may hunt criminals and oathbreakers as a unit, but it's the Sword of the Anvar'thaine, my sword, that weighs and passes judgement, unlocks the doorway to the magicless twilight world between the worlds, and dooms them to eternal punishment.

Trying to find anything of the Siorai he once was in the Grey's misshapen features is pointless. The Gloaming and Vheara have obliterated any traces, anything redeeming.

The Grey peels away from the pasture fence, turns, and shouts an order. His soldiers scurry to comply. One brings his horse. The rest wait while he mounts. Then they run behind him as he canters across the bridge towards the keep.

Beyond the road, the first plume of black smoke drifts skyward from the mill, thickening quickly before being chased by flames.

The destruction of the outbuildings has begun.

The first of the Greys has reached the gate. He disappears from view beneath the curtain wall, and I cross the solar and stand at the window that overlooks the empty courtyard.

Convincing the Greys of anything is the weak point in Flora's plan, although to be fair, I couldn't think of a better one.

The idea of avoiding a fight is one I'm still struggling to embrace. Riders *are* the fight. It's the reason we exist.

Flora hoped that by meeting the Greys at the gate, she and her armsmaster—a grand title for the grizzled old soldier long since beyond his fighting days—could convince them that there is no need to search the keep at all.

With the gate out of view, I have no way of knowing how the Grey reacts. Or whether Flora and Faolan are safe. Whether they are still alive.

The minutes tick by, and nothing moves in the courtyard. No one emerges beyond the gate.

Behind me, Flora's mother must finally feel my tension. She's fallen silent. I glance back at her, and her hands are clasped in her lap. Her face is pale, the skin thin in a way that suddenly shows her age.

How much of what is happening does she actually understand? There have been occasional flashes of shrewdness in her eyes that make me wonder if she has truly lost her mind, or if this refusal to acknowledge that her husband and sons are dead is a deliberate attempt to push reality away.

Partly out of sympathy and partly from a need to do something other than stand and wait, I point to her cup and then to the teapot on the table. She smiles and gives me an exaggerated nod, and after I pour out the tea for her, she pats the bench beside her. I march like a soldier and gesture towards the window. She purses her lips and looks away.

The Grey finally appears below me in the courtyard, followed by five of the six soldiers in the group. They fan out to the various sections of the keep: the chapel, the forge, the guard tower, the barracks, the kitchen. The Grey rides directly to the stable where the valuable horses are kept, dismounts beside the door, and disappears inside.

The rain has stopped, and the sun is out, though clouds still chase across it. I watch the area near the gate for any sign of Flora, the armsmaster, or the sixth soldier that never emerged. The Grey must have ordered him to detain Flora and Faolan until the rest of the keep has been searched.

Dread pools in my stomach, and the sound of my own thudding heartbeat is too loud. Then Flora darts into view with the missing soldier close behind. He grasps her arm. She wrenches free, and Faolan steps between them, trying to protect her.

The soldier draws his sword and holds it to Faolan's throat.

My hand finds the hilt of Flora's dagger in the pocket of my useless dress, and I search for enough magic to shadow-walk to the courtyard. The blade is cold and dead in my palm—a feeble mortal weapon instead of my own sword, but it was also the only weapon that Flora possessed. She put it in my hand along with her trust and walked out into the courtyard with nothing.

I have to help her.

Drawing harder at the three Veilstones, I coax more magic through them. Demand more. They scald my skin as the magic increases.

Flora catches the soldier's sword arm, every line of her body begging him to spare the old man's life. Miraculously, the soldier lets the blade drop, an inch, then two.

I feel a heartbeat of relief, but that soon changes.

Enraged barks ring out in the kitchen tower where the cook has taken the dogs for safety. The soldier seizes Flora and pulls her in front of him as he turns to face the noise. Flora arches her neck away from his blade. The sight carves me open.

The Grey emerges from the stable and peers in the direction of the commotion. Seeing nothing, he glances across to where the soldier is holding Flora in front of him like a shield.

Eyes locked on Flora, the Grey stalks towards her.

My fists clench, and the hair rises on my neck.

Throwing my mind to the shadowed doorway at the base of the stairs, I'm relieved when my body follows. But I'm still too far away, and the soldier would have too long to kill her before I could hope to reach them.

I stagger upright and search for another shadow closer to Flora. There aren't any. The soldier has her out in the open, and the cobblestones are steaming in sunlight that streams through a wide break in the clouds.

I pull back into the doorway to keep from being spotted by the Grey as he approaches. The soldier holding Flora has gone pale, his attention fixed on the Grey. Faolan takes advantage of the distraction and draws his sword. Steel rasps as it slides from the scabbard, and the soldier holding Flora whips around to face him, using Flora as a shield, the tip of his blade pressed into the hollow of flesh beneath her chin.

Faolan stops.

My mind races. I've seen soldiers like this—caught up in situations they can't escape. Even the slightest movement now risks Flora's life.

I'll need a weapon, every scrap of magic I can summon, and the element of surprise.

Calculating odds, I glance at the Grey. Then I step out into the doorway.

Flora spots me. Her eyes widen, and she shakes her head. A small shake, scarcely visible. She's telling me to stay back, and damn it, I don't know why. It goes against my every instinct.

The commotion in the kitchen tower spills into the courtyard as three black-and-white herding dogs bolt outside, teeth bared and bodies bristling with rage. Two bleed from gashes on their backs and haunches. Blood drips from their mouths.

Flora snaps an order, and they run towards her. Then they notice the Grey and launch themselves at him instead.

The Grey barely reacts. Eyes locked on Flora, he lifts his hand almost casually. The dogs jerk to a halt mid-leap, their throats caught by invisible fists of air. Legs thrashing, they hang helplessly suspended.

I flinch towards them, then make myself stop. The Grey is an air wielder, like I am, and his magic will feed on Flora's anguish. I have to be smarter.

The sound of approaching hoofbeats pulls my attention to the gate. The second Grey—the female—trots across the bridge. So now there are two to deal with.

The first one reaches Flora. The soldier still holds the sword at her neck. Her mouth moves, pleading with the male Grey, her hand gesturing to the dogs. Showing what matters to her.

The Grey turns his head—a slow, flesh-crawling motion like a carrion crow. Then his hand flashes out. The soldier holding Flora drops to the ground, unmoving, and his fallen sword is replaced by the Grey's hand clamping around Flora's throat.

My lungs squeeze shut. Rage roars in my ears.

The Grey whips Flora around and hauls her up against him, her toes barely on the ground. Her eyes are huge, round with fear.

And dammit, I can't bear it. I will end him for that alone.

A faint shadow passes behind the Grey as a thin cloud mutes a corner of the sun. I throw myself into it, praying to the Father of Light that it will be enough.

Pain and cold tear at my limbs. The shadow is too thin to accept me. Caught in the in-between, I try to force myself through. The pressure grows crushing.

I should go back. I push harder instead, stuck in an endless loop. Then the air finally sheets flat against my skin, and I'm released into the courtyard. I drop to one knee and drag a thin cloak of shadow over me, concealing myself while I try to pull breath back into my lungs.

The Grey is enjoying Flora's fear too much to notice me— or to kill her yet.

He turns her face towards the dogs and sweeps his other arm wide, unleashing a magic so ugly that it makes mine crawl beneath my skin.

The dogs fly ten feet, and their small bodies smash against the stone wall of the chapel with a gut-churning crack. They slide down in a heap of broken bones and fur.

They lie still. Then a woman screams.

It isn't Flora. Dangling where the Grey holds her, Flora

makes a raw sound—half snarl, half sob—and goes rigid in the Grey's grasp, her eyes fixed on the small, still bodies.

The Grey closes his eyes in ecstasy, feeding on her sorrow, her rage, her terror.

The wrongness of his magic hits me like a physical assault. It's dizzying, nauseating, making it even harder to force myself upright through the wave of weakness. My foot catches in the stupid skirt.

Then three things happen at once. Flora's mother breaks from the stairwell and rushes out into the courtyard. Flora screams, "No!" And the Grey twists his hand, releasing his air magic in a tight coil of power.

Flora's mother crumples to the ground, her neck snapped to an impossible angle.

The courtyard falls still, no sound, no motion. Flora's scream knifes through the terrible silence. The sound carves into my soul.

Fury pulls magic from me.

Drawing from the Veilstones with the last of my strength, I twist air into a cord of wind, wrap it around the hilt of the Grey's sword, and wrench the weapon from its scabbard.

I pull the sword into my hand, then lunge forward and plunge it through the Grey's back into his heart.

Flora stumbles as he falls.

The female Grey is off her horse and running. She flings a mist of black and red emotion at me—the remembered anguish of victims she has tortured. All their terror, pain, and loss of hope. I've seen this attack on the battlefield, seen how the red mist sinks into men and claws through their skin until they go mad.

But I've learned from that.

I send a burst of fire at the mist and sear it to harmless ash.

My body is nearly empty—weakness pulls at my limbs

until every step feels like I'm wading a river of mud. Desperate, I drag every last scrap of magic from the cooling Veilstones and use the stream of wind I crafted to slam the iron portcullis closed. Then I coil the stream around the female Grey and the six soldiers with her and fling them all back against it.

They slide down the portcullis and fall in heaps to the stones beneath. The men stay down, barely moving, but the Grey crawls to her hands and knees.

Every fibre in my body burns, the price of emptying myself of magic. The bandage feels wet against my chest, and I suspect I'm bleeding again. None of that matters. My knees buckle, but I force myself upright. Push myself into a run.

The sword I took from the male Grey is almost too heavy to swing, but I sever the other Grey's head before she can rise.

I can't tell how many of the human soldiers are still alive, but Faolan—the old armsmaster—is already beside me, his sword poised to finish them off.

Flora kneels on the damp cobblestones, tears flowing down her cheeks. She cradles her mother's body, shock and grief etched on her face and in her stillness. When she lifts her head and finds me, there is only pain where there should be accusation. She should blame me.

Her silence breaks me open.

I want to go to her, but I failed at the one thing she asked of me. Her mother lies dead on the cobblestones, and the guilt of that burns like poison within my chest.

The threat from the Greys is over, but some of the Queen's soldiers still live. I'll need to attend to that, but first I can offer Flora's mother the same respect that Flora showed back in the Sacred Wood.

Removing the borrowed shawl that hides my hair, I cross the courtyard to where her mother lies. The broken neck exaggerates the slackness of her face, the emptiness of the vessel without the soul that lived within. Death strips away all dignity, and it's up to us to give it back.

Flora looks up at me while I drape the shawl gently over her mother's face. I let my hand drop a moment to Flora's shoulder, and I wish that I had words that could offer any sort of comfort.

"I'm sorry," is all I manage to get out. Not nearly enough.

I've seen too much death. Meted it out too often.

But that's the one thing I am trained to do.

I hand her back her dagger and turn away to seek out the remaining soldiers, because it won't be safe to tend the living or the dead until they are gone.

It's almost a relief to spot them scattered around the courtyard, hanging back. The man by the chapel darts back inside the building when he sees me coming. The three others can't seem to decide whether to attack me or retreat.

Fighting humans is hardly a fight at all. I may be weak and empty of magic, but I've had centuries to learn my craft. And I am very good at killing.

CHAPTER 16

CHOOSE A SIDE

FLORA

The first dead soldier rolls into the Hall hearth with a sickening thud. The smell of blood, urine, and loosened bowels mixes with the char of smoke that's still rising from the outbuildings in the glen.

I refuse to break down, but tears leak anyway, and my throat aches with the effort of holding back my screams.

My mother is dead. The thought is a hole in my core, and I brace my palm flat to the hearthstone to keep from sinking to my knees.

I can't help thinking she wouldn't have died if I'd forced her to go with the women and children up to the shieling huts. That seemed too cruel and dangerous at the time—she would never have agreed to go. We'd have had to tie her to a horse, and she'd have needed to be kept in restraints. Otherwise, she'd have tried to walk back on her own, regardless of the danger. She would have hated me for it, but she would still be alive.

Catriona and I have dressed her in the gown she had sewn

for the last Yule celebration when the family was all together, and her body lies upstairs on her bed now, waiting for us to make time to bury her. To mourn her. Because the queen's horrors can't even give us that.

The mill still smoulders. Padraig's house, the old byre, the cottages. All of them are gone. I can only thank the Mother for the gift of rain that kept the fires in the pastures and fields from spreading too far up Glen Colm or towards the keep. And with the two Greys and all twelve of the soldiers dead, there's no one left to finish the destruction they began.

More will come, though. I have no doubt of that, so we must make sure that every trace of the soldiers and Greys we have killed today is removed as quickly as we can manage. When additional Greys arrive, I need to be able to convince them that the first group began their destruction, then realised that we were loyal and simply moved on to inflict their misery elsewhere.

Still, burning the bodies is a miserable job. I can't help wondering who they were and how they came to a place where they would participate in wanton killing and the destruction of homes and livelihoods that would leave innocent people to starve. How has Vheara turned men against their neighbours so completely that they can do such things? I'd like to believe that she and her Greys give them no choice, but that's almost the worst part of this war: that she and the king are making us hate each other instead of fighting them.

I wedge more kindling and peat around the bodies and smear them with tallow from the cask Morag brought up from the storeroom. But I can't bring myself to look at their faces.

These men were someone's sons or husbands or sweethearts. Somewhere, a family will miss them and never know how or where they died.

The fire catches, then roars. Heat slaps my face. An ember

scorches the back of my hand, and I hurry to brush it off. Smoke spirals up the chimney in choking gasps.

There's an old scar on one man's temple. I watch it burn away, watch until the men's limbs curl inward.

More bodies are burning wherever they'd fit: the bread oven, the kitchen hearth, the forge. Morag and Faolan have carted the two dead Greys behind the ridge, where Faolan will bury them deep while Morag gathers the boughs and herbs we'll add to the fires here to disguise the stench of burning hair and flesh.

I shouldn't dare to hope that this is the worst of what will happen to us at Dunhaelic. But hope is a vicious ghost, riding my back and whispering of things that cannot be.

The question I keep circling is whether I would make the same choices again, knowing what I know now. The answer frightens me, because it's this: There is no hindsight. I would help Chyr in the Wood regardless, because it was the right— the honourable—choice.

I would still bring him here. I would let him stay. I'm not sure whether that makes me principled or simply stupid, but I am what I am. Those are my values, and changing them would diminish my ancestors and all that I've been taught.

Behind me, Catriona enters the room, her tread slower than usual. She seems diminished, as if the grief has taken a blade to her, carving down her cheeks, deepening the grooves beside her mouth. Her hands are as filthy as mine from carrying peat, firewood, and bodies. Smoke clings to her clothes, to her greying hair, to the deep lines around her eyes.

"Here, love," she says, voice hoarse but gentle. "Let me tend this for you. The water should be hot now, but take a wee moment for yourself before you go back to tend the Ever's wound."

"I'm all right," I say, the smoke raw along my throat.

"Och, aye. You'll be fit as a flea in time, I've no doubt. But you aren't yet, and there's no need to pretend otherwise. Not for us. You're not alone here."

I am, though. I'm the last Domhnall of Dunhaelic, and alone is a word with thorns and spikes.

Catriona stands with her hands clasped awkwardly in front of her, as though she doesn't know what to do with them. I wrap my arms around her, and she folds me into a hug that feels like it may break my bones.

Something tears away inside me. A sob slips out—small and ugly—and I bury it in Catriona's shoulder.

Neither of us needs to say anything. Love stands beside you when war is coming, and it's there helping you burn the bodies. There's nothing more words can add to that.

I turn away, wiping my blood-blackened hands across my apron, but there's one more thing I have to know.

"Who killed the soldier in the kitchen?" I ask. "Was it the dogs or Morag?"

"The soldier deserved worse than he received," Catriona spits. "They all did."

I turn back to face her. "It's not for his sake I'm asking."

"Oh. Well, Morag wouldn't say." Catriona steeples her hands in front of her lips, debating what to tell me. Then she shakes her head. "Torin was always her favourite dog, though. If I had to guess, I'd say he defended Morag, and the soldier killed him for it, then Morag hit the man with a pot and knocked him down. Maybe the other dogs did the rest."

I nod, the ache in my chest twisting tighter, and I add this to the growing list of casualties. Morag still finds it hard to slaughter and dress a lamb. Killing a man will take its toll on her, whatever the reason. And Faolan and Chyr? They've both killed before, but I doubt either takes death lightly.

Something presses against my leg, a reassuring weight. I

look down, expecting to find Rab there, then I remember he's up on the mountain with Iain. Maybe it's wishful thinking, but I imagine I can still feel the other dogs around me, the tick of their claws on stone, their warm breath as they lie panting and watchful while I work. The sensation is so real that the hairs bristle on my arms.

The door to the receiving room is thick, oak-banded, and swings on well-oiled hinges. I'm relieved to see Chyr twitch to attention on the long oak bench opposite the hearth. The scent of boiled linen and the too-sweet smell of Ever blood mix with the resin smoke from the hearth. Flame shadows dance across the walls.

Chyr's chest and arms are bare—the dress he hated so much is finally gone. The heavy plaid of Domhnall tartan I wrapped around his waist earlier is slung low across his hips, the wool dark with damp. In the firelight, sweat sheens the beautiful curve of his shoulder, the thick corded muscles of his arms, the hollow of his throat.

"It's becoming a habit, me having to tell you not to tear yourself open," I say.

His grin is weak but valiant. "Maybe someday I'll follow your advice."

"You'd have less blood leaking through your bandages if you did."

He drops his head back to the bench, and I don't like his cool, pale skin or the rasp of his breath. But I have all I need laid out, and I wash my hands, then refill the basin with heated water and pour another dose of medicine into the cup.

"Father of Light, give me no more of that bloody medicine," Chyr says. "My tongue feels like an untanned hide, and my mind has turned to sludge."

"It's henbane, and you need it to ease the pain."

He grasps my arm before I can bring the cup closer. The touch is firm, his palm warm and calloused, and his fingers curve slowly over my skin, his thumb a whisper across my wrist.

"Flora—" His voice cracks. For once, he doesn't try to hide his hurt. The deep furrow between his brows, the flush along his cheekbones, the slow flare of darkness in his eyes...

Sliding his palm along mine, he folds our hands together. They fit easily, like two notes melding into a single, resonant chord.

"I'm sorry about your mother. I should have saved her. She—you both—deserved better from me."

My throat fills with an ache that stops my breath. An ache I have to fold away for another day.

"You couldn't have seen that coming," I manage to say. "I'm the one who was arrogant enough to think I could bluff my way through and keep everyone safe. I thought I understood what the Greys were like. I didn't."

A shudder rolls through me, and I shut my mind against the memories. The cruel enjoyment in the colourless eyes. The crack of bone snapping in my mother's neck.

I force myself to finish. "I saw a dead Grey on the battlefield where my father and brother died," I say. "That was a horror, but this was the first time I've seen one alive—if that's what you can call the state of them. I didn't expect the way they watch us, like vultures plucking out their next meal. The way we're almost dead to them already, so it's nothing at all to take a life."

Chyr's fingers tighten on my hand, his eyes brighter than they should be. "This is why I need my head clear." His voice dips low, nearly lost beneath the pop and hiss of the fire. "They need to be stopped, and I have to leave. Tonight, if you'll loan me a horse and do what you can to patch me up again."

"Why tonight?" I should pull my hand away, but I stare at him instead. No matter how I turn them around in my head, the words make no sense. "Are you *trying* to kill yourself?"

He draws a breath, though I can't tell whether that's from physical pain or the emotion of all that's happened. "The longer I stay here, the more danger you'll be in. And we're running out of time. We—*I*—have one chance to return to Tirnaeve and bring an army back to help fight Vheara. For that to happen, I need to reach Muilean on the western coast by Beltane Eve. Weak as I am, I'll need as much time as possible to get there."

I flinch at the name of the Sacred Isle—and the sacred date on the cusp of spring and summer when the Veil between the worlds is thinnest. It was at Beltane that the Cailleachans used to be held on Muilean to crown the Cailleach Queens, though the Sun King ended that.

"Why Muilean?" I ask, finally forcing myself to pull my hand away.

Chyr closes his eyes with a sigh, then answers: "Vheara changed the seals that lock the permanent doorways between our worlds to respond only to her magic. The only exception we were able to find was the doorway on Muilean that we came through last year. Either Vheara couldn't corrupt it, or she forgot about it. It only opens once a year."

"For the Maiden's Hunt—the Cailleachan." My tone is bitter. "But why would it open now? The Compact is broken and the last Hunt was four centuries ago."

Chyr pushes his hair back and rubs his temple as if his head aches. "Legal documents and magic are equally tricky, and the Compact is both of those. It states that the Master can call the doorway to open for the Anvar'thaine on Beltane Eve. That's how we came through, and I hope it's how we can return."

It's my turn to sigh as I pick up the cup of henbane again to offer it to him. The more I consider what he's said, though, the more fury creates a hard knot in my chest.

"You begged me to give you time because it would save us, all of us." The words come out of me in a rush. "But even if you could reach Muilean in seven days, wouldn't it be another year before you can come back and bring an army with you? Vheara would have ground the rebellion to dust by then—and every clan in the Highlands with it."

"I think—I hope—that the army is already waiting. Vheara had been working on her escape from the Gloaming a long time before she arrived in Alba Scoria, but no one in Tirnaeve knew that. There was no chance to ready an army to come through the doorway with us. Now Chulainn's had an entire year to prepare. Before we'd even left, he ordered his mages to find a way to send the reinforcements through."

"Yet no one has come," I say.

Chyr's eyes meet mine, then he looks away. "True," he agrees. "Not yet."

He's good at schooling his expressions, but his jaw gets harder the more he pretends he isn't bothered, and the pain is there, buried in the deep layers of his eyes, revealing the months of hope and heartbreak that he and the Riders must have lived through waiting for help that never came. There's also the toll that's taken in human lives, and I know Chyr feels that keenly.

"What if Vheara has managed to seal that doorway, too?"

"I pray that she's forgotten it exists. The Cailleach Queens and the Hunt for the Maiden are no more than a distant memory for most."

My knuckles go white on the cup, and something of my rage must show. Chyr struggles to sit up.

"Flora, I didn't mean—"

"Four minutes or four centuries, it doesn't matter how long it's been. You can pray all you like, but no one in Alba Scoria will forget a stolen throne or the fact that Fionn used the last Hunt to kill the queen and crown himself."

Of all our ancient stories, those about the ritual of choosing a new Cailleach Queen are the most revered. The Hunting of the Maiden was a chance for the Riders of the Anvar'thaine to prove they were worthy of the Maiden and for the Maiden to prove she was worthy to become the queen.

Neither the Sun King nor the Raven Queen was chosen. They simply took the crown as if it were theirs by right. The rebel king is trying to do the same.

Chyr watches me for another long moment, then shakes his head. I know he's going to say, "I'm sorry," again, but his apologies mean nothing.

I take advantage of his confusion to press the cup of henbane to his lips. "Drink."

This time, he doesn't argue. He drains it all, and I guide his shoulders back to the bench, settle myself, and begin to clean the wound that he's torn open.

The heat of his body releases the earthy scent of the bog moss I placed over the wound earlier to reduce the inflammation. There's also a hint of the spent lightning smell that comes from the celestial iron.

I peel the moss and bandages aside and cut away the remnants of the stitching where the wound has opened. There's more blackening than before, but it's a slow spread, not an infestation.

Lower down, whole sections of the flesh I stitched together have begun to knit themselves closed, and the pink seam at the bottom of the cut has healed well enough to fade to silver.

Chyr is doing better, but not well enough to reach Muilean.

As if he's heard my thought, his eyes find mine and hold them. "There's only a week left if I leave tonight. I need to give myself as much time as I can."

I pull my eyes away and concentrate on picking out the broken threads where my stitching has come undone. "And where is the king? The other Riders?"

Chyr pauses so long that I look up to study him. He's struggling with the pain again, and the faint scar near his mouth stands out stark silver against the rest of his skin.

I run my fingertip across it, and my breath catches traitorously when he shudders in response.

"Was this made by celestial steel?" I ask.

"It was. The wounds leave scars even though they start to heal as soon as the metal is removed."

I pluck out another broken thread from his wound, but he catches my hand suddenly and brings it to his lips. Then he holds it while I stare at him in shock.

The thought of him leaving makes me want to memorise his features, every curve and hard angle of them, and the layered depths of his eyes that hold as much danger as a selkie's invitation.

"You don't want to hear it," he says, "but I am sorry, Flora. For all of this. Your family. Your home. I know how it feels to lose the things that matter most. The choices I made in not telling you… We couldn't risk anyone knowing where we are going, not even General Mora, so we split up to lay false trails until we can all meet again at the doorway. If the army isn't there, I swear we'll make the—"

He cuts off with a muffled curse, and his chest arches up,

the muscles in his back clenching so hard that it bows his spine. Several of the black runes on his arm light up in gold, and the bands slowly crawl around the thick-veined muscles.

"What is it, Chyr? Tell me what I can do to help?"

He collapses back to the bench, sweat beading on his temples and his breath coming too fast. When he finally relaxes, he looks at me, and there's no expression on his face at all.

"Would you be willing to use your magic to heal me again?" he asks. "To pull out more of the celestial iron."

"You were dying then. You had nothing to lose—"

"I'm still dying, and it will have been for nothing unless I can reach Muilean in time. Vheara will win, and you won't be safe—no one in Alba Scoria will be. Stopping her is worth any risk."

"All I did yesterday was draw your fever. If you're asking me to draw all the poison out, you might as well ask me to give you the moon."

"Are you certain that's all you did?"

His eyes find mine, and my heart gives a thud at the expression welling in them. I'm not sure if it's pain or fear, but whatever it is, I hate to see it.

"I wouldn't know how to begin to draw poison out of your body," I say. "Where would it even have gone?"

"Your skin was smoking."

"You think I burned some of it away?"

"At least some of your magic must come from the Cailleach Queens, from the land and the Great Mother herself. I can't fathom how that works, but if it's anything like Siorai magic, it's not something anyone can teach you. Magic is as individual as we are, and there's no right or wrong to how we feel our way through learning."

"If I wanted to experiment, I'd begin with a broken bird's wing, not—"

"Not what?" He reaches up as I bend over him and cups the curve of my cheek with his palm. The heat of his touch pools beneath my skin, trying to draw out an answer I'm unwilling to give myself, much less to this man who sees and understands too much.

I don't want to believe in the rebel king. I don't want to support him, but after what I saw today, after what the Greys did, I don't have a choice because the Raven Queen must die.

As much as I want to stay to protect Dunhaelic and my own people myself, I can't stand back when there's much more at stake. The women and children in the hills will be no safer if I am here, and Faolan can see to the building of an escape out of the keep in case Vheara's army comes in force. We would lose Dunhaelic, but as long as Vheara is defeated, we can rebuild. If she remains in power, then all is lost.

I'll heal Chyr. I'll trade my pain to give Chyr strength. My pain to save him and let him get to Muilean so he can save what he can of my world. But I can't let him go alone, because he won't make it there without me.

The room feels like it's shrinking around us, and I pull away.

"I'll cut out as much of the blackness as possible again," I tell him. "Then I'll try to draw the rest out with magic. But I have a condition."

"Anything," he says in that voice that curls through me like peat smoke. "I'll give you whatever is in my power to give you. Believe me, I'm aware that I'm asking far more from you than I should."

"Swear it. Promise you'll give me what I ask."

"If it's in my power to grant it, I swear on my oaths and the Father of Light to give it to you. What do I have to do?" His eyes search mine.

My jaw set, I refuse to look away. "Take me with you to Muilean. Whatever the outcome when I try to heal you, you'll need me to make sure you get there."

"No." His tone brooks no argument.

"You swore, and you need me. I know the Highlands and the clans. Mainly, I'll be there to help if something goes wrong with your wound. If it isn't healing."

"Apart from the other dangers, we could all be walking into a trap if Vheara knows about the doorway."

"Today proved that staying here won't change anything. I can't save my people on my own. Vheara will send more Greys and more soldiers, and you won't be here to stop them."

Chyr's jaw tightens. "I'm sorry, Flora."

"Sorry doesn't change anything. No one I love will be safe until Vheara is dead, so I want to help. I can't fight her, but I can make sure you get to Muilean."

"No—"

"Yes. I've made the trip through the Ehrugael—the coastal area—many times with my father. I know the routes and the people know me. If you hope to make it in a week, you can't afford to turn away my help."

Chyr's eyes burn into mine, and he brushes his knuckles lightly against my jaw. That sends a spark of heat along my nerves, feather-soft and devastating, a warning that a journey with Chyr will be dangerous in many ways.

"I hate that you use my own arguments against me. There should be a rule against that," Chyr says with a twitch of his lips as though he's trying not to smile. "But if you insist, then yes, I will accept your terms. As long as we can leave tonight."

CHAPTER 17
DARK-EDGED HUNGER

CHYR

F lora's footsteps echo across the stone floor of the Great Hall beyond the door. I recognise their pattern, how they reveal her mood. The steps are slow now, heavy with grief, exhaustion, and what she perceives as failure.

I push myself to a sitting position on the long bench where I've been resting. The wound in my chest screams, but I'd rather get the worst of my display of weakness out of the way before she's here to see it.

The door opens without a sound, letting in the thick, greasy smoke and the stench of burning corpses that the burning juniper boughs haven't fully hidden. A glance at Flora's face is enough to reveal the damage I have done. She clutches a pile of clothing in unsteady hands, and the dark pain hasn't yet left those big, grey eyes.

"Flora, please sit." I make room for her beside me.

She shakes her head and refuses to meet my eyes. "I still have a hundred things to do before we leave. Iain and the women and children and livestock will need to stay in the hills, and I need flowers for the tomb—"

"Will you be strong enough to leave tonight? Be honest."

Her chin lifts. "You're the one with the gaping hole where your chest should be."

"Which isn't your fault. I asked too much—"

"I failed," she whispers as if the words are too hard to admit. "I couldn't pull all the poison out, and I couldn't even mend the flesh—"

"Lack of perfection isn't failure." I need her to hear me. "It was the first time you tried to pull the celestial iron out with magic, and you did knit some of the flesh together. Your stitching will hold the rest."

She stares at the wall, refusing to look at me. "What if that's not enough?"

I take her hand and tug lightly until I have her focus back. "I've made peace with dying, Flora. As long as we can get to Muilean by Beltane and open the doorway, you'll have given me more than I dared to hope for."

The oathbands don't like that answer, and it's a battle to keep the pain from showing.

"If I get weaker on the journey there, you'll be with me to help," I add. "Now, be honest. Are you well enough to ride tonight? There's only so much that strength of will can do to compensate for exhaustion."

"And there's the bee scolding the wasp for stinging." She forces a smile that doesn't extend beyond her lips, every line of her body set with determination as she pushes her long braid back over her shoulder. The firelight behind her streaks her hair in every colour of flame and moonlight, and I've never seen anything more beautiful than she is in this moment.

"Let's make a pact," I say. "We won't ask each other how

we feel. But if we can't go on, if we need to rest, we'll admit it. No pretence."

She nods. A small victory. Then she sets the bundle of clothing nearby and frowns down at me. I try to look innocent—something I haven't been in four centuries, more or less.

Motioning for me to slide to the far end of the bench, she removes a long length of plaid fabric from the pile she set down and shakes it out with a flick of her wrists. Starting near the centre, she folds it into wide pleats lengthwise, then lays it atop a narrow belt crosswise on the bench.

"Watch how this is done," she says. "I don't intend to dress you every morning while we're travelling. Hips go here so the kilt will hit above the knee."

She helps me ease my body down, then she drapes the woollen cloth over my lap, first one side and then the other. I lie perfectly still.

Then she makes it worse.

Beneath the thicker wool plaid, I still have on the shorter, thinner fabric she fastened around me earlier. She reaches to remove the pin holding it in place, and her knuckles skim the bare skin at my hip.

"Raise your hips for me," she says, her voice clinical. Soft.

But Father help me, my entire body tightens in response.

"Keep asking me that, and it will be dangerous." I mean the words to come out lightly. They sound like a growl instead, dark-edged with hunger.

Flora freezes, and the air between us thickens. Finally, she takes up both ends of the belt that will hold the plaid in place and hands them to me to fasten.

"You can sit up again," she says once I have that done. Her voice is gentle, but her hands still tremble as she picks up a shirt and a buff coat from the pile of clothing on the table.

"These belonged to my brother Rory. Like Catriona, he was a good bit rounder than you are, but that should mean they'll fit. Lift your arms."

The coat is the sort many Highlanders wear in battle, a short doublet-style jacket of tanned ox hides thick enough to stop a knife or glancing sword blow.

At the moment, I would welcome a simple fight. I'd take on all seven of the remaining Riders and let them remind me not to forget the reason we are here.

She starts to tug the linen shirt over my head, but, pain or no pain, I have enough pride left to finish dressing on my own. The shirt and coat are snug, but not so tight that I won't be able to swing a sword.

"Now, stand up, and I'll show you how the rest of the kilt is fastened," she says.

She's dangerously close when I push myself to my feet. I hope she'll step back, but she doesn't, and the bench behind me blocks my retreat. She tucks the shirt inside the kilt for me, and my skin comes alive as my magic responds to hers, drawn towards her as if it's as starved for her touch as I am.

The smaller kilt she'd left underneath falls to pool at my feet, and she stoops to pick it up. I hold my breath, not daring to move, but her breath sifts warm through the shirt and bandage on my chest as she rises again.

She doesn't look at me. Instead, she drops the small kilt on the bench, then gathers the excess fabric at the back of the great plaid and pulls it tight. The wool whispers as she draws one side across my right shoulder and slides it down my chest. She brings the other side up to meet it.

Her hand lingers along my collarbone, and she pushes a large pin in place to hold the folds. The heat of her palm remains like a haunting after she removes it.

I could bring my mouth down on hers. My body responds

at the thought, but that would change things neither of us can afford to change.

Would the oathbands consider that a violation? Or would they stay dormant? Not knowing what they'll react to is a threat all its own.

Flora steps back and hands me a second belt that contains a flat, round pouch and an empty scabbard. Thankfully, she allows me to put that on myself.

"Weapons?" I ask, my mouth still dry. "I've never seen a Highlander dress without an impressive collection of knives and daggers."

"I'll bring down what my brothers had that they didn't take with them," she says a little hoarsely, "and we'll pick up your sword on the way. Faolan's preparing my mother's...grave, but if you need anything else from the armoury, he'll give it to you when he's finished."

I wonder if Faolan has any self-control to lend me. Flora can't even say the word *grave* without breaking inside. She hasn't had time to grieve, and I'm pulling her away from everything she loves.

I refuse to take advantage of her vulnerability. But the way she tugs at my heart, the way I want her, the way my body remembers the shape of her hands—I've never felt this before.

We have seven nights to reach Muilean before the doorway opens. Seven nights in her company. Seven nights pretending I don't feel what I feel. Seven days trying to sleep when she's too close. How I'll survive that long without breaking my oaths or breaking one or both of us, I can't begin to think.

The candles gutter in the sconces as she shuts the door behind her. The route to Muilean may kill me in more ways than one.

CHAPTER 18

GIFT OF ILLUSION

FLORA

The moon rides low above the battlements of the Guard Tower by the time Chyr and I are ready to leave the keep. Ash and grief swirl through the courtyard air, dissolving into the ice-crusted puddles left by the overnight rain.

Throughout the keep, the fires still burn, the stench of corpses masked by herbs and juniper boughs added to the flames. By morning, Morag and Catriona will clean the fireplaces and toss the last evidence that the queen's soldiers were here onto the midden heap.

Faolan has already left to deliver messages in the village, and he'll ride from there to Ben Aran to help Iain build a shelter. The horses will need to stay away from Dunhaelic as long as danger remains.

All of them—Catriona, Morag, and Faolan—refuse to abandon Dunhaelic in favour of somewhere safer.

My goodbyes are said—to the living and the dead—and I

will not let them break me. My mother rests in the crypt beside my father, not far from all three of her sons. Whatever happens next, I will console myself that at least they will be together.

I wipe a fresh layer of ash from Bramble's mane and check our supplies. Bramble's bridle jingles as she stomps her foot, and her breath rises in a cloud. Eira, the pale mare I've chosen for myself, flicks an ear, watching wary-eyed as I check the girth on her saddle a final time. She's less sensible than Bramble, but she's strong enough to carry two while Chyr is too weak to ride alone.

After swinging myself into the saddle, I extend my hand to Chyr. His breath hisses as he pulls himself up behind me. He's in no condition for us to leave tonight, but he's right that we have little choice if we're to reach Muilean in time. Avoiding any routes the Raven Queen's patrols might use from here in the central Highlands to the western coast will push us off the main roads and take us longer than usual. Especially if we have to ride under cover of darkness to avoid being seen. Seven nights is barely time enough.

"Be careful," Catriona calls.

"You, too. All of you," I answer. "And make sure the escape tunnel is finished as soon as possible. I'll speak to Ailean about it on our way through the village."

I do my best not to cry as I walk Eira to the gate. Morag turns away with her shoulders shaking, and Catriona moves to fold her into a hug. They stand together, heads bowed and their woollen plaids pulled over their hair to protect against the falling ash.

Family isn't always the one you're born to. The wave of love I feel for this place, these people, catches in my throat. But living has to be more than surviving another day, another battle. Love is fighting with all I have to preserve a place in our world for the good and the light—love is not giving in to darkness.

The bridge creaks as we cross it, and Eira sidesteps nervously. Bramble crosses without a fuss, trailing behind us on a long lead rope tied behind my saddle.

Ahead of us, the moon gleams dark on the burned wood and blistered ruins of the outbuildings. I count the charred carcasses of cattle and sheep in the fields, letting the atrocities fuel my resolve. Then we reach the remains of Padraig's house and turn to follow the stream that runs up the back side of the Sacred Wood. I look back for a last glimpse of Dunhaelic Glen and the distant keep.

All my limbs go cold at once, and a lump of ice settles in my stomach. The bit clinks as Eira tosses her head.

Dunhaelic Keep has been destroyed. The buildings behind the outer curtain wall stand in jagged teeth of fire-blackened beams and piles of rubble, and where yellow torchlight glowed at the gate and the Guard Tower and the Lord's Tower when we rode out, now there is only dark and moonlight. Crenellations atop the battlements have fallen, and the stone is scorched and ruined by smoke.

"That isn't real," I breathe. "It can't be real."

Chyr tightens his arms around me. "It isn't. Lord, Flora. I didn't mean for you to see it like that."

I shake my head. "What did you do?"

"It's an illusion. A mask to keep the queen's hunters from paying attention if they come looking for the Greys and the soldiers I killed." Chyr's voice is a low rumble in my good ear.

My heart unclenches slowly, and for one wild second, I want to throw Chyr off the horse. "Why didn't you warn me? Great Mother, do you have any idea what I felt seeing that?"

"I can imagine, and I'm sorry. I tried to keep the magic from settling in place until there was no risk of you looking back. But it takes a lot to hold an illusion that size in my head, and I couldn't contain it any longer."

"Why not just tell me what you were doing?"

"Catriona said you would argue with me."

My heart speeds up again. "Why would I?"

Chyr remains silent long enough that I think he won't answer at all, and then he says, "It meant leaving one of the Veilstones to anchor the illusion."

"Are you out of your mind?" I twist in the saddle, trying to see his face in the moonlight. "Why would you do that? You need the ring for healing, and we may need you to use that magic if we run into problems."

"If you're coming along to keep me alive," he says in a voice that brooks no argument, "then I want to make sure the people you love survive until you come home again. This way, if any more of Vheara's forces come by, they'll see that the keep has already been destroyed, and they'll feel a suggestion that they don't need to look any closer. That's the least I can do for you."

For you.

Two words. They shouldn't mean anything.

But every wisp of magic Chyr has spent protecting what I love is strength he won't have available to heal himself. He'll pay for giving up the Veilstone, and the price will be measured in pain.

"I'm grateful," I whisper, and I hope he can understand how much I mean it.

Mist curls low along the ridge path, stirring with every hoofbeat. My chest still aches with loss, and my body sags from fatigue, but Chyr's presence is warm and solid behind me. I'm aware of his arms around my waist, the muscles of his thighs along mine, the rise and fall of his chest against my back.

The kilt and clothing he wears belonged to my older brother Rory. The kind one. The buff coat still smells of Rory, of nettle soap and heather that brings back a memory of him left over from the summer I turned eleven, when we'd hide side by side in the purple blooms, stalking red deer stags. It was Rory, soft, portly, and infinitely patient, who taught me how to hunt.

Chyr has none of Rory's softness, and even the scent is somehow sharper. The coat and the shirt underneath strain across Chyr's muscled chest and shoulders, and he's covered himself in weapons. Bracers fitted with knives encase his wrists, throwing dirks rest in his boots, and a dagger hangs beside the empty scabbard from the belt at his hip. He also wears the two swords he collected from the Greys across his shoulders.

We reach the willow tree by the stream and turn onto the deer trail that leads upward to the ridge. The bodies of the two Riders rest beneath the place I left them, and I rein Eira in and swing my leg over her neck to jump down first so I can steady Chyr as he dismounts. We end up standing too close, and it feels as though he means to say something. But his eyes are focused on my lips.

That look is a promise—and a threat. It portends a kiss, if not now then soon, and the thought makes me forget to breathe.

I need to guard my heart.

As much as Chyr makes my defences crumble, I have to remember that Evers are dangerous—and that he has a plan that involves him leaving in seven days. One that he hasn't fully shared with me. I'm certain there are still many things he hasn't told me.

For the moment, we are reluctant allies. We share a goal, and that is all.

Still, I almost feel that kiss between us.

Chyr clears his throat and turns to examine the ground, searching for the grave.

"It's here." I point out the uneven row of river-tumbled stones Morag left as a marker after she buried the bodies. The churned earth is covered over with leaves, and if not for the stones, the grave would have been invisible.

Chyr sinks into a crouch, his spine bowed as he touches two fingertips to the ground. He closes his eyes, and I realise how much I've come to rely on the small changes within them to tell me what he's feeling. His face itself gives so little away.

I move behind him and lay my hand on his shoulder, saying nothing. A touch can be more honest than words.

For a heartbeat or two, he doesn't move, but then he lifts his own hand and places it on top of mine.

The woods are quiet with the stillness of peaceful sleep.

Then the darkness stirs.

Two long shadows separate themselves from the trees and glide towards us, too impossibly thin to be human, but growing more solid as they approach. Their eyes glow blue in pale, nearly transparent faces that have no other features. They look directly at me.

They should terrify me, but my heart beats steady. The Sacred Wood and its creatures offer me no warning. There's something solemn and dignified about the shadows, something both reverent and familiar.

As if Chyr senses something similar, he lifts his head and looks directly at them. He gives them a nod of acknowledgement, and they nod back. Then they return to watching me and slowly incline their heads.

Chyr braces a hand on the ground to steady himself and pushes to his feet.

"Let's find the swords and go," he says, his breath rough.

The two shadows turn their attention to the grave. Unmoving and silent, they stand as though they're keeping vigil.

CHAPTER 19
GRAVES AND GUARDIANS

I've never seen a ghost. Can immortals have ghosts? Would they look like this, or are the two haunting figures something else?

It doesn't seem like the right moment to ask Chyr such questions, so I concentrate on digging up the three swords I buried. I hand them to him, and he slides the sword with the pommel of yellow crystal into the empty scabbard at his belt, and replaces the swords crossed over his back with those that belonged to the other two Riders.

We bury the Grey's weapons in the same place, covered with soil and leaves and marked with another rock. Faolan will know where they're buried in case they're needed. Then we mount Eira once again.

The Sacred Wood is thick with mist and darkness as we cross the ridge. It's senseless to miss Ari and his capricious temper, but as I loosen the reins to let Eira and Bramble pick their way through the roots and slippery moss down to the military road, I can't help myself. I miss everyone and everything I've lost and left behind, and we haven't yet left the boundaries of Dunhaelic.

We reach the military road before dawn, when the sky is already growing lighter and the night is at its coldest. The horses send clouds of breath into the air, their hooves crunching on flakes of frost.

I turn west and set Eira into a canter. Chyr's weight settles heavier against my back. Maybe it was seeing the grave and the ghosts that took the rest of his strength, but I suspect there simply wasn't enough reserve in him to travel yet. His thighs and chest feel too hot against mine, and whenever I shift in the saddle, his hand tightens at my waist, and he exhales as if it costs him. His every breath moves through me. With me. I can't escape it. Can't escape thoughts I shouldn't have.

We have hours to ride before we rest. The time that we remain on Domhnall land will be the safest portion of the journey—and the only chance to ride by daylight. We need to take advantage and cover as much ground as we can.

Once clear of the Sacred Wood, the road slopes downward, and the moor opens wide beneath us. Strangely, it's here that I feel our departure most.

The story of Lannraig, the seer who came too close to the Veil and let the magic destroy her, warns that magic is a trap. I can't help feeling that whatever waits for me is already set and baited, and I'm riding towards it like a lamb to the slaughter.

Here, at the end of the Sacred Wood, our path along the military road crosses the *betweens*. We're between wood and field, between night and morning, between everything we left burning at Dunhaelic and whatever waits at Muilean.

The nearer of the two Dunhaelic villages appears ahead, nestled against the hillside. A rim of fields lies scattered around it, and I scan them for movement, though ordinarily, it would be too early yet.

I pull Eira to a halt and jump from the saddle.

"You should ride Bramble until we clear the village," I say to Chyr. "Can you manage?"

He draws himself up as though the question's an insult. "Do I need an illusion?"

I look up at him. Dressed as a Highlander, astride one of our horses, he's still unmistakably what he is. Our warriors can be tall and broad, strong from work and battle. Some wear their hair much like Chyr, shoulder length with the top and sides pulled back into a warrior's knot. But physical beauty and the gravity of his injuries aside, Chyr is *more*, as though the extra lifeforce of his immortality is crammed inside him, his strength and magic barely leashed by bone and flesh.

"Can you make yourself look less like...?"

"Less like what? A Siorai? A giant's spinster aunt?" Chyr asks, sounding almost amused.

"Just less," I say with a sigh. "The village is one of ours. They're loyal, but it's best not to raise any questions."

I reach for his hand to help him down. He hasn't mastered the kilt yet, and it rides high on his thighs, revealing lean muscles as he steps down beside me.

"What were those shadows at the grave?" I ask. "Do Siorai have ghosts?"

Chyr sends me a startled glance. "You truly don't know?"

"The list of what I don't know could fill the keep. You'll need to be specific."

"The shadows were Hallow Keepers."

My hands close on the reins, and Eira pulls the bit in protest.

"Hallow Keepers?" I ask. "But all the magical creatures left before the High King of Tirnaeve sealed the doorways."

Chyr raises his eyebrows and shakes his head. "They follow you around, and you haven't seen them?"

He unclips Bramble and takes her reins while my brain spins in useless circles.

"Shadelings are part of the native magic of Alba Scoria," he says. "They wouldn't have survived in Tirnaeve, so Queen Nicnevin—"

"The Cailleach Queen who negotiated the Compact with the High King?"

"She took responsibility for them, but given the mistrust of magic that came from what Vheara and other Siorai had done, Shadelings generally prefer to remain unseen."

"The Hallow Keepers knew I saw them."

"They may have wanted you to, but it's also possible that your magic is strong enough to see through their concealments the same way Siorai can."

"And you've seen them around me before?"

Chyr's breath is shallow as he moves to stand at Bramble's saddle, and he doesn't try to mount. "Not Hallow Keepers specifically—various Shadelings at different times. Shadehounds guarded you in the Woods after I...attacked you, and Twilight Weavers tend your fires. That doesn't mean they are following you—they may be more restricted in where they live now that Vheara's made it too dangerous for them to use their shortcuts through the Gloaming."

The idea that Shadelings have never left Alba Scoria is oddly less shocking than the idea of magical creatures helping me without my knowledge.

I'd like to deny it, but I can't—I have seen them in the past. Hints and flickers, at least. The shape of a three-fingered hand in the firelight, a shadow that moves when nothing should. Whispers like intuition. Like my grandmother's voice. The stories say Whisperwraiths can do such things. Even the idea to turn my dagger into a sword to defend myself from my brothers came to me in a whisper. How else would I have known to try?

Chyr leans against the saddle, pinning me with that steady intensity that makes it so hard to look away from him. "They may also be drawn to your magic."

"Why mine? Why not my grandmother, or a hundred others in my family?"

"Can you be sure they weren't? Your magic was outlawed. And you did say your grandmothers could heal."

"One of them. Though now that you mention it, they would both leave offerings of herbs or flowers for the dark folk. Even Morag leaves out saucers of milk and bits of food in the kitchen. That sort of belief has never died."

"You see?" Chyr grips the saddle, one foot in the stirrup, and his muscles bracing to push off the ground. But he hesitates.

I duck around Eira to help. "I knew you weren't well enough to leave yet."

"I'm perfectly capable."

"If you were, then you'd be in the saddle instead of arguing."

He huffs as he swings himself up. "I was distracted. I'm crafting a mask to make myself less handsome. Drastic changes take more magic."

"Try making yourself a little more humble while you're at it."

"It's hard to be humble when you think I'm pretty," he says, grinning. His voice is still laced with pain, but there's also that low purr in it that makes my next breath too slow.

"Don't do that," I snap. "And don't pretend you don't know what I mean."

I glance at him, and he no longer looks like Chyr. The perfection of his features is suddenly carved more roughly, and his skin looks two decades older—harder and more weathered.

He looks mortal and ordinary, which is what I wanted. I find that I don't like it, and his mouth twitches at the corners as though he knows.

"Don't forget to change the sword," I say. "It's too distinctive."

"The sword can't be enchanted, but I'll keep the pommel hidden." He twitches the drape of his plaid to cover it.

The village is stirring already, though it's quieter than usual. Blue peat smoke rises from a handful of chimneys. Hens scuttle through muddy yards, a door bangs, and a dog barks once, then quiets.

Ailean limps in from the nearby field as we approach, wiping his wrinkled, work-roughened hands against the skirt of his plaid.

His eyes flick over Chyr, taking in every weapon and every muscle as well as every feature. "You've hired a guard for yourself, is it?"

"For the journey I have to make," I say. "Did everyone get off safely?"

"Aye, or nearly so." Ailean turns his attention back to me. "Only a few who're too stubborn to go are left. Most were happy to follow their wives and bairns to the hills when Faolan came with the message. But it will chafe at them, mind you. They'll not want to stay away too long."

I sigh and take out a small flask from my pack and hand it to him. "I wanted to bring another supply of the hawthorn and motherwort cordial for your granddaughter's heart. Morag can make up the rest of what anyone might need."

"Thank you." Nodding, Ailean accepts the flask.

"I'll be gone a couple of weeks, but Morag, Catriona, and Faolan will remain. Will you make sure the escape tunnel is dug as soon as possible? You can bring everyone back from the hills once there's a safe way to get them in as well as out if needed.

We should post lookouts on both ends of the road as well to give ourselves time to get to safety."

"I can take care of that. And you want the escape route to run out to the dry moat from the crypt, Faolan said?"

"With some hidden footholds up the side of the dry moat into the thickest part of the woods. Meanwhile, there's livestock enough, and we have supplies in the storerooms. But warn our people not to be fooled if they see a ruin as they approach—the appearance isn't what it seems. Faolan will open the gate when he recognises friends."

Ailean digests that for a moment, his eyes narrowing. Then he nods. "Magic, is it? And past time, too, for the Mother to send us something useful. What should we say if an outsider asks what's happened?"

"Tell them a dozen of the queen's soldiers passed through here with two Greys and a number of our best horses after they destroyed Dunhaelic. They were riding quickly, but you've no idea where they went."

Ailean runs a hand through his wiry grey hair, then folds his arms across his chest. "I'll ride to the other village and tell them the same. But without wanting to add more worries to your plate, you should know I was told the Clan Council would be meeting soon—without you."

"Was it the stewards from Ceapaich and Gleanngaradh who told you so?"

"Aye." Ailean nods. "But the Council would be bloody fools to try."

I keep my voice level. "The promise of power can make men foolish. That's no surprise to anyone. Can you hold them off for a couple of weeks? Send word to anyone who'll help."

"Don't dismiss the danger, my lady. And if you don't mind me saying, it may be time to choose yourself a husband—before the Council chooses one for you."

"Not you too, Ailean?" My stomach clenches. "I'm not a prize filly to be auctioned off."

Something flickers at the corner of my eye, and I cast a quick look at Chyr. The illusion he's been wearing drops away momentarily, giving me a glimpse of the Ever before the human male is back.

Ailean doesn't seem to have noticed, and I want to keep it that way. "Is there anyone in particular," I ask him, "you have in mind for me to marry?"

"Ceapaich is a horse's ass, but he won't play by any rules. The Gleanngaradh heir is a man who'd suit you better. He's older and not much to look at, that's true enough, but he's good in a fight, and he doesn't lack for sense."

Chyr makes a low growling sound that turns into a cough as Ailean casts a glance in his direction.

Then Ailean steps closer to me and lowers his voice. "All of us here would make our oaths to you, husband or no. We know well you're the one who's managed Dunhaelic long before your father and Rory died. And you were right about the war when the Council and your father were wrong. Plenty of us will say as much to the Council if you let us."

"Let's fight one war at a time, shall we? But thank you." He's a good man, and I give him a genuine smile. "If the Council tries to call the meeting before I'm back, don't tell them I'm away. Simply remind them that I buried the last of my family in the crypt last night. And if that doesn't work, tell Faolan to close the gate and make it clear I'll hold Dunhaelic until I decide I wish to leave."

Ailean's mouth twitches. "With pleasure. Peace to you on your journey, my lady, and to your mother on hers as well."

"Peace to us all," I say. "Stay safe, Ailean."

The route I mapped out for our journey turns off the military road beyond the village, climbing a track into the wilder hills. Two strange cuts scar the terrain above, one atop the other like a pair of ghostly roads. No one remembers their meaning, and an unsettled energy stirs within them. Not power, but the memory of something powerful, as though the land remembers more than those of us who live here.

Chyr's face is white and drawn. He can scarcely keep upright in Bramble's saddle. I pull Eira to a stop as soon as we're out of sight of the village and tie her behind Bramble. With some awkward wriggling, I settle myself into the saddle in front of Chyr so that he doesn't need to dismount.

Frost laces the heather, and patches of old snow linger in the shade higher up the braes. A red deer startles at our approach, vanishing through the yellow blooms of furze.

Chyr leans on me more heavily, and I'm soon exhausted from trying to hold his weight. We've ridden only a couple of hours more before I spot an old turf-roofed bothy tucked low against a rise.

If we're to be sure of reaching Muilean on time, we should ride several more hours before we stop. But I decide to take a chance.

Chyr is too weak to argue much as I help him to dismount.

His breath comes hard and shallow, and his lips are pale. He's shivering, and the heat of his skin makes it clear his fever has returned. The hut's stone walls are half-collapsed, but it's hidden beneath a pine overhang, and the inside is cold but dry.

I unroll two of the extra plaids we brought and lay them out on the ground to protect against the chill, then I set the remaining plaids nearby to use as blankets.

"I gave you my word, so I won't ask how you are," I say.

"Why does that seem like a question?" His eyes lock onto mine, and his lips curve into a tired half-smile that's pulled crooked by the scar at one corner.

Everything about him knocks me off balance. His vulnerability makes me want to take care of him, but beneath that, there's a flush of heat and want that's been building the whole time I rode with his arms around me.

"Look how well you avoid the subject," I say a little hoarsely. "We can stay here until dark, so you should try to get some sleep."

I pour him a cup of willow bark tea from the flask I brought, and he sips while I build a fire. Once a few of the larger pine branches are burning, I descend the hill in search of peat.

My boots sink deep into soil still slick with rain, and my mind is full of disjointed thoughts. Too many decisions must still be made, and too much has happened. I focus on the immediate task, trying not to think at all as I find a good section of peat bank and unsheathe my dagger to slice through layers of black-brown sod. Pulling the first slab free requires both hands, but I finish and set it aside to carve out another.

The air shifts, tainted by something sour. Something that raises the hair on my arms.

I have the feeling of being watched, and the attention doesn't feel curious or benign. This is a creature with malice—and patience. Then faint dots of red appear in pairs behind clumps of brush above me on the hill. They glow like embers, but they're shaped like eyes. As soon as I try to look at any of them directly, they disappear.

I move farther downhill, hoping to draw whatever it is away from Chyr, but I don't see the red eyes again. If they were ever there at all.

After retrieving the peat blocks, I return to the bothy as quickly as I can and find Chyr asleep. His weapons lie within reach beside him, and he's fully clothed, curled on his side with the covering plaid pulled low.

The fire has dwindled to embers, and I find myself staring at him while I wait for the peat to catch. Rory's shirt pulls tight over Chyr's biceps and wide shoulders, the white linen stark against his sun-drenched skin. Even in sleep, there's a furrow between brows that, like his lashes, are darker than usual in someone with pale gold hair. But then, there's nothing usual about him.

There's still an unused plaid. I could take it and put some distance between us. Instead, I watch him until the peat finally begins to glow and a thin reed of blue smoke wafts upward. Then I tell myself I'm cold and I lie down beside him, my back pressed against his back to let his heat seep into me through the layers of wool and linen for a little while. I draw the remaining plaid over both of us.

He rolls over in his sleep and wraps an arm around my waist. My breath catches, waiting for him to wake. To pull away. Grief, fear, and rage still roil within me, and the warmth and strength of his arms are both comfort and distraction.

I should pull away. But I've never been held like this. Never been as aware of the difference between muscles and curves, of the silent reassurance of lying beside a man. I breathe in the sweet-salt of his scent, and I finally understand why the seer Lannraig traded her visions for a single hour of human connection.

Chyr's heart beats in a quickened thud where my head falls back against his chest. The whispered hum of magic coming through the Veilstone rings is harder to ignore. It's amplified in the silence, and the power feels different coming through Chyr than when I was carrying the rings myself. It's hotter, brighter, as though something in him changes it, tempers it. I can't tell where the magic ends and he begins. Both are too addictive.

I don't move away. At some point, I drift into sleep, lulled by the heat, the hum, and the patter of rain outside.

Then Chyr jolts awake. He lurches to his feet, groping for his sword. Breath rasping, he staggers towards a low growl coming from outside the bothy door.

CHAPTER 20
HOUNDS AND BLADES

CHYR

The baying of Ravenhounds jerks me awake—a low, broken curse of a sound I've heard too often. My sword is nearby as always, but now I strain to lift it. By the time the familiar hilt is secure in my hand, I've oriented myself again in the gloomy herder's hut.

Flora rolls to her feet beside me. "What is it?"

"Some of Vheara's less pleasant pets have come to play. Stay here."

By now, I should know better. Flora follows me out the door. She doesn't bother arguing.

I squint against the rain that drives sideways against the slope. The Ravenhounds rush me—black shadow bodies and molten teeth. Ember-red eyes that burn with rage and hunger. I meet the first mid-leap, steel biting into its ribs. A second knocks me to the ground. I hit hard and roll through a puddle, slashing the creature's throat, then I shift to avoid the corrosive spill of blood.

The mud is slick and treacherous as I struggle to my feet.

Cursing my weakness, I reach for magic through the Veilstones, draw what little I can, and scrape the last dregs from within myself. I manage to forge a thin stream of fire and hurl it at several of the hounds. They howl as they ignite.

A new snarl cuts through the storm, closer than it should be. Flora jumps in front of me, her braid flying like a whip. My knees buckle as I try to get there first.

Her dagger is masked as a sword again, the same illusion she used before. More brave than sane, she circles, searching for the beast as though she can't find it either. I drag myself forward, my heart stuttering as the snarl comes again from her left. She spins to the right.

The beast leaps at her, and I throw myself between them. Teeth rake fire down my leg, and I twist and drive my blade through the monster's skull. It goes still, but when I try to rise, my leg collapses beneath me.

Another Ravenhound drives me to the ground. Fetid breath and drips of spittle hit my face. My blade shakes as I try to lift it to meet the attack, and all I can do is brace myself.

But the monster yelps and falls away, blood splattering from its gut as Flora stabs it—saving me yet again.

She doesn't look at it. Her eyes search for mine.

Rain sluices down my face, muddy loam cold against the fire that burns the back of my thigh. Moss slicks under my palm as I reach for purchase.

"Don't move." Flora presses one hand against the wound while the other holds me still. My flesh heats, burns, but the cold, magicless emptiness inside me gnaws at every bone and muscle as her breath whispers across my skin.

"They're all dead?" I force the question out.

"All of them."

The fire of her hands drags the pain in my leg away. Only

my leg. My thigh is the only part of me that feels the heat of the healing she's pouring into me this time, not my entire body.

She's learning. Growing stronger and more precise.

That's my first lucid thought, even as she shifts me onto my back. Her hair has escaped the thick braid, the copper and moonlight strands darkened by the rain. Water runs through streaks of blood along her cheeks, but I don't see any injury beneath them.

Her eyes are closed in concentration. Then her hands press against the soaked linen of my shirt and the bandages over my wound. Her magic rises again—a surge pushing into me then tugging at the dark, alien agony that's been sitting in my chest.

Smoke rises from her skin, thicker and darker than the two times she's healed me before. She pulls harder, and the cold darkness claws outward through my flesh. My muscles clench, every instinct fighting that pull. Then something loosens, and the sensation is gone.

My chest throbs, but it's a dull, dry ache instead of an insistent scream. Yet she's still pulling, shaking with the effort of it.

"Flora, stop. That's enough!" I push to my feet and back away, and it's only once I'm standing that I realise I shouldn't have the strength to do that. She gave me the strength.

Her eyes meet mine, and she knows. Those grey eyes are alive with the awareness of what she's done, and a small, astonished smile hovers on her lips.

I'm gripped by an insane impulse to kiss her, but she's trembling like a rabbit, and I want to pull her into my arms and hold her until it stops. I want...

But she draws a deep, shaking breath and turns away.

"What were those things?" she asks, her voice hoarse.

I wipe the blade of my sword on a clump of moss. "They're called Ravenhounds, and there may be more of them. We need to go." I catch her hand in mine and kiss her palm. "Thank you. You keep saving me."

"You keep doing your best to die. Please stop."

The laugh that spills up my throat sounds rusty. How long has it been since I laughed?

Flora goes still at the sound, her eyes finding mine. Something shifts in her expression—surprise first, then a softening, and something more...I want to stay in that look, to deserve the feeling behind it, however fleeting.

Then I spot the beast she killed, and she sees me note it. Her expression hardens.

The hound's carcass lies a few feet away, its abdomen cleaved by Flora's sword that rests discarded on the ground beside it. The blade is covered in the black, treacly gore that lives between the bones and shadows of Vheara's Ravenhounds. The most important aspect of the sight registers only slowly.

The sword is still a sword—not a dagger.

Illusions disappear when they're no longer fed with magic. Yet the sword is there, gleaming in the wet light, coated with the dark blood of the Ravenhound she killed to save me.

"That's not an illusion. *Your sword is real.*" The words come out more like an accusation than I intend, and I clear my throat and start again. "That shouldn't be possible. There's not enough metal in the dagger for that—not to make a blade strong enough to use."

She tilts her head. "What's the point of a useless sword? And I told you it wasn't an illusion. I can't help it if you didn't believe me."

I close my eyes at her innocence and my own blindness, shaking my head as I hurry back inside the hut to strap on the rest of my weapons and gather our things so we can leave.

She did tell me. I assumed that she was bluffing.

She's *human*. Is this the sort of magic the ancient queens were able to summon? Few Siorai are powerful enough to draw metal from the earth, if that's what she's done. Created something from nothing. Even now, I don't think she grasps how impossible that should be.

Few Siorai can call tremors from the earth. Or heal as Flora heals.

None of it should be possible for her, but Flora excels at impossibilities.

The two of us each pull an extra plaid around us for warmth and fold the remaining plaids into the packs, then we saddle the horses quickly. Flora's movements are sluggish, and she tries to pretend that her hands aren't shaking.

The magic she poured into me—magic that I can still feel coursing through my veins—came at the expense of her own strength.

I should be grateful to her, but I'm terrified for her instead.

She's only beginning to touch her magic. Whether that's Siorai magic that the Veilstones or I have woken, or it comes from the ancient Cailleach magic, or some combination of the two, she doesn't understand it. She can't control it, and even if my oaths don't seem to see it yet, that makes her doubly dangerous.

What wouldn't Vheara do to have that sort of power?

What would Flora become if Vheara turned her?

The questions slide through me like ice.

Vheara can never learn that Flora exists, and yet I'm about to drag her into territory that will be crawling with Vheara's eyes and ears. Flora's magic could make the difference in reaching Muilean on time, but my oaths—No, I refuse to think like that.

I give her a leg up into the saddle, and she looks at me with her brows creased.

Another Ravenhound bays somewhere in the distance.

I think of the way she threw herself into the fight to save me, and something thickens in my throat and slips down into my chest, making it hard to speak. It's impossible to miss the shadows beneath those clear grey eyes, the way she clutches the reins to keep her hands steady.

I wish I could let her rest. It's still hours before nightfall, and travelling through the day is riskier. But we can't stay here.

Where there are Ravenhounds, Vheara's Greys may not be far away. The hounds not only serve as scouts—the Greys also use them to drive prey to slaughter.

After tying Bramble to Eira's saddle, I mount behind Flora, and we both adjust our plaids to cover our heads against the rain. I settle my arms around her to keep her steady. She sits determinedly upright as we first set out on the long traverse across the slope, then the effort becomes too much. She slumps back against me.

The icy rain stiffens my cheeks and turns Flora's hands red as she grips the reins. Her soft warmth feels good in my arms, and the floral hint of bog myrtle that clings to her is bright and heady.

Her curves are maddeningly close.

My body responds without permission. She must feel it, because her breath hitches. The tension between us becomes a torment as she guides the mare along a faint trail heading west and uphill through gorse and bare boughs of heather.

I watch the slopes for signs of Ravenhounds or Greys. Their baying calls echo through the hills now and then, and Flora and I are both careful to say nothing above a whisper in case our voices carry. Then, finally, we have some cover among the trees. The rain slows beneath the branches, but water streams off the leaves overhead.

Still keeping her voice low, Flora turns her head slightly

towards me. "The Ravenhounds," she says. "Where did they come from? Or are they something Vheara created the way she made the Greys?"

I'm not even surprised that she's figured that out for herself. "They were Shadehounds before she turned them, which makes them far less dangerous. Vheara and the other Greys retained all their Siorai abilities, but their strength is limited only by the amount of suffering they can inflict and absorb."

"Other Greys… Wait, are you saying that Vheara is like the Greys? But I thought…They say she's beautiful."

"That's vanity. Illusion. Beneath the mask, she looks like any other Grey. Corrupting magic will always exact a penalty."

I can almost feel the way Flora's mind spins as she considers what I've said.

"Maybe it's more than vanity," she says after a bit. "No one in Alba Scoria would have supported her against your rebel king if they'd seen what she is."

"Never underestimate what people are willing to overlook if it means they get what they want."

"People like my father. Is that what you're implying?" Flora sighs. "I doubt he tried very hard to see the truth beneath her mask."

Her voice is full of pain, and I know how much she loved her family, how deeply she loves everyone in her life. I tighten my arms around her as Eira picks her way across a shallow stream.

"Don't judge him too harshly. It's hard for people who aren't naturally cruel or self-serving to see those qualities in others, and Vheara has always been careful to hide the evil at her core. She flatters others into believing in her. Even Chulainn—the High King. He didn't see what she was doing until she threatened him directly. Then he ordered Fionn to banish her. That's what set the chain of events in motion."

"I don't understand."

"Vheara wanted a position at court, and when Chulainn denied her, she tried to dethrone him. That's when he sent Fionn and the Anvar'thaine to hunt her."

Flora goes rigid in my arms. "The same Fionn who became the Sun King?"

"Yes, Chulainn's brother. He was Master of the Anvar'thaine, and Chulainn trusted him," I say, fighting through the ice and fire that the oathbands send through me.

Flora's tension passes to Eira. The mare snorts and throws her head. "Is that why the Sun King was never punished? He murdered women and children—*babies*—and your High King did nothing for four centuries because Fionn was his *brother*?"

Pain shoots through me and forms a vice around my skull. My mouth goes dry.

The cursed oathbands pick up what I'm thinking before I even form the thought.

I try to go around them from another direction. "I'm not defending Fionn," I say, balancing on a dagger's edge, "but there's more to it than I can explain. The main point is the timing. Fionn banished Vheara before the Compact was created, and no one had ever escaped from there before. The Gloaming has no magic, and magic is as essential to Siorai as breathing air or seeing light. Most Siorai go mad within a century or two of being sent there."

"But that's cruel—" Flora begins, then stops herself.

Eira's hooves slip on the boggy hill track that's so faint I can barely make it out. The rain has stopped, but water still sheets off the yellow-blooming gorse, and the slope rises steeply ahead. The sky glowers as more storm clouds gather.

"By your standards, maybe it is, but when you live as long as we do, punishment has to be cruel enough to ensure that oaths and laws have meaning. Until Vheara, no one had ever escaped the Gloaming. But she had studied more about runes and magic than any banished Siorai before her. She found a way to drain the dregs of magic from any Siorai and Shadelings she found there, and the Gloaming became her personal hunting ground."

"Why would you banish Shadelings?" Flora twists in the saddle, distracting me beyond patience as her backside shifts against me.

"Stay still, please." My voice is strained. "No, we don't banish them. Shadelings are creatures of the *betweens*, and the Gloaming is a place of shadows, a world between worlds. It's full of small doors and shortcuts the Shadelings used before Vheara began to capture them and force them to feed on suffering. Terror, anguish, panic, hate, and rage—this war is a feast for all the creatures she corrupted."

Flora's gone silent, her every muscle tense. At first, I believe she's reacting to the shock of what I've said. Then I realise her attention has shifted elsewhere. The wind is rising, and it carries the stench of smoke.

My throat tightens as if it's already clogged with soot. I'm afraid I already know the answer, but I don't know the countryside enough to be certain.

"Whose land is that?" I ask.

Tears strangle Flora's voice. "Camhrain of Locharn. He and his clan rose for the king from the beginning, and they've given him more than almost any other clan. Now they'll pay the price."

CHAPTER 21
CASTLES BURN

Our priests would say the gods spare no thought to human suffering, but those are our gods. Siorai gods. The mortals have their own who've turned their backs on them. The destruction of their religion is another sin to lay at Fionn's feet.

Fionn and—

The oathbands lash out, sending ice and wildfire roaring through my veins. I fight to keep hold of the name, keep hold of my thoughts. It's bad enough that the king's oaths control my actions, but I'll be damned if I concede them my mind and conscience, too.

Gradually, the runes release their grip, but a hard knot settles in my chest, and I'm left with a bitter taste on my tongue.

Camhrain of Locharn was—*is*—a good man. He and his clansmen fought at our backs for the best part of a year, and despite his own losses on the battlefield, he never took revenge once the fighting stopped. In Glashu, where the population supported Vheara, Locharn kept our army from sacking the city in punishment until the Riders and I arrived to help. They still ring the bells there on Sundays to honour him. More personally, he's a friend. This past year, he's grown closer to me than anyone apart from the Riders ever has.

My throat aches at the waste and the cost of this bloody war.

"Locharn was wounded at Culodur," I say. "We saw his men carry him off the field. After that, I don't know what became of him."

Flora's shoulders go soft, and she takes a ragged gulp of breath that I can feel against my chest. "I hadn't heard that."

"Did you know him well?"

"He's as good as an uncle." Her voice breaks. "I haven't seen him recently. He and my father fell out about the war. Locharn tried to argue him out of supporting the queen, and— at least at first—he was one of the few who agreed that we shouldn't fight on either side."

"He thought we didn't have enough men to win against Vheara. He was right, but even believing that, he invited us to stay at Aknacaery with him while we waited for the clans to rise. Then we persuaded him to change his mind."

Flora leans back against me, her hair soft beneath my chin. We both sink into our thoughts, lulled by the steady rhythm of hoofbeats and the occasional tick of rain against our plaids and saddles. A hawk screeches overhead and circles low above us.

The hills grow steeper, turning vivid blue-grey in the rain. Picking our way through scrub and fallen pines, we turn south and east again to avoid Vheara's garrison at Dun Uilleum before passing a signal beacon site that's nothing but cold ash where a fire should be stacked and waiting.

No sentries. Only silence where men should be standing.

Flora stiffens, and both of us fall silent as we pass. The track through the glen below and over the next few hills feels increasingly hushed and ominous until the roar of a red deer stag cleaves the silence.

The skittish mare jitters, but Flora controls her as she looks around.

"A signal?" I whisper.

There's no time for her to answer. On the hillside not ten feet from us, two men leap up from where they were lying in wait. The drapes of their plaids are drawn over their heads to blend in with the brush and yellow furze. I'm off the horse in a stride, my blade drawn and ready.

"No, Chyr!" Flora jumps down to stay my hand. "They're Camhrain men. Friends."

The men turn to her and incline their heads, throwing back the plaids to reveal their faces.

"Lady of Dunhaelic," the shorter one says.

He's broader and shorter, with dark hair worn short and a thick jut of forehead and deep-set eyes, while the other is red-headed, lanky, and narrow-jawed. I don't recognise either of them, but I see the moment they realise who I am.

The redhead's gaze drops to my sword for confirmation. "You're the—"

"Rider, yes," I acknowledge. "And I'm sorry for what you've suffered. Is there news of Locharn? We lost sight of him when he was carried off the field."

The men stare a moment too long before the redhead replies. "He was alive the last we heard. They got him out before the Raven bitch and her Butcher—" He spits on the ground. "Before they made the wounded beg to be allowed to die."

Flora inhales sharply, and her hand closes around my forearm. Her face has lost its colour and for an instant she lets herself sag against me before catching herself again.

The shorter, darker man nods at her. "There were

Dunhaelic men coming south with him," he says more quietly, "a fair number along with ours, but I don't know any names. We've heard nothing these past two days."

"Aye, the news is slower than the Raven's redcoats and filthy sorcerers," the redhead says, then spits again. "The Butcher's here already."

"The Butcher himself?" Flora rocks back on her heels. "We saw the smoke. Was it Aknacaery burning?"

"The castle, aye, and the villages and farms around it." The redhead's voice is raw, and he swallows slowly. For the first time, I can see how young he is, still more boy than man.

"The Butcher swept in too quickly," the other man says in a voice that comes out shaking through gritted teeth. "They flayed the skin off the men before they killed them, then drove the women and children into their own houses. Burned them alive."

Flora makes a thin, raw sound and sinks as though her knees are giving out. I go to catch her, but she raises her chin and pushes me away. Rain softens to a hiss through the gorse growing on the hill.

"What do your people need?" Flora asks the men. "I can send word to mine. We've no labour to help you rebuild, but we still have sheep and cattle."

"Not much sense in rebuilding until we know it's over, and there are deer and rabbits in the hills and fish in the lochs. We'll make do." The darker one lifts his chin with that fierce Highland pride that still believes Vheara, her Butcher, and all her Greys will never tame them.

I shouldn't give them hope, but maybe that's exactly what they need. A sense that all the pain hasn't been for nothing.

"Momentum may still turn," I say. "Help could come. But whatever happens, know this: neither Clan Camhrain nor Locharn himself will be forgotten."

The men study me as if testing my words for meaning. I meet their eyes, and after a time, the redhead pulls his plaid back up to cloak his head. The rain is coming down again.

"The queen's bastards are still about. We can see you safely through if you're heading towards the pass," he says.

With a smile of thanks, Flora shakes her head. "You have more than enough to tend to on your own. We'll avoid the Butcher's men if we can, and if we can't, then we'll do our best to kill them."

Both men give her toothy grins. "Stay close to the loch then and keep to the trees when you can," the redhead says. "They keep lookouts on the ridges, and they're using our signal fires against us."

They bow lower this time, to her and to me. I clasp their forearms and hold their eyes, making sure they see my gratitude.

"Safe journey," the darker one says.

"Long life to the king," says the redhead.

Flora barely disguises a grimace hearing those words, and we ride on in grim silence as the scent of smoke hangs thick in the air.

Near sunset, I spy a pair of rabbits on the hillside and whip out a dirk to throw. Flora stills my hand with a gesture.

"We can't afford a cookfire here," she says, "and we have hours of riding left before we stop."

"We need to take food where we find it—Muilean and Beltane are still a long way off. And I can manage to mask a fire after the healing that you gave me. I'm a Rider, not an invalid."

I throw the dirk, and it flies true. A quick, clean kill.

Flora's silent as I retrieve the body and tie it to Bramble's saddle. Having reasserted my independence to that small degree, I consider telling her I will ride the rest of the way on my own to make it easier on the horses. It's no exaggeration to say that I feel well enough for that. But as strong as Flora has proven herself to be, riding through the evidence of what the Butcher has done will be hard. If nothing else, I can offer her a bit of comfort to take away from the cold ache of seeing the atrocities and knowing that more are coming.

By midnight, we descend towards the eastern end of the loch. The castle and various points around the long, narrow water still smoulder an angry orange and red. The stench of scorched fields and charred flesh cuts deeper than the wound in my chest, worse—a thousand times worse—for knowing that women and children burned.

These reprisals, every one of these deaths, is another mark upon my conscience.

Flora's shoulders tremble as we follow the rough trail. Her tears drop to the bare skin of my arm around her waist. She fights to hold herself together, but eventually sobs shudder through her in gulps. She's crying for more than the ruins of Aknacaery. It's the loss of her mother and the destruction at Dunhaelic, the loss of her father and brothers, and so many of her clan—and the fear of what's happening elsewhere.

I draw her closer, and she tips her head back against my chest. I reach up to brush her cheek, and my fingers come away wet with tears.

There doesn't seem to be a limit to my rage. It's bottomless, ravenous. It grows with every atrocity Vheara has committed over the past year—over millennia. My sword begs to answer her cruelty with blood. My soul *craves* her death.

"Vheara needs to pay," Flora says, echoing my thoughts almost exactly. "The Butcher needs to burn."

"They will. I swear it."

"What if you go through the doorway and don't come back?"

The oathbands warn me—cold and fire flashing from the

runes until I manage to bank the fury that veers too near what Chulainn has forbidden.

"I'll drag myself out of the Pit—the Gloaming—if that's what it takes," I say. "Killing Vheara is not a task I'll leave undone."

Flora thinks a bit—I can *feel* her weighing my words, measuring my conviction. "You can have Vheara and the Greys," she says eventually. "They were Siorai, so that's a task for the Anvar'thaine. But the Butcher is human. It needs to be one of us who kills him. Slowly. In pieces carved off his body strip by strip, then cooked on the fire while he's forced to watch."

"That sort of revenge requires conviction. It isn't justice."

"I'll be plenty convincing given the opportunity."

I smile in spite of myself. "Oh, I've little doubt."

It says nothing good about me that Flora's thirst for blood distracts me with a flash of desire. But nothing can keep our minds from the desolation we're riding through for long. The senseless torture, the gratuitous infliction of pain, is too visible.

We're both spent as dawn approaches. "We should look for shelter," I suggest. "It will be too dangerous to keep riding once the sun comes up."

Flora nods, but a light rain has begun to fall, and the thin woods of birch and alder trees don't provide anywhere for us to sleep. Every rustle and creaking branch has us searching for scarlet coats and booted feet. Flora's shoulders get tighter and her spine more rigid with every mile.

We stop to let the horses drink at a small river flowing through an open field of boulders. We ride another half hour while the stars dim and the sky fades to grey.

Then two faint shimmers of light bob down the slope to our right, slowing to float briefly three feet above the ground in front of us before darting a short distance back up the hill, inviting us to follow them.

"Whisperwraiths," I say. "Do you see them?"

Flora reins Eira to a halt. "Should we follow them?"

I should know by now that Flora rarely reacts the way that I'd expect. "Can you hear them whispering?"

She gives a slow nod. "Although it's not words, is it? Not even voices, unless you're hearing something different than I am. It's more as though they've whispered an entire idea into my mind. As if it's my own thought. That should be terrifying."

"Isn't it?"

"No..." Flora rolls the word around on her tongue as if she's testing it.

I wonder if I should be concerned that she's not afraid. "Of all the Shadelings," I say, "Whisperwraiths are the ones that worry me."

"I've heard stories about what they do to people they don't like—the way they can put ideas in people's heads."

"Most magical creatures answer cruelty with cruelty, and Vheara has turned some of them, too. Used them to make our soldiers attack each other."

"These don't feel dangerous."

"I'm not sure whether to admire you for being brave or shake you for being too trusting."

"Is that what Siorai do? Shake women? I am not your sister or your wife."

"It's an expression, and trust me, I am aware you're not my sister."

She turns in the saddle to look at me, but she says nothing and simply nudges the mare off the trail to follow where the Whisperwraiths lead us.

The bracken-covered slope ends in a rockface that climbs almost vertically a few hundred feet. The Whisperwraiths dart behind a copse of stunted pine trees to the left. Hidden from the track below, a wide rock ledge juts from the granite crag, providing a natural shelter from the rain. The ground beneath the ledge is flat.

Briefly, the Whisperwraiths hover inside, then they give a sudden dip and wink away.

"Do you suppose they've been following us all this time— since back when you said we needed to find a shelter?" Flora asks.

I dismount and hold out my hand to help her down. "One or the other of us should have been able to see them. Then again, the Riders and I never saw them on the battlefield either. We only found out later that our soldiers heard them whispering in their heads."

The overhang is too small for our horses, but a hidden gully nearby provides water and forage. We unsaddle them and rub them down in the fading darkness, then I clean the rabbit and cook it over a small fire before we settle ourselves in the shelter beneath the ledge. I'm more careful than usual to lay my swords and knives within easy reach.

"Let me check the bandage again," Flora says, and she steps closer to untuck the fabric of my shirt from beneath the kilted plaid and push it upward. Her fingers leave trails of heat along my skin.

She seems to have no idea of the reaction she provokes, or at least she ignores it, as we have both had to ignore her effect on me when she moves unexpectedly in the saddle.

I stand still, force myself not to reach for her. Something in the moment shifts between us, and she looks up at me, her lips so close that I can feel her breath.

Conceding defeat, I step back to put more space between us. "It's far better since you healed it again."

"You're still feverish," she says.

"I am many things, but cold has rarely been one of them." I spread two of the extra plaids on the ground just as she did the last time we stopped to rest.

It's insanity. Sleeping beside her will only be a steady drip of torture.

I almost hope she'll argue—snatch the remaining two plaids for herself and make a bed somewhere out of reach. Instead, she stands and watches until after I'm stretched out on my back. Then she lies down on the farthest edge of the heavy fabric, as far from me as possible.

My jaw tightens, and I draw her closer until the remaining plaids cover us both. That's all I allow myself before I turn away.

"Goodnight, Flora."

"It's daylight," she says. "Sleep well."

She's at once too close and too far away to make sleep likely. The heat of our bodies releases the smell of wet wool and hints of old smoke, but that doesn't drown out the faint scent of rosemary and bog myrtle soap that still clings to her clothes and skin.

She lies unnaturally still, her every shallow breath brushing my back, her spine curved, and her muscles as taut as bowstrings.

Does she feel any of the pull I feel between us?

The thought that she would throw herself away on a man who doesn't love her—on a man who could hurt her, control her, try to take away her fire and spirit—sends anger clawing at my chest.

I roll over onto my back and stare at the granite slab above our heads. "You're not actually thinking of marrying someone your Clan Council chooses for you, are you?"

"Dunhaelic is my home. It's my responsibility. How do I walk away from my people and trust that whoever comes in will treat them well? Dughall wouldn't." Her voice sounds flat, as though she's already given up. Then she rolls over, too, and lies on her back beside me. "I know my limitations, Chyr. I can keep good accounts and raise fast, sturdy horses, but I'm no warrior. Dunhaelic needs strength now more than ever. More strength than I can offer. Look what happened at Aknacaery."

"What happened at Aknacaery is all the more reason you shouldn't betray yourself," I say. "Your life is too fragile to waste it on someone you do not love."

Her answer is slow in coming. "That's survival," she finally says, "not betrayal."

"It's madness, and you deserve better."

"What do you know about what I deserve?" She pushes herself up on one elbow to look at me, her breath coming faster. "You don't know me. You don't know us. You know nothing about having your choices stripped away, because *you're* the ones who've stolen them from us."

She's right, but she's also wrong. She's prey caught in the cage of her circumstances, but I'm trapped just as surely by the layers of oaths that bind me.

"What I know is that marriage should be sacred, and that keeping Dunhaelic will take more than strength. Leadership isn't defined by the sword alone. Don't regard yourself so lightly."

"Don't pretend that Siorai never marry for convenience. The Compact required the true queens to take Riders as companions. That wasn't about love."

My oathbands flare a warning.

"I'm aware of the oaths I took, believe me."

"If those oaths still follow the Compact, then you agreed to marry without love, if need be. To make a personal sacrifice for something greater, something you believe in. You have no right to judge me for doing the same."

Her voice cracks on the last word, and her face begins to crumple towards tears. Something cold and bleak settles in my chest, but she catches herself and smooths her expression back to a semblance of calm as though the mask had never broken. I've seen it now, though, and I recognise what that control must cost her.

I've worn that same sort of mask my entire life, never letting anyone see that there's something vulnerable underneath. Showing weakness only gives your enemies the ammunition to defeat you.

My breath hitches, and my hands ball themselves into fists. It's all I can do not to curse. Or to close the short distance and kiss her until we both forget. The silence draws out between us until eventually, I'm forced to admit the truth.

"I'm not judging you," I say. "I'm angry for you. I'm *breaking* for you." *I hate the idea of you with someone else.*

She exhales, watching me with her eyes nearly black, the pupils blown wide open. Her breath is a whisper against my cheek, the long braid of her hair a rope of silk against my arm.

I want her to say something, to break the tension. To give me permission.

A long moment. Neither of us breathes.

Instead, she turns away.

I can't blame her. I'd be a fool to expect she wants me.

We lie back-to-back again in the heavy silence as the sun climbs higher outside. I feel every gossamer breath Flora takes, every minuscule shift of her body. It's a sweet and bitter torment.

Then she clears her throat, her body tensing even more.

"Would you...could you roll over?" she asks, her voice so soft I'm afraid I heard her wrong. But it unravels everything I've tried to hold together.

I turn and pull her against my chest, my arm sliding around her waist as though it knows where it belongs. I would scarcely need to move at all to claim her lips. She can't be so innocent that she doesn't know she's tempting me.

"Does that hurt?" She tilts her head back to look at me, and it takes a moment to realise that she's asking about my wound.

"No," I say, and it's not a lie because it's not my injured flesh that pains me.

Flora isn't mine. She never can be, and I can't allow myself a single lapse of self-control. There's too much at stake.

Lying still, I count her heartbeats until their rhythm slows and my hunger has become a steady ache.

CHAPTER 22

WAKING THE BOG

FLORA

We leave again before full dark. The Peathan Pass will be a hard ride, and we've spent nearly two full days on the road already. We have five days and half a night left to reach Muilean.

The glen is still, Loch Airceig an ink-black spill between steep braes. I switch horses, putting us both up on Bramble to give Eira a rest after she carried us most of the day yesterday. We hug the shore, the horses splashing through the shallows where trees force us to the water. I start to duck under a low branch of moss-covered birch, but Chyr catches it and pushes it aside for me.

When he's sitting this close behind me, every one of Bramble's strides rocks me back against Chyr, pushing a flush of awareness through me. I steady my hands on the reins.

There's more strength in Chyr's arms now, and he balances himself more easily on Bramble's back, but I'm not sure how much of that new strength is due to my healing as opposed to the Veilstone rings.

He wears a Veilstone on each hand, and my body draws in the warm hum of magic as his arms wrap around my waist. Like the touch of his skin, that awareness is a constant tingle beneath my skin. It vibrates through me like the low purr of his voice against my good ear.

He knows, somehow, without my having asked him, to speak to my right ear and not my left. Knowing he's pieced that together for himself pulls at something inside me with unnerving insistence, only adding to the tension that's been growing between us. I don't know how I can bear more hours of lying beside him with my eyes closed and sleep eluding me. Wanting him has become an ache that refuses to away.

Bramble stumbles as we cross a shallow ford. Chyr tightens his arm around me, his hard chest pressing closer against my back. My breath catches, and we're both still.

He doesn't release me straight away, and I don't pull away.

"What's it like in Tirnaeve?" I ask, curious, but mainly trying to break the tension. "Is it beautiful?"

"Yes and no. Not like this." He gestures around at the loch and the braes that are growing steeper. "The shimmer of magic makes the colours brighter, the contrast sharper. The untamed places are glorious, but we only have a few small pockets of them left. Siorai like to claim things and change them for their own amusement."

Wind skims over the loch, throwing up drops that hit my cheek. I try to imagine a place where the earth and water have all been tamed, and it strikes me as heartbreaking.

"What do Siorai build instead?" I ask.

I can feel Chyr's smile as the muscles work in his cheek. "They shape their dwellings from living trees and crystal or marble or precious stone, decorated with cascades of water and flowers that never lose their blooms. Every home is a competition to see who can create the most magical, the most original, the impossible. And nothing is ever finished. There is always something new to copy, outdo, or create."

"Do you miss it? Home?"

He's quiet, as though it's a question he's never asked himself. "The Anvar'thaine and the other Riders have been the closest thing to a home I've ever had. Our barracks are part of the Palace complex, but we're rarely there, and the place itself isn't anything special."

"And your family? Do you have sisters? Brothers?"

His breath snags and holds a moment before he lets it out. "I didn't see my father often, and I don't remember my mother. My uncle took me in when I was small. Maybe that's where my appreciation for simplicity comes from. His home always has to be the most spectacular."

There's a bitter note to his voice that says more than words ever could. The arm banded around my waist tightens and keeps me from asking more, but I imagine a small, vulnerable version of Chyr, alone in a house made of gems and marble. A house that's beautiful and heart-achingly cold.

The light drizzle that had been falling earlier has finally stopped, and the sky is clear. Above us, the brightening stars shine almost as bright as the moon. They press close as we reach the loch's end and turn towards the Peathan Pass.

Wind stirs with the scent of peat and rain-soaked ferns, and fallen pines slow our path, but the chances of running into the queen's soldiers on this rough-bound stretch of track should be diminished. The terrain's a natural defence.

The moon is starting its descent by the time we come to a wide stretch of bog hemmed between a steep slope strewn with boulders and a wide, babbling stream. It's a green trap of water and loose vegetation glowing in the moonlight.

"We'll need to cross here," I say. "The map showed a hard climb to the pass, so we should also let the horses rest."

Chyr swings his leg over Bramble's flank and slides to the ground, then he holds his arms up. His hands are firm on my waist, his eyes holding mine a moment too long before he lets go and trusts me to stand alone. He swallows visibly, and my heart beats faster as I drag my eyes away.

We tie the horses at the stream to keep them out of the bog, and I spread more of our dwindling ration of cheese and oat bannocks out on a flat rock nearby. Chyr crouches by the water, fingers brushing the surface.

He goes still, listening. Bramble raises her head from the stream, water dripping from her muzzle. I surge up, dagger drawn, but a flicker of movement draws my eye, a twitch of ears, a pale shape hopping. Then Chyr's dirk flies from his hand, and the rabbit goes still.

I feel its death, a pinch like I felt at the rabbit's death yesterday. Nothing like the scale of the loss and emptiness I felt when we passed the pyres of Aknacaery and the surrounding homes and fields, but an acknowledgment of something passing. It's unfamiliar enough to confuse me.

Chyr picks the rabbit up by the ears, smiling until he sees me. "What's wrong?"

I shake my head. "Nothing."

"Good, because I'll take rabbit over oatcakes any day." He grins at me again, and I realise it's a smile that's free of pain, a genuine smile. I can barely remember when life allowed for joy.

Then a sharp bark echoes off the cliffs above us, and we both go still.

The air shivers, a feeling like teeth on skin. The bark is answered by several more.

Chyr's sword sings as he draws it and turns to look behind us. I unsheathe my dagger, and my magic answers when I call it. The dagger changes, growing and broadening, but there's none of the effort or pain as the magic moves through my veins. That's different, but I set it aside to consider later.

The horses snort, their ears pinned back against their heads. They thrash, trying to pull loose from the trees where they're tied beside the stream.

A low growl sounds somewhere close. Too close.

I turn, and the Ravenhounds are easier to see than those we fought beside the hut. Their eyes are like burning coals, their teeth dripping fire, and their dark bodies gleam like bog water, thick and lightless. They crouch low as they creep towards us through the brush on forepaws the size of milking basins. I count seven of them, working together like a hunting pack.

"Stay behind me," Chyr says, moving to intercept them. His sword is already whistling as he swings it, and the bold grace of his movement is stunning.

I edge towards the stream and put myself between the hounds and horses. Two of them detach from the group and circle around Chyr to follow me. Then, as if responding to a signal I can't hear, they spring in unison.

Chyr shifts to cut off the two that are coming towards me, leaving the rest at his back. But I don't need him to save me.

I run forward and attack the closest one. They're less solid than they look: bone, shadow, and something that ripples when I strike. My blade catches on bone. I strain to pull it free so I can swing again.

Chyr finishes off the last of the Ravenhounds as mine goes still. He turns, his eyes raking me head to toe, searching every limb for bites, scratches, anything broken. Finding none, he breaks into a swift, wide grin, and our eyes hold long enough to force me to acknowledge the connection between us. My throat tightens as the truth hits me.

It's a connection I didn't expect or want. I've fought it, but the truth is that Chyr matters to me beyond getting him to Muilean, beyond him bringing back help against Vheara.

I drag my eyes away to check that he's undamaged. Another bark sounds, and we both turn to look.

Five more Ravenhounds run shoulder to shoulder up the slope, with a second row of four more approaching close behind them. They work as a pack, fanning out, circling us to cut off escape.

Dread drags at my limbs. I raise my sword and prepare for another fight. But nine Ravenhounds are too many at once, and I won't be much help to Chyr.

Then again, if they hunt like dogs, maybe they'll chase what runs.

I turn and bolt. My stomach heaves with the stench of blood and the sour, metallic smell of the bog. But the bog is what I know.

I race past the horses, then I slow to search for furze and saplings and the darker green patches of moss that grow on solid ground. Bit by bit, I thread my way deeper into the bog. Water splashes, loose moss sucks at my ankles, wanting to pull me down.

Fear keeps me looking straight ahead. I'm afraid the Ravenhounds aren't coming. And equally afraid they are.

Then I hear splashing nearby, and I push another five feet farther.

But now I'm trapped. There's nothing solid in front of me, and no way out.

I turn, and the Ravenhounds are plunging after me, too intent on the chase to note the footing. The bog pulls at their feet. Three of them tumble into deeper water and try to swim, claws scrabbling for purchase. Their heads swivel too far on their necks as if bone and sinew were badly joined.

The fourth is the last to arrive at the edge of the bog, so it has time to realise what's happening to the others. It slides to a stop with a chilling, distorted howl.

I can't trust that none of them will climb out.

Drowning them is the only answer.

Panic is not an option, but my heart pounds at my ribs, desperate to escape. Drawing in a deep breath, I push every other thought out of my mind so I can concentrate.

That's when I feel it. Not a voice. Not even a whisper. A thought that prompts me to feel for what's around me. To use it.

I bite my lip, doubting the magic, doubting myself.

Two of the Ravenhounds are paddling closer. One scrabbles at the edge of a tuft of earth and peat, pulling its front legs up. The edge of the sod breaks off, leaving a fresh, dark ridge of soil. The hound yelps and splashes back into the water.

Reaching for the pulse of magic that lives in the earth, I follow it down into the bog. It moves sluggishly through the water, like a spoon pulled through porridge. Despite the resistance, I feel no pain.

I let go and allow the magic to flow through me, let myself float away on it. Eyes closed, I sort through what I sense within the bog, the peat and various plants, and the power of the water itself.

Magic and moss breathe beneath my feet. Sticky sundews and butterworts wait to capture their prey, and the stalks of cottongrass bow in the wind, faint brushes of white only hinting at the fluffy heads to come. None of that is useful, but the toadstail moss at the edge of the bog is exactly what I need.

Untangling the long roots and creeping stems, I drag them towards me, then wrap a strand around the nearest thrashing Ravenhound and drag him down beneath the peat. I loop it around a few more times, anchoring it so it will never come up for air.

The next Ravenhound yelps as it disappears beneath the water. Its legs churn as it tries to save itself. I pull more toadstail, but whatever excess magic I had is leaving me. The effort is harder, and the pain of using it returns as I anchor the second hound beneath the peat.

The third hound gives up and sinks beneath the surface. It feels like I'm scraping my own flesh away as I make sure it can't come up again. I barely manage to wrap a few roots around its legs.

Pain roars through every nerve, but the bog is still, as if it's waiting with me.

I look up, and Chyr stands at the edge, the last Ravenhound motionless at his feet. The remaining hounds lie bloody and scattered where he killed them all.

His face pale, he steps towards me. "What in the Pit was that, Flora? What did you do?"

"Stop! The bog's not safe."

"*You're* not safe. You made the Ravenhounds chase you when you knew there was no way out. Why didn't you let me kill them?"

"You killed twelve of them. That wasn't enough for you? Anyway, I'm not that good with a sword. Drowning them seemed more efficient."

I'm not going to argue with Chyr. I feel drained and exhausted, but also proud. Not for taking lives, though I'm not sure the Ravenhounds were alive at all, but for stopping them, for removing something from the world that is so terrible it should never have existed.

Chyr's mouth opens and closes soundlessly, and then he laughs. It's a deep, low sound that echoes off the hills. A laugh that shivers through me, more dangerous than the Ravenhounds.

He holds out his hand, and I will my feet to move. Picking

my way back through the bog towards him, step by step, I search for solid footing. When I reach him, he pulls me close with such force that I fall against his chest, and he holds me as though I'm something precious and breakable. I'm neither of those things, but as usual, when I'm around him, I feel too much, too many conflicting emotions.

Pressed against his chest, I feel the even beat of his heart, a contrast to the wild pace of mine. Both of us are breathing too fast.

I step back and open Chyr's coat to check for blood. "Did you reopen your wound? Did they bite you?"

He says something, his face drawn into sudden lines of worry. His hand cups my face. His lips move, but I can't hear anything over the ringing in my ears.

"I'm fine," I try to say. "We should—" The ground tilts. I lock my knees, blinking hard, and my hands won't stop shaking. Every part of me is shivering, and then the dark closes in.

CHAPTER 23
DEPLETED

FLORA

I wake with my head in Chyr's lap and his fingers rubbing circles along my temples. It's still dark, still raining. My head throbs as if a smith is pounding the inside of my skull with a hammer.

"Back with me?" Chyr asks. Not waiting for me to answer, he presses a flask to my lips and tips a dribble of water on my tongue. "Slowly now. That's good. How do you feel?"

"Possibly better than the Ravenhounds. Possibly not."

His lips twitch at the corners. "The Ravenhounds you drowned in the bog? I doubt they feel much of anything now."

"Lucky Ravenhounds." I move, and every muscle in my body groans in protest.

The weakness is more than physical. I'm shivering and scraped empty inside. I try to pull magic from the earth, but nothing happens.

Chyr tightens his arms around me as though he feels my panic, and the Veilstones on his hands hum against my skin. I curl into his warmth, and he brushes a strand of hair off my cheek and tucks it behind my ear.

"I take it you've never depleted your magic before?" he asks.

"I've barely known I had any to deplete," I say, and that doesn't lessen the wave of panic that hits me at the thought of losing it. "My magic has been getting stronger since I've been around you. Around the Veilstones. Does that mean it will come back, or is it gone for good?"

Chyr shifts his arm around my shoulders to help me sit up. "It should come back. The process is slow at first—your body needs a certain amount of magic to attract more to you."

"Then why didn't I feel this bad right away?" I ask.

"You used it all so fast that your body didn't have time to understand it was gone. Then the lack of it hit all at once."

He straightens his long legs on either side of my hips and pulls me back against his chest, wrapping his arms tight around me. I grit my teeth to stop them chattering while Chyr rubs my arms and wraps every bit of himself against me.

The warmth of his magic seeps inside me. It's more than the Veilstones, which are a steady flow when Chyr's hands touch me. This is different—a bright gold warmth that's Chyr himself. I press close against his chest, letting the sensation steady my breath.

Then I realise what he's doing, and I peel myself away.

"Stop. You don't have magic to spare." I set my palm on his wrist, and his pulse is pounding.

He gathers me closer. "I'm stronger since the last time you healed me."

"I'll believe that when I see it." I shake my head, which is a mistake because it makes me dizzy and threatens to turn my stomach inside out. "Anyway, we can't stay here. There will be nowhere for us to shelter on the stretch leading to the Pass. We need to make it to the other side by daybreak or we risk not making Muilean on time—and there's too much chance of being spotted."

"You're right. With that many Ravenhounds hunting, there are definitely Greys nearby, and possibly the Butcher himself, based on what the Camhrain sentries told us." Chyr releases a sigh. "Wait here, then. Don't even think of moving. I need to try to get rid of the bodies."

He strides back to the horses and returns with the rest of the spare plaids, which he wraps around me with a single-minded attention that makes me breathless. I watch him, taking in the way he looks up at each step to search my expression, to check on me.

When he's done, he stares down for a moment as though he's going to say something. His jaw clenches, and he turns on his heel, then strides to the nearest of the dead Ravenhounds. He picks up the body and throws it into the bog before moving on to the next.

Mud gurgles. Dark water closes, but the Ravenhounds sink too slowly. I try not to think of those glowing red eyes and teeth that drip with blood and fire, of how I felt when they were attacking Chyr.

I'm a little stronger by the time he returns. Warmer, at least. I climb to my feet and roll the extra plaids back into wet bundles. Chyr takes them from me and packs them away again, then ties the dead rabbit to Eira's saddle. He lifts me as if I weigh nothing at all and sets me on Bramble before swinging himself up behind me.

The irony isn't lost on me. The position is the same as how we've ridden these past days, but Chyr takes the reins, and the sensation of riding with him is entirely different when I'm not in control. It makes me even more aware of his body pressed against mine and how weak I feel. He settles my head against his chest and curls an arm around my waist, his hand splayed. His warmth seeps through my clothes, and the Veilstones are a soothing hum.

That shouldn't feel safer, but it does.

We cross the stream and scramble up the bank on the other side, then climb between rocky outcrops towards the gap that lies between the mountains. I've stopped shaking, and that hollow feeling inside me is ebbing away. Still, when we reach the top, Chyr lifts me from the saddle and sets my feet on the ground beside him.

"Now," he says, "if you're feeling a little better, we should set some boundaries. You have taken care of me because I was injured, and healing is your strength. You are guiding us because you know the territory—"

"And I can read a map."

"And you know the people and the allegiances, which is more than I could glean from a map. But since I'm no longer dying—"

"That remains to be seen."

His jaw works in annoyance. "I'm not dying *today*, so kindly leave the killing to me. That is literally my job, Flora, and I'm good at it. It's not that I don't appreciate what you did, but in the future, please trust me to ask for your help if I need it."

"Are you as good at admitting you need help as you are at killing things?"

He stares at me and sighs. "I'm male, so probably not. But I promise I will try to do better if you promise not to try to give me heart failure the way you did tonight."

"Fine," I say, reminding myself that feeling a connection doesn't mean that I should trust an Ever. That is still who Chyr is, and when we've reached Muilean, he'll be gone. Wind lifts the damp hair at my neck.

"Good," he says. "Fine."

Here on the western side of the Pass, the mountain forms a sheer cliff behind us. Already, a faint silver ribbon stretches south below us, moonlight spilling across Loch Seil between rank after rank of darkened hills. It's still well before dawn, and while nothing stirs on the wide expanse of slope below, watchfires glow red and amber in more than a dozen places, blurring as my eyes tear at the thought of what that means.

Chyr crosses his arms over his chest as he studies them. "The Butcher's men, or Vheara's soldiers from Dun Uilleum, most likely. They're spread out more than I'd hoped. Vheara may be trying to block access to Muilean."

"It could be more of what we saw at Aknacaery. Those are mainly Domhnall, Camhrain, and Leithe lands. The Cymbeuls allied with Vheara have been trying to steal them since the true queens fell. I wouldn't be surprised to find the Cymbeul chief has sent his militia out to seize whatever land he can."

Chyr turns to me, and the tension in his shoulders and the sharp glitter in his eyes echoes what I'm feeling. But he says nothing and strides off instead towards a sheltered spot between the cliff and a mitten-shaped thrust of rock where he builds a fire that won't be seen. He makes quick work of skinning the rabbit and spitting it over the open flames to cook. Fat hisses, and smoke rises low and thin.

I'm still weak, but both my strength and magic are returning, the way wet peat expands after being compressed. Cautiously, I reach into the earth to draw more magic, but I can't take more than a shallow pull, as if my body is wrung too tight to hold more than that.

I can't put off the questions any longer. Not understanding my magic is a danger, and I need to learn.

"Can you tell me how the Veilstones work?" I settle myself beside Chyr with my back against the rock. "I've been stronger since I touched one. Stronger the longer that I'm near them. Are they giving me more strength for the magic I can already use, or are they giving me access to magic I've never had? I think it must be the Veilstones. Some remnant of Siorai blood in me using the magic from Tirnaeve."

Chyr pivots where he crouches low beside the fire, his eyes widening. Then any trace of emotion is quickly tamped down, leaving his expression blank. "Do you feel like you're pulling magic through the stones?"

"Not on purpose, but when I'm near you, I can feel them, almost the way you pushed magic into me earlier. Their temperature shifts, and the hum gets louder."

He nods, a line creasing deep between his brows. "They run hotter the more they draw, and go cold when my own magic is too drained to attract any." He flexes his fingers and straightens them again, watching the rings as he speaks. Fat drips from the spit and sizzles as it hits the fire.

I tip back my head, searching for words to explain ideas I don't understand. "I used to think transforming my dagger was the only magic I had. I'm not sure calming a horse counts—"

"It does."

"But what I did in the bog today—"

"Did that scare you?" Chyr prompts after I've been silent too long.

I bite my lip, still thinking. "When I was eleven, one of the big larch trees fell into a pasture fence in a storm. The mares got out, and Iain came to my father and brothers for help. My mother insisted it was too dangerous for them to go, but Iain and some of the men went out anyway. I snuck away on my own to help, and I found one of the mares sinking in a bog. When I went to lead her out, I became mired as well. I thought we were both going to die."

"You made the earth obey you then? The way you did

tonight?" Chyr asks. The fire reflects through the layers in his eyes in a way that makes it seem the fire is caught inside him.

"Earlier, you asked me if I'd ever depleted my magic. I haven't thought about that night in years, and I've never suspected it had anything to do with magic. But I remember how desperate I was, and then the mare was free. We both were." I shrug. "I was a child. Children don't think about what's possible. I got the mare out, and Iain found me curled on the ground unconscious with her standing over me. It was days before I was strong enough to get out of bed."

Chyr stares down at his hands. They're splayed on his thighs, the graceful fingers slightly weathered. "I'm acquainted with how it feels to empty myself, but I'm Siorai, so I can't die from it. That wouldn't apply to you."

"How do I know I'm using too much?" I ask.

"Stop when it hurts. Sounds simple, doesn't it?" Chyr catches my chin in his fingers and tips my face so that I have to look at him. "You're terrifying. Even if you learn your limits, I've no doubt you'll push yourself past them."

The hold of his fingers is gentle, and his eyes slip down to my lips. Heat from the fire warms the air between us.

Then Chyr drops his hand and shakes his head. Something shutters behind his eyes. Pivoting back to the fire, he turns the rabbit on the spit. "You asked about the Veilstones, and the truth is, I can't explain it. How did you learn the trick with the sword? Did someone teach you?"

"I'm starting to wonder if it might have been a Whisperwraith."

Chyr's brows shoot up. "What? Why?"

"My grandmother had healing magic, but that was easy to pass off as knowledge of herbs and salves. The Sun King would have killed her if anyone had known, and my father made me swear never to show anyone what I could do." My heart squeezes at the memory, at the reminder that he's gone, and I close my eyes a moment before continuing.

"And the Whisperwraith?"

I sigh. "My younger brothers liked to torment me with their wooden swords when they began their training. Until then, we'd done everything together. Then suddenly I was a girl, and they were *men*, and I was supposed to treat them with respect. I wanted to learn to fight back, but no one would give me a sword of my own."

"So you made one for yourself. Something told you that you could."

It makes me smile that he understands. "Not only did I have a sword, but I had it whenever I needed it—and no one knew it was there. It took me months to learn the trick, and it felt like I was pulling shards of glass through my veins. But it was worth it. The look on my brothers' faces when they trapped me—I made them both bleed a little, and they never tried it again."

The memory doesn't bring the wave of satisfaction it used to before they died.

Chyr catches my hand and threads his fingers with mine. His grip is careful; the Veilstones hum faintly against my skin.

"Does it still hurt when you use magic?"

"There are moments when it doesn't hurt," I say, "I thought maybe that was because of the Veilstones."

"Whatever Siorai blood you've inherited must recognise them. But the magic you had before—was it harder after Vheara came?"

I nod, and the small crease between Chyr's brows deepens. He pauses to pull the rabbit from the fire and checks it before sliding it back to roast again. Fat falls into the fire with a pop. A thread of smoke curls upward.

Chyr finally shifts around to face me. "The Veilstones were

made to give us access to our magic while we're here. But the runesmiths wouldn't have known any descendants of the Riders would still have enough magic to use them."

I huddle deeper into the warm plaid that's trapped my body heat, thinking of the Veilstone that Chyr left at Dunhaelic. Thinking of possibilities.

"I've seen you use air and fire magic and jump from one place to another," I say. "And create illusions. What other types of magic are there?"

Chyr raises his head, shadows from the fire playing across his skin, and he studies me more closely. I force myself not to look away.

"All Siorai can shadow-walk, work illusions, and do basic mind-tricks—change perception, shape dreams and memories, plant suggestions or compulsions—"

"The things the Compact outlawed."

Chyr's sigh is barely audible. "Some of them. More powerful Siorai can work with one or two of the elements. The way that you do." He casts a quick look at me. "I've seen you move the earth, and your sword transformation is probably tied to earth magic, too. I suspect you can also work with water."

I think of the feeling of the water in the bog, the power in it. My heart gives a quick thump. "Earth is all I know to reach for."

"Healing is a water magic. We can try experimenting when you're feeling stronger. That and teaching you to use the Veilstones properly, since you've been doing that anyway."

There's no inflection in the way he says the words, but heat floods my cheeks. "You said the Veilstones were made for you—but there must have been something similar back when the Riders were consorts for the Cailleach Queens."

A muscle jumps at Chyr's temple, and he closes his eyes a moment as if fighting with himself.

I can't help pressing the point. "Magic was the reason the Cailleach Queens married Siorai companions in the first place. If sealing the doorways cut off most of the magic that came from Tirnaeve, then the consorts would have been too weak to be useful."

"I wouldn't say that." Chyr says the words lightly, and he smiles at me, but there's still tension in the line of his jaw.

"But there was something—wasn't there?"

"Flora, I wasn't much more than a child when Fionn killed the last queen." Chyr sits back deeper on his haunches, and his jaw tightens.

His fingers are deft on the hot flesh as he takes the rabbit from the spit and lays it out on the oilcloth left over from our cheese. He doesn't look at me.

He's hiding something. When he told me that Siorai can't lie, he warned me that doesn't mean they tell the truth. I should be angry, but I've seen his oathbands, and all those rows of runes that represent promises he has to live by.

"Something other than Veilstones," I say. "What was it?"

Chyr settles himself beside me, his back to the mitten-shaped rock, and lays the cloth with the rabbit on the ground between us. I can feel the tension that tightens every one of his muscles. His fingers clench, and his voice sounds like gravel when he finally answers.

"Chulainn had a Hollow Crown made when he sealed the doors—similar to the Veilstones but much more powerful."

My breath hisses as I draw it in. "That's not in any of the stories."

Chyr doesn't look at me, and his expression is carefully blank. "No one but Chulainn and the Anvar'thaine knew what the crown was meant to do."

His voice sounds strangled on the last words, and tendons stand out in his neck as if someone has pushed a hot poker into the middle of his back. That alone tells me as much as all he's ever said to me so far.

My heart pounds furiously in my chest. "The Compact was created to make the Cailleach Queens and their descendants powerful enough to protect Alba Scoria *against* Siorai. Against those like Vheara who came from Tirnaeve to exploit us. But if the consort's magic was limited to what came through the Hollow Crown, then all of it was a lie."

The wind gusts, and the fire blows sparks into the air with a hiss and crackle.

"I can't answer that," Chyr says.

His movements are painfully slow as he busies himself tearing off a rabbit leg. He offers it to me without looking at me, which is confirmation in itself.

My blood chills as I think it through. A Veilstone ring swirls on each of his hands, the gold threads of magic dancing like sunbeams through a cloud.

"The Compact was a trick, wasn't it?" My words are cold, and my hands are numb. "It let the High King seal off the doorways so no more celestial iron could be brought back to Tirnaeve, but the Siorai blood of the consorts was never meant to strengthen *us*. It gave the High King more control over us than he'd ever had. He never gave us a single thing he couldn't take away."

My eyes burn, and my breath comes too fast. I reach for Chyr's arm and squeeze hard enough that he's forced to look at me.

"Tell me I'm wrong, Chyr," I insist. "Say it."

His eyes have darkened to a brown gold, and his hands are fisted at his sides as if he's fighting with himself. Slowly, he shakes his head.

His body convulses in wave after wave, muscles straining beneath his skin. Sweat breaks out on his forehead, and his face is as pale as it was when I was carving out his flesh.

Instinct has me reaching to pull his coat open and check his wound. But he catches my hand and pulls it aside.

"The pain is from my oathbands. It has nothing to do with the wound," he says.

His voice is hoarse, and instead of dropping my hand, he wraps his fingers around mine. We sit in silence while he struggles.

I can see the tremor in his fingers even after the convulsions stop and the muscles in his neck and arms relax. Then he tips his head back against the damp rock, sweat still beading across his brow.

I've seen how much pain Chyr can tolerate without complaint. If the oathbands don't want him discussing the true reason behind the Compact, that only confirms what I was saying.

The Compact was never equal. Never real.

I need to re-examine every story I've ever heard about it— and everything Chyr has told me. It's time to think more carefully about what he might have been leaving out. What he might have been unable to tell me and why.

Wind sweeps up from the valley, colliding with the rock behind us. It leaves a cold chill that makes me shiver. In the distance, dozens of watchfires bleed red against the darkness. The war is here.

CHAPTER 24
TIME TO CHOOSE

FLORA

We descend towards Glen Fhionain, and shortly before dawn, we find a deep cleft between two outcroppings of granite on the hillside.

Fallen rock overgrown with vegetation overhead creates a deep cavern and protection from the rain. Better yet, a thicket of birches below hides the entrance, and a nearby stream falls from a natural pool, giving us a sheltered place to bathe.

A pre-dawn silence blankets the glen, and a low-hanging mist dims the glow of the watchfires on the far side of Glen Seil. The danger is still there, but the moment is peaceful enough that I can almost push it from my mind as I water the horses and let them graze. Then I steal the first turn to take a bath.

The water is cold but as clear and soothing as moonlight. It makes me think of the difference between my own magic and Chyr's, his bright, steady heat against the pale warmth I'm starting to recognise at my core. The magic I draw from the earth is entirely different—wilder, cooler, grittier, dark and rich with life.

I run my hands through the water, testing it against my skin, searching for a connection to help me understand it.

The magic in the water *wants* to be understood. I cup my hands, trying to contain it at first, then pouring it from one hand to the other. It wants to spill over and fall back into the pool, but I give it a mental tug to pull it back into my palm. It almost answers. The potential is there, then pain tears at my veins, reminding me that my magic is still too empty.

Shivering, I wash my hair and wring it out, then rinse my clothes and lay them on a rock out of sight to dry. The sky is softening to gold and rose across the moors. The first notes of birdsong sound from the brush. With the plaid tucked tight around me, hair still dripping down my back, I leave the horses grazing and return to the cavern where Chyr has already built a fire. Smoke veils the damp air, and the granite floor is cold and rough beneath my feet.

Chyr looks up from where he's crouched by the fire, his eyes gleaming like stars. He steals my breath, and his attention feels like a living force that pulls me towards him with such intensity it's like a hook sunk into my chest.

His gaze shifts back to the fire, and the pull eases. My breath still comes too fast and shallow, and I concentrate on removing clean clothing from my pack.

"I'll check your wound when you're finished bathing," I warn. "Don't try to remove the dressing yourself."

A muscle twitches in his cheek, and he studies me, his jaw clenched, his mouth a harsh slash bracketed by the small silver scar at one corner. But Great Mother, he is beautiful.

His lips part and the sharp line of his jaw softens as if he means to say something, then he shakes his head and turns his back. Moving with practised efficiency, he strips off the various swords and knives he has strapped to himself and then unpins the plaid from his shoulder and peels off the buff coat and the shirt beneath.

He's left in nothing but the kilted plaid and the thin bandage wrapped around his chest. The wide expanse of his back tapers from broad shoulders to his narrow waist. My fingers twitch, wanting to trace the long groove of his spine between the ridges of muscle. He turns and snatches up a spare plaid in one hand and his sword in the other.

Heat flares in his eyes as they meet mine. An answering burn spikes somewhere deep inside me.

Six feet separate us. My throat is dry, and I swallow slowly. Chyr's chest rises and falls. His attention drops to my lips, and he takes a step.

Then he stills and curses beneath his breath. Striding past me, he leaves the cavern.

My hands shake. I sink cross-legged to the ground, my knees unsteady and the damp plaid puddled around me. I will my heart to slow down, my breath to calm.

Relief and disappointment tangle into a knot beneath my ribs.

I've known what Chyr is. I've felt the attraction—I'd have needed to be dead not to feel it. Still, it has grown deeper, become more, and when I'm pressed beside him, wrapped in his heat and the hard strength of his arms, I can't keep pretending that all I want is warmth and comfort.

He comes back faster than I expected, and I've made no effort to change my clothes. I'm still slumped on the ground wrapped in nothing but the damp plaid, my hair dripping, and my feet numbed from cold.

If I'm honest with myself, that's by choice, not neglect.

Chyr crosses the cavern in a rush, then he crouches and tips my chin up. "Are you hurt? What happened?"

I shake my head, the roughened pads of his fingers scraping against my skin. "I was making a decision."

He rocks back on his heels. "Thank fuck. I don't think I can take you depleting yourself again."

His hair is damp and tousled, falling loose around his face. The fire has burned low, turning his eyes to bottomless honey-gold. They linger on mine, pinning me in place.

The edge of his thumb brushes my bottom lip, skims over my cheek. I can't—I don't—look away.

He groans and pulls me to my feet. His hand slides to the back of my neck. I push forward as he leans closer, and our lips crash together. His teeth nip until my mouth opens, and he dips his tongue inside, coaxing mine to dance. I run my finger down the hollow of his spine, and he shudders and pulls me closer.

Then just as quickly, he pulls back. "We can't," he rasps. "You don't want this."

"You don't know what I want."

He sets his jaw and shakes his head. I stare at him, but he gives nothing away, and finally I raise my chin and stalk back to retrieve my dagger. He's standing where I left him, his head bowed.

"I still need to change your dressing," I remind him.

I'm gentle as I slice through the knot that holds the bandage in place and unwind the layers of cloth—more gentle than I feel. I can't even say why I'm angry, because he was right to stop me.

Wasn't he?

I'm not naïve. I've heard women talk as they work together, sharing their burdens and turning their complaints into sly jokes about their husbands. I'm aware that once I'm married, I'll be lucky if my husband gives a damn about what I want. Or gives me the option to say no to what *he* wants.

Chyr watches me unwind the strips of linen bound around

his chest. There's a dark hush between breaths when my fingers brush his skin, but bit by bit I'm more certain of my feelings as I touch him.

The final bit of bandage strips away, and I see the wound for the first time since I healed it yesterday. After his pain earlier and the battle with the Ravenhounds, I expected it to be reopened. Instead, new red skin stretches the full length of the wound, indented deeply over the worst of the injury. It's fully sealed, though, and lower, where the wound was shallower, most of it has faded from pink to silver so that it's barely visible.

My throat clogs, and my lungs squeeze.

I did that. My hands. My magic.

Too many thoughts crowd my mind at once: how it's possible, what it means, whether it will last.

But I'm so, so tired of thinking.

I touch the healing skin with my fingertip in case it isn't real. Chyr sucks in a shaking breath, and I like the power of knowing that I can bring out that reaction. My finger traces the wound lower. He shivers and places his hand over mine to still the movement.

The plaid is wrapped low around his hips, slipping below the sharp angle of his hipbones. Firelight catches on the hard ridges and the trail of gold hair that disappears beneath the wool.

Chyr is so tense that I feel it in his stillness, in the sudden release of the breath he's been holding.

"There's no point in keeping this bandaged." I manage to sound calm. "But now that we can't see beneath the skin, we can't know how much the poison is spreading underneath."

He takes hold of my hand as I step back. "Flora."

I look up.

"You've done more than I asked," he says. "More than I had any right to expect."

His eyes are warm, his smile gentle. But I hear the words he isn't saying, the reminder that all he asked of me was time. Weeks, not forever.

I don't want to give myself to Ceapaich or Gleanngaradh or any other Domhnall man. I want Dunhaelic in my own right, and I want to keep my people safe. I'm no longer naïve enough to believe I can have any of those things.

I can't trust Tirnaeve or the Siorai. I'm as certain of that now as I am that none of us can trust the Raven Queen.

But Chyr is honourable. I believe that. Despite the cold way he was raised, there's warmth at his core, and the four harsh centuries he's spent as a Rider haven't exhausted the well of kindness in him. He feels the mistakes he makes, and he regrets them, and I've come to see that he's harder on himself than anyone I've ever met. He's shown loyalty in the way he refused to leave his friends after they died, the way he asked me to help him bury them. And the way he gave up one of the three Veilstone rings to take care of Dunhaelic and give me peace of mind... Even if I felt nothing for him, I would admire all of that.

I can't lie to myself and say that I feel nothing. I feel too much.

My hands tremble, not from fear but from the hunger growing low within me. My life is not my own, and I don't know what the future brings. Now, though, I want a man I choose, a man who looks at me as if he fears breaking something precious. A man who gave up his own magic and strength to protect the people I love.

I want to feel something that isn't fear or loss, and I want to feel it with Chyr.

He shakes his head. "Don't look at me like that."

"Like I want you?"

"Like you might let me have you. It's been a long time since

I've been with a woman, and I've come to care for you. To want you. I'm clinging to my last shred of self-control."

"Then don't. You've shown more care for me than any man I've ever met. I want this as much as you do."

Then his mouth is on mine, and everything both of us have been holding back is unleashed. The kiss is punishment and absolution. It's fire.

His arm circles my waist until I'm arched against him. He catches my hair in his fist and pulls my head back, tracing the curve of my throat with his lips, his tongue.

Reaching between us, I tug at the plaid he has wrapped around his hips until that, too, slides to the floor.

"Flora?" Chyr's voice is a growl, a whimper.

"If I have to marry someone, give myself to someone, then I want to have this first, with someone I'm attracted to, someone I want. Is that selfish? Is it unfair to ask you to give me that?"

"Not unfair. Unwise."

"I'm tired of thinking about every step I take, worrying all the time. Whatever happens, whoever I have to marry, I'll try to make the best of it, but I'd like to have something to remember."

My chest heaves as his teeth nibble at my ear.

I reach up to wrap my forearms around his neck and bring his lips back down to mine. He untucks the fabric holding the plaid around my chest, and the wool falls to my hips, caught between our bodies. The calloused warmth of his hands moves from my shoulders across my breasts. His thumbs brush over my peaked nipples without stopping, without relief. He lifts each aching breast to meet his mouth, his tongue circling, teeth scraping.

I moan, my eyes unfocused, my breath ragged.

His hands continue their burning slide past my waist. My

plaid falls from my hips with a whisper, and his thumbs meet on my stomach, then slip lower until they brush the low crux where desire coils.

I'm naked, and part of me is conditioned to believe I should feel shame or fear. He looks at me with half-lidded eyes that hold both reverence and hunger, and he drops to his knee. I feel no shame, only wonder and a consuming need.

"What do you want?" he asks with that rasp and purr in his voice that is like a feather slowly rolling up my spine.

"A moment out of time. A memory," I say, knowing that's only part of it.

"Are you certain?"

"Never more so."

His gaze doesn't leave mine again, not even when he leans in to press his lips against the hollow where my thigh meets my hip. His touch is a promise.

But I want to see him, too.

I step back to admire him. Every one of these muscles looks earned, a tool in service of his oaths. In service of who he is.

With a soft curse, he surges to his feet. He's erect and large, and I never imagined that the shrivelled little things my brothers were so proud of could look like *this*.

He stoops and lifts me with an arm beneath my shoulders and another beneath my knees. He smells of sweat, the sweetness of Ever blood, and heady, musky desire.

The fire has guttered to embers, but the cold around us only makes the heat we're creating all the sweeter. Chyr spreads out one of the plaids and lays me down on it, kissing my shoulder, my throat, the hollow beneath my ear. Teeth scrape my lower lip. He takes the weight of my breasts in his palms again, caressing the undersides with his thumbs, teasing, his gaze holding my suddenly unfocused eyes.

"I want to give you so much pleasure you'll forget everything else."

His mouth comes down slowly, so slowly to my nipple, and he takes it between his lips, draws it in. My body shudders.

There's warmth—heat. More than the heat of his breath and his tongue. I recognise the bright gold threads of his magic as they echo every suck and rasp of his mouth, spreading across my stomach and down between my legs as though he's there as well.

I gasp, and he laughs. "You like that? I can do more."

Then he's everywhere, and the sensation is bliss like I never imagined feeling. My hands are wrapped around him, my nails clutching for purchase as jolts of pleasure shake through me.

"Spread your legs for me, Fierceness. Let me see you. Let me taste you."

I pull my thighs wider, making room for him, and then he's there with his mouth and his magic, moving even deeper inside me, until my entire body is throbbing. Magic makes slow teasing circles at my core while he dips a finger inside me carefully, then adds another.

"More," I demand. *"Please."*

He releases more magic, molten and tingling. I explode, hips bucking, back arching, mind a daze. The world narrows to our heat, to the hum of magic singing through my blood.

Chyr spreads my thighs even wider, watching me as if he's turning me inside out, reading every twinge of my muscles, every quickened heartbeat. He brings his mouth back to mine.

"Are you certain this is what you want?" he murmurs against my lips. "You don't understand what I am. I haven't told you everything."

I can't begin to catalogue all that's in his voice. Grief, shame, tenderness. It makes me realise how very alone he's been. Maybe long before his friends died, before this war began. Far

227

longer than I've known him. Duty, responsibility, honour—all of those are a devastation of loneliness.

And that is a place in which we both have lived.

I lift my hands and cup his face. "You asked me once if I knew what you were, as if that would make me fear you. I know that your allegiance is not the same as mine. But at least for the moment, we can take comfort in each other. Let me show you that you're more than oaths, duty, and whatever you were born to be. Those things are only part of you."

Something softens in Chyr's face. Something that looks like hope. But he says nothing, only kisses me fiercely and eases himself inside me. There's a pinch, and he pauses to give my body time to adjust. I draw him deeper until he fills me. Then all thoughts of gentleness vanish as we surge together, our bodies and our magic melding until I can't tell where I end and he begins. Pleasure builds to a crest, and I fly apart, shuddering, unravelling. Chyr convulses, his breath ragged, and he holds himself propped on his arms, looking down at me.

"You will haunt me, Fierceness. I'm afraid that you will haunt me."

I shouldn't like the sound of that name, but I do. I want to believe I'm fierce enough to save my people, and I want to be brave enough not to regret my mistakes. Yet I feel too much, and the intensity of it scares me as we collapse against each other.

"Is it your wine that's behind the stories of mortals who become addicted?" I ask. "Or is there something else? Something about Siorai themselves that makes mortals feel addicted?"

He pulls me against him tighter. "Wine, compulsion, lust, love. Wishful thinking." Then his head lifts, every hint of softness gone. "Wait. You think I've *compelled* you to want me?"

"I'm asking, that's all. They say those who've been touched

can never be satisfied, that they'll do anything anyone wants of them in the hope of feeling the same pleasure."

"And you think I would do that? To you?" His honey-gold eyes are dark, burning into me, waves of energy seeping out of him as though he's too angry to contain it. His hand clenches into a fist, and he strikes the shifting bands of runes that circle the thick muscle of his arm.

The blow lands with a thud. The force of it ripples through the cavern. My ears pop, and the fire gutters.

"These oathbands enforce my obedience to the Compact. I swore to them because I believe in them. I don't believe in taking advantage of someone weaker, whether the weakness is physical, magical, or otherwise. There is nothing desirable about using force. I won't pretend I don't want you, Flora—I've proven how much. But not like that. Never like that."

His voice is rough, and the energy coming from him tightens my lungs. But I haven't finished.

"Is there any other reason why humans would be attracted to—would crave—Siorai?" I ask.

His mouth twists, and there's something lost and a little broken in his expression. "I swear to you I have no desire to take your power or will away from you. The thought of you giving yourself to a man who wants you for what you can give him instead of loving you for who you are—it makes me want to gut every spineless male in that council of yours.

"No one should ever try to make you less. Or make you doubt yourself. They should be awed by every careful, calculated cogwork of your mind. You're brave and fierce, measured and loyal and kind—beautiful enough to haunt a man's dreams. I know what it's like to have to live without love, and that should never be your fate."

His words open a sluice gate, setting free a torrent of all the things I haven't dared to let myself feel after losing my entire family and every soul who ever loved me. Everyone who belonged to me.

I reach for Chyr, my hands tangling in the silky strands of his hair and dragging his mouth down to mine.

He kisses me deeply, intently. Beyond the cave entrance, the sun breaks the horizon, changing the colours of the world, but inside, the light is even brighter. Our skin, his skin and mine, glows with a soft, amber light.

Every part of me that felt filled feels hungry again, craving him. I'm alive and awake, and whatever I was before I found Chyr in the Sacred Wood, I will never be that again.

Outside, the wind quiets, and Glen Fhionain holds its breath. Briefly, the watchfires, the war, the long ride to Muilean—it all retreats, leaving nothing but heat and hunger.

CHAPTER 25

MASKS AND PROMISES

CHYR

Warmth blooms from Flora's skin. She sleeps nestled against me beneath the tangled plaids that cover us, and for a moment after waking I hold very still and simply let myself feel everything: the shape of her, the scent of her hair, the quiet fact that she is here and I am here and neither of us is dead. The joy of it is uncomplicated for exactly those few seconds. I've never wanted a woman—body, mind, and soul—as much as I want Flora. Which is exactly why I never should have touched her. She makes it impossible to think, impossible to keep my distance.

The depth of my betrayal crashes into me all at once. How selfish it was to take her.

Flora will be furious when she learns the truth. She won't care that I tried to warn her.

As if she feels me watching, she opens sleep-soft eyes and blinks up at me, her colour rising as the memories surface.

"Hello," she whispers with a fragile smile.

The sun is setting, warming the light within the cavern and setting her hair on fire. I drink in the sight.

"How do you feel?" My voice sounds rough.

"Good." She tips her head, considering. "Stronger. Your magic did more than give me pleasure, didn't it?" Raising herself on one elbow, she places a palm across the healing scar that cleaves my chest. "Did you give me more than you could afford to give?"

"No." I trace the line of her jaw, then cup her cheek. She relaxes into the contact, and I lean in and claim her lips. She answers for the space of a heartbeat, meeting my hunger with her own. Then she draws back and catches my hand, turns it, and kisses my palm before letting it drop.

I'd like nothing better than to pull her back to me, to kiss my way back down her body until sounds of pleasure escape her lips. But she gets up, taking the plaid with her to wrap it self-consciously around herself as if she wants to hide her body from me.

Without the plaid, I'm bare. Flora blushes furiously and starts to turn away. Then she stops, and her eyes trace a slow path from my head to my feet instead, as though she's painting a memory of me in her mind. I grow harder at the thought that she wants to keep some part of me, and a smile of something like pride tugs at the corners of her lips.

I don't want the moment to end. I lie back, arms folded behind my head, letting her look. "It's still early. We could find new ways to use magic that we didn't try last night."

Her eyes widen, and her lips part slightly, then she goes still. I see the war inside her. Denial and duty, but also curiosity, temptation. Passion. That's there in everything she does.

Flora holds nothing back—except from herself.

That self-denial is what wins out this time, too. I see her pulling away even before she shakes her head.

"We need more food," she says too quickly. "There's a village not far from here, but we'll need to get there before everyone goes to bed."

Her voice is flatter, and she doesn't meet my eyes. The distance between us suddenly feels more than physical.

Outside, the sun hasn't yet fully set. Pools of light and dark still stripe the cavern floor, and I shadow-walk to stand beside her. Clasping her chin, I turn her to look at me, then I shift my hand to lay my palm along her cheek.

"What's wrong? Do you regret what we did, sweetheart?"

She groans and tilts her head, leaning into my hand, chasing the contact. Then she rises on her toes and wraps her hands around my neck to bring her mouth to mine. It's a deep kiss, claiming and angry, but it's over too fast.

Her grey eyes are glazed and stormy. "It was unfair of me to ask that of you."

"I can speak for myself. Did I not give you pleasure?"

"Too much." She blushes again, pink racing up the long column of her throat and spilling across her cheeks. "I needed a choice, a memory, and you gave me that. I will never regret what we shared, but it can't happen again. I have to marry—"

"No. You don't."

"I *do*." She shakes her head and gives me a smile that tugs at my heart. "I *will* have to live with another man, and I have enough good sense to know the limits of what I can bear. The more I give myself to you, the more I'll hate having to give myself to someone else."

The thought of another man touching Flora drives a spear of ice through my chest. That's followed by an ache of loss as I think of never being able to touch her again, never burying myself inside her or losing myself in her fierce, generous heat. Never waking with her in my arms again.

I swallow the blow, but it burrows deep.

Still, I've never yet had to talk a woman into my bed, and I won't start now.

"If that's what you need, that's what will happen." I drop a kiss on her hair, pretending to both of us that it will be as simple as that when we both know there's still the rest of the journey to get through.

How do I turn the clock back on what I'm feeling?

I brought the horses in before we went to sleep, and I bedded them down with forage I gathered for them. Now the cavern smells of wet stone and manure, but the mares are still drowsing, their right hind legs resting on their toes and their hindquarters steeply angled. A tail twitches, and even that small sound suddenly seems too loud.

My eyes are locked on Flora's, arguments milling in my head. Arguments aren't what she needs, though.

I manage to smile and nod. Then, taking a clean shirt from the pack, I leave her with a bit of privacy while I retreat to the pool farther along the hillside and wash up as quickly as I can.

The dress, shift, and stockings that Flora left laid out on a rock in the sun are still too damp. I use a bit of magic to dry them with heated air before returning to the cavern and giving her a turn to bathe.

My regret at the situation between us hasn't diminished, and I'm angry at myself for having allowed things to go so far. I should have expected that Flora would have regrets—and I wasn't entirely honest with her. That thought alone unmans me.

I pack our supplies and saddle the horses while Flora has her bath, and by the time she is dressed and ready, I have my expression well-schooled and my feelings buried. I won't make this any harder for her than it has to be.

Yet the blows keep coming.

"You should probably ride Bramble on your own now that you're well enough," Flora says when it's time to leave.

She watches me carefully, biting the inside of her lip as if the suggestion makes her nervous. As though she expects me to argue.

I find my fist itching to crack the stone in the cavern wall. Not because of what she's asking. I hate that she feels she has to tiptoe around me. I release a long, slow breath.

"If that's what you think is best," I say.

"With the watchfires on the far side of Loch Seil, we'll need to take the harder route along this side. We'll stand a better chance of outrunning patrols if we don't ride together."

We both know that's not her only reason.

Partly from necessity and partly to help smooth the tension, I remove Oran's Veilstone ring from my finger.

"We were going to experiment with your magic tonight," I remind Flora. "And test the way you've been diverting it from the Veilstones—"

She looks up, her expression panicked. "No—You mean I was stealing magic from you? I didn't think of it that way."

"I'm not accusing you." I shake my head. "But since you're getting stronger, it makes sense for us to see what else you can do. We need to understand how closely your powers mirror Siorai abilities."

Her hands are so small that the ring is too big for her thumb, much less her fingers. She folds her fist around it. "Does it matter where I put it?"

"If we're right, you've been drawing on it even when you weren't the one wearing it."

She tucks it between her breasts and laces her bodice

tight. I drag my eyes away, feeling as callow as a half-grown cub.

We ride out as the last of the sun fades, keeping to the birch woods as long as we can. A last few glints of gold and red still gleam on the dark water cradled by the shadowed hills.

The low knoll at the head of Loch Seil is too familiar, its memories tainted by trampled banners, defeat, and broken promises.

I pull Bramble to a halt, and Flora stops a few steps ahead, looking back at me with her eyebrows raised.

"This is where we planted the Sun King's banner," I say, "and the chiefs of the clans who rose for us came to take their oaths."

"My father was there. He wanted to hear what the rebel had to say."

I hate the dismissive tone she uses. "He has a name."

"One that his followers use with a title he hasn't earned in front of it. He's king of nothing yet."

"Vheara has to be stopped, regardless."

"I won't argue that." Flora's eyes are as hard as flint. "But we'd have had a better chance of stopping her before so many lives were squandered at the altar of another pretender with a pretty flag."

My oathbands warn me that's another dangerous topic. I take a breath and steer the subject in a slightly different—but no less painful—direction. I can't avoid the truth.

"Vheara will consider both Bhoradail House and Gleannadail to be targets for retribution for their owners' part in the war. It's probably best to avoid passing near them."

"We'll need to avoid everyone—regardless of who they fought for. For their safety as well as ours. All the Domhnalls in Ehrugael rose for your king—"

"And I don't want them dying for it." The words come out

more forcefully than I'd meant to. My cheeks heat, and Flora studies me with those calm eyes that see too much.

"There are no settlements on the eastern route along Loch Seil until we reach the southern tip," she says. "It won't be travelled much this time of year."

She watches me as though she expects me—dares me—to argue, and the wind blows back the plaid she wears wrapped around her shoulders. She's magnificent, and the risks I'm taking with her suddenly kick me in the chest. I'm gambling with her life and so much more.

She shouldn't be here. Not with me.

"If you show me where to find the track, I can follow it on my own," I say. "Regardless of settlements, you've seen the watchfires. We're getting to the most dangerous part of the journey."

She wheels Eira around, her hair whipping like a battle flag as she halts beside me. The mare shakes her head in protest, making the bridle jingle.

"You think I'd give up now?" Flora asks. "After what the Butcher did at Aknacaery, I'm not leaving you until you are through the doorway, and I can assure myself that you'll be returning with an army at your back. I've lost my whole family—as have too many others. Killing Vheara and the Butcher is the only way to redeem the suffering, and the schedule hasn't changed. If you want to reach Muilean by Beltane Eve, you can't afford to waste time getting lost."

She doesn't wait for me to reply. Instead, she nudges Eira into a canter and leaves me to follow.

As much as I wish she was wrong, the Riders and I travelled by boat from Muilean after we arrived. The route overland is unfamiliar, and with only five days left to reach the doorway, I don't have time to make mistakes.

Flora's pale mare flies like a wraith through the dusk as I

chase her, and perhaps I'm lying to myself when I force myself to accept Flora's choice. I don't have the right to set boundaries for her.

I can only hope she doesn't end up regretting that as well. Hope is a stubborn beast and slow to die.

The track along the head of the loch leads past the ruins of a church. The traditional large standing stone guards the entrance, but someone has long since scratched out the crescent moon symbol of the Cailleach, the Great Mother, until even the shape of it is all but gone.

A pair of Hallow Keepers, the silent Shadelings who guard the sacred places, emerge from the shadows of the building and incline their heads as we pass. Flora places her hand to her heart, but she doesn't look back.

Beyond the church, the windows of the rush-thatched cottages in a small hamlet are starting to light, yellow flickering in one window and then another. Chickens peck in the gardens, and a Shadehound uncurls itself from the nearest doorstep and trots to meet Flora as she approaches, its feet making no sound on the hard-packed track.

Flora puts a tentative hand out for the hound to sniff, then pats its head while I weave an illusion to mask myself to resemble an elderly human male. Flora and the Shadehound watch me with identical expressions of mild amusement.

"Do I look harmless enough?" I ask.

"As harmless as a man with a magic sword can ever look."

I arrange a broad section of the great kilt to hide the crystal pommel. Then Flora knocks at the cottage. A young woman answers with a baby on her hip and three boys—none of them more than five or six—peeking around her skirt.

She looks wary as Flora introduces herself and asks where we might buy some food. "It's only me and the boys here, my lady—and my father Donal. But you're welcome to share our meal."

Flora smiles at the children, and they smile back shyly, then one darts forward and tugs at my plaid for attention before his mother pushes him out of the way. Stubbornly, he pauses a short distance away. "Have you seen my father, sir? He was fighting—"

"Hush, wee man. Mind your manners and go play with your brothers," the woman says, turning back to Flora.

Flora tries to smile. "Your offer is very kind, but we've a fair distance to go yet. I hoped we might buy whatever you or your neighbours can spare. I know that's not much these days."

The old man stands up from the table where he's seated. "Won't be safe for any Domhnall to travel through Ehrugael. Especially you, Lady of Dunhaelic. There's Cymbeul militia about, and the Butcher himself."

"The Butcher? Where?" I ask, somewhat sharply.

The old man is missing an arm at the elbow, and he's younger than I thought at first. I search my memory, trying to place him. His eyes are a clear blue and sharp. They narrow as he looks me over, then his attention comes to rest on the pommel of my sword. He starts to drop to his knee at the same moment that I realise the boy tugged the drape of my plaid aside.

I catch his good arm to keep him upright. Our eyes meet, and I give him a small shake of my head. "Have you seen the Butcher yourself?"

The old man studies me a beat too long, and I notice Flora watching us both. Her face has lost all expression.

239

"He rode through on the way to Gleannadail House, Your—" He swallows visibly. "Sir. But more militia and the queen's red-coated peacocks arrive every day. Too many for Dun Uilleum to hold, so they're quartering in all the larger houses. Meanwhile, they thieve and rape, pretending to search for...the king and his Riders. The Butcher's offered £30,000 in reward—enough for a man to buy most of Ehrugael. There's not a Domhnall here who'd take it, though. You can believe that." He glances at Flora and gives her a nod. "Don't matter what side Domhnalls fight for, we'll not betray anyone."

"Good man," Flora says. "And what of Alasdair of Gleannadail? Is there news of him and his family?"

The man's face turns sour. "Red coats took him and his son to Dun Uilleum in chains. Put his wife and two girls on a boat—claimed to be taking them to the Tower in Dunfithic."

The young woman returns with two bundles of oilcloth in time to hear his words. She pauses and looks at her father, then turns to me with her brows raised.

"This is more than I hoped," Flora says, taking the bundles from her gently. "We're truly grateful." She holds out a gold coin.

"We don't take charity in this house." The woman draws back, her chin raised. "My husband will be back soon, and my own back is strong."

"What's your name?" Flora asks.

"Mairi, my lady."

"I'm Flora, please. And I'm paying what the food is worth to us in this moment. You'd do me a kindness to accept it and take your family away from here while you still can. If you can travel as far as Dunhaelic, ask for Faolan and tell him that I sent you."

Mairi holds out her palm to take the coin, but her father catches her hand to stop her. "We'll accept no coin for helping either of you," he says. "But we'll go to Dunhaelic and find a way to make ourselves useful until you're home again."

He shifts his gaze from Flora to me, holding my eyes until I nod.

Flora kisses Mairi on the cheek, then steps back. "I hope you and your boys stay safe, and that your husband and all the Domhnall men will come home soon."

"Thank you for that, and may the Lord Father save the king," the old man answers, glancing from Flora back to me. "It's in my heart to hope that the king knows that every true man in Ehrugael will still stand with him whenever it's time to fight again."

Flora drapes the plaid over her head as we return to the horses and put the food away. She's quiet, her face averted, and no sooner has she swung herself into Eira's saddle than she kicks the mare into a run and retraces our path back towards the eastern side of the loch.

I push Bramble to follow, my mind racing and only half aware that the Shadehound from the village has picked up a friend and they are both running behind us. We pass the old church at a canter and approach the birch-covered hills that slope down almost to the water.

A heavy drizzle begins, with clouds blotting out the moon. It's too dark for the pace Flora has set, so I urge Bramble to catch up. Flora refuses to look at me until I reach for Eira's reins in desperation and pull her to a stop.

"Tell me what's wrong," I say.

Flora draws her dagger and presses the blade to my wrist until I drop her reins.

"Were you ever going to tell me?"

My heart thuds heavily. "Tell you what?"

"That you're the rebel king masquerading as a Rider."

The oathbands constrict in warning—a brief moment of ice and fire in my veins. I can't ignore them, but I know Flora won't betray me. Drawing a deep breath, I search for an answer that they will let me give her.

She stiffens in the saddle with every passing moment I don't speak. Picking up her mood, Eira paws at the ground, the bit jangling and dripping froth as she works it with her tongue.

"You don't even have the courtesy to admit it, do you?" Flora snaps. "So much for truth and honour. But at least help me understand. Does a would-be king outrank the Master of the Anvar'thaine in Tirnaeve? What about a messenger? The king's errand boy?"

The oathbands clench again, and the pain is nothing to the shame. I say the words I've already said to Flora too often. Words that won't change what's done.

"I'm sorry."

"Apologies are meaningless. I can understand why you might not have wanted to tell me at the beginning. But after I healed you? Haven't I proven you can trust me?" Flora's eyes grow colder. "The Camhrain sentries recognised you, didn't they? You stopped them from saying it aloud, just like you tried to stop Mairi's father from taking a knee when he recognised your sword. *The king's sword.*"

"The Sword of the Anvar'thaine. The Master's sword."

"Am I the only fool who doesn't know the rebel king is the Master of the Anvar'thaine?"

"Does it matter what people call me? I'm still myself, Flora. Still king of nothing."

I want to remind her that she said she knows who I am—regardless of *what* I am. That's not fair, though, and I know it.

I should have found a way to tell her I'm oathbound to win the throne. Until this moment, I didn't know how much her acceptance matters. How much I care that she sees me for myself.

She's thawed the ice I'd built around my heart and made me dare to feel again.

I hate that I've hurt her. That I've lost her.

"I wish I *had* told you. I thought there was too much danger—"

"For me? Or for you?" Flora snaps.

"For both of us."

"Nothing about you being here is safe. Not for a single soul in Alba Scoria." She nudges Eira closer, until we're stirrup to stirrup and our knees are touching.

I feel the fury rolling from her. The Shadehounds growl behind us, and the wind rises, rain-soaked and edged with smoke.

"This," Flora continues fiercely, "*this* is the exact reason why it's impossible to trust an Ever. You don't lie, but you aren't honest. Not because you can't be. Not because of oaths or promises. Because you *won't* tell the truth. You dole out information like sweets to small children, and you expect us to be grateful for the crumbs."

It's the pain behind Flora's rage that makes my heart ache.

After Culodur, I swore I wouldn't drag anyone else into danger for me. That I wouldn't cause more pain. That vow means as much to me as the oaths that bind me to the Anvar'thaine.

I've seen the damage Vheara and I have done to Flora's people and the others in Alba Scoria. What my father has done to them. Still, the oaths that bind me to my uncle are a leash I cannot shake.

When Flora confronted me in the woods, I was fighting not to have to kill her. I tried to save her, and instead, I've taken away nearly everything that she cared about.

"You are the last person I ever wanted to hurt. Please believe that if nothing else."

"Am I?" she asks too quietly. "Tell me, did you have to bed me to keep your oaths? Did you have to prove I can't believe what I feel or who I trust? Or was that just a bonus?" She searches my face for a moment, then nudges her horse forward without waiting for me to answer.

The question echoes, and hearing that cold, dead tone in her voice is when I know that what I've done—what I've broken— is beyond repair or mending.

I bedded Flora because she burrowed into my heart. Because she's become a craving. I bedded her in spite of my oaths. But I can't deny that if what I am starting to hope proves to be true, she will be hurt even more.

And that will break us both.

CHAPTER 26
THE SHADEHOUNDS KNOW

FLORA

S cant light pierces the canopy of white-trunked birch trees that stand like wraiths in the darkness. Chyr creates a small, round scoutlight that illuminates the ground in front of us. It's enough for me to give Eira her head, and the mare picks her way through the moss, roots, and fallen branches along the slope. Rain patters on the loch and drums on the leaves above us. I'm glad of the excuse not to talk, because if I say anything more to Chyr, I will regret it.

I let myself behave recklessly with him, and despite his warnings, I believed in the wounded Rider who was trying to save my world. I failed to see he was only claiming it for himself.

He gave me his true name, Cóirneach, and he told me his friends call him Chyr. I should have known then that something was wrong. True names have too much power. Why would an Ever give one away so willingly?

Unless he needed it to hide behind.

Chyr is the rebel king. Teàrlach Solas, the man his supporters call the Bonnie King.

The man to whom I gave my body is the son of the Ever who took everything from us, from my family, from women, from Alba Scoria. Our lives, our gods, our right to rule, our magic, our self-respect. He ripped what was left of our bloodline from our islands and drove us into the hills.

I believed Chyr when he spoke so earnestly of oaths and promises. If those meant anything, his father would have been banished the moment he broke the Compact—but Tirnaeve did nothing. For four centuries, the Sun King lorded over us from his stolen throne.

It took Vheara killing Fionn for Tirnaeve to send Chyr and the Anvar'thaine—not to save us. To take the kingdom back. To the Evers, we have never mattered.

The Raven Queen should never have been our war. We shouldn't have to spill our blood to stop her or die to put an Ever—any Ever—on the throne of Alba Scoria.

The beat of the horses' hooves through the birch woods is a war cry to my anger. Rain soaks through the plaid I've wrapped around myself as a cloak, and water streams down my face. With Chyr behind me, I feel even more alone.

As though they sense my mood much in the way Rab would, the two Shadehounds who followed us from the village stay close, like sentries keeping to the edge of the soft light Chyr is casting on the ground.

The trees thin eventually, opening onto an old drovers' track. I push Eira into a canter while we have the opportunity, until we come to a burn swollen by rain and snowmelt. The water is a dark strip, its depth a mystery, but there's no going around. I give Eira a long rein and pat her neck as she plunges in.

Water churns above her knees. She moves cautiously,

stopping to test her footing until she scrambles up the opposite bank. Chyr is faster on Bramble, and he stops ahead of me on the track.

"We could eat here," he says. "You've had nothing since the rabbit last night, and the horses need to drink."

He's right, though I don't want to acknowledge it. I want to grieve what I felt for Chyr, what I believed about him. What I was starting to believe about myself.

I search for somewhere to sit out of the rain and far away from Chyr's brooding silence. The wool of our plaids grows warmer when it's wet, but tonight, there's ice building in my chest, and the chill seeps into my bones.

There's nowhere to shelter, so I huddle on a narrow rock along the riverbank, with my knees pulled up as I watch Eira and Bramble drink. Chyr unwraps one of the oilcloth bundles, puts half away again for later, and hands me more than my share of the rest. I refuse to argue with him. I take it, and hunger makes the cold mutton, cheese, and bannocks taste like the best meal of my life.

Chyr stands with his back and one foot braced against a tree behind me. I can feel him waiting for an opportunity to talk.

"Don't," I say. "Whatever you're going to say, I don't want to hear it. Leave me to settle what's happened in my mind without making the situation any worse."

"Tell me how I can make it right between us."

"Asking me how to mend your betrayal is another betrayal," I say, even as some ruinous part of me still wants him. I tear off two morsels of the mutton to give the Shadehounds.

The hounds show no interest in the meat, so I offer them bannocks and cheese instead. They've no interest in those either, edging over shyly to let me pet them. It's like touching silk through water, their substance shifting beneath my fingers, their grey fur dripping shadows that blur their outlines. They smell cool and misty, like the moors and braes at twilight.

Watching me intently through dark eyes ringed in a pale gold that glows like the moon, the smaller female whines softly and thumps her tail. The male divides his attention between me, Chyr, and the woods around us.

They make me miss Rab. I miss home, my family, my people. My place.

I wonder if Chyr understands how important place is to us in the Highlands, the earth beneath our feet that's been tilled and tended down the centuries by those who share our blood. We're a people of place: Domhnall of Dunhaelic, Domhnall of Gleanngaradh, Domhnall of Ceapaich, Domhnall of Gleannadail.

Chyr's father stole our places from us, and in doing so, he forced us to become something other than who we were born to be. Chyr made me believe in him, believe in myself. He changed me, and now he's stolen that new beginning and taken my self-respect. I don't know how to get any of that back.

Chyr and I finish eating, and I wash the meal down with enough water to make me forget my stomach's been empty too long. Then we ride on with the Shadehounds padding beside us through a misery of driving rain. Bogs at the edge of the loch force us to detour upland or risk skirting the dangerous edges where false ground can kill in an instant. Eira dances too close for comfort several times as she veers off to snatch bites of heather or grass.

With no moonlight, it's hard to gauge how long we've been

riding. Finally, the sloping woods give way to gentler hills covered in blooming furze. We traverse three or four of these, and then the Shadehounds shoot forward at a run.

Chyr and I glance at each other. He extinguishes the scoutlight, and as we crest the next low rise, we're hit with the smell of smoke.

My chest tightens, and a sick feeling turns my stomach. But the smell isn't the harsh, greasy smoke of destruction. It's pine sap and iron, a watchfire built outdoors to withstand the rain.

Chyr slides silently from Bramble's saddle and tosses me her reins. "Take the horses off the track," he whispers. "I'll go have a look."

Eira dances sideways, but Chyr is already moving, his footsteps silent. I dismount and lead the horses into the thin pines and rowan scrub. My heart is thudding, and I'm relieved when the Shadehounds return. But I don't give a damn about Chyr's order.

"If you two can understand me, stay with the horses. Stay." I hold out my hand in the palm-down gesture I use for Rab. "Stay. Guard."

They tilt their heads, then drop to their haunches and wait as I tie Eira and Bramble to a twisted pine. I move quietly through the brush in the direction that Chyr took, and when I look back, the Shadehounds are still where I left them, which fills me with both relief and wonder.

Seeing no sign of Chyr, I follow the smoke. I round a bend and spot the soft orange glow of a fire flickering in a hollow between the hills.

The glow vanishes behind trees and brush as I move closer, until I crest another moss-covered hillock. Then it's suddenly right ahead. Crouched behind a narrow birch, I peer into a gully where a lookout post has been dug in. Three lean-tos covered in oilcloth stand in a row, swords and equipment scattered in front of them. Within each one, two men in scarlet uniforms sleep on cots, and a seventh man stands by the fire, watching the slope below.

My fingers curl into my palms, nails digging into my skin. The vantage point gives a clear view of Loch Seil and the Domhnall territory beyond it. It also overlooks the drovers' track where Chyr and I would have passed if we hadn't smelled the smoke.

As if I've conjured him by thinking his name, Chyr appears behind the sentry. Clamping his hand over the sentry's mouth, he makes a clean slice over the man's throat and lowers him to the ground, where he lies unmoving.

My heart twists. There's a pang of loss similar to what I felt with the rabbit's death, a faint echo of the sense of loss at Aknacaery. But instantly, Chyr pivots towards one of the tents, and I understand what he means to do. It's necessary, I can acknowledge that. Eliminating the watchpost will reduce our risk and the danger for everyone in Ehrugael, but the men are sleeping, and that's an ugly kill.

As angry as I am, I know Chyr enough to know he'll carry that guilt with him. And he shouldn't have to shoulder it alone.

I run to the camp, moving as silently as I can.

Chyr is inside the first shelter when he sees me, and he shakes his head, warning me away. Ignoring him, I tiptoe to the lean-to farthest from him.

He kills again. I feel the loss of the life he's taken just as I reach the structure. Forcing myself to set that aside, I crouch beside the first of the red-coated soldiers. But I can't kill him in his sleep—I can't. With my dagger poised at his throat, I cover his mouth with my other hand and wait for him to wake.

Confusion dulls his senses when his eyes first open. The delay is long enough for me to carve a deep slice across his throat. The wound wells red, blending into his coat, and blood pumps with the last beats of his heart. He stills.

The death isn't a pang in my heart this time. It's a rip in my soul, swift and raw. Trying to ignore it for the moment, I move on to the second man. My hands shake as I kill him, and by the time I emerge, Chyr is in the third shelter already. He scowls when he sees me.

I don't know which of us makes some small sound. Perhaps neither of us does, and it's sheer ill luck. Across the shelter from Chyr, the second soldier bolts up from the cot and darts towards the watchfire, fumbling for something at his throat—a stone of some sort on a leather cord. Yanking the necklace free, he flings it into the fire and screams a word that I don't know.

The fire hisses and flares, and the smell of pine pitch cuts through the scent of rain.

Flames erupt on the ridge above us, a long beacon ripping through the darkness. Chyr dives at the man, but the soldier grins as if he's already won.

That smile makes me ignite with rage.

Vheara's soldiers are using our own hilltop signal fires against us. They kill our warriors, torch and spoil our fields, slaughter our animals, rape our women, and burn our children. And all the while, they *smile*.

Magic comes before I call it, roiling in the air around me as if the fury I feel is echoed by the earth and sky. It begs to be used, whispering insistently, calling out not to the power of earth that I know, but to something that pulses in time with my heart, something that is a part of me as surely as the air I draw into my lungs. It's the ancient powers that whisper: the ancient gifts of land and sun, of rain and fertility and wind, and the cool nights when the silver eye of the Cailleach's moon provides a respite.

I reach for rain the same way I would reach for earth. My

face lifted towards the swollen clouds above the hill, I sift through the water's magic the way I did back at the pool, separating it from the lighter air. The cloud is cool and patient. Fine droplets turn to swollen drops, gather and hesitate, and then give way—first mist, then rain, then the hard downpour that drowns the flame.

The signal fire snuffs out.

I search for Chyr. He has the soldier by the collar of his unbuttoned uniform coat. With a flick of his dirk, he makes a clean slice through the jugular, and he strides to me before the corpse even hits the ground.

"Are you hurt?" he asks, his eyes scanning over me.

"No." I'm surprised that it's the truth. My shoulder burns as though a stray spark hit it, but the magic came without the usual rake of pain. It never even touched the ember of Siorai magic that lives inside me.

Breath returns slowly to fill my lungs.

"We should leave," I say. "The beacon will bring someone."

The air grows chill, and the darkness thickens. The hair rises on my arms as if it wants to crawl away.

"It's too late to escape already," a low voice growls.

A Grey appears behind Chyr, holding a Ravenhound that strains against its leash. The dark blade of a sword hisses as the Grey thrusts it towards Chyr's back.

CHAPTER 27

POWER AND PRICE

FLORA

Chyr spins from beneath the Grey's blade, flame bursting from the tips of his fingers like an extension of himself. The movement is so fast it's glorious—a dance of limbs and light. The Grey screams as fire hits her, blinding her. Chyr drives in for a deathblow to the heart. She darts aside.

The Grey's ashen skin is charred black and angry red around her uncanny eyes. She drops the Ravenhound's leash and flings fire back at Chyr. He bends and whirls. His blade slashes, severing her hand at the wrist.

Eyes burning, flames dripping from its teeth, the Ravenhound races towards me. No time to draw my dagger.

I throw my hands up to shove the Ravenhound away, reaching for air the way that The Grey's ashen skin is charred black and angry red around her uncanny eyes. She drops the Ravenhound's leash and flings fire back at Chyr. He bends and whirls. His blade slashes, severing her hand at the wrist.

Eyes burning, flames dripping from its teeth, the Raven-hound races towards me. No time to draw my dagger.

I throw my hands up to shove the Ravenhound away, reaching for air the way that Chyr does, for the power of air I felt earlier when I reached for rain.

The air doesn't move.

The Ravenhound leaps to attack. With a whispered prayer to the Mother, I throw my hands up. And suddenly there's resistance against my palms. The air feels as if it has weight and substance. I gather it and slam it into the Ravenhound's chest. The monster hangs mid-leap, unable to reach me.

Then Chyr's sword flashes, and the Ravenhound falls.

I stand staring, my chest heaving.

Chyr runs towards me. "Did it bite you?" he asks. "Are you hurt?"

I shake my head.

Movement surges from the trees. My heart misfires and my breath snags as I turn. But it isn't another threat, only the two Shadehounds I left to guard the horses.

The Ravenhound hasn't moved. The Grey lies crumpled on the ground, her body a heap of misshapen limbs, her head lying a foot away.

My stomach heaves, and I double over to vomit the remnants of my dinner. I stay there, hands on knees, bile stinging my throat, gasping for breath.

Chyr comes to stand beside me. I don't dare look up.

If he offers me sympathy, I'll break. If he offers me some male word of so-called wisdom, I'll break him.

He gives me another moment before he speaks.

"I have to check the top of the hill and find out how the amulet worked. They may have more patrols and beacons. Can you look through the ashes to see if there's anything left of the amulet?" The lines of his face are drawn, his skin leached of colour. His hand reaches towards me, then he drops it to his side.

I straighten, spit, and wipe my mouth. Push my shoulders back. "Signal fires are meant to be answered by another beacon. I didn't see any others, so maybe no one was sure they'd seen the fire lit."

"We'll talk about how you did that later," Chyr says grimly. "My bigger concern is how the Grey arrived so fast. It's dark— no light, no shadows. They must have some new way to travel."

My hands clench back into fists. "You think more are coming?"

"Maybe." His hair has come loose from its warrior's knot and falls around his face. He rakes a hand through it, then shakes his head. "Find the amulet, then wait in the woods until I come back. Will you do that? Hide in case more Greys arrive."

I don't bother arguing. He should know better than to think I'll ever hide.

I'm shivering and weakened, but the flame inside me feels bright and hot, untouched. I have more magic than I should, considering how much I've used—as if the magic has come from somewhere else.

I've killed two men, and I'll let that unravel me later. But the magic? I'll claim that now. For the first time, the magic feels like it's truly mine, an extension of myself that connects what I am—who I am—to the world outside, to the earth and wind and sun and rain.

Chyr gently lifts my chin to make me look at him. "Stay safe. Do you hear me? You're stronger than either of us suspected, Fierceness, but you're not invincible."

Heat sears my cheeks at the memory of the purring growl in his voice and the look on his face when he said it.

"Spread your legs for me, Fierceness."

Shame threatens to buckle my knees, but I refuse to show

it. Turning away, I search the ground for a stick to stir the ashes of the fire.

Chyr's gone when I look up. The clouds overhead have thinned as if I've drained them, but the sky still offers little light. I scan the steep gully that climbs towards the beacon hill. Nothing moves, and I cross the few steps to the fire pit.

The ashes are hot and dry. Chyr must have smothered the flames, with air magic or something else. Yet another question to set aside for later.

The broken amulet isn't hard to find—two shards of green serpentine, the colour of new birch leaves, veined through with butter yellow. Sacred stone from our Sacred Isles. Even the runes etched into it are similar to the talismans of fertility and protection passed down through my family.

I rub the pieces on the hem of my skirt, but there isn't enough light to read them, even if I knew how.

What I do know is that Vheara is corrupting even our stone against us.

Tucking the shards into my pocket, I turn and find the Shadehounds behind me, Shade and Shadow, the male large and dark, the female smaller and lighter grey.

"So much for guarding the horses like I asked," I say. "But you came to protect us, didn't you? I can't fault you for that."

Shadow edges forward and presses her cold nose into my hand. Shade cocks his head hopefully, as though asking my forgiveness.

I scratch them both behind the ears, wipe my dagger on a

clump of moss, and slide it into its sheath. Then, although I tell myself I'm not following Chyr's orders, I walk back into the trees and sit on a fallen log, my back against a young birch that grows beside it.

The Shadehounds lie down nearby, and I am wondering whether it's worth trying to convince them to return to the horses when they stiffen, jump to their feet, and growl.

Silently, I move behind the birch trunk and pull my dagger out again.

I wait. For a minute or two, I hear nothing. Then there's a sense of intrusion, a presence. The feeling swells, and I try to isolate it, opening myself to the air and sky and the small creatures and growing things. The woods have fallen into a hush. Then I hear a low murmur of voices that grows steadily louder, until they're close enough that I can make out words.

"I swear I'll kill them when we finally catch up," a male voice says. It's deep with a hint of a growl to it.

"It isn't them. As injured as they were, they couldn't be moving this fast," another male says.

"I feel Chyr nearby, and who else is it going to be? We've been tracking bloody great explosions of magic all over the place for *days*. The Greys wouldn't be fighting each other like that."

"That doesn't change the fact that it doesn't all feel like the Greys' ugly magic—or ours."

"Then maybe you should have paid under the table to have my sister do your runes after all. The ones the palace smiths gave you must be fucking useless."

"Will you two shut up, for Pit's sake?" a third male snarls. "If you don't stop circling around the same conversation, I'll ram moss down your throats so deep you'll be picking it out of your asses. Now pay attention. We're getting closer."

The Shadehounds growl softly as three Evers emerge from

the woods above us. The first is the tallest. He's dark-skinned and russet-haired, his stride sure and soundless. The two others follow immediately behind him, one with dark hair and the other with bronze-gold hair that shines in the dim moonlight that's beginning to ghost through the thinning clouds. All three wear boots, breeches, and coats like those Chyr and the dead Evers wore when I found them in the Sacred Wood.

They drop to a crouch as they spot the camp along the gully. The blond vanishes so fast he must have cast an illusion to hide himself, but the others stare at the camp a long while, then there's a whispered conversation I can't make out.

The tall one moves ahead, bent low but walking fast, his hand resting on the hilt of his sword. Runes gleam silver down the back of his neck, revealed when the wind stirs his russet hair. The dark-haired one follows. He's built less powerfully than the blond, but he moves with a feral, elegant grace as he creeps in the direction of the camp.

Intent on watching the Evers, I don't notice the fox at first. It's a large female, nearly the height of the herding dogs. She trails the Evers out of the trees, but pauses when she spots the Shadehounds. Then she sees me and gives a high-pitched yelp before ducking back among the birches.

I probably shouldn't, but I'm curious, so I follow the Evers, keeping low and moving between rocks and clumps of brush for cover.

They reach the camp and find the bodies. Giving up on being stealthy, the blond makes himself visible again. The tall one crouches to examine the Grey and the Ravenhound, while the others check the sentry and the soldier who threw the amulet. Then they separate to check the three shelters where Chyr and I killed the sleeping soldiers.

They emerge, and the clouds part to reveal the moon. Light glints on the blond's shining hair and a row of runes etched from one side of his jaw to the centre of his chin and down the column of his throat, marks that remind me of the glowing runes in the oathbands around Chyr's arm.

The dark-haired one hurries to join them. He pulls out a knife from somewhere, and flips it idly across the back of his hands and into his palms like a nervous tic as the three engage in a heated conversation. Runes glimmer on the knuckles of his hands, a couple of them glowing gold as the knife skips across them.

I'm more surprised by my reaction to the Evers than I am by the knowledge that they are Riders. Or rather, my lack of reaction.

In their own way, each of them has the same fearsome beauty as Chyr. There are differences: a long, lean face compared to a broader one, a sharper chin, hooded eyes versus ones set deeper, darker skin or hair versus lighter. But I've spent time with Chyr now. I've discovered the danger in that beauty, learned the way Evers can lure you in.

None of these three has the pull I felt almost from the first with Chyr, but I sense the power they all wear as easily as a cloak. Seeing them makes me think of Chyr's grace, his speed and strength as he killed the Grey, the fire streaming from him as if he was part of it and it was part of him. His pain and weakness hid most of that in the beginning and made him seem less dangerous.

I turn to go back to the cover of the trees. The fox is still there, watching me. She yips another warning.

All three Evers are staring straight at me when I dart a glance back towards the camp. They sprint towards me, the tall one only fifteen feet away.

It's too late for me to escape.

Heart thudding, I palm my dagger and stand up from behind the clump of furze. The tall one stops, watching me as though I'm a deer he's afraid to spook.

The dark-haired one has no such worry. "Well, now. What have we here?" he drawls, approaching me with a hint of swagger to his step and the knife now held lightly in his hand. "Who are you, sweetness? And where did you come from?"

"Leave it to Chyr to find the only mortal as beautiful as a Siorai," the blond one says, coming up beside him. "You suppose Chyr brought her with him?"

"She has his smell on her," the dark-haired one answers, with a dry drawl.

"Shame. I wouldn't have minded," the blond one says.

"There's no one you *would* mind, Daire," the dark-haired one says.

"Not you, Lorcan. I do have standards."

"Shut it, the both of you," the tall one snaps. He shifts brown eyes from me to the two growling Shadehounds who have come up behind me to stand like andirons on either side.

There's intelligence in the way he studies me that reminds me of a wildcat on the hunt. And like a cat, his colouring—from his bronze skin to the rust-red hair tied back with a leather cord—is taken from the shades of earth.

Where he's restrained, the other two seem more reckless. That along with their power and arrogance make them doubly dangerous.

Seeing them, what General Mora wrote in his letter to the rebel king—to *Chyr*—suddenly makes more sense. My teeth clench at the thought of my brothers, the rest of our warriors, having to fight beside Evers so self-important that they feel comfortable talking about us *mere mortals* as though we aren't standing right in front of them.

Something of my thoughts must be written across my face. The tall one holds his hand out towards me in a calming gesture. "Easy, love. We aren't going to hurt you."

His voice is pitched low and soothing—with the same inflection I would use to settle a wounded animal.

It has the opposite effect. I turn and run back towards the horses as if I'm the half-feral creature they believe me to be. I'm not even sure why I'm running. Only that I must. That the earth and air and magic around me *need* me, dare me, to run.

The pain in my shoulder flares like it did when I put out the signal fire. My blood thrums in my veins, drums calling me to war.

Footsteps sound—behind me, I think—as someone gives chase. That only makes my legs fly faster.

CHAPTER 28
WILL YOU RUN AGAIN?

FLORA

The Shadehounds flank me as I run, Shadow staying close, her breath like cool mist against my calf. Shade darts ahead a short distance, then pauses to look around before catching up again.

Fury is a prod in my back, driving me deeper into the trees. The Riders are making no effort to be silent as they chase me. I hear them arguing.

"Hold up, you idiots! Don't go after her yet." That's the tall one.

"Nothing like a good hunt." The dark-haired one again, that dry drawl. "I know you feel it, Ronan."

"Wait for Chyr," Ronan—the tall one—says. "We can't do anything without the Master."

My stomach coils into a knot. Their voices fade as I run. My eyes blur, and I stumble on a branch in the dim moonlight spearing through the trees. I catch myself, a hand scraping against rough bark. One of the Shadehounds whines and nudges me to keep going. My palm is slick with blood, but some part of me is numb, and the pain is distant.

Somewhere, a horse whinnies. I don't think it's coming from where Eira and Bramble are tied, but I can't be sure.

Lungs burning, I sprint faster. And the longer I run, the more I understand the instinct that warned me to escape, the reasoning my body grasped before my mind could even think it through.

As long as the Riders hunt me, I have to run. It's more than their arrogance and condescension I'm escaping. If they decide I know too much about Chyr, they might kill me to protect him. I can't risk that. Too many people depend on me. With Mairi, her father, and her children, I've added even more.

My breath comes in gasps by the time I reach the horses. Then there's another choice. Another goodbye.

No horse can carry two Evers for any distance, and the moon is already descending. If I take both horses, Chyr would never reach safety by dawn, much less Muilean by Beltane Eve. Then there'd be no army coming from Tirnaeve. Chyr and his Riders may have little regard for us, but Vheara has none at all.

I'll leave Chyr a horse because I have no choice, but that's another heartbreak. It will have to be Bramble. Eira's more likely to hurt herself or throw a rider she doesn't know. But Bramble was one of the first foals I helped deliver. I dried her off myself the night she was born. How can I leave her behind?

My hand shakes as I reach for her. She snuffs at me, and I press my forehead to hers. "Be good for the Ever, and come back to me somehow," I whisper. "You'll always be my best girl."

The tears I've been holding back spill down my cheeks, my breath as ragged as my thoughts. All I can hope is that Chyr will find a way to send her back to me. I have to trust him at least that much.

I mount Eira and turn her back towards Glen Fhionain with the Shadehounds trotting behind me.

Spiderweb clouds still chase over the moon, the light dimming at inconvenient moments. Without Chyr's magical scoutlight to guide me, I'm forced to slow down. We've barely topped the second furze-covered hillock before hoofbeats pound closer after us.

I nudge Eira into a copse of trees to let the Riders pass. A scoutlight flares, and four horses crest the rise behind me. Chyr's with them—I can sense him—and the light gives him speed I can't match.

Then Eira makes hiding pointless. She whinnies as she picks up Bramble's scent, and Bramble answers. Chyr changes direction, riding towards me. The other Riders follow.

I reach for power in the air, hesitant at first. But I understand the feel of that magic now, and the wind gusts as I push it through the trees to cover the sound of my escape. Angling uphill, I cut towards the pass above Glen Fhionain. The wind howls behind me. Trunks groan, and branches snap.

We plunge into a narrow glen and through a stream, the Shadehounds splashing across behind us. Eira stumbles coming out on the other side.

A stone dislodges, knocking into another with a staccato snap that echoes off the braes. I keep the wind blowing, channelling it around me instead of through me. That takes less effort, and the Veilstone barely heats against my skin.

Reining Eira to a stop, I let the wind drop and listen for the Riders, feel for them. One of the Shadehounds gives a soft growl. I sense the horses before I hear them. They're close. Closer.

I whip the wind back through the birch-covered hills and kick Eira into a hard canter, darting back among the trees.

"There, up the slope. Catch her!" someone shouts. It sounds like Chyr. My heart squeezes in recognition, but that only makes me more determined.

Hoofbeats sound closer. A vice of panic grips my chest.

Siorai magic writhes within me, eager to be released. But I reach for the power in the air and the water, Cailleach power. Grasping the clouds ahead, I gather them and drive them behind me to form a cloaking mist. With the clouds thinning ahead, the moon reaches through the trees and lights the way in front of me.

Eira and I race downhill, back to the drovers' road around the loch. She has speed on the flat. I lean forward, my weight in the stirrups. Her mane lashes my wrists. She stretches her neck, giving me everything she has. Unable to keep up, the Shadehounds drop back into the grey mist I've created.

Another goodbye.

The low clouds muffle the sound behind me. I open myself up, let my senses expand around me, carried away on currents of air. Magic pulses in my veins, beating to a heartbeat that isn't mine. I feel things beyond sight—I steer Eira around obstacles that are barely visible. I sense the rise and fall of the hills ahead, and I know we're approaching the deep burn before I hear the water.

Eira launches off the bank and lands partway across, icy water soaking up my skirt as we splash to the other side. I pull more clouds down behind us.

The drum of hooves comes from multiple places now. I let my senses stretch again, searching for that sense of presence, of intrusion. The Riders have split in four directions now: one farther up the slope and three staggered behind me.

Eira gathers herself to jump a fallen log, and my focus snaps back into place. We clear the log and turn back towards the loch. The Riders follow. I know it's Chyr, and goosebumps erupt across my skin.

But I've lost my focus, and with it, I've lost the clouds. They're drifting higher into the sky. I can see the scoutlights now: Chyr on the road, moving fast; two Riders on the hill behind me, and the third descending in front of me to cut me off.

They've fanned out like hunters flushing game to kill.

Eira's hooves gouge into the wet spring growth. Heather and brush rasp against her legs, the fragrance sharp and bittersweet. She stumbles and falls to her knees, and I dismount briefly to check that she's all right. Then I push back into the saddle. Her flanks heave with every breath. But it's not the running alone that exhausts her. She feels my fear.

The more the Riders chase me, the more I'm sure they'll never let me go. Why else would they keep coming? And where fury fuelled my magic, fear chokes it and makes it weak. The realisation slams my heart against my ribs.

At my core, I'm nothing but fear. I can pretend all I want that I'm good enough, or strong enough, or brave enough. The magic feels my doubt.

I steady my breathing and walk Eira forward. The Riders are drawing closer. Their hoofbeats create vibrations, and the four males are bright spots of energy, a sense of otherness, as if the land is showing me they don't belong.

The bog ahead gleams darkly in the moonlight, a wide, visible trap that smells of stagnant water. But it's far shorter across than skirting around it. Cutting through might give me a chance—as long as my magic doesn't run out.

Throat raw and dry, I send Eira into the bog. Her head shakes, and she bucks, trying to throw me off. I pour a stream of calming magic into her, enough that I can feel the Veilstone heating against my skin. She quiets and runs on, her ears still pinned flat against her head.

An eerie glow ripples across the water ahead. There's less solid ground here, and the variations of green are harder to pick out at night. I rely more and more on magic, reaching down into the bog to sense what's there and drawing power from deep within the earth.

The earth magic is gritty and raw, but comfortingly familiar. Its pulse throbs in my veins, the heartbeat of Alba Scoria. I use it to compress peat and stack it in layers on top of the highest ground, building a trail under Eira's feet.

She squelches forward. The bog is greedy, sucking at her legs. Her nostrils flare, and she shakes her head. I talk quietly, calm energy following my voice as I stroke her neck.

But then I can't find enough peat nearby to continue building the path.

Black water swirls on either side of us. Eira's head jolts up, disoriented. She veers off the trail, and I catch her just in time. Swimming's too big a risk—a pocket of mire could easily suck us down.

I slide off and walk to Eira's head, then nudge her backwards until I find a route that gives me more peat to build on. Finally, we're moving forward again.

"Chyr, stop!" A cry rings out, and I whip around.

The Riders have reached the edge of the bog, and three of the horses are skidding to a halt.

Chyr isn't stopping. His height and width are stark against the darker background of the slope. Magic swirls around him, and his hair glows in the moonlight. The image burns itself into my mind. This is how I'll remember him, dream of him.

Pain and regret and fear taste like blood on my tongue, emotions I can't afford to feel.

Step by step, I build my path and keep Eira moving across the bog. Calming her must be using my Siorai magic, and that takes a toll. The flame inside me is guttering, dwindling to an ember. I swallow a rush of fear.

"Flora!" Chyr's shout echoes over the water. "Wait. Stop, for the love of—"

A horse's scream cuts across the words, a high-pitched squeal of terror. I turn and slip in the muck. My arms flail in an effort to regain my balance.

Chyr has followed me into the bog—no regard for his own safety. Or Bramble's. My heart twists and leaps into my throat as I see her hind legs sinking. Water and clumps of peat churn around her. Her forelegs flail for solid ground that isn't there.

She's panicking, her eyes rimmed white in fear.

Chyr throws himself from the saddle and catches the noseband of her bridle. He sinks to his hips in muck.

My heart plummets. I channel the magic around me and reach deep into the earth to lift the ground beneath them. The bog boils, and moonlight smears the moving water.

Raising the ground is harder across the distance. Yet the thought of losing them, of failing…I can't give up.

"Steady, Bramble." Chyr's voice strains. "Steady—"

She twists, foam-flecked muscles rippling. The move knocks Chyr aside. He falls, and water closes above his head.

Someone screams—no, *I* am screaming.

I search inside myself for calm and push an enormous wave of it at Eira. Even then I'm not sure I can trust her not to move.

"Stay here, sweet girl. Don't budge a hoof. I swear I'll come back to get you."

I run back along the trail I've built to save Chyr. But his head breaks the surface. He gasps, coughs, sucks in air, and swims a few strokes towards Bramble.

He glances back at me, wild-eyed defiance warring in his expression with something that looks like shame. "Help the mare," he says. "I'm safe."

He won't be safe if he tries to pull himself up on anything that isn't solid. But Bramble screams as water reaches her hindquarters. Her legs are mired too deep to move.

I send the last of my magic out under her, searching for anything solid to hold her weight. The bog is too deep beneath her.

Wild magic swirls around me, an enormous living force that's begging for me to use it. Only I don't know how. I don't know what to do.

Bramble screams again, the water nearly to the top of her hindquarters. Her front legs are almost floating while the bog drags her hind end under.

Panic washes through me, clogging my throat and wrapping around my heart like a cold, hard fist.

I ignore what my mind tells me—that the earth is too far under Bramble, that I can't help her. I only know I must. Letting the wild force around me flow, I drag the ground up inch by inch.

Water churns and separates around Bramble's hindquarters, and they finally break the surface.

She's still flailing. I croon to her as I make a trail for myself back to the bit of solid ground where Chyr had stood beside her.

"Hush, lovely girl. Stay quiet, love. I'm here."

I grasp her bridle and lay my other hand on her neck in reassurance. I've no calm inside me to give her, and the ember of Siorai magic is cooling. I reach for the Veilstone and pull. The ring warms in my bodice, but not nearly enough. I give Bramble everything that I have left.

Chyr is still in the water, but he isn't sinking.

I stroke Bramble's nose and scratch at the spot she likes beneath her mane. At the same time, I keep building up the ground beneath her.

Water and flecks of peat sluice off her flanks. Her struggles weaken. I count her breaths against my own until she's steady, until I can see her hocks rising, then her knees and ankles sluicing water.

When she's free, I nudge her backwards. Her muscles bunch. Pushing back against the muck is easier than trying to pull herself free. I get her back to the solid footing of the path I made earlier.

I take a closer look at Chyr. I want to be angry when I see him.

Mainly, I feel relief.

All of this, Chyr coming after me, putting Bramble in danger—all of that is down to me not having had the courage to face my shame. To face him. To trust him.

But he came after me.

"Stand, Bramble." I leave her with a last pat on the shoulder.

Testing every step, I retrace my path to where Chyr has pulled himself up to his elbows.

The ground rolls from under him when he tries to climb up. He clasps the hand I offer him, his palm wet and slippery. He puts one foot on the path as I pull, but I'm doing little more than steadying him.

He pauses with his hands on his knees, his shoulders shaking. He's soaked and shivering. His breath comes in ragged gusts, his entire body trembling with effort. I can't help remembering when his wound was bleeding, and I was afraid that he would die.

That's not true any more. The force of him, the magic that rolls through him and crackles along his skin... A shudder rocks me as he straightens. His eyes burn gold, boring into mine.

"Why did you run from me?" he asks.

Is it hurt or anger that fuels the question? I can't tell. Maybe both. I don't know the answer. There are so many reasons, and I want to admit to none of them. Yet my cowardice doesn't excuse me from telling him the truth.

"I woke up in the cavern, wondering how I could marry anyone who wouldn't give me as much of himself as you had. Someone who wouldn't see me as an equal. Despite being an Ever and a Rider, you never made me feel that I was *less*—until I discovered everything between us had been a lie. Then I overheard the Riders talking, and they made no effort to hide their contempt for humans. For me."

I hate the hurt that bleeds into my voice.

Chyr's breath comes hard, and his voice is a rasp. "I'm not them, Flora. You've never been a coward, so I don't believe you ran because Daire and Lorcan indulged in their usual self-absorption. Why didn't you wait for me?"

"Because what if you *are* like them? What if even that is a lie between us?"

"Don't you know me better than that?" Gently, he taps my heart with two fingers. "In here, you know how I feel about you."

"I know I feel more than it's safe to feel. You're the rebel king. You hid that from me because your safety depends on no one knowing. What if the other Riders want to kill me for knowing?"

"I will never let that happen." There's no inflection in the words, but the way he says it leaves no doubt.

He traces two fingers up my throat to my chin, then cups

my cheek. I want to sink into his warmth. My eyes want to close, but I pull back.

"Are you going to run again?" he asks. "Because if you are, I'm going to need a minute before I can follow you."

"You don't need me. Your Riders can get you to Muilean. And here." I reach into my bodice and pull the Veilstone ring from between my breasts. "You'll need this. Only promise me that when you bring your army back, you'll treat us better than your father did. Don't exploit us the way Tirnaeve always has. We won't stand for it this time, so don't expect to find us weak."

"You're the one who underestimates yourself. You mistake fear for weakness when it's no more than a boundary to test your courage. The compassion you've shown me, your honour, intelligence, and refusal to give up no matter the odds, those are all traits Siorai once admired. In you, I see a reflection of who my people used to be. You and this war have shown me how far we've departed from truth and justice. We twist both until they're a hairbreadth from breaking."

I search Chyr's face for evasion or deceit, for distortion. His expression is naked, the tendons standing out from his throat, and pain etched starkly in the lines around his eyes. The silver scar stands out more clearly at the corner of his mouth.

He threads his hands through mine. "You and I—that was truth. A moment out of time I'd lay down my sword to live in with you forever. Whatever happens now, I need you to remember that. You matter. You're the reason my heart still beats."

I'm choking on my grief, but I shake my head. "Be careful, Chyr, for all our sakes. And when you get to Muilean, find a way to send Bramble home to me. Don't let Vheara's soldiers or the Cymbeul militia take her."

I turn to leave, but he doesn't release my hands. "Are you running away?"

273

"I'm walking," I whisper, stepping back.

With one sharp tug, he catches me and wraps his arms around me, capturing my mouth in a kiss that starts gently, sweetly. In spite of what I tell myself, I want to kiss him back.

One last kiss.

I give in, and he groans. His hands rake into my braided hair. The kiss deepens, and I'm falling, drowning. The world spins. Heat floods my limbs, boils through my veins, leaves me tingling with every nerve ending alive at once.

Chyr pulls back, and his hands drop to my shoulders. But the heat doesn't stop.

My whole body catches fire.

The sensation pours through me, agony worse than running out of magic, and the skin across my forehead sizzles as if it's been branded.

I slap at it, trying to stop it. But I can't feel anything there.

A green haze flashes across my vision, and all that pain and heat concentrates into narrow points. The reek of the bog rushes at me, far too strong.

My heart lurches into a sprint as if it can outrun whatever's happening.

"I'm sorry, sweetheart." Chyr stares, his skin bleached white, a muscle clenched in his jaw. He catches my wrist. "I am so, so sorry."

"What have you done?" My voice trembles.

His eyes hold such raw sorrow and rage that it makes me stagger. He drops his arm to my waist and holds me up.

"I have failed you in so many ways." His voice is grim and hoarse. "I hoped I was wrong—or at least that we could wait until we reached Muilean and Beltane. But I should have found the strength to warn you. And to tell you what I feel for you while there was still a chance that you'd believe me. I understand how much it means to choose for yourself. That's what I regret more than anything. I'm sorry that this will take so many choices from you."

His finger shakes as he brushes the tip across my forehead precisely where it hurts. The burn throbs with the thunder of my heart.

A shudder rolls through me. I try to take a breath, but the air is too thin, and it refuses to fill my lungs.

I want to demand that he tell me what he sees.

But I'm afraid I already know.

I'm afraid I should have guessed days ago. That deep down, I already suspected.

I can almost hear my grandmother's voice, hushed against the crackle of the flames in the hearth behind her as she told the story she'd already told us so often that my brothers and I, and every child at Dunhaelic, could repeat the words by heart.

No one ever knew who among the queen's blood might be chosen. The land took the Domhnall woman it needed when the time was right, and it marked the new Maiden with a crescent moon on her right shoulder in glowing silver—the Great Mother's own symbol—so that the Cailleachan would be called to begin the tests. Three tests and three crowns had to be won before the Maiden could become the Cailleach Queen.

The bog holds its breath, and I stand a moment, listening to the pulse of power in the still night air and hearing it echoed by the answering thunder of my heart.

That shouldn't be possible.

None of this is possible. Every fibre of my being wants to scream out my denial.

CHAPTER 29
VINE AND FLAME

CHYR

Flora looks broken—I have broken her. I've pushed her from one shock to another, one betrayal to another, and my oaths won't let me stop.

I don't know how she can take much more. Even her magic must be near-depleted, and I recognise the despair trapped behind her eyes.

The green circlet of thorny vines and leaves etched on her brow is a gift from the land, glowing like the runes of my oathbands. But like those, the Crown of Vines is a lifelong sentence.

Her lower lip is trembling. Her hand flies to the mark, feeling for it.

"It can't be the Crown," she whispers. "That isn't mine. There's no queen, and I'm not the Maiden. I've never been the Maiden."

Silence hangs thick over the bog, as if the gods are waiting.

There's a splash of mud on Flora's cheek and a small twig

tangled in her hair—not to mention a crown etched in green light across her brow. She's never been more beautiful or fierce. Yet she's a cornered cat spitting at a pack of wolves.

I pick the debris from her hair and brush the mud away with my thumb. She draws a thin, unsteady breath as I touch her, and I wait for her to exhale, to push me away.

When she doesn't, I can't resist.

"Come here," I growl, opening my arms, tucking the top of her head beneath my chin when she takes a step, drawing a deep breath to take in the scent of her that underlies the smell of the bog—Flora's own salt and heat and fire and magic. I wish…I wish so many things.

She trembles against me, still holding back. She makes me want to have been born to another life so that I could be better for her. I'd give anything to give her different choices. But eventually, I have to let go.

I hold her at arm's length and look down into those grey eyes that are no longer calm. I'm not sure whether it's the moonlight shining into them or something wrought by magic, but they've turned from grey to a molten silvery-gold—the colour of the moon.

"Will you let me see the mark?" I ask because she won't believe it until she's forced to acknowledge it.

I ease the cowl of the heavy plaid back from her shoulders and loosen the laces of her bodice.

Her eyes are puzzled, not furious, and she makes no move to push my fingers aside. That alone unmans me, but I don't let my fingers linger. I hold the bodice closed for her as I slip the sleeves down her arms, making sure the dress doesn't fall.

She bites her lip while I turn her around. I'm not surprised to find a small crescent moon etched in glowing silver on the back of her right shoulder. Like the crown, the mark is smooth as I drag the pad of my finger across it, but she draws a sharp breath at the touch.

"Does it hurt?" I ask.

"It can't be there." She flinches away from the contact. "I don't want it. I refuse."

"But you knew it was there at some point? When?"

She blinks as tears spill over. "At the camp, when I put out the beacon fire. My shoulder burned, but I didn't think it meant anything. This isn't Muilean, and there are four more nights until Beltane. It can't be the Hunt."

"For your sake, I wish that was true." I pull the sleeves back up and cup her shoulders with my palms, holding them in place while she reties the bodice laces. "Our oaths felt it when you ran. We had to chase you. You're the Maiden, and we are the Anvar'thaine. You ran, and I caught you—"

"You were drowning. I *saved* you."

"I caught you because I knew you'd save me. That's who you are. You'll sacrifice yourself for others every time—that's why the land chose you."

I spin her back around, and her eyes are enormous in the moonlight. Drowning in them, I cradle her face in my palms and give her one last kiss, a barely-there kiss. I've no doubt it will be the last, because she'll fight us tooth and claw through what comes next.

The Crown of Vines is only the first of the three she must win to become the Cailleach Queen. The second is the Crown of Flame, and for that she'll need the Father's blessing. Then there's the third crown.

It must all happen by Beltane morning.

Then there's the doorway—and with luck, an army waiting.

I rest my forehead against hers, my lips still tingling from her kiss. Her heart beats like a caged bird, frantic to escape.

"Forgive me," I whisper again, my heart imprisoned along with hers.

The silence echoes when she doesn't answer.

The Sword of the Anvar'thaine scrapes free of its scabbard. Moonlight catches on the yellow crystal, and Flora goes rigid. I hold her in place and press celestial steel against her throat.

"Don't," she begs, eyes brimming. "Please, Chyr. I don't want it." Her pulse hammers visibly beneath the blade.

My lips still taste of Flora's kiss while the words spill from me in a voice that isn't mine. The whole ritual is an oath etched into my arm.

"Father of Light, the Master of the Anvar'thaine commends this soul to your eternal judgement, her fate to your wisdom. Bless her with flame—or condemn her to the sword."

Flora's eyes bore into me, sharp enough to cut through skin and bone. I can't reassure her. I can only watch my sword and believe, to my core, that the crystal pommel will catch fire. Flora is the best of us. Still, the gods are fickle, so I hope. I pray.

Father help me, I don't know how to kill this woman. Yet if it has to be done, I would rather the last face she sees, the one she blames, is mine. The other Riders are oathbound to do it if I refuse, but they don't know her.

They don't know that light freckles show on her nose when she's frightened, or that she speaks to horses as though she knows they understand every word. That she is braver than any Rider I've fought beside, even if she herself can't see that. The Riders don't know *her*, and I will not let her die without the respect she's owed.

No moment is more vulnerable, more intimate, than the cusp of death. If I can't save Flora, I can at least ensure that the man who kills her will understand what the world is losing with her death.

CHAPTER 30
STOLEN CHOICES

FLORA

F lames erupt inside the yellow crystal that forms the pommel of Chyr's sword, and the entire stone glows orange-red, the colour of a midday sun. At the same time, pain scalds across my forehead. The same place as before.

My head is on fire. The heat spreads, prickling down my neck, along my arms, through my chest. The moonlit sky closes in around Chyr's face, everything fading grey, then black—into nothing.

A warm exhale of breath drifts across my cheek. I'm cradled in strong arms, and I feel safe, although something lurks at the edge of my consciousness like a monster in the dark. I don't know what it is, but I don't want to know. My eyes stay closed.

"Flora?"

Chyr's face swims back into focus, those honey-gold eyes intent beneath furrowed brows. Beyond him, Eira and Bramble are waiting, and I need to get them back to solid ground. My pulse stutters as the memories filter back.

"Was I judged?" I touch my forehead, half-expecting my fingers to burn. There should be a ridge, a scar to mark it. There's no change except that I'm warm instead of cold, and the ember inside me is an inferno. I swallow hard, forcing down a scream.

Chyr adjusts his arm beneath my shoulders, and I realise I'm draped across his thigh as he rests one knee on the peat. Great Goddess, how long has it been? I've no strength left to get us back to the edge of the bog if the path I made earlier has drifted away. Not magical strength—it's physical this time. I struggle to get up, but Chyr holds me tighter.

"Let's make sure you're all right before you rush to stand," he says. "And yes. The crown is still three vines woven together, studded with little leaves, but it's changed from a green glow to gold with flames that flicker across your brow."

The sky spins, stars blurring. My mouth is filled with ash and fury.

"The ritual isn't finished, though, is it?" Even as I say the words, I am certain it will never finish.

It can't.

Vheara has no intention of giving up the throne of Alba Scoria, and if Chyr hasn't been able to defeat her, then I stand no chance. Even if I did, would Chyr's oaths force him to take it from me?

Can he let me become the Cailleach Queen?

Whatever jest the gods are playing will tear us both to pieces. I'm not naïve enough to believe it has anything to do with deserving to wear a crown. I'm no more than a pawn in a game between the gods and Tirnaeve.

Well, nothing says I have to play along.

"Cóirneach." I speak the name in a broken whisper, but Chyr's head snaps up, his eyes flying to mine. The reaction makes my heart beat faster, and the word hangs in the air as heavy as bog-mist.

"What are you doing, Flora?"

"If I say your true name three times, you can't deny me what I want. True or false?"

"Mostly true—"

"Cóirneach, Cóirneach, Cóirneach." My voice is a rasp, my body aching with the plea. "Take it back, Chyr. Reverse the crowns and the Hunt. I'll get you to Muilean and you can win the war."

"I can't," Chyr says, and the pained tightness in his face pierces straight through me. "You may hate me for this even more than for all the other ways I've failed you, but even my true name can't undo the will of the gods and the oaths that bind me."

I twist away, trying to wrench free of his grasp. "Let me go."

"I have to take you to Muilean, Fierceness."

"You don't."

"Neither of us has a choice."

"Have we ever had one?"

His grip on my arms is gentle. That makes it no less impossible to escape. And the other three Riders are still mounted on their horses, waiting at the edge of the bog.

A bit farther on, staying well clear of the Riders, Shadow and Shade are pacing back and forth along the water's edge.

Even they must have known.

I shove down the swell of panic that seals my throat, my

heart running away as I try to think. But I can't escape. Not now. I've no magic, no strength, no plan.

That doesn't mean I'm giving up. There *will* be a time for me to get away. All I have to do is wait for an opportunity.

When I speak, I manage to sound quite calm. "Dawn will be here soon. We need to get the horses out of the bog safely, and we'll have to find shelter before daybreak. Otherwise, no one will reach Muilean."

None of that's a lie.

"Do you promise me that you won't run?" Chyr asks, his eyes so intent that I feel them like a physical touch.

"I swear I'll do exactly what I said," I answer. Which isn't what he asked, but let him puzzle out what it means.

He releases me, and I retrace my steps to Bramble. Chyr must have given me some of his magic while he held me, because I don't feel nearly as empty as I did before. While it feels like the Hunt and the crowning must have taken years, it can't have been more than an hour. The bog and the position of the moon, the horses, and even the Riders all look much the same.

Most of the solid footing that my magic built through the bog is still passable, and I use as little magic as I can to help us all return to the drovers' track. Not because I feel depleted, but my magic feels strange. Unfamiliar.

The three other Riders say nothing when I reach them. But they stare at the Crown of Flame with expressions somewhere between disbelief and awe until I raise the plaid from around my shoulders and drape it low over my forehead to hide the mark.

The pair of swaggering bastards—the blond with the silver runes along his jaw and throat, and the dark-haired one with the lazy drawl and the vicious humour—don't look at me at all after that. The tall one with the russet hair seems kinder, and his smile looks genuine.

"Some of us are well known to have no manners, so I'll apologise on their behalf—and mine," he says. "We didn't know who you were at first. Although—as Chyr has pointed out—that's no excuse for being offensive. I'm Ronan, and the two idiots are Daire and Lorcan."

He points them out, and Daire, the blond, glares back at me with fury smouldering in his blue, otherworldly eyes. I look away, then steel my spine and stare back at him with my brows arched. His build is stronger than the other two, and his wide jaw tapers in a sharp triangle to a stubborn chin. The fact that he's glowering down at me from his position in the saddle only makes him more intimidating.

Lorcan, the other one, sits his horse with an easy grace. He's pretty—even for an Ever—and his strength is leaner, his features more delicate beneath dark, silky hair. He doesn't glare openly, but something cunning swims behind his hard, emerald eyes that warns of a sharp intelligence I shouldn't underestimate.

I'm in no mood to feign forgiveness or mince my words.

I turn back to Ronan. "I'll accept your apology, but I don't see the point of forgiving someone if they can't be bothered to speak on their own behalf."

Turning away, I stoop to check Bramble's hind legs for any sign of injury or heat. She seems all right, so I give her neck a reassuring pat and walk back to Eira.

Chyr tries to help me mount, but I'll be damned if I'll show more weakness in front of the Riders.

I tuck the front of my skirt deeper into my belt to keep it out of the way, then I push my foot into the stirrup. My knee and thigh shake with effort as I swing myself up, but eventually I drop into the saddle with a bit of dignity intact.

"I hate to suggest it since it sets us back another night, but we should go back to the cavern where Chyr and I slept yesterday. If we try to ride on, we'll be too close to the enemy camp at daybreak, and we'd be hard-pressed to find anywhere big enough to conceal us all."

"If we do that can we still make it to Muilean in three nights?" Chyr asks sharply.

"I can't promise anything. It won't be easy either way, and we don't know what might be waiting for us between here and the Loch of Rebirth. But if we're caught in the open when the sun comes up, we won't get there at all."

The Riders look to Chyr for his reaction. His face is pale, and tension rolls off him in waves as he gives me a silent nod. Then he swings himself onto Bramble's back.

"We should ride through the trees wherever we can. We don't want to lead anyone to us," Ronan says. "I'll cover our tracks wherever we have to use the trail."

"You can do that?" I ask.

"Earth magic. A little loosening of the soil here and there, a bit of dust scattered across the tracks. Simple enough." Ronan winks at me. "I can be more impressive, if you like."

Chyr shakes his head. "Your idea of impressive might be different from Flora's. Her earth magic threw me into the air on her first attempt."

The Riders stare at me, and I set Eira into a trot. We follow the drovers' track along Loch Seil back towards Glen Fhionain. The Shadehounds dart in front of me and seem content to run slightly ahead of the rest of us.

The sky lightens, gradually fading to the grey-blue that precedes the dawn. We push the horses faster to beat the sunrise, but the closer we come to the cavern, the more I dread going back.

The cavern is where I claimed a sliver of freedom. Then I gave myself to a man who took my freedom from me.

CHAPTER 31

OATHS AND BANISHMENT

CHYR

The cavern hasn't changed. Even the scent of intimacy lingers, along with the smell of horse and damp. Only twenty-odd hours ago, Flora lay here in my arms and gasped my name in hunger. If I close my eyes, I can almost feel her mouth on mine, the curve of her spine arching into my hands, the way the magic curled between us.

Now she refuses to look at me, and I can feel her thinking, plotting. I keep her beside me when we all split up to water the horses and gather forage so we can get out of sight before dawn breaks. Until then, there's no time for anyone to talk.

But once the chores are finished, Lorcan's dark voice cuts the silence first. "Explain," he demands, stepping in front of me. "What in the Pit just happened?"

I turn and lift the saddle from Bramble's back and carry it to where Flora is already setting Eira's saddle down. Lorcan huffs and follows me. As he nears Flora, the Shadehounds shift uneasily where they've flopped down near the cavern entrance, their heads lowered while they weigh whether he's a threat.

Flora straightens, and the Crown of Flame across her brow paints gold and red reflections on the cavern wall. She stares at them, her back stiff and her shoulders tense. I reach for her, but she shifts away.

"Answer the question, Chyr. We deserve an explanation." Lorcan squares his chest up against the saddle that I'm holding, forcing my attention back to him. His dark hair is tangled, and there's no hint of the amusement he likes to hide behind.

Already frayed beyond recognition, my self-control shatters. "You know what happened," I snap at him. "We Hunted the Maiden, and we've invited even more chaos into this war for the sake of the damned oaths that own us. We've taken all of Flora's freedom from her."

Flora's head turns towards me, tears shining in her eyes.

The Pit take me, I didn't mean for her to hear the ache in my voice, the despair. But I'm damned if I know how to hide them. The knowledge that she must hate me shatters me to my soul.

Daire has stripped off his coat and rolled up his sleeves. He's crouched by the ashes of yesterday's fire, coaxing dried moss and kindling to light, the flame turning his gold hair nearly the same shade as Flora's and making the dormant power runes glow silver across his jaw and down his throat.

Soft-footed as a wraith, Ronan stops beside him and drops a load of knotted old gorse roots as thick as his wrists to the ground. Then he turns to me with his arms folded across his chest.

"We'll discuss the Maiden later," he says. "First, tell us how Tuirse and Oran died. Tell us where you left them."

One of the horses releases its bladder, and there's a long cascade of piss streaming against the stone.

It feels appropriate—this is one of many conversations I've been dreading. With the Hunt compelling us to go after Flora, I delayed giving them the details. There's no way around it now.

I set the saddle down with the fork resting against the stone beside my foot. "When you left to draw off the Greys that followed us—"

"When you *ordered* us to leave you," Ronan says.

"We were slowing you down," I respond. "The Greys would have picked us off as soon as they caught up. I gave the only order that gave all six of us a chance to survive."

"Then why are they dead?"

"Are you accusing me of something, Ronan?" I pull myself up to snarl at him. "Speak plain."

"Great Mother, what is wrong with you?" From where she is rubbing Eira down with bog moss, Flora whips towards Ronan. "Aren't you supposed to be the next best thing to brothers? Chyr was a thread away from death."

Ronan barely glances at her, his jaw tight and his teeth gritted. "Siorai don't die of wounds like that. We've all had worse."

"Any given week," Daire says.

"But again, Oran and Tuirse are dead. Chyr isn't." Ronan shifts his attention back to me and rakes a hand through his russet hair. "So how is that?"

"Because of her." I wave in Flora's direction. "We were dying from the moment we were ambushed—the swords that wounded us were coated in a fine dust of celestial iron."

My throat closes at the thought of how much Flora has given me and how I've repaid her. Shaking my head, I try to push away the guilt, lock it away along with the anguish of those long final miles with Tuirse and Oran. It will come back—guilt always does.

"Tuirse could barely sit up in the saddle," I continue, "but he was telling a joke about what Vheara's Greys wore under their uniforms. Oran was leading the dappled mare and walking beside me. I heard Oran laugh, then the next thing, he was dead on the ground. The mare tried to carry them both, but Tuirse insisted on walking. He fell and didn't get back up."

"*Fuck.*" Daire's shock is mirrored on Ronan and Lorcan's faces.

"Dying of a wound after leaving the battlefield? That's never been a possibility," Lorcan says, pulling out his favourite knife and tossing it blade over hilt, the way he does when he's excited or upset. "I guess that almost makes us mortal."

Ronan shoots him a filthy look. "Chyr isn't, apparently."

"Flora healed me. She buried Tuirse and Oran when I couldn't, and she hid me when the Greys came. She's kept me alive ever since."

The three of them turn to stare at her, but she ignores them. Little does she know that's the surest way to get Lorcan and Daire's attention.

"What do you mean, she healed you?" Daire stands up now that the fire is crackling. "You said you were poisoned by celestial iron."

"She cut out most of the infected flesh, used magic to draw out the iron, and knitted the wound back together. Think about *that* the next time you cretins are inclined to be disrespectful."

Flora's pretending not to listen, but even in the dim light I can see the blush blooming in her cheeks.

She finishes grooming Eira and has moved to work on Bramble, and we all watch her silently. Exhausted, furious, scared—she's clearly all of those things. She's also the damned Maiden, and the most fierce and beautiful woman I've ever seen. I know better than to ask her to sit down and let me take care of the horses for her—especially in front of the others. I beat down the impulse, and I swallow the growl that fights its way up my throat at the way the Riders are looking at her.

As if he's heard it anyway, Ronan snatches up his bow and quiver and strides to the cavern entrance. "I'm going out to hunt," he says. "There's another storm coming, and the Maiden will need to eat."

He vanishes into the early light, and I suppose I can't be surprised. Ronan's first instinct when he adopts a wild thing is to feed it.

Thunder cracks outside. Within the cavern, the silence stretches. Lorcan and Daire exchange one of their long, silent looks. Daire shakes his head.

"Chyr, tell me this," Lorcan drawls, ignoring him, "we all know you'd rather burn your own eyes out than sit on Fionn's throne. But you expect us to believe you happened to find a Maiden in the woods when there hasn't been one in more than four centuries?"

I haven't had a good brawl in a long time, and I indulge myself in imagining how good it would feel to sink my fist into Lorcan's smirking face. He spins his favourite knife across his knuckles, blade over hilt. Nervous.

"Believe whatever you like," I say.

Thunder rolls outside, and the fire crackles.

Daire flashes me one of his saucy grins. "You're thinking about hitting him, aren't you? Go ahead. I'll watch."

Flora rests her arms across Bramble's back. "He isn't entirely wrong, though, is he, Chyr? You made it sound as if you played no part in any of this. But when did you first suspect I might be the Maiden?"

At the back of my jaw, the muscle twitches into a knot. "I didn't know, Flora. It made no sense. Too many things argued against it, but that your magic wasn't Siorai."

"Not what I asked."

I let the silence stretch. "Then I'm not sure what to tell you."

"And there it is. You Evers—"

"*Siorai*," Daire snaps, his knuckles whitening on his fists.

"You Evers," Flora repeats, calmly, glaring at him. "You pick and choose which truths to tell, which laws to enforce, which oaths to keep—"

"We have to keep all our oaths," I say. "Unless they conflict."

She turns her eyes back to me. They're still different from the calm grey of before, still the same silvery-gold as moonlight, but now they've hardened to steel.

"You've said that before," she says. "But if you've sworn to enforce the Compact, how is it you left your father sitting on our throne all these years? How is it that your oaths never called for you—the Master of the Anvar'thaine—to banish him for that?"

The oathbands flood me with ice that makes it impossible to breathe. But even if I could tell her the reasons, they'd make no difference.

"No answer, Chyr? Any of you? Nothing to say?" Flora prompts.

Daire's jaw works, a muscle jumping. Then he lunges at her. The Shadehounds growl and run towards her, Shade moving faster even as I run to knock Daire aside.

Daire gets to her first, his arms caging her against the wall. I wrench him back. My fist connects with his face, and when the momentum whips his head aside, I follow with a punch that doubles him over. Shade stays and growls at him.

"Don't ever touch her." My voice is soft.

"Why?" Daire wipes the blood from his lip. "Because you're the only one allowed to do that?"

"Because *she* decides. Always. Do not touch her. Do not threaten her."

The two of us glower at each other, but because it's Daire and it's impossible to contain his chaos, he turns to glare at Flora again. Shadow has pressed her body tight against Flora's legs, fangs bared and hackles raised as if she'll take down anyone who dares to come any closer.

Daire's lip curls as his attention shifts from Flora to the Shadehounds and back again. "Are you really that naïve?" he asks her. "Do you think Chyr *chose* not to punish his father? Fionn was Master of the Anvar'thaine before Chulainn forced Chyr to take that role. Chyr and the rest of us all took our vows at once because Fionn murdered the other nine Riders who served with him. It wasn't an *honour* for Chyr to be chosen."

"Enough." I catch Daire's arm, my fingers digging in.

Daire shakes me off, reaches back to grasp his shirt at the back of his neck, and strips it off. He leans closer, teeth bared, and points to the single row of runes that circles his arm.

"This—*this*—is the oathband of the Anvar'thaine," he says. "But that's not what Chyr's uncle had burned into Chyr's skin. Chulainn made Chyr the Master to punish him. To force him to fail so he'd be banished to the Pit, where he couldn't be a threat. Chulainn made Chyr Master to *control* him.

"Chyr was barely nineteen—little more than a cub and without the experience to understand the oaths he was forced to take."

Lorcan steps between me and Daire and sets a hand on Daire's shoulder. "Chyr's right, Daire. She doesn't need to hear this."

"She has no right to judge him," Daire snaps.

"Actually, she does." I turn to her, and she's still backed against the wall, backed into a tiny corner of the rest of her life with no chance to escape. I want so desperately to find a way to change that. "You don't understand what I've done to her."

"Can you stop being such a bloody martyr?" Daire's voice

is low. "If you didn't want me knowing your secrets, you shouldn't have taken my sister to bed."

I glance back at Flora, and our eyes crash together. Her expression is unreadable, and I'm not certain what I even expect or hope she feels.

"Riadan's a runesmith, remember? And there are no secrets between us," Daire continues, unaware. "She read your arm, Chyr. She told me about the petty, personal oaths your uncle made you take: never challenge him, never be disloyal, never disobey him, never believe or speak ill of him, never question him—especially about your father—never believe ill of him *or* your father. That's not the worst, though, is it? Chulainn bound you never to speak before the Assembly, seek the throne of Tirnaeve, or enter the mortal realms without his explicit permission. And he bound you to accept *his* interpretation of the Compact as the final judgment."

A horse shifts—an iron shoe scraping against the stone.

Daire's challenge is there in the way he watches me, but if he thinks I was unaware that Riadan had read my runes, he's much mistaken. Not only that, but I was *glad*.

I *am* glad.

It's been nearly fourteen months since I took the risk of showing her, and I had begun to believe—to despair—that she hadn't told Daire before we stepped through the doorway. Now, finally, the words I can't speak myself have been said aloud.

Flora stares at me, her skin turned pale. She presses back into the cold stone of the cavern wall, her breath catching. "How could you swear to that?"

"It was that or be punished for Fionn's crimes," Daire says.

I rock back on my heels—that's something not even Daire's sister could know. How did she find out?

Ronan clears his throat and steps into the firelight. He's

soaked to the skin and carries the limp bodies of four rabbits strung on a leather cord slung across his shoulders. Twigs of rowan are tucked into the crook of one arm.

"Since we're having this discussion now," he says, "let's set aside Chyr's oaths to his uncle for a moment." He drops the rabbits and the rowan beside the fire and crosses to where Flora is still backed against the wall, while leaving her plenty of room so she doesn't feel like she's being crowded. "The rest of us aren't compromised by the king's politics, and we are still the Anvar'thaine. Our oaths bind us to uphold the Compact. If any of us—including Chyr—breaks those oaths, the rest have no choice but to banish them to the Gloaming. Do I need to explain that to you?"

The wind outside is rising, blowing in through the entrance. The fire cracks and sparks. It takes all my control not to seize that wind and make it howl, not to whip the fire into an inferno to match my rage.

I was going to give Flora a little time before I broke this to her. But this is another of Ronan's talents: he sets a trap and waits for the wild things to come to him. Now he's the first to grasp what the others haven't fully processed.

Lorcan likes to fancy himself the clever one in this group, but it's Ronan who often sees what others don't.

Still, Flora doesn't know enough to fully understand the situation yet, and she doesn't trust him. If he's hoping for an advantage, he won't get it.

She slides along the wall towards Bramble. "I assume the point you're making," she says, "is that you all have to make very sure I get to Muilean."

"True, and all of us have to offer ourselves to you as companions," Ronan says. "You can't choose Chyr. You do see that, don't you? Not with the oaths that have him tied in knots."

Wind drives rain into the cavern mouth. Fat droplets bounce off the stone.

Flora's eyes find mine again. All the colour has drained from her face, and I can see the exact moment Ronan's words land—not the horror of the crowns and the Compact and being chosen, but the specific, personal cost of that. I see her understand that the one choice she thought she made for herself, the one decision in her life and in this entire war that should have been hers alone, has been snatched away from her along with so much else.

Every tear that spills down her cheeks unmans me.

My chest squeezes, flattened under a mountain of regret.

This is how it feels for my heart to crack under the weight of all these oaths.

If I'm honest, though, I can't blame my oaths, my uncle, or the war. I should have found a way to stop this. I should have sacrificed anything and everything not to break her. I'm the one who's responsible, and now Flora is drowning in the fate to which I've bound her.

CHAPTER 32
REFUSE AND DIE

FLORA

I want to melt into the cavern wall and disappear. That's an idea I haven't considered yet: whether my magic would let me transform myself to interact with the landscape. The concept is distracting enough that I let my overwhelmed mind dart after it like a dog after a hare.

Still, the tears keep falling. I wipe them with my fists. Beside me, the horses chew their feed, their bodies radiating heat while Shade and Shadow guard my front from Daire and the other Riders.

All too soon, I'm back to thinking about Ronan's warning. My nails dig into my palms. I don't want Chyr—or anyone—as a consort, but that doesn't change the way my stomach seizes at knowing I can't choose him. The idea of having to accept any of the others makes me lock my knees to keep them from giving out.

I watch Chyr through the haze of wet-wood smoke, the angry set of his jaw, the unhurried efficiency with which he unpacks plaids and rations, the way the Riders angle their bodies towards him, keeping him in sight. When he speaks to them, they lower their eyes a degree, even when they argue.

They respect him. He's the Master, and they don't doubt he'll do his duty.

I can't doubt it either. Even if that duty means my death.

Bramble swings her muzzle to me, and I unclench my fists to scratch her on the nose. "At least I have you back. That's one good thing—and having Shade and Shadow with me is another. We will be all right."

The mare nudges my shoulder, her big brown eyes half lowered as if she doesn't believe me. Which is fair enough. I don't believe me either.

I've dredged my brain for every scrap of knowledge, every snippet of story I've ever heard about the Maidens and the crowning of the Cailleach Queens. If there's a way to stop this nightmare, I haven't remembered it yet.

The Maiden can refuse the Hunt. She can fail the test, and the land will release her and choose another Maiden. That's all in the ancient stories. But I didn't realise I'd been chosen, that I was being Hunted. I didn't know anything until I already wore the Crown of Vines—and by then, I had no options.

Cold rain blows into the cavern. A gust of wind shears along the walls. That's not why I shiver.

Finding a solution isn't optional. I *will* find one.

I wear two crowns, and unless I choose a Rider and make my sacrifice at the Altar of the Moon, I'll be dead by Beltane morning.

Even that might not save me.

Chyr's father was the last Rider chosen to be the consort— and he killed the queen who chose him. I won't let myself be dragged to Muilean like a lamb to slaughter. If I have to go at all, then somehow I will turn the time to my advantage.

It would help to find an ally among the Riders. Someone who'll defend me when Chyr cannot. Of the three Riders, Ronan seems most likely for that.

As if he feels my eyes on him, he turns and smiles. "I thought we could take a moment to say goodbye to Tuirse and Oran," he says. "Flora, do you want to join us?"

He stoops to pick up the sprigs he dropped beside the fire earlier. They're entering the sweet phase of rowan, when they smell of marzipan.

The mood in the cavern changes. Daire stops trying to look intimidating and drops his arms to accept the two sprigs Ronan holds out to him, then Lorcan takes his. I expect Chyr to step up, but he stares hard at Ronan first.

Ronan holds out the next two twigs to me.

"You didn't know Tuirse or Oran, but you buried them," he says. "That matters."

I open my mouth to protest that I didn't, but when I think it through, Chyr didn't *lie*. Not by Ever standards.

Those who did the burying are my people, loyal to me, employed by me. I approved the burial, and in that sense, I did bury them. I also dragged their bodies up the hill myself, my face inches from theirs. Then I helped Chyr say goodbye. In those ways, they will always be a part of me.

The realisation pushes my feet towards the fire. And maybe this is also a chance to show the Riders that I'm more than a prisoner. Something other than the Maiden.

Wiping my cheeks again, I push myself from the wall and walk to the fire. I keep my head high, as if I've earned the crowns I wear.

Shade and Shadow trot behind me, sticking close to my heels.

"Thank you." I accept the rowan, and I gift Ronan with a smile. The one I rarely use.

He blinks, but he's as wary as the others. I think my tears have scared them more than swords or magic.

Lorcan shifts closer to Daire, and Chyr is coiled so tight that emotion quivers in the air around him.

We circle around the fire, and the Riders turn to Chyr expectantly. Firelight plays over his cheekbones and the sharp angles of his jaw. His eyes swallow the flames.

"Oran was the quiet mountain of the Anvar'thaine," he says, his voice quiet and solemn like the Chyr I had started to believe I knew. "We all leaned on him, and he died the way he lived, gently laughing at a bad joke one of us used to disguise their pain. Without Oran, we wouldn't have become a team."

Chyr throws a sprig of the rowan into the fire, and the rest of us do the same.

"May Oran be long remembered," the Riders say in unison.

The fire crackles, and the sugared-almond scent of burning rowan fades too fast, leaving only bitterness.

Chyr shifts his feet, his eyes heavy-lidded. My feet want to go to him, my fingers want to slide between his and squeeze them in reassurance. I clasp my hands in front of me.

"Tuirse made us laugh without ever making any of us the butt of the joke," Chyr says. "His kindness had no limit. Tuirse was the heart of us, the buffer between strong personalities. I can't count the nights that he sat beside me, reassuring me that however bad things seemed, he always had my back."

"May Tuirse be long remembered," Daire, Lorcan, and Ronan say, as we all cast our offerings into the flames.

Their Ever traditions are not mine, so I say nothing. But Chyr's eyes bore into mine.

"They died as warriors." It's the same tribute I said at their grave, but after hearing Chyr's story, I believe it.

They fought death and Vheara's poison. They fought for each other and for Chyr.

Hot tears slide down my cheeks and clog my throat. I watch the rowan burn, thinking of my mother, my father and brothers, and all the goodbyes I've had to say—the goodbyes too many of us have had to choke out as we laid our loved ones in the ground.

Vheara is far from finished. There will be more.

The only way I can honour the people who are gone is by fighting with everything I have to get back to those who remain.

Back to Dunhaelic.

Ronan clears his throat. "I saw a group of Vheara's soldiers pass on the drover's track along the lake, riding fast. Several Greys were with them. Showed no interest in looking for tracks, but that'll change when they find the bodies at the camp."

"You covered our steps," Lorcan says, "and even if they have a Grey with magic-sense, Flora's the only one who's used any since we left the camp. That would only lead them as far as the bog. We'll be long gone by the time they search this far."

"Unless they can sense her crown," Daire says glumly.

Chyr catches his eye and shakes his head. "We'll be all right here today, and the rest we'll worry about tonight."

I swallow a sick feeling that he's tempting fate with those words. In the aftermath of the Hunt, I'd almost forgotten that the hunters are being hunted.

"We'll have to go by the camp again," I say.

Lorcan scoffs at me. "We'd be idiots to try."

"Then we'll have to be idiots, unless you have magic that lets you fly. There's no safer route for us to take." I smile at him, enjoying the flare of his nostrils and the flush of red rage that spills into his cheeks.

Lorcan is the hardest to read of all the Riders. He's silk and charm and gleaming teeth on the surface, but I suspect the temper he showed with Chyr earlier is only the second of many skins he wears, each more cruel than the last.

"Can you explain it to them slowly, Flora?" Chyr pulls a knife from his belt and picks up the brace of hares Ronan brought back for dinner. "Use small words as if they're children. I'm going to take these outside to clean so we can eat."

He leaves me alone with the others, and that's deliberate, although I'm not sure what he thinks it will accomplish. To be honest, I'm too tired to care.

"The Butcher is staying at Gleannadail House," I explain to them, "and Alasdair Domhnall has been taken to Dun Uilleum in chains. Vheara's troops and Cymbeul militia are demanding quarters in homes across Ehrugael, but we've also seen dozens of watchfires burning, which suggests there are camps between settlements."

Frowning, Ronan pushes his russet hair off his forehead. "Why would the Butcher come here? There are still patrols searching all through the north and the Highlands. And with the losses they took at Culodur, the clans in Ehrugael would be easy enough to break without him."

I try to ignore the fact that those clans are mostly *my* people, and remind myself that the Riders do not know. Logically, they could assume I'm a Domhnall, but then again, I'm human. Evers don't concern themselves with who we are or what we need.

"Is it possible he knows you're here?" I ask. "The queen could have been sent to make sure you don't reach Muilean."

Daire and Lorcan exchange a look that I can't read.

"True," Lorcan says, "and you could be leading us straight into a trap, taking us past that camp. Have you thought of that? If the Butcher knows we're here, he could be deliberately pushing us to take this route so that he can try to pick us off."

I release a sigh. "He could, but whether that camp was part

of a trap or simply the work of a prudent commander doesn't change our situation. There's no track along the western shore of Loch Seil, and the hills come down right to the water there. We'd lose too much time and miss Beltane Eve by at least a couple of days. Beyond the hills, the terrain is even worse: either too open or too hard to pass through quickly. It's unfortunate that we've given ourselves away by murdering the sentries, but we'll have to go around any new patrols."

"It's not murder when they're enemies," Ronan says, tilting his head to study me.

"It felt like it." I refuse to look away.

"Ah, a soft heart to go with that pretty face," Daire says. "How deliciously unsurprising."

"Because I don't enjoy killing people in their sleep?"

"Because you're a shiny new toy."

"A toy *and* a prisoner. Better and better," I say as thunder cracks outside.

Daire's grin is too sharp for humour. Or charm. "Is it really so terrible here with us, little flower? You don't seem the type to sit at home gossiping over your embroidery."

Unintentional or not, it's a gut punch, and tears sting my eyes as his words conjure an image of my mother in her solar. The way she used to be.

Furious, I make a show of letting my eyes travel over Daire, from the silver runes along his jaw and throat and down the wide chest and the defined muscles that disappear into his breeches. Then I lift my attention back to his face and shake my head.

"I would have better options for entertainment at home," I say, "and the scenery is prettier. Also, death-by-crowning isn't exactly a dream come true."

Lorcan bursts into laughter, and Ronan chuckles. Daire waits a beat, then lets his grin widen wolfishly. He bends too close, his breath warm on my ear. "Something you should know about me, love: I can never resist a challenge."

"Learn," I snap, stepping away. "Self-control is part of growing up."

"Oh, I am all grown up." Daire shifts closer again, forcing me to take another step. Then he glances around at the others. "See what happens when you give a woman a crown or two? Suddenly, she gives orders like a queen."

I raise my eyebrows at him. "That's *Maiden* to you, *love*."

Daire's eyes drop instantly to my lips. "But are you?" he whispers. "Still?"

A hot flush crawls up my cheeks, and I step past him, circling around the fire.

In the rare event that I'd ever need a reminder of how much I loathe the Evers, a minute in Daire's company will take care of that.

Lightning flashes and thunder cracks outside again, and at the mouth of the cavern, something moves. A fox slinks in and stops a few feet inside the opening, red fur dripping with rain and golden eyes dull with fatigue. Her tongue hangs from the side of her mouth.

"Rua, you're back!" Grinning, Ronan strides past me to meet the vixen, his arms opening wide for her. She jumps into them and joyfully licks his face.

I'm not even surprised that the fox I saw back at the camp is Ronan's pet. My capacity for astonishment has been exceeded.

All I want now is sleep. As much as I wish I could run back to Dunhaelic while the Riders rest, I am wearing proof that the gods are real. The two crowns are burned into my skin, and I don't know how to hide from that. At least, not yet.

CHAPTER 33
SOVEREIGNTY'S MAID

FLORA

The rain has stopped. After the violence of the storm, the near silence and the stillness of the air feel expectant, like the pause before something worse.

I am curled up alone in the same spot where, a day ago, Chyr and I slept tangled in each other's arms. He is sleeping at the back of the cavern with the other Riders, leaving me with all four of our plaids to make my bed. That shouldn't soften my feelings towards him. But it's another example of his kindness, and I do know he feels things deeply.

Maybe I'm a fool, but despite all the things he deliberately didn't tell me and everything he let me mistakenly believe was true, Chyr's sense of honour is the one thing I cannot doubt. That has nothing to do with his oaths—it's who he is at his core.

In some ways, he's a prisoner as much as I am. It might be impossible for him to choose between his oaths, and while it still feels like betrayal, what he's told me has been threaded with care. He's made me no promises, and I never asked for any.

I can't help reaching up to touch the crown at my brow—but there's no physical bump or ridge for me to find. I've barely slept for thinking of it. My mind churned with trying to find an escape, reliving what's happened and worrying over what's still to come. And even at the back of the cavern, the Riders' presence loomed too large, their breathing and snores too loud. The very fact that they slept while I did not was galling.

By Beltane, I will need to choose one of them. One of them will be chosen. How can they sleep so easy?

My wakefulness brought home the loneliness of where I am, and where these crowns will take me.

Nothing in the ancient stories could ever have prepared me for that.

I roll over and check on him and the others. The sound of steady breathing fills the cavern. I've slept in my clothes, so I'm dressed already. I wrap a plaid around my shoulders, pick up my boots, and tiptoe towards the light that streams in from outside.

Ronan's tame fox, Rua, is still curled up near the cavern mouth where she fell into an exhausted sleep last night. Her head is cushioned on her tail, and she opens her eyes as I sneak past her. Shade and Shadow pad silently behind me. The fox pays them no attention.

"I'm only going out for a bit," I say. "No need to move."

I walk as far as the mouth of the cavern and pause in the shadow of the overhang, blinking against the light. Another between. I'm neither in nor out, neither the me I knew nor the me I must become.

I'd like to be just Flora again, a woman with choices. Good or bad, I used to believe I had them. But already, I feel the changes within myself.

It's past midday. I don't need to check the sun's position to know that—the heightened senses that connect me to the landscape haven't left me.

The hills are swollen, the earth rich and dark, leaves glistening, and puddles gleaming silver among the rocks. But wind still lashes the bracken, whipping the branches together with a sound like gnashing teeth.

I scan the glen below. A corner of the church near Mairi's village is visible in the distance, and beyond it, a long column of black cattle moves north in the direction of Dun Uilleum, surrounded by dots in the scarlet of the uniforms Vheara's soldiers wear. Plumes of smoke, thicker than the peat of chimney fires, rise skyward in various places. Not Mairi's village—the smoke is all farther away than that—but I've no way of knowing what is burning.

My arms tingle as the hairs rise along them. Pressure swells within me, and I want to seize the wind and pick up every one of Vheara's soldiers and blow them out to sea, wipe them from existence as though they've never been.

Standing here, helpless, the cavern walls close in. I glance back at the Riders before slipping out onto the hillside, but no one stirs.

Two steps later, Lorcan materialises beside me. "Did you think no one was keeping watch?"

My heart skips a beat. "For the enemy or to keep me from leaving?"

He shrugs. "Either—both."

"I'd be stupid to try to get to Muilean on my own."

"I don't know you."

"You haven't given me a chance."

He steps closer, the ever-present knife rolling absent-mindedly across his knuckles. Hilt and blade skip bone to bone without drawing blood, then flip to land flush in his palm before he flicks the knife again to repeat the process, faster and faster with a whisper of steel on skin.

Like Chyr, he towers above me. The Evers all do, but there's something in the green of Lorcan's glittering eyes that makes my mouth go dry, and not in a pleasant way.

He leans in closer. "Your very existence forces Chyr to choose between his oaths to the High King and his honour and loyalty to the Compact. You'll damn him to the Gloaming or destroy him. Destroy *us*. What more do I need to know?"

I turn my back on him and start to pull on my boots.

"Where are you going?" he asks.

"To get the clothes I washed earlier. To get some space."

Without taking his eyes from my face, Lorcan stills the knife and holds it against his side. I don't retreat.

"I won't let you be his downfall," he says very quietly. "Chyr is the best of all of us, and he's paid the price for others all his life. He accepted all the guilt for Fionn's crimes as if he deserved to be punished for the sin of being his father's son. We were the only ones in his corner then, and we'll protect him now."

I give a slow nod of acknowledgement, my heart hurting for the wounded young man I've glimpsed within Chyr occasionally.

"What happened to his mother?"

"No one knows." Lorcan slides the knife into a sheath at his wrist. "But all the things you think Siorai are? That is who Fionn *was*. If Chyr's mother is still among the living, and she managed to escape him, I wouldn't blame her."

"I can. Who would leave a child with someone like that?"

"Fionn never bothered himself with Chyr except to use him as a whipping boy, someone at whom to focus his rage on the rare occasions he was even there."

"All the more reason." I finish tugging on my boot. "And Chyr's uncle?"

Lorcan stares past me, down into the glen. "Chulainn was no better. He's more careful than Fionn, that's all. Power can do wonders for a reputation."

Except for the cold glitter in his emerald eyes, Lorcan's face holds no expression. I tighten the plaid around my shoulders to keep myself from shivering.

"Why are you telling me this?"

"I need you to understand what Chyr is to us—to every one of the Riders." He glances down at the Shadehounds, and they watch him coldly with their moonlight eyes. Shade steps forward, but Lorcan ignores the large male and bends until his nose nearly touches mine. "We would die for him. Kill for him. Crush little flowers without a second thought."

"Thank you for the warning." I manage to keep my voice steady. "But flowers can be poison. Be very careful with them."

With as much dignity as I can muster, I cross the hill to the stream where we watered the horses. It's only after I round the bend out of sight that I give in to the shudders that rattle my teeth.

Leaning back against the overhanging cliff above the bathing pool, I take deep, gulping breaths. Lorcan has made it clear I'll need to watch my back. The Riders may be oathbound to make sure I reach Muilean, but if it will save Chyr's life, that's an oath Lorcan, at least, is willing to break.

That moment when the soldier lit the beacon on the hill and smiled, the moment the pain first seared my shoulder, fury filled me just as it does now. But it wasn't my fury alone. The land itself was angry. Magic rose within me to answer then, and the wind has risen in response to my anger now.

Gusts beat at the cliff and sweep through the yellow furze. Wind swallows the burble of the stream that tumbles on the rocks.

I feel the wind's fury, the crushed furze, and the battered

stone. They match the way every part of me is being pummelled.

The thought makes me pause, and for the first time, the connection makes sense. I don't understand the Crown of Flame yet, but here beneath the cliff, listening to the wind and water, I finally *feel* how the land and I connect.

That's what it means to wear the Crown of Vines.

Alba Scoria didn't choose me because I deserve it. She chose me because I'm needed—because I share her fury and her grief.

Vheara and these Evers are causing more damage than Fionn ever did, and I can't defeat them. I can't even protect myself from the Riders.

But I am not alone. If the gods believe I have the strength within me to make a difference, then there must be a solution. I need to think harder and use every tool that I've been given.

Letting out a slow breath, I try to still my mind. I don't reach for the wind—I don't reach for any magic at all—but the air begins to calm. I let my mind drift, trying not to control my thoughts.

The stream slows, too, into a gentler burbling over the rocks, down into the pool, and then cascading down again. The water is clear in the way it can be only when it's icy cold, but the rock near the edge has been soaking up heat since the rain stopped earlier. I let my feet drift towards it.

Lorcan's energy is a spot of heat by the cavern mouth, well out of sight. Deciding to ignore him, I drop the plaid from my shoulders onto the dry ferns on the bank. Seated on the rock, I remove my boots, shift, and stockings.

Shadow crawls forward to sit beside me, while Shade turns his back and flops to the ground, watching the direction of the cavern.

"Tell me if anyone comes," I tell them, and I wonder how much they understand.

I gasp as the water chills my naked skin. The pool is only three feet deep, but that's enough to let me float on my back and soak in the sun's warmth. Submerged in the water, the world is quiet again.

Until now, I've fought for every drop of magic. Reached for it, torn it from the earth and sky, pushed it to do my bidding.

The Riders have limitations, the same way I do when I force magic to obey me. I pay for it in pain, but is that an Ever trait? The Riders haven't thought to take the Veilstone away from me—not yet. Most likely, one of them will.

I think back to the moment when I first reached into the cloud above the signal fire and felt the droplets of water forming, back to the moment in this same pool earlier when I felt the water wanting me to understand it.

Instead of using my magic to control it, I let myself sink in, savouring how it feels, how the droplets huddle together and drift as one. Acknowledging the darker, cooler water flowing beneath the surface, I concentrate on the warmth near the surface and bask in the light that pours magic from the sun into the earth. Then I stop moving the water with my hands and simply trust that it will flow around me.

The whole pool becomes a gentle eddy. I'm not pulling it in; only increasing its own momentum. Accepting what it already is, not what I try to make it. Accepting what it offers.

A shadow falls across my face. Releasing the water's magic, I crouch deeper in the water, hands crossed over my chest. Then I turn to face the bank.

"I didn't mean to scare you." Chyr has his back turned. "Lorcan was worried you've been gone a long time." His voice sounds thick and hoarse.

A boot scuffs against stone, and I can't tell exactly where. Shadow's ear flicks, then settles. Chyr's breath roughens. Mine does, too.

I want to test what I feel about him, examine my conflicting emotions the way I studied the warmth and the chill of the water.

311

Trusting myself is even harder than trusting him. Releasing control is the hardest thing of all.

"I came out here to think," I say. "But I can go back inside."

"No need, but I'll sit just around the corner to be sure you're safe."

I picture Chyr as the young man left alone to face his father's betrayal, people whispering, judging him, his own uncle trapping him with rings of oaths. No one to comfort him.

"Do you want to come here?" I ask.

His shoulders go still, as if he's stopped breathing. "After you're done?"

"Now. With me."

"Nothing has changed, Flora. You must know how I feel, but I've betrayed you."

"I hate the others."

"Exactly what every man wants to hear. Anyway, they'll know—"

"They'll survive."

He turns slowly. "Is this fear or anger? Or punishment?"

"It's desire," I say, though I'm lying to myself and afraid to admit to more. "My body is the only thing I control. The only thing that's mine to give away, share, or keep to myself. You gave me your name for the same reason once. I know that forgiving you is complicated, dangerous even. But what's between us feels honest, even if it can't change whatever happens next."

I lie back and let the water float my legs out from underneath me, baring my breasts and stomach to the sun. Closing my eyes, I listen to the water ebb and flow, trying not to wonder what Chyr is doing, what he'll choose. Hoping he'll choose me, at least for this moment—not because I need him to, but because I have decided I am allowed to want this. Want him. Not as the Maiden, nor as the Domhnall of Dunhaelic, but as myself.

Whatever the crowns and the Compact make of me before all this is finished, I can still have this one last choice of my own. But he has to choose it, too.

Then I feel the water eddying around him as he lowers himself into the pool and pushes towards me.

He stops before our bodies touch. I arch my back, my hair streaming behind me as I lift myself back onto my feet.

His breath catches, and I soak in the sight of him: the broad planes of his chest, the width of his shoulders, the need in his eyes. The scar of his healing wound has faded even more. Less of it is that angry, life-threatening red. My fingers ache to trace it, to make sure the healing is real.

Knowing our time together is fleeting, I want to touch every inch of him. Touch him with my lips, my tongue, my fingers, until I've committed all of him to memory. Until I've made him feel as wanted and beautiful as he made me feel before who we're being forced to become came between us.

His fingers tremble as the back of his hand brushes my cheek. "Do you have any idea how magnificent you are?" he whispers.

"I'd rather be fierce," I whisper.

"You could never be anything less."

"Tell me what you want, Chyr. Can we steal half an hour for ourselves and pretend that we have choices?"

"I'd give anything to pretend our circumstances are different. You know about my oaths and the reasons I couldn't tell you who I was. But the truest reason I didn't tell you is this: when I was dying, I couldn't bear the thought of you looking at me with hatred or disgust. I believed those moments with you would be all I would ever have. My last chance to have someone see me for myself. And I needed your kindness, your warmth. If I was going to die, I wanted that to carry with me, because I didn't even know how much I'd missed having that in my life until you offered it to me.

You filled an emptiness in me. Gave me a gift I'd been searching for all along without knowing what to call it. Something that wasn't for Tirnaeve or my uncle or the Riders but only for myself."

It's the admission of a child who grew up lonely in a cold, cruel home. My heart breaks for him all over again, and I rise on my toes and tangle my hands in his hair, pulling his face down so I can kiss him, claim him. Not as a consort or a king but for *him*. For the child he was and the man he made himself. For the way he's fighting—because I believe, I have to believe, he is.

I kiss Chyr with every bit of the hunger I am feeling, and he drinks it in like I'm offering him water after days of thirst. His hands slide down my back, over the curves of my bottom, across my thighs. He lifts me until I wrap my legs around his waist, low enough to feel the hard length of him where I'm most sensitive to pressure. He walks towards the rock at the edge of the pool, then sets me on my feet and bends me backwards until my spine lies against the sun-warmed stone. Pushing my legs apart, he steps between them.

The contrast—silky water and skin against hard rock and muscle, fire and heat against the cold—brings my every nerve to life.

A shudder runs through me. I trail the edge of a nail down the hollow of Chyr's throat, down the carved muscles of his chest, around one flat nipple, then the other. He trembles again, his pupils dark in eyes that burn with fire.

His next kiss is a question. He tastes of temptation and sin, and my tongue answers, sliding over his. When I nip his lip, he smiles.

"Fight or share?" he asks. "What can I give you?"

"A fight I can win," I breathe.

"Then pay attention, Fierceness. Eyes on me."

He catches both my wrists in one hand and stretches my arms above my head. The position lifts my breasts, forces me to trust, to surrender. Rock grates my knuckles; the sting turns bright. I lift to meet it.

His tongue traces my jaw, then slides down my throat, lower, lower.

The movement is slow. He pauses, his gaze searing into mine. "More?"

I moan, because words won't come.

His hand slides down, palm splayed over my ribs, my stomach. Lower. His calluses are rough, like the rock behind me. The sun is warm on my face, and the water is cool and yielding.

"Good?" he asks, his thumb circling. "Too much?"

That hand and the things he's doing with it. The way his fingers curve inside me, the way his thumb moves.

"Good," I whisper. "So good."

My hips buck towards him. My breath shortens. I twist my wrists—not to escape, but to reach him, to take his head between my hands, to lift higher or pull him where I need him most.

But he doesn't set me free.

"You're still in control," he says. "Tell me to stop. Tell me to be gentle. Tell me what you want. Anything."

I shake my head. I don't want gentle.

What *do* I want? I want to rewrite history. That's what I need. What we all need.

Chyr sheathes himself inside me, pushes in slow enough to make me feel the stretch, fast enough to steal my breath, shaking me to my core. He isn't sweet or tender, not like the last time. His magic isn't warm; it's fire followed by a breath of cold, a hundred points of pressure pulsing and driving and pounding while his tongue glides between my breasts and down to trace the outline of his fingers across my stomach. The magic is wild, and his tongue is maddeningly thorough until it's almost too much to bear.

The pressure builds.

Chyr moves faster, harder, his gaze locked on mine.

I shatter, pleasure rushing through me in wave after wave. It's too much, and I try to retreat. He holds me like he'll never let go. And I tip over the edge again—climbing, falling, floating.

I feel Chyr's heat, his weight. The stone is rough against my back, the wind cooling the sweat and water along my skin, the sun reaching down in fingers as thin and sharp as needles to ignite fire somewhere deep inside me.

I lose myself in all of it, allow myself to drift until I'm not sure where I stop and the earth and sky begin.

Chyr thrusts harder, and I climb one peak after another. Then he spills himself into me, and I plummet off the edge of the world, determined to change the very shape of it. To reforge it into something new.

Everything Chyr feels for me, everything he is, shines from his eyes, and I brush his damp hair off his cheek. "I forgive you," I say. "For misleading me. For catching me."

"Because of this?"

"Because you did the best you could in the moment, just as I will do whatever I must. And because I want to."

Because I love you.

The water hushes to a silver whisper, and sweetness rises from the yellow furze and damp wool drying on the bank. In the distance, smoke is rising.

Whatever the rules of the Compact were more than 1,600 years ago when it was written, they're less clear than what I always believed. I refuse to accept there's no solution. Why would the Cailleach mark a Maiden after four centuries and take away the one man who has ever made her understand her strength?

There must be a way through this, and I will find it even if I have to bend the rules into a shape I can accept.

Having to choose one of the other Riders is unthinkable. After Chyr, how could I bear it?

CHAPTER 34
TAKE THE STEEL

CHYR

M ist coils along Loch Seil's calm surface, and the night is chill. After the hour spent outside with Flora, I miss the sun and the warmth all the more, but Flora comes to life in the moonlight, magic shining from her.

We ride single file, silent save for the rhythm of hooves and the creak of leather, our way lit by scoutlights and the glow of the swelling moon. Rua threads through the woods above us, her tail low, and the Shadehounds pace behind Flora like soundless shadows.

The wind brings the scent of smoke now and then. Beneath the thick plaid she has pinned around them, Flora's shoulders tense every time. Her attention shifts from the woods to the hills or the trail ahead as if she hears things that we don't.

A mile out from the camp beneath the beacon site, she stiffens in the saddle, and Eira flattens her ears in response. Up ahead, Ronan gives a soft whistle and halts under a cluster of slender birches. The Shadehounds melt up the slope, and we all dismount.

Bent nearly double, Ronan ghosts forward, a dark shadow slipping between pale trunks until he's out of sight. The rest of us crouch where we are, our swords already out, until he comes back to report.

"Six humans and a Grey," Ronan says. "Likely a picket of sentries for the camp. If that's the case, there will be at least that many in the camp itself, and likely another group of sentries farther on."

"Did they hear us?" Flora whispers.

"No sign of that. Which doesn't mean they can't be waiting for us." He turns to me. "How do you want to do it? You stay here with her, and the rest of us go? We can't risk having her taken."

"I'm right here, and I make up my own mind about where I go and who with." Flora tips her head back to glare at him. "Also, it's pointless for us to split up. The men are down on the track. We can cut higher on the hillside and get past them. Can any of you muffle the sound of the horses?"

Lorcan gives her a dismissive smirk. "Leave the soldiering to the adults, love. We can't risk leaving the enemy at our back—we could end up trapped between several Greys."

"Killing those soldiers and the Grey yesterday is what brought the extra sentries here. But I doubt whoever's in charge knows a Rider was involved, or they'd have sent even more men by now. That will change if you take out more Greys. Vheara's troops will start hunting you here in earnest."

"We would be clear on the other side of the loch by then," Daire says.

Flora's silver-gold eyes turn to steel. "A signal beacon can outrun any horse. They'll have more than enough time to have an ambush waiting for us."

"We can kill them before they fire the beacon," Daire says, pulling his hair back and refastening it in a tighter braid behind him.

I shake my head. "The men have amulets with fire runes."

"Going around the camp reduces our risk," Flora adds. "Why give them more reasons to look for you here—or to retaliate against the clans?"

Lorcan bounces on his heels, eager to go. "You don't know Vheara if you think all the clans aren't due for retaliation already," he says. "Especially in Ehrugael."

He turns to me, expecting me to side with him. And he speaks for all three Riders. They prefer action, and Flora's caution will never sit well with them.

In the end, it's a strategic decision, not an emotional one. I have no choice.

Aware of the Riders watching, I offer Flora what small measure of comfort I can.

"Your reasoning is sound, Flora, but Lorcan isn't wrong either. Our best chance to save lives is still to get back to Tirnaeve. Every Grey we kill now is one we don't have to worry about later."

Flora holds my eyes briefly, then turns to the other Riders one by one. Finally, she drops her chin and shrugs. "Fine. What do you want me to do?"

I give her a nod of appreciation and make a quick decision. Although Ronan is not the best of fighters, he's our best scout by far. I could use his expertise, but I can't trust Daire not to goad Flora into something rash. And I don't trust Lorcan with her at all.

"Stay here with Ronan in case there are more of Vheara's troops behind us or scattered in the wood."

"There aren't." Flora's tone is confident, but the set of her chin suggests she doesn't intend to explain.

Her power is growing, and I'm pleased because we need it—*she* needs it. That doesn't change the fact that she's more dangerous—and in more danger—until she understands and embraces what she's becoming. And every secret she keeps pulls her farther from me.

"You'll watch over her?" I ask, sidling close to Ronan.

He nods, and the Shadehounds fall back to Flora's side as I slip off the track up into the trees, motioning for Daire and Lorcan to follow.

"I'm surprised you'd leave her alone with Ronan." Lorcan throws me a sharp-eyed glance.

"Shut it," I snap. "Focus."

"I'm only saying I don't think I would in your shoes," Lorcan drawls. "You can see he likes her. Who knows what she can talk him into doing?"

We slip into the trees, and I swallow down a flash of irritation. Lorcan's the hardest to predict of all the Riders. He's played the dangerous flirt too long, armoured in the careless cruelty that some women mistake for charm. It took me years to realise that cruelty is the most honest thing about him. When it comes to having our backs, I trust him without question. With others, though, he's calculating and patient, content to study his prey until he identifies their deepest fears, their greatest vulnerabilities. Then he'll sweep in for the kill.

I've seen the cold gleam in his eye as he watches Flora. I suppose I should have realised that spending more time in her company would only make him more determined to save me from her. Whether he'll decide that requires seducing her or killing her, though, I can't be certain.

The trees thin on the hillside above the picket sentries. We use the cover while we can as we position ourselves above the enemy. The moonlight is faint, but various power runes that Daire's sister has given him glow gold along his jaw and throat as he activates the spells within them.

"Try to save your magic if you can," I say, not surprised when my voice sounds inside my head instead of being audible. Daire has runes for each of the Riders that let us communicate with him and each other.

His answer returns to me the same way. "We'll need to deflect their attention from what's happening around them to keep them from activating the fire amulets before we've killed them all. And I need to silence the fight so we don't alert the camp. It would be far easier if we had some way to block the amulets, but since we don't know exactly how those work...I don't think we can risk assuming that anything we try would block the magic."

"I've been thinking about that," Lorcan says. "If the amulets are tied to a particular signal fire, whoever is creating them must be close enough to have been at that site. Here, in other words."

I glance from him to Daire. "There's no other way to do it?"

"There are always other ways." Daire shrugs. "But it would take a runesmith with more skills than most."

"You think Vheara has Greys that good?" I ask.

"I think the better question is why she would waste runes that powerful on a beacon fire in the back of beyond unless she was expecting us to pass this way," Lorcan says.

We all fall silent as we consider that.

We descend the slope towards the group of sentries. There's no doubt that Flora's presence will change the dynamic among the Riders in ways I'm only beginning to calculate, but it feels good to have Daire and Lorcan beside me again as we move to attack.

It's a familiar rhythm, stalking our prey, setting the trap, snapping it closed. I've missed their swords at my side and those moments when the power runes allow us to hear each other's voices in our minds. I've missed them, and this is the first time I can admit to myself how much I feared that I would never see any of them again.

A Grey and six soldiers—four men and two women—are hidden among the trees below us, a few feet uphill of the drovers' track along the loch. The spot is well-chosen for an ambush on anyone passing by. Escape to the front and rear is easily blocked, and a narrow strip of bog on the loch side of the track will prevent escape in that direction.

The Riders and I use the same advantage against them.

Daire activates another rune to let us communicate silently with each other. Then circling ahead, Lorcan blocks the route to the nearby camp. I will hold back to cover the rear and keep them from retreating towards Ronan and Flora. Daire will drop in directly above them.

"Ready." Lorcan's signal is a whisper in my mind, and Daire echoes, "Ready."

I give the order to go.

We spring the trap, and I signal that the Grey is mine. My gut tightens, my mind sharp in that moment of anticipation when the enemy is an unknown quantity, and I don't know what sort of magic I might face.

The Grey raises his hand as if for an elemental attack, his ashen skin seeming to absorb what little light the moon provides. I surge forward, my sword swinging. The eerie eyes with their strange, colourless irises widen in panic, and the mouth opens to scream, but his head falls silently to the ground.

Two of the women have their swords drawn and circle towards me. I'm good at killing, but I don't enjoy it. I've seen too much death in the past year, and I can't help wondering whether these soldiers would fight for Vheara if they had a choice. Is it naïve to hope they wouldn't?

I give both women a quick, clean death, then hunt down a man who tries to escape into the trees.

There's no sign of a signal fire on the hilltop yet, but we hurry in the direction of the camp as soon as the last of the sentries is dead. Where the trees break and the slope descends into the gully, I signal for Daire to scout ahead while Lorcan and I wait at the edge of a clump of pale-barked birches.

The wind is gusting, blowing scattered clouds past the waxing moon and rustling the brush in the rock-strewn gully as Daire slips across. We're close enough to see the men moving around the camp, and where there were three shelters yesterday, there are seven now.

"Three Greys and eighteen men," Daire's voice whispers in my head. "Also three Ravenhounds."

"Damn it." I release my grip on the hilt of my sword and turn away. "That's too many. Too much risk of the beacons being lit. Come back, and we'll regroup."

"It's one Grey apiece, and a few men," Daire says. "Perfect odds, just about."

Lorcan opens his mouth, then thinks better of it, and merely studies me with his green eyes glittering as we start to retrace our steps.

"Where are we going?" Lorcan asks as we pass the spot where we killed the sentries.

My boot snags in the thorny gorse, and I pause to kick it free. "We'll leave the camp alone. That many reinforcements says they're not taking chances. Killing one Grey and a few men could have been the work of Highlanders who happened to get their hands on celestial steel. If we take them all out tonight, we'll have a fight on our hands all the way to Muilean and the doorway."

"Are you going soft on us, Chyr?" Daire asks.

"It won't matter how many Greys we've killed if we miss the doorway because we didn't get there on time."

Some of the tension drains from Daire's features, but Lorcan's silent disapproval hangs over us the entire way back to where Flora and Ronan wait. Then we round a bend and spot the two of them seated side by side on a log beside the track, heads bent together. Her scarf and his brown forearm brush as they lean in, speaking too low for their voices to reach us.

My blood pumps hot, and I stretch my fingers to relieve the tension.

If any of the Riders would be suited to Flora, it's Ronan. He's steady where I am not, warm where I am guarded, and he never pinned her to the ground against her will or withheld the truth of who he was. His oaths won't place her at risk. Still, I have to clench my jaw to keep from saying something I won't be able to take back.

Flora's eyes cut to mine as if she knows exactly where I am, and she says, "You didn't kill them all."

How can she know that?

I feel both Lorcan and Daire focus their attention on her more sharply.

"Only the sentries," I say. "We're going to have to leave the camp alone and sneak past the other sentries. Can you come and dispose of the dead so no one finds them?"

She gives me a slow appraisal, checking for injuries first, then studying my expression. With a sigh, she pushes to her feet.

I'm not looking at Ronan—I haven't dared look closely at him yet. Instead, I watch as the Shadehounds peel themselves away from the hillside above Flora and stalk towards Lorcan, their grey fur bristling and dipped in shadow. They tilt their heads when they reach him, and their lips curl until their teeth gleam. Then they vanish.

Daire waves a hand through the air where they were standing, and a low growl makes him jump back.

"That's a message for you, Lorcan," Ronan says.

"What? They're watching, and I won't see them coming?" Lorcan doesn't sound amused.

Ronan shrugs. "Seems you're smarter than you look."

The wind has shredded the clouds, and the moon casts a pale glow that ripples across the black water beside the track. We all stare grim-faced at the Grey's crumpled body and severed head. Facing the corpse is like staring down into the Pit, a mirror of what any of us could too easily become.

"Don't break oaths, is the moral of that story," Ronan says, echoing my own thoughts.

Daire picks up the Grey's sword from where it lies in the moss and prepares to fling it out into the bog.

Flora catches his arm. "Don't."

"It's celestial steel," Daire hisses.

"Yes, and we'll need every scrap of that to arm our warriors if we want to have a chance of defeating Vheara."

Lorcan's eyes narrow. He studies her, then stoops to retrieve the Grey's head by the hair. "It's not a bad idea, but there are laws about giving out celestial steel."

"Do any prohibit me from giving it out?"

"Well, no—"

"Good." Flora slides the sword through the straps of her pack behind Eira's saddle.

Lorcan watches her a moment longer, then draws his arm back to throw the head. "Any objection if I throw this? Thought I'd better ask permission."

"Lorcan, don't be an ass," I snap.

"As it happens, we should leave the Grey," Flora says.

Daire cocks his head, thinking it through. A moment later, he gives her a slow, admiring smile that makes me want to cuff the back of his head. "You want to make it look as though the soldiers killed the Grey and ran away. Then all we have to do is sneak past the camp and the picket of sentries on the other side."

He cuts me a look I can't quite read, and it occurs to me that Daire hasn't stoked Lorcan's anger a single time since we left the cavern. The impulse to turn emotion into chaos is embedded so deep within Daire that it's a reflex, which makes me wonder what he's thinking.

Flora moves to the edge of the bog. The rest of us pick up the red-coated bodies, then follow as Flora picks her way through, searching out the solid ground and creating it where none exists.

"You can drop them here," she says. "It's deep enough."

"Strictly for the sake of curiosity, why aren't we throwing them in the lake?" Lorcan asks when he comes back with a second soldier.

Flora doesn't so much as glance at him. "The loch is shallow a long way out, and the water may be stained with peat, but it is clear."

She leaves him to reason the rest out for himself, and I can't help noticing that Ronan grins. Daire doesn't bother to hide a smirk. When the last of the bodies has been dropped, Flora watches the scarlet coats sink into the moss, peat, and tar-dark water. I move back towards the shore, but a strange prickle of magic raises the hair on the back of my neck, and I turn back.

The crown burns brighter across Flora's brow, red and orange flames mirrored on the water below. Power spills outward, and the loch shivers—ripples skimming the surface— while the charged air blows her hair back and billows her shawl.

Ronan cuts a look back at the camp, and Daire hastily taps a rune along his throat. I can only pray that none of the Greys nearby have enough magic-sense to feel Flora's power across the distance. But then I realise that what I sense doesn't feel like magic, not in any way more than the magic in the wind or the sunlight or the spring leaves unfurling in the birches.

What she's doing now is different from what I've seen her do before, and I'm not the only one intrigued.

Daire, Lorcan, and Ronan all stare at her with varying degrees of awe.

And hunger.

Siorai are creatures of magic and lust, and one begets the other. Whatever Flora is becoming, there's no denying her effect. Watching her makes me hard, and I would bet the Sun King's bloody throne I'm not alone.

The thought raises a growl in my throat.

It's primal, this tie between sex and magic and battle.

Caught deep within it, all four of us lose the one rule by which every Rider lives or dies.

Never, ever, let down your guard.

The air still hums with her power when the first hoofbeats reach us. Before we notice them, the four horsemen approaching at a gallop are close enough that the Shadehounds turn with their hackles raised.

CHAPTER 35

ILLICIT MAGIC

CHYR

Hoofbeats pound the earth, coming fast. The four of us wait, blades ready, magic primed, for whatever comes galloping from the darkness. A half-second later, I recognise Niall with Sean, Cathal, and Fergal riding hard behind him.

The pressure in my chest unwinds, releasing more completely than it has since I asked the four of them to lay a trail towards Eireen while the rest of us went south. It's a relief to see them—and an added worry.

Niall and Fergal vault off before their horses have fully stopped. Fergal reassures his mare with a parting touch, a gesture so familiar—so much a part of him—that it makes my grin stretch even wider. I hurry to meet them, and Niall's smile mirrors mine as we clasp hands and forearms.

"Thank the Light," Niall says. "Sean's had us chasing after your magic across half of Alba Scoria. Does that mean you have the Hollow Crown? But how? And what of the Raven witch?"

Niall looks worse than the rest of us, unshaven and haggard as if he's been running for days. The dark shadows under his eyes make the grey almost as light as the new silver-gold of Flora's.

Fergal looks noticeably thinner, too. Without a doubt, he'll have been insisting on sharing the food rations equally with the others despite his extra bulk.

Even Cathal is unusually quiet, his dark skin paled to an undertone of ash. His attention has already slipped past the four of us to the dead Grey and then to Flora.

Then there's Sean. It isn't fair for me to treat him any differently because of General Mora's accusations. Sean doesn't deserve that—or at least I hope he doesn't.

I grip his forearm and clasp his shoulder briefly, and he does the same. But I see a flicker of disappointment in his eyes, which means I didn't manage to hide my hesitation.

"Unfortunately, we don't have either the crown or Vheara," I say.

"Not that crown at least," Daire says with relish.

Ronan flicks him a look, then shifts his attention back to Niall. "What made you think we had it?"

"That." Sean points at Flora, who's still working in the bog to anchor the bodies of the soldiers we killed. "She has our magic corrupted with something else. And what's that on her forehead? It looks like the Crown of Flame."

I'm teetering on the edge of exploding at Sean's words and the way they all stare at Flora with alarm and distaste, as if Sean's accusation of corruption makes her no different than the Greys. I force myself to exhale because grabbing Sean by the throat will do none of us any good.

The crown shines on Flora's brow, and her hair blows lightly around her face. Her magic feels nothing like the Greys, and I still can't feel anything of Tirnaeve in the power she's using. But Sean's magic-sense is legendary—innately clearer than mine and further enhanced by one of the power runes on his temples. What he senses from Flora may be different.

I open my mouth to explain, diplomatically—but Ronan beats me to it.

"That's Flora, and yes, that's the Crown of Flame, so don't be disrespectful." Ronan's voice carries a quiet threat.

Niall casts him a sideways glance. "What's she trying to do in the bog?"

"That's your first concern?" Cathal throws Niall a scornful glance. "'Where did you find the future Cailleach Queen?' is the better question." Cathal sounds bemused. "Assuming one of us will have her and she's willing to make the sacrifice." His expression is fascinated as he watches Flora, as though she's an intriguing puzzle he needs to study.

Fergal smacks the back of Cathal's head with a paw the size of a warhammer. "If she wears the Crown of Flame, we're oathbound to marry her, you oaf. Except we can't, can we? There is no Cailleach Queen. There's a king, and he's standing right beside you." He turns solemn blue-grey eyes to me. "This isn't good. It means at least one of us will have to decide which of our oaths to break, either to the Compact or the Master."

"I'll need to re-examine every word of the Compact." Cathal rubs his hands together. "I've always taken the text literally: '*The Master shall open the doorway to the Sacred Isle on the Night of Rebirth, and the Anvar'thaine shall Hunt the Maiden.*' But that can't be literal, or the woman wouldn't have the Crown of Flame already. Assuming you've completed the Hunt without reaching Muilean—"

Sean glowers at him. "Leave the Compact to the bloody scholars in Tirnaeve to debate, would you? What does it matter? Whatever that woman might be, she's no Maiden, and she'll never be the Cailleach Queen. She's a fraud and an abomination."

"Sean, enough." My voice is quiet enough to warn him I've reached the limits of my patience. "You don't understand anything yet, and I won't tolerate more insults."

Sean draws himself into his most forbidding stance, a habit when he's feeling out of his depth: legs wide, arms folded, nose high, lips thin, eyes hard. His gaze snags for an instant on the flames at Flora's brow, then he snaps his attention back to me. The six power runes he bears glint along his temples, three on each side.

Fergal steps between us. "Fists and arguments later. Explanations first. What is the woman doing, and why is there a dead Grey on the path? More importantly, where are Tuirse and Oran?"

I shake my head, and Fergal turns away to drop down to his haunches, head in his hands. Cathal strides off with his back turned, and Niall's pale brows slide together into a frown. "What happened, Chyr?"

My lips are dry, and my hands shake. I'm not ready to go through it all again. But Ronan speaks before I can.

"Their wounds never healed," he says. "Their swords were coated in powdered celestial iron."

The night is suddenly colder, and the darkness closes in around us, making the jingle of the horses' bridles and the rustle of leaves through the trees unbearably loud.

"Fucking Vheara." Sean kicks at a clump of grass, then rests his forehead against his horse's saddle.

For four centuries, the ten of us have hunted together, fought together, bled together—survived together. And now we haven't.

Grief has weight and pressure. It's a bitter taste on the back of my tongue. Apart from me, none among the Riders has lost a parent. Sean lost his twin sisters, but that was long before I knew him. Fergal lost his betrothed shortly before joining the Anvar'thaine, and I remember the way he used to wall himself off from us in the beginning, his face turned to stone and his eyes like chips of ice.

He looks like that now. Even Niall has his shoulders hunched around himself as though the news has gutted him physically. Rage has replaced the usual studious disinterest on Cathal's face, and Sean's fury is even worse.

He shrugs off the hand I place on his shoulder. "I told you we shouldn't split up," he snaps. "You wouldn't listen and insisted on having your way!"

I resist the urge to snarl back at him. "The three of us were as good as dead after the ambush. That magic you sensed was Flora's, and if it hadn't been for her, I wouldn't be here either."

"You think a human healed you from celestial iron poisoning? Are you insane?" Sean glares at me, then has the good sense to drop his eyes to the ground. "Your General Mora did more than shake your loyalty to your brothers. He's shaken all the sense straight from your head."

"Sean," Niall warns, "that's far out of bounds."

Sean turns to him with a snarl that makes the horses raise their heads and shift their legs. "No. With only eight of us left, Chyr needs to stop wasting time considering how *humans* feel. We could have won at Culodur if he had trusted me over Mora, but he's still turning a blind eye to their evil. We've all seen the atrocities they commit against each other. And now here's this creature who endangers everything we're trying to do, and he acts as though she *isn't* an abomination."

Fury as sharp as steel rips through my chest. "She isn't—"

"You know the High King would condemn her." Sean flings the words at me. "Think, Chyr. You're bound to protect the Compact. Protecting Alba Scoria from illicit magic was the main reason the Compact was created. The old queens are dead, and apart from the Shadelings and us, any magic left in this cursed place is illicit. We're oathbound to remove it—which means we've no choice except to kill her."

"That is not what the Compact says or what our oaths require. *She* is more righteous than any of us." I seize Sean by the shirt and pull until we're standing nose to nose. "Make a move to hurt Flora, and I will bloody well end you. Do you hear me?"

I feel her behind me before she speaks—both the charged energy of the magic she's been wielding in the bog and the quiet, leashed throb of her anger.

"That's all right, Chyr," she says, her voice deadly calm. "I don't need you to defend me, and your Rider is only drawing the battle lines more clearly." She steps around me and squares up to Sean with magic still billowing her hair. "Let me be equally clear. If you want to kill me, try it. I'll defend myself, and I may not be able to kill you outright, but I can make damned sure you spend eternity looking up at the world from the bottom of the bog."

CHAPTER 36
THE HUNT BEGINS

FLORA

Daybreak approaches too fast after the delay with the soldiers at the picket and the arrival of the other Riders. There's a ruined Domhnall castle on the coast that I'd planned for us to use as shelter, but there's a long stretch between the end of Loch Seil and Castle Tchirum that won't be safe to cross in daylight. If we can't make it the whole way before dawn, it will cost us another night that we do not have.

I've spent the hours since the bog watching the four new Riders, trying to assess and sort them. Sean, who wants me dead, has reasons I can understand but not forgive. Cathal studies me the way Iain taught me to assess a horse at market, leaving my emotional reaction entirely separate. Niall seems steady, but unreadable. Fergal's care for his horse makes me disposed to like him, and when his eyes catch mine, they aren't unkind.

Not unkind. High praise indeed these days.

We've no time for stealth, but as we approach the camp, Daire touches a couple of the runes along his jaw and throat. They turn from silver to glowing gold, and a pulse of magic shimmers across my skin.

"What is that?" I ask.

"He's using a rune to create a bubble of silence and darkness around us, and another to keep us from being noticed," Chyr says. "You can speak normally as long as we stay close to him."

Daire winks as though I should be impressed, but based on what was said back at the cavern, I imagine the runes are his sister's magic and not his own.

If I'm impressed, it's with her and not with him, so I merely shrug. We set the horses into a canter and pass beneath the camp without any problems. The second picket is a bit more complicated.

The six human soldiers are spread along the track, and the Grey that accompanies them has climbed a few yards up the slope. The terrain around him is strewn with scree and boulders, and Daire shakes his head, gesturing for us to skirt the soldiers on the right, between the loch and the drovers' track.

All the Riders veer off in that direction, but the gleam of moonlight catches on thin seams of dark water between hags of peat.

"Stop!" I shout, too loudly.

The Riders rein in, unconcerned—at least not about the noise.

"There's no firm footing there for a horse." I point to where the ground is treacherous. "I can make it stable, but you'll need to ride single file behind me."

Chyr nods, and I reach into the bog. Power rushes up to meet me. The peat is mostly solid, but deep water-filled troughs lie between hard banks, and the empty space goes deep. I push the banks together and use my magic to sense the areas that look solid even though they aren't. The squelch beneath Eira's hooves goes quiet, and the ground holds, creating a narrow bridge for us to pass.

We're almost clear when Daire's mare gives a ragged scream as an edge of the peat bank gives way. She drops to her hock in water and twists, and Daire falls with a splash, his head plunging under.

Lorcan shouts and dives off his red gelding, rushing back to help him. I push magic around Daire and pull him to the bridge.

"Heads up. Company's coming, and Daire's runes have failed," says the blond with close-shorn hair—Niall, his silver-grey eyes almost matching the colour of the inactive power runes on his wrists.

He and Cathal, the one with runes etched into the shaved scalp above his ears, both touch various runes on their own bodies. The runes flare, glowing gold as their concealing magic ripples around us.

The damage is done already, though. There's shouting, and the soldiers are running. The Grey in the trees jumps down onto the drovers' track and gestures to the loch. A wave of water rises and builds, sweeping towards us. Lorcan pushes both hands at it, and the wave breaks in sections instead of sweeping over us all at once.

And on the ridge above the camp, the signal beacon flares. I search for another way to smother it, but it's too late. Another beacon answers farther down the ridge, and then another, and another, and another, an endless line of signals burning hill to hill, warning all of Ehrugael that the rebel king and the Riders have come.

The line of beacons flares too quickly for us to hope to reach the end of Loch Seil before Vheara's patrols know to be on high alert—before we risk being caught in a trap. Now every second counts.

Lorcan pulls Daire up, and they throw themselves into their saddles. We drive the horses hard, staying off the track as much as we are able. There's no sound of pursuit behind us, but the loch narrows ahead, with too many possible choke points.

Emotions swirl in my chest, a sour brew of guilt and too many other things to name. My heart tries to keep pace with the staccato beat of hooves until fear exhausts itself.

Until we stop to rest the horses, none of us tries to speak. Then Sean throws himself off his black gelding before I've even managed to rein Eira in.

"What the fuck was that?" He stalks to my stirrup, stopping with his face red and twisted and close enough that I could kick him if I had a death wish.

I swing down beside him, feet splashing in the mud. "Back away and do not shout. Are you asking why Daire fell—or do you have a better question?"

"Why should anyone trust your magic?"

"My magic didn't fail."

Sean darts a glance at the long line of beacons burning behind us and ahead, then locks his eyes on mine. "If it wasn't your magic, it was your judgement. Either way, your trail was too narrow."

"That's hardly fair." Ronan comes to stand beside me.

Sean gives a humourless bark of laughter. "Adopting another wild thing, are you, Ronan?"

"Enough!" Chyr commands. "We'll lead the horses on foot until they're rested, but the stars are fading. We're wasting time. Flora, do you sense anyone nearby?"

"Not yet, but we should cross to the other side of the loch. There's an island a short way ahead. We can use it to break the distance the horses have to swim."

Chyr is silent as he digests that. "Can we still make it to Castle Tchirum?"

My throat is dry as I shake my head. "We would need at least two more hours of darkness to have any chance of reaching it," I admit. "We have to look for shelter somewhere closer. This puts us another day behind."

The stink of smoke grows stronger as we ride south. We swim the loch and find a narrow burn that flows into a deep wood of willows and birches on the other side of Loch Seil. We splash through water stained as dark as tea, the horses slipping on mossy stones and tree roots, but walking the horses in the burn eliminates our tracks.

I can sense soldiers now, many of them, along with the Greys whose presence makes my magic crawl whenever my senses brush across them.

Chyr sends me small smiles as if to remind me not to take it to heart. Ronan and Fergal grin at me a few times, too, and I wish I had the energy to pretend that I'm fine.

I'm not.

My hands won't stop shaking, and as much as I hate to admit it, Sean was right. It's not only my magic that can fail— it's me. I'm the one who doesn't know how to control it or use it to help us. I *should* have made the bridge wider, and now any chance of getting to Muilean unchallenged is gone.

Deep in the woods, Chyr gestures to our left. "We should fan out here and see if we can find somewhere to get a few hours of sleep."

"We'll need more than a few hours." Sean spurs his gelding up beside Chyr. "Or are you planning to let the witch drive us directly into the Butcher's arms?"

"We might have made better progress if you'd spent less time arguing," I retort.

Sean glares at me and opens his mouth to spew more venom, but Chyr sends him a hard look, and Sean reins his gelding back.

Lorcan may come in a close second, but Sean is the worst of the Riders. Even if I hadn't read General Mora's letter accusing Sean of betraying the king, I doubt I would trust him. I can't quite see Lorcan as a traitor. Not to Chyr, at least. But Sean? There's something between him and Chyr that pulls my eyes to Sean at every opportunity.

Ignoring Sean would be like trying to ignore an adder that's coiled and full of venom.

"Chyr's right," I say. "There's a storm coming, so any sort of cover from the elements would help."

A couple of the Riders look to the sky, and I can feel their doubt. The stars are nearly gone, but it's light enough now to see that the clouds are still thin and scattered. I *feel* the storm, but that's not something I want to say. Not in front of Sean and Lorcan.

Chyr scowls at Sean, and the big, blond snake drops back as the Riders leave the burn. The horses scramble up the gravel shelf and a steeper, bent grass-covered bank to where a deer trail leaves an opening in the vegetation.

The wet earth swallows sound. Dew clings to brush and low-hanging leaves, depositing cold drops into our hair and shoulders with every accidental brush.

I spot a potential shelter before we even separate to search. A fallen oak rests on its root plate and the bare branches of its crown, leaving a narrow tunnel underneath that could be draped in plaids to form a tent. Multi-stem clusters of hazel trunks form a living screen of stems and leaves behind it, with several more hazel clusters along the front.

Reining Eira in, I signal for everyone to stop. "That's as good as anything we can find," I say, gesturing towards it.

Chyr scans the area, then gestures for everyone to dismount. Rua, who has been draped like a scarf across Ronan's shoulders, raises her head, looks around, and launches herself to the ground. Feet silent on the moss and rotting leaves, she vanishes into the undergrowth. Shade and Shadow glance at me, tilting their heads as though asking for permission.

"Go on," I say. "Have fun."

They take off after Rua at a sprint.

Cathal, who's scarcely said two sentences since he and the others joined us, pauses to survey the area before swinging himself from the saddle. He's as much a warrior as the others—strong-muscled and fierce-looking, his dark hair worn braided close at the top of his head before falling in a glossy curtain below his shoulders. His grey-blue eyes are a stark contrast against his deep brown skin, and the way they absorb everything around him seems more thoughtful than tactical. A row of power runes begins at each temple and follows a shaved line above his ears before disappearing beneath his hair at the back.

"We should at least try to look for something more suitable than this place," Sean says to me, making no effort to get off his horse. "At the very least, it's only prudent to scout the area. But if you and the woman are too tired, the rest of us can go alone."

Nothing in Chyr's expression overtly changes, but something behind his eyes goes cold and as still as a stalking cat. "This is your last warning, Sean. No more digs. No more disrespect."

"Or what?" Sean leans in. His massive forearm is braced across the pommel of his saddle.

Chyr lifts his hand, palm out, and a blast of air knocks Sean from the saddle.

Sean lands hard, and Chyr is on him before he can stand, driving a bruising punch to Sean's throat. Sean falls back, gasping for breath, eyes wide.

Silence thickens like a mist. The burn chatters over stone, and the wind stirs the rushes and willow leaves.

Chyr straightens and looks down at Sean with terrifying calm. "This past year—especially the past two weeks—has reopened old wounds for you. And I'm sorry to see you in so much pain. But you need to set that aside. You're too good a Rider—too good a man—to let what happened almost two millennia ago cloud your judgement."

"You want me to 'set it aside'? How the *fuck* do I do that? Why would I want to?" Sean kicks to his feet in one fluid motion.

Chyr doesn't give an inch. He presses a finger into Sean's chest. "Why should you *want to*? Because you have a job, Sean. You took oaths, and being a Rider is about justice—not revenge. Have you lost sight of the difference between enemies and friends?"

Sean points at me. "That woman is not your friend. She's your destruction. And if you don't see that by now, then she'll destroy the rest of us along with you."

It's too much emotion, too much anger, and I can't bear to listen to any more. I strip off Eira's saddle and exchange her bridle for a halter and rope, then walk her around the back of the fallen tree behind the screen of clustered, thin-trunked hazel trees furred in moss and lichen.

It's almost a taunt from the gods that we're in a hazel wood. Hazel is the tree of knowledge, and eating hazelnuts is said to grant wisdom. The Mother only knows I could use a bit of that. All of us could.

I don't know how Chyr keeps his calm—because what he did with Sean just now, and what he did back in the cavern with Daire and Lorcan, *is* a form of calm. He saw his men coming apart and reeled them back in with the blend of violence and kindness that they needed in that moment.

"Are you all right?" Ronan's voice startles me, and I find he has moved up beside me so quietly I didn't notice.

"Compared to what?" I ask.

He grins. "Fair. But Sean is—" He sighs, and I suspect that's because Sean has already shown me who he is. "The Riders can overwhelm me sometimes, and I go off on my own somewhere quiet. To the woods more often than not. This is a good place to get away, if that's what you need. But I'd like to come with you—for protection, nothing else. You can pretend I'm not here."

My smile is reluctant, which has nothing to do with him. "I don't mind your company, Ronan."

"You don't?" His eyes light up. "I'm not usually good with people."

On impulse, I stand on my toes and kiss his cheek. "Rua likes you. Animals have better taste than people do."

Ronan tips his head. His grin widens, and walking there in the hazel wood, I realise that both his eyes and his hair are the colour of hazelnut shells.

Having confirmed that there is enough space to spread the horses out behind the screen of hazel trees, I turn back towards the burn to let Eira drink while I collect bent-grass for fodder.

"What happened to Sean's sisters?" I ask.

Ronan's footsteps falter as he paces along beside me. "I'm not good at those sorts of stories," he says. "Anyway, it would give you nightmares."

I have enough images in my head already without adding more, so I don't press him. I tie Eira where she can reach the water, and Ronan and I harvest armloads of the thick, tufted grass that grows beside the burn. He helps me carry it back to the sheltered area behind the hazel. When I return to take Bramble down to the burn, I find that Chyr and the others have tented blankets over the oak trunk and a frame of woven hazel stems. Crushed bracken fronds soften the ground near the upended root plate, and another plaid is laid on top of that.

"That's for you," Niall says, running a hand gruffly through his pale, close-shorn hair and looking down at the plaid as though he's embarrassed to look at me. "There's room for two more there, so you can choose who'll make you least uncomfortable."

"I've spent the most time with Chyr and Ronan," I say, weighing my words carefully. "But I'm not the only one who's uncomfortable. I'll take two more horses down to drink and leave it for you to decide among yourselves."

"Is Ronan going with you?" Chyr asks, glancing from me to Ronan and back again.

"I can," Ronan says. "But I should hunt."

The two of them exchange a glance, then Ronan peels away to pick up his bow and quiver, and Chyr takes two of the Riders' horses while I lead Bramble and another mare. Eira nickers as she hears us coming, and we quickly rub the horses down while they drink, then gather more grass for forage.

Chyr slides worried glances my way when he thinks that I'm not looking, but he doesn't push me to talk. I'm grateful to him for that.

It isn't until after we've taken care of the horses and left them all tied with plenty to eat that he catches my elbow and turns me to face him. A muscle tics in his jaw, but his honeyed eyes soften as he searches my face.

"You're worried," he says. "More than yesterday. If it's about Sean, I promise he won't hurt you."

"It's not that," I say, though that's part of it. "We're even more behind, and it's my fault. It will take time to find enough boats to carry us and the horses, and half of Vheara's armada lies between us and Muilean. And if we can't bring the horses over, there's no chance that we'll be able to cross to the sacred place on time. And where would we leave the horses so that they'll be safe? I can't lose Bramble and Eira, too."

"Flora." Chyr bends his knees so that our eyes are level, and I'm forced to look at him. "I understand that you don't want to think about the Crown of Moonlight, but this is life or death. You have to be prepared to choose a Rider."

"Do you think I don't know that?" I hate that my voice cracks and comes out too small, too soft.

Chyr presses on as if he has to get the words out. "Ronan is a safe choice. He'd be good to you. Both Niall and Fergal would be as well. Cathal less so, but more from neglect than any intent to harm you."

The way he watches me breaks my heart. I can feel all the things that I want to say to him pressed into a hard lump in my chest.

What would he say to me if his oaths would let him?

He lets his head tip forward to rest his forehead against mine, and he clasps my hand and places it against his heart.

"You have to pick someone, Flora."

"If I can't choose you, how can I?"

CHAPTER 37
OUTRUN THE BEACONS

FLORA

S leep is elusive. The presence of the Riders charges the air, and I miss the comforting sound of Chyr's heartbeat against my ear and the warmth of his arms around me. Yesterday, sleeping across the cavern from him and the others was easier. Here, he is close enough for me to sense him a couple of feet behind me. Close enough to feel his absence.

I'm relieved when Niall wakes him for his turn at watch. Chyr pauses to look at me before he leaves, as if he knows that I'm awake. But instead of speaking to me, he whispers, "Watch her," to Ronan and snakes through the narrow opening of the shelter.

I wait until he's gone, half-afraid Ronan will shift closer and take Chyr's empty spot. When he doesn't, I whisper without turning, "Is there so much danger you need to watch me?"

"No—yes. I don't know," Ronan whispers back. "We don't know. Chyr's right, though. You need to be careful."

"Does it bother you not to trust your brothers?" I ask. "I imagine trust is the most important thing between you."

Ronan is silent for so long, I'm convinced he's going to ignore me. "They could just as well wonder why they can't trust us."

"I don't want to come between you."

"You haven't. None of us is responsible for the roles we're born to. Now try to get some rest."

Despite my arguments to the contrary, we start saddling the horses as soon as the sun is gone. The ride to Castle Tchirum is three to four hours at most—along Loch Seil to its end, then following the river overland to Loch Moadar, the large sea inlet that surrounds the island castle and flows to the Sea of Islands.

There's no sense in hurrying. I will need time to hire the boats once we get there, and I can't do that before dawn. Or with a slew of impatient Riders at my back.

"What's the point of waiting to speak to anyone?" Cathal asks. "It's far too risky, and we can simply take the boats. We'll need every moment we can scrape together to cross Muilean and reach the doorway on time. If you're squeamish about it, we can leave a bit of gold for whoever owns the boats. But we don't want anyone coming with us."

"We'll need at least one pilot who knows the coast, tides, and shoals," I say, biting off a sigh.

Cathal draws himself up, his expression smug. "We all know how to sail. It isn't difficult."

"Is that so?" I place the saddle on Eira's back and make sure it's set smooth so it doesn't pinch. "Can you navigate out of

Loch Moadar in the dark, in swells that will lift us sideways? Can you time the ebb beyond the point, read the riptides, and navigate the shallows close to shore to avoid Vheara's patrols? Do you know the hidden landings on Muilean?"

"Why not cross directly over the Sound? It's shorter," Chyr says.

"Vheara would be stupid not to have ships waiting at both ends, ready to pounce on any vessel they spot. Even if they're not looking for you, there will be others trying to get to Eireen to escape the queen's reprisals."

Chyr can't be surprised by what I'm saying, but he isn't asking for himself. He's giving me the chance to explain my logic to the others. They don't know me, and I haven't earned their trust.

No one argues, though they don't look convinced. I'm not sure they understand how hard the crossing will be at night.

We start the ride towards Castle Tchirum in wary silence, weaving carefully through the willow scrub to circle around a camp of soldiers not far beyond our own. Two other camps slow us as the salt tang of the sea begins to replace the wet pine and peat of the wood and the river. The moon is still high when grit and damp sand begin to whisper underfoot, muffling the dull thud of the horses' hooves. Shade and Shadow leave footprints like wisps of mist that vanish almost as soon as they pass.

At our backs, a cold wind blows down the river, carrying smoke from the watchfires that glow orange in the distance. Ahead of us, kelp drifts tangle along the flats that line the great sea loch of Moadar that empties into the Sea of Islands, and the ruined walls of the old Domhnall castle rise from the small island at the centre of the loch like a broken fist.

I don't sense anyone inside, which means I was right to hope Castle Tchirum would be a safe place for us to shelter. But as I look at the ruins now, they're a reminder of how long our clan has been fighting against the Everfolk, struggling to save what should be ours by right. Four centuries ago, my people destroyed the greatest Domhnall stronghold before it could fall to the Sun King to be used against us.

Yet memory is fickle. I remember playing among the castle ruins with my brothers when we were children. I've never forgotten how Dughall of Ceapaich damn near drowned me here in the salty water while my younger brothers watched and laughed. Rory, my older brother, rescued me from Dughall and lifted me to his shoulders as he splashed along the causeway back to the mainland.

What I've failed to recall until this moment is that the causeway is submerged except when the tide is low, which, by the look of it, won't be for several hours.

Dark tongues of current slither over the wet sand ribbon that's barely visible beneath the water. A curlew gives its lonely, fluting call as I rein Eira in and stand to watch the tide.

My fingers clench on the reins, and my cheeks flare hot as I feel the Riders looking at me.

"Brilliant," Lorcan says, reining his horse hard enough that the red gelding throws his head up. "Shall we set a watchfire of our own here on the beach? Maybe put up a war banner, too. Just in case we're not visible enough as we twiddle our thumbs and wait to cross."

Sean, who has been glaring at my back for the second straight night, snorts at that. "I told you the woman was trying to kill us, didn't I?"

"Daire can make sure we won't be seen," Chyr says, sending a scathing look at both Sean and Lorcan.

Fortunately, that shuts them both up.

Chyr shifts his attention to me, his eyes softening. "How deep is the water, Flora? Can your magic do anything?"

"Can I split and hold back the tide?" I gape at him, thinking he's lost his mind.

"Can't you?" He raises his brows and gives me that slightly crooked smile I've come to know. Then he shakes his head. "You wouldn't need to do it alone. Sean is skilled with windshear and vortices. My own air magic is better with cords and short bursts—and Niall's is more about precision than force. Daire and Lorcan have water magic. And all of us can lend you strength."

"Nothing that can hold back the ocean," Daire says. "And why would we trust her magic?"

"I'll settle for someone holding back your mouth long enough for Flora to concentrate," Ronan says, and Rua gives a big yawn where she's curled across his shoulders.

"Father of Curses," Sean growls. "Do you all hear yourselves? We're not here to save this woman from her own stupidity." He jabs a finger in Chyr's direction and sweeps a look around at each of the other Riders. "We don't know what will be waiting for us before we reach the doorway. Not to mention what is waiting for us in Tirnaeve. We can't afford to waste any magic. Not on her."

"I'm sorry." Heat floods my cheeks, and my breath comes too fast and shallow to fill my lungs with air.

Fergal stares at me, sets his jaw, and kicks his horse forward, sending it splashing out onto the causeway.

"Fergal, stop," Chyr orders.

Before Fergal can rein in, though, a wave washes his mare off her feet.

She tries to swim, nose high, and her eyes are panicked as the tide sweeps her farther from the causeway. Fergal dives from the saddle and paddles towards her head, but he's not a strong swimmer either. Another wave pulls him under.

I don't stop to consider whether holding the sea is

possible—I focus on what's least impossible. Instead of trying to force the water back, I steal the motion from it, stilling a section before it reaches the causeway above Fergal and his horse. It only holds a few moments before it breaks, but I try it again, and it feels firmer, as though my grip on it is stronger.

Between the causeway and Fergal and the mare, the level drops, and the rush of current slows. Water streams around the barrier, doing its best to fill the empty space, but both the Ever and the horse find their feet. Fergal crouches on the sand, a few inches of water still eddying around him.

Racking coughs shake his body. Then he shakes himself and reaches the trembling mare. He pats her on the neck, pulls himself into the saddle, and rides her back in the direction of the causeway.

And now that I'm holding the water, I can't help thinking about it.

Holy Goddess—I am holding back the tide.

The reflection of the pale moon ripples on the water, nearly full, and the air is heavy with magic and brine and smoke. I shiver, and cold sweat beads across my skin. I can practically feel Sean's gaze boring into my back, sharp as an executioner's axe.

The magic doesn't feel wrong. It doesn't feel forced, not in the way that magic used to be painful. It's as though I'm asking and it answers.

I don't know how much I have inside me, or how much I am spending. Whether I'll have enough to get everyone to the other side. All I can do is test it.

"Stay here," I say.

Kicking Eira into a run, I charge out onto the causeway, pushing the barrier forward as I ride.

"Go! Everyone!" Chyr orders behind me. "Now!"

Water splashes as the Riders send their horses forward at

once, a trained unit charging. That's not what I wanted, and my hands tremble.

Instead of the narrow space needed to calm the water for a single horse, now I have to hold back enough water for all of them.

My jaw sets so hard it aches. Fear bangs against my ribs with every heartbeat, as loud in my ears as the thunder of the horses and the crash of the sea. Fergal leans forward in the saddle and jumps the mare back up onto the causeway, reining her around beside me, and we run until we reach the other side. We come off the causeway wet to the knees, the castle a black hulk against the sky.

The heavy weight in my chest eases once we're all on firm ground again. Then I notice the dark look Sean gives Chyr, the look he throws around at the other Riders. The fear in his eyes when he stops his gelding as far from me as he can.

Illicit magic—I can almost hear his words hanging in the air.

I know they aren't true. Nothing about my magic feels wrong or tainted.

But Sean wants to take the easier path. For the Riders, killing me would be safer than waiting to see what I might do to hurt them. Just as Catriona believed it would be safer to let Chyr die.

I told Catriona that we were better than the Evers. Sean and Lorcan are the worst of what I feared.

And the way Cathal is studying me from the back of his horse, I'm not sure I'm a person to him at all. He watches me more as if he sees my magic as something he covets, something he'd like to have for himself.

Kelp stinks on the stone beach around the ruins of Castle Tchirum, and the wind off the sea loch carries salt and cold and the chalky taste of old ash coming back to earth. I look back for Shade and Shadow, needing the reassurance of their presence. Catching sight of them always makes me miss Rab, and I wonder how he and those back at Dunhaelic are doing. More than anything, I wish that I could be home with them instead of here.

The seaward arch of the castle stands open, the door long gone. We dismount and file through into a weed-choked courtyard where moss and damp creep up the walls. The roofless inner structure has a tangle of grass and stinging nettles growing around the edges. They'll be itchy to sleep on but food for the horses if we cut them, bruise them, and let the sting leach out of them for an hour.

Cathal, Sean, and Lorcan stride off to inspect the inner ward and climb to the highest structurally sound corner, though I'm not sure what they hope to see. Ronan checks the stone-curbed well in the floor of the keep, which still contains a derelict bucket.

The well is choked with reeds, and the bucket leaks as he dips it down and brings it back up, but there's at least some liquid left. He takes the bucket out of the castle to scrub it out with sand, then searches for a trough to fill so the horses can drink.

Ronan brought down a roe deer in the willow wood last night, and we eat the remnants of that along with the last of the cheese and oatcakes Chyr and I bought from Mairi back in the hamlet near Glen Fhionain. I leave the Riders huddled around a fire that someone has masked with an illusion to suppress the smoke and glow, but I will need to be up again before dawn to find a boat.

The Shadehounds and I find a place to lay my plaids

wedged between fallen stones in the innermost portion of the ruined hall, out of the way of wind and sea spray. Shadow belly crawls closer until she's pressed right against my side, her nose resting on my knee. Shade places himself like a guard at my feet.

I don't need to hear Shade's low growl a short while later to know that Fergal has come to stand nearby, but for such a boulder of bone and muscle, Fergal moves with surprising stealth.

"Can I join you?" he asks.

"Why?" I sit back up and draw the plaid I was using as a blanket around my shoulders. Shade and Shadow sit up, too, watching Fergal with wary caution.

"I wanted to thank you for what you did," Fergal says. "With the water."

I shrug that aside. "I meant, why did you ride out on the causeway?"

"The others were talking in circles, and you seemed upset. I didn't think the water was deep enough to be a problem."

"It's not the depth—that's what I was trying to explain when I said we'll need someone on the boats with us who understands the currents. But thank you, Fergal. It was kind."

I sense him blushing more than I can see it in the dark.

"Sean's feelings against humans," Fergal says, "I'm not excusing him, but there's a reason behind it. His mother liked to visit here long ago—before the Compact. She was here with his twin sisters when the human reprisals started after Vheara was exiled. Sean's mother escaped, but his sisters didn't."

"More of us died than Evers—"

"His sisters' heads were placed on spikes in the village square. Someone Sean knew recognised them weeks later. That's how he found out. Seeing what the Butcher and others have done here—even some of Chyr's supporters—it's brought all the emotion back to the surface for Sean. Not only the anger, but the grief, too. The pain."

Tears spill over before I'm even aware they're coming, before I can think to hold them back. A cold wash of grief and rage settles over my heart as I think of my own mother and what the Grey did to her.

Terrible things have been done on both sides—and they're happening again. While that helps me understand Sean's behaviour, I can't excuse it.

My tears keep falling, for my family, for him, for all of us. For so many wasted lives and so much potential wiped away. For all the people left behind.

"How old were the girls?" I ask.

Fergal sits down beside me, and Shade and Shadow happily trot away as if they've decided they don't need to stay with me now that he is here.

"Siorai age faster until we're in our thirties," Fergal says, "though that's still not nearly as fast as humans. Sean's sisters had lived for twelve years, but in human terms they looked like they were only five. He loved them fiercely. All children are a miracle for us, but twins especially. They're so rare that they're revered."

"Did you know Sean back then?"

"I did. He wasn't always such a broody bastard."

"I'll have to take your word for that, and the information doesn't change anything. I'm not going to let Sean kill me because I feel bad over something that happened nearly two millennia ago. I'm never going to be easy to kill."

Fergal laughs, a deep rumble that bursts from his chest, and the sound makes me look at him more carefully. He's massive, though I'll never make the mistake of assuming that makes him less intelligent than the others. But neither is he any sort of a gentle giant. His hair is a dark auburn that curls around his face, and his eyes are a calm, blue-grey. There's a dimple in his chin that looks like a child dented it with a finger.

"There's nothing easy about you," Fergal says. "That's not a bad thing. The gods don't hand out crowns for *easy*. They give them to people who challenge the sun and the moon and make the universe pay attention."

Leaning closer, he picks up my hand and brings the back of it to his lips. Then he's gone without another word, a boulder who moves like a wraith.

Stunned and with no idea whether I should trust him, I sit with my arms wrapped around my knees for a while once he's gone.

The conversation has made me restless. Winding the plaid tighter around my shoulders, I cross to an empty window in the wall that overlooks the sea, and stand staring out at the moonlight drifting across the water.

The Riders are scattered in various places around the castle. I feel them like different points of light, and I recognise Chyr's as it moves towards me. It seems brighter than the others, warmer. I wonder whether that's because I know him better, or whether that's somehow a reflection of who he is.

The salt wind lifts strands of his pale hair, and his eyes look less gold in the moonlight. "I'll sleep with the Riders and keep them away from you if you want. Unless you'd feel safer if I'm with you?"

My heart gives an unwelcome thud. "What would the others think of that?"

"I've threatened to kill more than one of them if they hurt you. I doubt they'd be surprised."

"So you don't threaten them over a girl every other day of the week?"

"No." He smiles ruefully. "Not as a general rule."

I'm silent for a moment, then I say, "Fergal told me

something about how Siorai children age. When you joined the Anvar'thaine—when your uncle made you take those vows—how old would you have been in human years?"

"It's not quite as simple as that."

"Make it simple."

"I don't know. Thirteen? Fourteen? But don't make excuses for me."

"If I didn't already see you, that answer would show me who you are. Bad people don't go out of their way to seek out blame."

"Royalty is royal from birth. We don't get the indulgence of growing up soft and waiting to take on responsibilities. How old were you when you started helping to manage Dunhaelic?"

"That was my choice, and I'm not royal."

"You're wearing a crown. Two of them."

"I was twelve."

"You see?" Chyr's voice is that deep, dangerous tone that curls around my spine, and he smiles and reaches down to brush a thumb across my cheek.

The truth is, I find everything about Chyr dangerously attractive. I'd like nothing more than to have a year to figure out all the ways he sets me on fire.

Something in the air shifts between us, and I take a steadying breath.

"I have to do the honourable thing," Chyr says. "Make it easy for you to choose one of the others. That may kill me, but if it means you survive, I'll do it. I'll do whatever it takes." He turns me to face him, his hands splaying at my waist as he holds me tight. "Trust me, Fierceness. We'll find a way through this. I have you."

CHAPTER 38
GREYS IN THE MIST

FLORA

Fog blankets the sea as dawn approaches, but the tide is at its lowest. I wrap a light scarf low across my forehead under my heavy plaid to keep the Crown of Flame well hidden. Chyr has cloaked himself in the mask of an old man again, but this time, he's traded his sword for Ronan's so that it can't give him away.

We saddle the horses while the Riders lean against the wall nearby, and Chyr gives me that rare grin that makes his eyes shine. Even through the disguise, it makes my heart skip a beat.

"Almost there," he says. "The end's in sight. One way or another."

"Don't invite more trouble. It dogs our heels close enough already."

He gives me a look that's pure Chyr, and it's so strange to see it on an old man's face. But it makes me realise that Chyr is Chyr no matter what he looks like. That terrible beauty isn't what matters. That's not what makes me want what I can't have.

My heart kicks in my chest, a rhythm that's as wild as the crash of the waves against the rocks. We lead the horses towards the ruined gate of Castle Tchirum with the Riders trailing behind us.

Chyr bends close to my good ear. "You don't mind trouble as much as you pretend," he says. "Admit it."

I'm not sure he's wrong, but time is moving too fast. I want to make the most of what we have left together—even if it's only a quick ride to find a boat or two and men to guide us.

The Riders follow us to the shore, and as we stop at the gate, Sean can't resist sending me a filthy look before he turns to Chyr.

"Let someone else play nursemaid," he says. "Or let her go alone. It's stupid to risk yourself, Chyr."

"Flora needs someone along to send back a message after she finds a boatmaster. And I'm familiar with what to expect from Domhnall clansmen."

"You're the bloody king, not a messenger." Sean's brown eyes are icy in a way I never thought that colour could be.

"Chyr once told me that's exactly what you have all become—the High King's messengers and errand boys," I say quite calmly. "I know Lorcan would kill me to protect Chyr, and the others will do whatever's needed to keep their oaths to the Compact. But where are your loyalties, Sean? Why do you read things into the Compact that the others don't?"

Seizing the opportunity, I turn to Cathal. "What exactly does the Compact say about illicit magic?"

Cathal's grey-blue eyes narrow, and his cheeks pinch as he inhales. But he touches a finger to one of the dozen runes along the shaved line of scalp above his left ear, and it flares gold.

"It isn't much," he says. "'*None shall work compulsion, mind-bending, illusion, or other magic to affect the Peace of the Realm or alter the minds of mortals in Alba Scoria, except in the Realm's defence. Whosoever takes up illicit magic that imperils the Peace shall be subject to the justice of the Cailleach Queen, or failing that, the justice of the Anvar'thaine.'"*

"That's the only reference?" I ask.

Cathal shoots an apologetic glance at Sean. "No other explicit reference."

"Prohibiting illicit magic was the *intent* behind the Compact," Sean says.

"Was it?" I lift my chin, meeting his glower. "Because from my family's perspective—and to be clear, that would be the Cailleach Queen mentioned in the Compact—the *intent* was to keep Siorai from continuing to abuse humans. Are you saying the High King's intent was something else?"

Sean steps closer, his shoulders thrust forward until he's looming over me. "I'm saying you are subject to the justice of the Anvar'thaine."

"And I'm saying—for the feeble-brained among us—that what Cathal just quoted makes defence of the realm an exception. Or how else do you justify using your illusions and runes? Also, the queen's justice takes precedence over the Anvar'thaine. You, Sean, are not the queen. You are not the whole Anvar'thaine, and you are not its Master. You don't get to invent jurisdiction and carry out judgement in a single breath."

I mount Eira before he can answer, and I ride towards the causeway at a canter with Shade and Shadow at my heels.

The wind sweeps in, raising the swells in Loch Moadar and

flinging seawater in our faces as we gallop across the wet spine of the causeway from the castle ruins. Back on the mainland track, we keep to the left-hand verge, moving south. Peat fires mingle with the distant smoke from enemy camps and the smell of kelp and brine.

The nearby fishing village is little more than a smudge in the fog at first, a crescent of turf-thatched cottages, net sheds, and the frames used for drying fish set along the remnants of the river where it flows into the sea. I notice nothing amiss at first—I'm still too angry, too rattled. Chyr spots the problem at the same time I do, too much movement at the shore for the early hour. He holds up his fist, signalling for me to stop.

We rein the horses in, dismount, and walk them towards the cover of a scrub of willow and alder on the north side of the river that separates us from the village. Chyr's face takes on the stillness and concentration that tells me he's building an illusion to keep us from being seen.

After leaving the horses tied out of sight, we approach the village, hugging the riverbank that offers the only cover.

The fog and the sea drown out the screams at first. But we hear them as we draw closer, shouts and cries, the sound of mallets pounding, children and women wailing. The shore is a blur of scarlet coats and the plaid uniforms of the Cymbeul militia, dotted among the smaller figures in white shifts and nightclothes with unbound hair flying in the wind. The soldiers whip women and children in front of them, forcing them into the surf, bare feet slipping, skirts dragging through the brine, hands bound in front of them.

At first, the double line of wooden posts pounded into the surf almost resembles an odd sort of fish trap. My mind's eye can almost see nets strung between them.

But that's only my brain refusing to process the horror.

A scream rises in my throat. Chyr pulls me against him, his hand across my lips.

The queen's men shove *children* against the first row of stakes. The smallest of them is a blonde girl, her chest deep in the water with spray lashing against her face. The women kick and thrash. A soldier cuffs one across the face, then lifts his dagger.

Another scream builds, and Chyr tries to turn me into his chest, holding me tighter.

My limbs have gone numb, my heart pounding so hard it feels like my ribs are rattling. But I make myself watch, trying to think of a plan.

Instead of stabbing the woman, the soldier splits the front of her shift to her waist and drags it off her shoulders. Then he ties her, nearly naked, to a stake in the back row positioned deep enough that she will drown as the tide comes in, but not so deep that it will happen quickly.

It's only then that I spot the two Greys on the beach. They're the ones for whom this whole horror is being staged, and they aren't watching the women and children at all.

The men of the village—husbands and fathers—are staked out along the beach facing their wives and children. Gagged and bound, they will be helpless as the tide comes in, as the women they love are forced to watch their children slowly drown before being drowned themselves.

Already the Greys pace along the line of men, drinking in their anguish, their terror, their rage.

Power gathers in cords that crackle along my skin. This close to our goal, the stakes are so high that we can't call attention to ourselves. But I can't watch women and children being slaughtered.

I twist out of Chyr's grasp, earth and air and water pulsing with my fury, wind whipping, the sky darkening.

Dragging the water back from where the women and children are tied, I raise it into a wall six feet high, stealing its momentum and pinning it still. In front of the stakes, the tide drops below the children's knees, and the surface smooths to glass. Then I swing my arm wide and turn the wall into a weapon, curving it around the women and children and knifing it along the beach towards the two Greys, who are too intent on gorging themselves on the men's agony to see what's coming for them.

The soldiers see it. They shout, then scream as they try to run.

I push the water between the Greys and the stakes where the men are tied. But someone is moving between me and the water—Chyr. Sword raised, he's running towards the stakes, and I try to calculate whether he's too close.

My concentration breaks. The wall of water starts to collapse, froth churning as it breaks into an enormous wave.

Fear freezes me in place. Water rushes towards the stakes where the men are tied.

Then Chyr sends a blast of air to crash against the churn. Spray and foam shoot skyward, and he holds the water back.

Shaking myself, I reach for the water again—gather it, pull it vertical, rebuild it. I loop the wall back around the two Greys and as many of the soldiers as I can capture. Then I close my trembling fist, and the water mirrors the motion. The water squeezes until the mass and pressure and the force of my horror and fury crush—until the Greys are broken. Then I snap the water back out to sea like a whip cracking. The ocean boils and froths, crimson uniforms and cloaks tumbling in streaks like blood through the wake.

I feel the mortal lives snuff out. Maybe like Daire suggested, they're the enemy and I shouldn't care. But it's not enough to be better than someone else. We have to be better than ourselves.

Each of those soldiers chose obedience over death. They chose the wrong side, not caring what happened to others. But I've taken away the option for them to ever make better choices.

The sky gutters darker. The wind beats against the shore.

Cries rend the air as Chyr sends ropes of air to capture the remaining soldiers and Cymbeul militiamen who have tried to run away. The Shadehounds have revealed themselves, snarling and snapping at the heels of the escaping men. Half the soldiers run, but the rest are too terrified and fall to their knees with their hands covering their heads.

I leave Chyr to finish them and run forward instead, drawing my dagger to saw through the ropes that hold the villagers still lashed to the stakes. I free the children first. Hemp rope bites deep around tiny wrists. The shocked, still eyes of the little ones have my stomach roiling and my chest aching with pain and fury. By the fourth set of wrists, my palms are slick with the blood of innocents. Sound comes back far away, as if I'm underwater. Time narrows to the scrape of my blade on rope and the taste of salt. When the last knot gives way, my hands won't stop shaking.

The beach is calmer. Women have pulled up their soaked, tattered dresses and carry the smallest children towards the shore, older children helping younger ones. I stand a moment, tears pouring down my cheeks, my breath coming in great, dry gasps.

Then I realise no one is moving. I turn, and the women are kneeling in the sand and nudging the children to do the same.

I blink, wiping my eyes, and stare back at them blankly.

Chyr steps up beside me, looking like himself again because he can't keep up illusions while using his active magic. My mouth opens to ask a question, but he runs his thumb gently across my forehead.

My scarf has blown back, and the Crown of Flame is no longer covered.

It's too late to hide it—and I'll never be able to take this moment back.

This is the first time I've come face to face with what the crown still means, not to the Evers, not to me, but to *us*. To the Domhnall. To mortals, to Alba Scoria. And the weight of that burden threatens to drag me to my knees.

"Please get up," I manage to say, gentler than I feel. "Help your little ones, and untie your men."

The women stare at me, then my words seem to fall in place for them. They climb to their feet while I stand and try to keep myself from trembling.

Then I turn and follow the women who have moved towards the line of stakes where the men are tied. Chyr comes with me, and we shift from one stake to another, our daggers sawing through the ropes that bind the men's hands and feet and the rags that were meant to hold back their screams as their families drowned. Every snap of rope, each gasp of release, feels too small and comes too late.

CHAPTER 39
FOUR BLACK PILLARS

FLORA

The sea is calm now, but it won't stay that way. The Greys aren't dead. I crushed them, drowned them, but their heads and hearts remain intact. Sooner or later, they will rise from the sea and resume their torture.

I stand alone at the shore watching for them, with Shade and Shadow pressed against my legs. Once I'm gone, the village will need to keep a lookout along the waterline. I will give them the sword of celestial steel I took from the Grey by the camp. I only wish I'd thought to collect the weapons sooner.

I've made too many mistakes. Not merely the things I've forgotten to do, but what I've done—and nearly done.

If it hadn't been for Chyr's magic, the wall of water I summoned would have hit the men the Greys had staked along the shore. I could have killed them because I lost control.

Sean keeps calling my magic illicit. What he means is *dangerous.*

I am dangerous.

The one saving grace is that the other Riders weren't here to see it. Chyr has returned to the castle to get them now that several of the village men have agreed to take us to Muilean, but the truth is, maybe it isn't the Riders I should fear.

My hands are shaking. I curl them into fists, but I can still feel the power coursing beneath my skin and humming in the air around me. Waiting. Wanting.

That magic kept Chyr from dying. And it nearly killed the men I was trying to save.

What if I can't control it?

I've been preparing for the Riders to try to kill me, preparing to die for refusing to accept the final crown. More than any of that, what frightens me is the knowledge that I've no idea what I'm becoming. And whatever that is, I don't want it. The magic begs me to use it, but it's wild. It isn't meant to be controlled.

Siorai magic has rules and limits. The magic of earth and wind and sun and rain is nearly limitless, and I have to be strong enough—and smart enough—to set my own boundaries. In that, it's more like Vheara's magic. There will always be a temptation to reach for more.

No one should be trusted with so much power. It's too easy to find an excuse for giving in to what we want, a reason for claiming more than we deserve.

Behind me, the village is quiet as the women try to comfort the children and the men go to gather the boats and supplies they'll need to take us to Muilean as they've agreed to do.

Salt spray hits my face, and wind billows my skirt. Out on the Sea of Islands, Vheara's patrols are already at work, grey-sheeted silhouettes in the shredding fog. A single-masted cutter, low and fast with sharp triangular sails, dips and rises, vanishing and reappearing behind the waves. Farther west, a deeper-hulled sloop beats the outer edge of the channel, hunting any boats that dare a run towards Eireen. More silhouettes haunt the fog, too distant to see clearly.

There's no sense waiting for night to fall. With the two Greys unaccounted for, the queen's forces could return to the village at any time.

That's what troubles me most. What will happen when the redcoats and more Greys come? How can the village defend itself?

An old woman wrapped in a black shawl approaches me cautiously. "Can I speak with you, my lady?"

Something about her tugs at my memory, and I wonder if I've met her before when we stayed with the Domhnall of Raghnall. Her face is as wrinkled as a winter apple, her dark eyes hooded with age but still quick and bright. They linger on the crown across my forehead.

"Is it the Bonnie King you've chosen to take as consort?" she asks.

Her bluntness startles me. "You recognised him?"

"My husband and a few others did," the woman says, giving me a one-shouldered shrug. "Not all of the men who met in Glen Fhionain could go to fight, but they thought he seemed a good man. As far as Everfolk go. And we've suffered from the Cymbeul militia worse than ever since they allied with the Raven Queen. Your father..."

My eyes well up, and I blink back the tears. "My father didn't mean to ignore your people, I'm certain. He didn't see the Raven Queen for what she was, and he didn't think it likely that the king would win."

"Did he know that you had magic when he did that?" the old woman asks. "That you might be the Maiden?"

"How could any of us have suspected that when the old ways were as good as dead? And no, to answer your other question, I can't choose him."

"Good." The woman's face lightens, and she makes the sign of the horns, as though pushing evil back. "I don't mean to tell you your business, it's only…"

"Only what?"

"I'm afflicted with the Sight. Now and again. I saw your death when the Bonnie King touched your crown. Both of you will die."

My heart jolts, and my hand presses to my chest. But I can't make decisions based on fear.

"What did you see exactly?" I force myself to ask.

"Blood pooling in two shallow bowls carved into a heavy, moon-grey altar on four black pillars." The old woman ducks her head, looking down at the sand instead of directly at me. "You and the king lying dead on the ground in front of it, looking no different than you look now, same dress, same plaid. But there's a wound in your chest, blood soaking into your clothes all around it. I didn't see a reason for the king's death. No blood. No wound. But he didn't move, and he didn't breathe."

The oaths. I hug my arms around my waist, burrowing deeper into my plaid. "Are your visions final, or can they still be changed?"

"The Sight is fickle. It shows what it wants me to see and no more. And the visions never come a second time." She presses her lips together, then glances down at her muddy shoes before looking up again. "The future can be as hard as stone, but find a crack and you can break it."

The thud of hooves on wet sand makes me turn. Chyr and the Riders approach at a canter.

I've ridden with them, but I haven't seen them like this— the full might of the Anvar'thaine riding. Everyone else must feel it, too. The importance of it. Children stream from the cottages in the village, running towards the beach for a glimpse. The men and women walk more slowly, but they also stream to the shore.

Shivering, I turn back to the old woman. "Thank you for letting me know."

She catches my hand and holds it between hers in a grip that's surprisingly strong. "You won't discount the warning, will you? Seeing the Maiden walk among us, what you did for us—you give us all hope. That's what we need."

Hope is a cruel illusion. It lets you put off decisions, deluding yourself that solutions exist even when they don't.

"I won't discount your vision," I say, "but we can't rely on gods and prophecies. The Greys from this morning will be back. And more will come. The village won't be safe for you, so take everyone, retreat into Castle Tchirum, and rebuild the gate. Ultimately, we'll need more celestial steel. Until the Greys and Vheara herself are dead, every small victory will only bring more danger."

CHAPTER 40
CHOOSE YOUR RIDER

The sun drains white behind the clouds as we put out to sea, but the wind blows hard, shredding the concealing mist as fast as Daire and Lorcan create it with their water magic. Aboard the two cattleboats that carry the horses and the Shadehounds, Sean and Niall do their best to still the air and keep the fog thick around us.

We keep the three boats close to shore. Even without her sails, the twelve-oared birlinn that carries the rest of us outpaces the cattleboats that drag lower in the water. The oarsmen raise their oars every fifth stroke to slow us down.

The horses are restless in the pitch and throw of the swelling sea, and Flora stands to the side of the helmsman at the back, her knuckles white on the rail. Whether that's fear or anticipation, I can't tell. Her hair streams like fire and moonlight in the wind—she's never bothered to refasten it—and her shawl has long since been forgotten. Even with the Crown of Flame shining on her brow, she's never looked more lost, and the need to gather her in my arms is almost more than I can bear.

It's impossible to ignore what I feel for her. She sees her fear as weakness when that's what gives her strength. From the moment she found me in the woods, she has shown kindness and compassion to everyone around her except herself. Our journey deprived her of sleep, food, and comfort, and she accepted it all, enduring pain that could make a Rider weep. Her mind is endlessly fascinating, her power makes me hungry, and I could sink myself into her body for an eternity, but it's her heart—that fierce, courageous, impossibly kind heart of hers—that I love the most.

Leaving the remaining Riders to watch for patrols and manage the weather, I thread my way past the rowing benches to join her at the stern.

"What's the matter, Fierceness? You're quiet in a way that's never good."

She flicks a glance at me, her eyes glowing like moonlight in the mist. "I'm trying to work out what you want and how long you've planned it."

I push away a twinge of fear. "We're still trying to reach Muilean. That hasn't changed."

The skin tightens at the corners of her eyes. "Not now. Overall. I understand that you're limited in what you can say—what you can think. Part of me is afraid to articulate my suspicions, even to myself, for fear of causing you pain and triggering some damnable consequence from your oaths. But I can't help feeling you want more than the throne of Alba Scoria. I want to believe your sense of honour is pushing you towards a different solution."

I step up to the railing, my shoulder brushing hers. "A man sailing through fog doesn't always have a plan. That doesn't mean there isn't a destination."

"Is that you agreeing?" Flora tips her head, giving me the solemn, considering look she has when she's thinking deeply. "All right. Tell me this. What will happen to Alba Scoria if you and I both die? What would the High King do?"

The birlinn heaves as a wave hits, sending a plume of spray across the deck. I grasp Flora's shoulders and turn her to face me. "Your death is the last thing I want."

"That doesn't mean it isn't what needs to happen."

It's not the time, but if I don't do it now, there may never be a chance. I bend and claim her mouth with every defiant bit of hope that still clings inside me. Without words, I tell her all the things I hope and want. What her world and mine both need.

Her mouth tastes sweet as she kisses me back. Groaning, I pull her hips tight against me, holding her there even once I lift my head and look into those quicksilver, moonlit eyes. They still hold a few remnants of the deep calm grey that belonged to the Flora she used to be.

"Don't ever give up," I say.

She blinks and shakes her head. "But there's no way out."

"You found an answer to Sean's claim of illicit magic."

"Did I?" She arches an eyebrow at me. "The way I lost control of the water this morning, I'm not sure he was wrong."

A cold lump forms in my chest at the idea that she can doubt herself to that extent. "You lost focus for an instant. Your magic is a gift from forces more powerful than any of us, and it isn't given lightly. The gods know who you are better than you do."

She dips her head, evading the hold I have on her eyes as she tries to escape the truth. "I'd like to believe you're right."

"Then think. What did you do when you needed an argument against Sean?"

She looks back up at me, her focus sharpening. "I asked Cathal for the text of the Compact."

Turning without waiting for me to answer, she staggers forward to where Cathal and Fergal stand watching the sails of a distant cutter. Cathal frowns as she stops beside him.

"Tell me exactly what the Compact says about the final crown," she says.

Cathal's eyes narrow above his high-bridged nose. A vein throbs under the brown skin at his temple.

"Tell her, Cathal." Fergal offers Flora one of his shy smiles of encouragement. He's ready to trust her. He's always been able to see the truth in people more easily than the others can.

Cathal cuts him a glare, but he activates the power rune above his ear that enhances his memory. "There are several."

"Just answer the damn question, you pompous ass," Fergal snaps.

"The first one is this," Cathal says, looking grim. "'*The Maiden must wear three crowns to become the Cailleach Queen: the Land shall crown her in vines if she proves herself worthy; the Father of Light shall crown her in flame if she is true; and if she takes a Rider to hunt beside her and they sacrifice their blood upon the Altar of the Moon, the Great Mother shall crown her in the light of rebirth.'*"

"What if she refuses?" Flora asks.

Cathal sighs. "'*Once marked with the Crescent Moon, the Maiden may refuse the Hunt or fail the test, whereupon the land will release her and choose another. Once she bears the Crown of Vines, she must wear the Crown of Moonlight before the moon sets on the Night of Rebirth. If she fails, her life will expire with the rising of the Sun.'*"

None of this is new, but still the words are a knife twisting in my gut. Flora's eyes catch mine for the briefest of moments then cut away.

"That's a bit harsh, isn't it?" Fergal asks.

Flora's lips twitch into a mirthless smile. "I suspect that's the way your High King wanted it. But one of my less-than-brilliant ancestors fell for it."

"Careful," Cathal says. "That's perilously close to treason."

In the distance, the cutter changes course, coming towards us as it tacks against the wind.

"Cathal, stop stalling," I snap at him. "What else does the document say?"

Flora nods. "What happens if the Rider I choose refuses or fails to make the sacrifice?"

Cathal's eyes simmer with resentment. "Neither of you understands how legal documents work—"

My hand is wrapped around Cathal's throat before he has time to flinch. The pressure is light, barely there, but it's a warning that's long past due.

"Cathal, I have no patience left for games."

"All right, yes," Cathal says, then he rubs his throat and glares at me when I release him. *"'Whosoever among the Riders forsakes the Compact, forswears their Oaths, breaks a Law of Tirnaeve, or refuses a Lawful Order given by the High King, the Assembly, or the Master of the Anvar'thaine, shall be banished to the Gloaming for the duration of their lifetime.'"*

Flora's teeth dig into her lower lip. "What if," she asks, "the oaths conflict?"

The ship heaves and groans as a wave hits us broadside, and an instant later the lookout shouts, "Queen's cutter approaching starboard and sailing fast!"

Cathal spins away, eager to escape.

I stay only long enough to grit out the answer Flora needs. "That's why you have to choose your Rider carefully," I say. "He may not be able to save himself, but he can choose to let you live."

My magic is still low after the air I wielded back at the village this morning, and I need to conserve it if I can. I join Niall and Sean at the bow, where they've been trying to contain the fog despite the ripping wind.

"Has the concealment failed enough for the cutter to have spotted us?" I ask.

Niall peers ahead through the fog, but the white sail of the cutter ghosts through the mist, here one moment and gone so thoroughly the next moment that she seems like a hallucination.

"I can't be sure, Chyr."

No sooner has he said that than the boom of a cannon answers the question for us.

We're approaching the mouth of Loch Moadar where it joins the Sea of Islands. A faint line of waves marks a sandbar or rocky reef, and the channel snakes perilously thin. Even if the cattleboats weren't behind us, there'd be no room for us to swing about, and we've no hope of running past the cutter. She is built for speed and armed for war.

The helmsman fights to hold the tiller against the wind. Old scars stand out white on his knuckles from previous battles where the tiller has fought him back.

"What do you want to do?" Sean asks.

The birlinn is a trader, not a ship of war, but the Domhnall men have grown accustomed to evading Vheara's ships.

"Prepare for battle," I order.

"Aye, Your Highness."

To conserve weight, there's no coxswain aboard, so the helmsman shouts the order himself.

The drum pounds, and the oarsmen stow the oars. Two of them run to brace the mast. Others throw up shields along the gunwales and ready javelins that will have little effect against a ship armed with cannons.

"Sean, Cathal, with me." I run to the back, and Cathal presses a power rune on the dark skin above his ear to let me reach out to Daire. Cathal's runes are not as strong as Daire's, so his range for mind-speak is more limited. I let out a breath when I can hear Daire's voice in my mind.

"You need me up there?" Daire asks.

"There's a cutter closing fast. We'll need both wind and water to push it back."

"And Lorcan?"

"Lorcan, can you hear us?"

There's no answer. Then I feel Daire's rune flare, and Lorcan's voice sounds in my mind. He and Daire have a rapid-fire conversation in our heads to coordinate Lorcan covering both his own position and Daire's on the cattleboats.

Sean creates a bridge of air for Daire to cross over to the birlinn. Sweat beads on Sean's brow, and the precision rune at his temple glows brighter as he strains to hold the air still long enough. The rune makes it easier for him, but I bloody well hope he won't be close to spent by the time he's finished. Precise magic, like a bridge, costs far more to create and hold.

His hands tremble. Air eddies within the bridge's span, starting to bleed off along the edges. He grunts as he tightens it up and anchors it in place.

I set my jaw and watch Daire's every step until he's close enough for me to grasp his arm and heave him up. Wasting no time, he runs forward the moment his feet hit the deck, with the rest of us close behind.

Flora is there already, working. She's forcing waves of

water and wind against the cutter, driving it away from us. Then the cutter's cannons fire again.

The blast steals my hearing. A black hail of grapeshot flies towards us, threatening to shred through sails, mast, and flesh. I rush to Flora, my hands up to deflect the bits of iron, but the birlinn lurches and slides backwards through the water, knocking me off balance.

CHAPTER 41
SAILS IN THE STORM

FLORA

I've heard that the queen's ships fire canvas bags of projectiles from their cannons to shred everyone aboard an open vessel like a Highland galley or our birlinn. Still, weapons like those are so far removed from the way our warriors fight that it takes me too long to process what's hurtling towards us.

I shove harder at the wall of wind and water I've been driving towards the cutter. It's too broad to be of any use against what looks and sounds like a swarm of iron bees. The swarm pierces through it, and the force I've used pushes back against our ship.

The deck bucks beneath my feet. Sean slams back into the mast.

And the swarm is still coming.

Breathing deeply to calm myself, arms shaking with effort, I try to think. Then grapeshot hits a wall of air and falls into the sea in front of us. A ball of fear in my throat leaves a bitter rasp behind as it fades into relief.

Glancing beside me, I find Niall with his hands up, as though he has commanded the shot to stop. He has three power runes along the back of each wrist, and one on each arm is glowing. As soon as things stop flying at us, he catches my eye, grins, and steps closer.

"Can you push against the cutter's hull to turn her to starboard?" he asks. "If we can fill her sails, we can use them to force her onto the rocks." His eyes flick from the sail to the skerries and back, measuring the distance.

I can't speak for fear of losing control, so I nod instead and concentrate on narrowing the wide thrust of water and wind into a narrower fist directed against the cutter's left.

"Good," Niall calls. "Keep going."

It's an odd sensation when his magic brushes against mine—similar to Chyr shoving the water back for me this morning, but different in the way that one batch of ale can vary from another. My ears fill, and the hairs on my arms lift as his power presses in.

He pushes air into the cutter's sail. I shift my focus to aiming the ship at a row of rocks that bare their teeth near the point of the island on our right. The ship starts to turn.

"You two are working well together." Chyr comes up beside us and braces himself against the rail, his right thumb rubbing the pommel of his sword.

"Flora's adapting quickly," Niall says as the cutter—the one we're driving towards the rocks—moves beyond the lee into the churn, where the tide turns on itself and spits spray into the air.

We need to push the cutter a little farther. I can't let up, but the thrust of my magic against the water is creating a backwash that reaches beneath our birlinn. The ship slews sharply, and oars bang the gunwales. A horse screams on the cattleboat behind us.

I struggle to adapt the force I'm using, but unlike Siorai magic that risks running dry, the magic that comes from my Crown of Vines feels like more than I can harness.

The cutter's crew swarms the deck, desperate to pull down the sails that Niall's magic has filled with air. Sheets of canvas plummet from the mast. Then Niall's magic has little to manipulate. But Daire moves behind me and places his hands on my shoulders to help me guide the water along the cutter's beam.

Inch by hard inch, we press the ship to the jagged rocks. Spray stings my cheeks as our birlinn finally slips out from the cover of Loch Moadar into the open sea. Wind whips against us. Daire and I crowd the cutter until she hits with a thunderous bang and the screech of splintering wood.

The cutter shudders, then the whole hull tilts sideways. Men spill from the deck, and the mast snaps with a gunshot crack. The next wave lifts the carcass and drops her again. She grinds harder against the rocks. Bits of railing and jagged sections of beam break off her hull, and she's finished.

I feel it as each life dies, like threads snapping from my heart. How many men are on the cutter? Part of me doesn't want to know, but I can't shed the responsibility. They're dying by my hand. They have families—someone who loves them regardless of the orders they follow.

A few men crawl up the shore and fall, heaving against the sand.

"Boat!" someone cries.

I whip around, tasting blood from where I've bitten into my lip.

All ideas of stealth have vanished now. The crew of our birlinn hoists the sails. Chyr shouts orders to make a run at a sloop-of-war approaching port side. The sloop is larger than the cutter we broke on the rocks, but the birlinn heaves around to pursue. Then someone mutters a curse, and a Cymbeul longboat noses out from a pocket bay on the island. Men in the queen's crimson coats mix among the blue and green Cymbeul plaids, rowing on the open seats.

"I'll take the longboat," Daire says as the sloop fires a broadside at us.

I shake my head. "Let me. You and Niall are more used to working together. You'll defend against the cannons better."

The thirty-foot longboat is low and wide, built for twelve. No sail billows from the narrow mast, nothing to catch any wind that I could send. But here I don't need precision.

I raise a swell of water, pulling it higher and higher. It towers above the longboat, kelp fronds streaming from it like grasping fingers.

A handful of the rowers scream and dive out of the boat, swimming back towards the island even before I let the wave break down onto the longboat's spine.

The longboat is done. It plunges underwater, then shoots back to the surface in three separate pieces. Water plumes back into the air around it, and the churn tumbles men and wood. An oar pops up as if the sea has spit it out.

The sloop-of-war hammers a second round of cannons at us. Chyr and Niall stop the swarm of iron before it hits us, but a few stray bits of grapeshot pierce through. An oarsman grunts as he's hit, and splinters fly from the mast as iron embeds in wood. The rest of the stilled balls hail harmlessly into the froth around us.

I step onto the gunwale between Niall and Daire and wait until the sails of our birlinn carry us past. Then we work together to turn the sloop broadside. We're farther out from shore, but rocky skerries at the mouth of a sea loch crush the sloop as we push her against them until she sinks.

We can't make a run for Muilean; we need to defend the cattleboats. But the cannon fire has alerted Vheara's fleet, and I have only a short breathing space in which to draw the grapeshot from the injured oarsman and heal the wound. As we clear a point of land that juts out into the sea, a second sloop-of-war bears down on us with little warning.

The second sloop is close enough to land that we're able to break her and beach her in a matter of minutes. But a new group of sails coming hard across the open water raises an alarm from the lookout.

"Frigates! Two of them—forty-gunners at least. Approaching dead to starboard."

"Push the cattleboats ahead into the bay where that second sloop was hiding," Chyr orders. "We'll cover them and draw the frigates close to shore where it's easier to sink them."

A shot cracks from a new longboat that's appeared from behind a jut of rocks along the shore, spitting splinters from the rail of the closest cattleboat. I hear one of the Shadehounds yelp, and I run to the back of the birlinn. Chyr runs with me.

Shade is down, blood seeping onto the planks beneath him. Shadow stands over him, her hackles high.

My ears ring, and a paralysing stillness fills me. I can't lose anyone or anything else. I won't.

But I can't think how to reach him. Shadow whines loud enough that I can hear her above the ocean's wail.

"Sean, get over here," Chyr orders. "Pick the hound up and bring him here."

Sean sets his jaw in a stubborn line. "It's a Shadehound. Not worth the magic. You want him here, you do it."

"You have the rune—it will cost you less magic."

"Still not bloody worth it. You want to appease the witch, do it yourself."

Chyr steps towards Sean to stand chest to chest. For a heartbeat, the crash of the ocean is the only sound.

Sean doesn't move. He's taller and broader, his body built

to intimidate. But Chyr's strength is in his mind as well as his muscles. Force of will blazes from his eyes with an air of command that Sean can't match.

My eyes flick from the two of them to Shade, and I feel useless. Despite all the magic I can summon, I can't trust myself to use it. Not with Shade's life at stake.

Then Sean loses the stare-down between him and Chyr, and with a muffled curse he steps to the aft railing of the birlinn and activates one of the runes along his temple. But there's no gentleness in the way his air magic picks Shade up and carries him from the cattleboat to drop him onto the birlinn's deck.

"Thank you," I grit out as I drop to my knees and reach for Shade. But Sean is already striding off to cope with the two frigates. Chyr squeezes my shoulder, then follows him to help.

My hands pressed lightly above Shade's haunch, I use my magic to sense for the iron that's not supposed to be there. I pull the metal towards me until the misshapen shot works free, leaving broken bone and torn flesh behind it. I mend the damage, knitting bone and muscle and skin a piece at a time. The sensation is familiar now, more controlled. The magic pours from me almost as if it follows a channel I've already carved in my mind.

As if he knows not to move, Shade lies still on the deck, head flat but his one moon-pale eye watching me. Trusting me. Then it's done, and his tail thumps once against my boot.

I pat him on the head. "I'm not letting you go. You're mine. You and Shadow and everyone else."

He licks my hand, then lurches to his feet and gives himself a shake. A broadside from one of the frigates screams towards us only to be stopped by a wall of air.

Ships and battles blur together. Between the skirmishes, we sprint as fast as the cattleboats will let us along the coast to Muilean. At some point, Lorcan replaces Daire beside me, and Sean comes to take Niall's place. Chyr's magic is more familiar when he works beside me, but he's better at sending a whipcrack of air to break a mast than he is at filling a sail and moving a ship towards shore.

We're clear of the patrols eventually. Those we can see, at least. What lurks in the Sound, or approaches from the direction of Eireen or the western isles, we cannot guess.

Chyr and the Riders have spent most of their magic and need to rest, Niall so much so that Chyr has given him the extra Veilstone. He's white and trembling, his short, ash-blond hair damp with sweat and seawater, plastered against his skull. Apart from the muscles, the six discrete runes on his wrists, and a quiet aura of deadly power, he has none of the affectations of some of the other Riders. He doesn't play with knives the way Lorcan does, hoard weapons like Chyr, or wear his hair in complicated braids. He doesn't complain. He's steady and solid, and I find that I like him very much.

And without him or the other Riders to help me fight in case we need to, and with nothing immediately threatening us, I decide to take a risk.

As Muilean's western cliffs come into sight at last, I ask Niall and Daire and the other Riders to help me understand the process of raising a storm. I don't have an existing cloud to bring down rain, but I understand water enough now to know that I can use salt to seed the droplets and create the dark sheets I need above the water. And the wind—I can create that already.

"How do I make lightning?" I ask.

Chyr grins suddenly, that crooked smile that makes my heart swell. "Fierceness, lightning is so far outside my skills I've never dreamed of it. But you wear the energy of the sun in the Crown of Flame. Fire is there inside you already, and from what I've seen of your magic, you need only to understand how lightning relates back to that."

"It doesn't. Flame and lightning are not the same," I say. My voice comes out thinner than I like, and I rub the gritty salt from my fingers against the damp fabric of my skirt.

Ronan comes up behind me, with Rua once again a warm band of red fur and watchful eyes wrapped around his shoulders. "Fire is energy—it's life itself. The memory of summer's heat, the heart of the earth, and the food we eat. It's there in the warmth of our breath rising on a cold winter day. Think of it like that."

"Lightning builds in the pressure of warm air racing up and cold air pressing down," Cathal surprises me by adding. "I'd imagine the Crown of Flame gives you everything you need. Push it's heat out into the air, send it up, and you'd make lightning." He counts the steps off on his fingers—one, two, three—as precise as if it's all logic and study and nothing else.

"I don't know how to make air cooler."

"If you can add heat, you can take it away," Chyr says.

I nod as if that doesn't sound overwhelming. Maybe that's the biggest difference between my magic and Tirnaeve's. The land and the gods have already given us all the gifts we need. They're already there, waiting for me to understand how they connect—and what they give and what they cost.

Creating a storm is too much at once, but I manage to form a cloud bank out of nothing, and I drag it along the water.

The clouds are thick enough to conceal us from any more of Vheara's patrols and cover our run up the long, narrow sea loch that takes us as far inland as the western shore of Muilean allows.

We all breathe a sigh as we clear the first thin sliver of channel and approach the end of the loch. We slide past the small island that sits dead in the centre of the natural harbour.

Then we see six longboats pulled up onto the beach.

CHAPTER 42

RACE ACROSS MUILEAN

CHYR

We slide silently towards the harbour, not knowing what awaits us. Flora has laid down thick clouds at our backs, and the wind swirls eddies of mist around the ships.

A cormorant cries and takes wing off the jagged rocks at the easternmost end, and for a moment, I'm relieved, thinking that the bird signals a deserted shore. Then I see the empty longboats pulled up above the high-tide mark.

Alarm whispers mouth to mouth back across the birlinn as the others see them too. Daire taps his power rune to pull silence around us, and Flora draws the cloud in closer to keep us from being seen. On the rowing benches, the men raise their oars, water sluicing down the blades as they await an order.

"Flora?" I turn to her. "You've sensed people before. Can you feel anyone now? Or is it too far?"

She stills. Sensing may not be the right word for what she does, but it's a closer fit than *listening* or *seeing*. Her beautiful face loses all expression, and what remains is pure Flora: strength, power, and the fierce goodness that shines from her as brightly as the flames dancing across her brow.

Beyond the boats and the wet, rushy meadows of the low ground, there's a slight rise where the dark-thatched roofs of a small village float above lime-washed walls that blend into the cloudbank. There's no smoke. No movement.

It feels like a baited trap, and the hilt of my sword provides little comfort as I rest my hand against it.

Flora steps up beside the boatmaster. "You said it was a Leithe village, but loyal to the king?"

The boatmaster is short and square, with greying russet hair and a deep chest that's starting to sink towards his gut. He stands in the gunwale, peering through the cloud.

"Aye, so it is," he says. "Cymbeul swine seized the land long since, so anything those traitors want, the Leithes will choose the opposite. But loyal or not, no man on Muilean can keep the militia out, you ken. Nor the bitch-queen's army. But I can go to the village and have a look who's there."

"No. There's a Grey with them. It could be a routine patrol, or they could be hunting for the king. Either way it's not safe for you." Flora gestures to a stretch of shore immediately to our right. "Set us down there, and we can skirt the village without a confrontation."

The oarsmen beach the birlinn and the two cattleboats up on a thin stretch of sand and pebbles with a hiss of wood and stone.

I look around at the others. "Carefully," I order. "Take nothing for granted."

Flora's adopted Shadehounds leap to the shore and bound towards each other. Shadow licks Shade, and he rubs himself against her. Then they both run to Flora through the surf, their enthusiasm nearly knocking her over sideways. She laughs, and I should caution her to silence, but it's a sound I've heard so rarely that it goes to my heart like a lance. I miss its absence when it's gone.

The Pit take me, but I want—I need—this woman to have a chance to laugh.

I need her to live.

"Shade, Shadow—show yourselves, both of you," Flora says, noting how the boatmaster and the others are watching her. "You're making these poor Domhnall men think I'm seeing things."

I hold my breath, waiting to see if the Shadehounds obey her—whether they understand her. We know so little about these magical creatures that were abandoned in Alba Scoria when the Compact sealed the doorways.

Since I can see them at the moment, it's hard to tell, but they must do as she asks. The boatmaster and crew stare, and several swallow visibly. Flora notices and pets both hounds on the head. They turn to follow her as she helps unload the horses.

We give our thanks to all the men and watch as the boats head back down the loch. They've said they'll pull into an inlet nearby and try to wait for us.

"If the patrols spot you or anyone poses a threat, don't wait," Flora says. "And if we're not back by dark tomorrow, get home the best you can. We're grateful for all you've done."

"We wouldn't have the choice to help you if you hadn't saved us," the boatmaster says, and several of the others nod.

The boatmaster's eyes shift from Flora to me and back to her, to the Crown of Flame etched in magic across her brow, at the way the light flickers across the twisted vines and leaves like living fire. And Flora is the one he bows to, making his choice between us clear. Then he signals to the other Domhnall men, nods his head to me and the other Riders, and turns to float the boats back out onto the loch.

Sean scowls after him in disapproval, then shoots a glare at Flora. Lorcan does a triple flip with the knife he's been fondling before dropping it back into its sheath, and a rune flares on his left knuckle as his eyes meet Sean's in a silent conversation that sets my teeth on edge.

"Daire," I call out softly. "Stealth and inattention, please."

He triggers two of the power runes along his jaw. The first creates a bubble of silence that will muffle the horses' hoofbeats, the jingle of bridles, and the sound of our voices. The second rune pushes focus away from us in case we're seen, and makes it difficult for anyone to notice we are there.

Daire and Niall are both still spent from the magic they used on the boat, but Daire's sister has spent years etching the runes for him. They're far more powerful than the runes the others purchased from Chulainn's palace smiths for the better part of three years' wages.

In the open country here, when we know there's a trap set for us, it's worth asking Daire to push the small amount of magic his runes require to activate. At the same time, that power makes the runes a two-headed axe.

We pay for that convenience; even "low-cost" runes leave a wake. A Grey with magic-sense will feel them from a long way off.

Proof of that arrives soon enough when one, then three, then five of the purple witch-lights Greys like to use wink into existence in the nearby reeds. The glowing balls sweep across the shallows towards us. We kick the horses into a run, and our silence holds, but a signal fire flaring on a nearby hilltop brings us to a sudden halt.

"I have that," Flora says, and she gathers up clouds the way she did when the soldier triggered a fire amulet to start the beacon. The process is faster this time—she's gotten better. It takes her only moments to focus a downpour onto the flames to put them out.

I'm not sure that was fast enough to keep it from being seen, but I stand a few minutes watching the surrounding hills for other beacons. When nothing else lights, I catch up with the others as they ride down the soldiers hiding in the reeds. Fortunately, there's only a single Grey with them. With Daire using his runes to baffle the traces of magic and the sounds of battle, we manage the deaths with minimal loss of time apart from a small delay when Flora insists on healing a minor cut that Daire sustained from an ordinary sword.

"It's nothing," Daire says.

Flora arches an eyebrow at him. "Like your dead Riders' wounds were nothing? How do you know the blade wasn't coated with celestial iron?"

Daire shakes his head, rage kindling in his eyes. "Fucking Vheara."

"Exactly." Flora's lips tighten. She checks the wound, but there's little to see, and when she knits the flesh, there's no sign of smoke rising from her skin. I'm not certain whether to take that as a sign that there's no celestial iron present, or maybe only that there isn't any fever.

Either way, Flora is magnificent, and I see the way the other Riders watch her. Even Lorcan—maybe especially Lorcan. I wouldn't trust him an inch with her, but the glaze of lust in his eyes at the power she's using is undeniable. Apart from Sean, who hates her with a ferocity I do not understand, and Cathal, who I suspect has never lusted for anything that wasn't written in a book, the others have all worn that same dazed expression at one time or another.

We continue riding single file through alder and willow along a burn that flows into the loch. Ronan rides first, scouting ahead with his farsight rune activated on the back of his neck and Rua running in front of him on silent feet. Moonlight slicks his bronze skin as he signals for caution whenever something seems out of place. I ride behind him, followed by Flora so she can try to sense men and Greys around us. The Shadehounds keep close beside her. Fergal won a brief argument with Daire about who would ride at Flora's back, and Daire—being Daire—throws half-hearted jabs at Fergal as they ride. Daire's usual chaos.

The remaining Riders follow at a greater distance, but I'm aware that Cathal occasionally crowds close to Sean to continue an ongoing conversation.

I'd hoped that seeing Flora working with them might have softened both of them towards her, but I can't think what else they would be discussing. I catch Niall's eye as we skirt the village and angle my chin back in their direction. He nods, letting me know he's aware of it as well, though I'm not sure whether he can catch anything they're saying.

There's no time to stop and force a confrontation. We have fifteen hours before dawn.

Fifteen hours for me to open the doorway. Fifteen hours before Flora dies if she hasn't earned the Crown of Moonlight.

We pass the village without sighting a Grey, a redcoat, or the Cymbeul plaid. A dog barks once, but more than likely, that's nothing to do with us.

We cut inland along a river, weaving in and out of the water to muddle our tracks. Silt sucks at the horses' hooves, and alder catkins stipple the sluggish current.

Ronan's hand snaps up, signalling for us to halt. A deadfall rigged with turf and a cut spruce trunk blocks the deer track up ahead. Lorcan's knife flicks out to slice the rope, and Daire's silence rune is still active, so it contains the sound.

The silence is a reminder that we've relied on Daire's magic for too long already.

I turn to look at Flora. "Can you raise a mist? Daire will need time to recover his strength."

She nods and pulls fog from the river to travel with us while Fergal and Ronan trade off using their silence runes to keep us from being heard. The mist has the disadvantage of keeping us in a cloud of cold and unrelenting damp that seeps into our bones.

Vheara's forces are out in strength. Ronan points out sloppy footprints along the riverbank, and as we pass a cart track, the mud is churned by men and horses. Fergal uses his earth magic to smooth our tracks, and Lorcan draws water from the mud to create puddles where we crossed so that the lack of prints doesn't seem suspicious. We stay to the trees where we can after that, weaving through birches and alders, but it's less than an hour before Flora warns us to stop.

She's sensed a group of men positioned strategically where anyone crossing this side of the island could be spotted. They melt into the gorse and heather, even when we know they're on the hill above us.

We dismount and wait while Ronan shimmies his way closer and comes back to report there are two pairs of redcoats together with enough Cymbeul militiamen to make a dozen, all of them hidden in a thicket. One of the men is watching for movement through a spyglass, but the rest are either sleeping or playing dice.

"I'd say it's a safe bet Vheara anticipated we'd be coming," Sean comments sourly. "We'll need to assume we'll be fighting through a force at the loch, so we should avoid distractions. This patrol is easy to detour—and we're not coming back this way."

Flora shoots him a measuring glance, then looks away. Her expression is unreadable, but I can imagine what she's thinking.

If we can reach the doorway, and I manage to open it, they'll all expect us to go through together—except for the Rider Flora chooses. If she chooses. Even then, they'll expect Chulainn's oaths will force me to kill her.

As if she feels me watching her, Flora glances over, then takes a step towards me. But it isn't time yet. I can't give her too much time to think about what I'm going to ask her to do. She'll hate it, but I have to make her see that it's her only option.

I order Lorcan to leave the men alone. With silence and attention-deflection in place, we give them a wide berth.

Once past that ambush, we stop to let the horses and the Shadehounds drink at a stream choked with birch roots. Then we find a ford downstream a short distance, and emerge with the horses dripping and our own legs wet. Ronan whistles for Rua and drapes her across his shoulders when she comes back to him.

A storm is rolling in, the clouds thickening high above us. That makes it easier for Flora to pull them around to cloak us. We hunch into our clothes as the rain begins. I'm luckier than the other Riders in my thick plaid and the leather buff coat, and I'm starting to appreciate the clothes, and that's only one of the many reasons I've come to appreciate the Highlands. It's a loyal, fierce culture. The men are warriors, and the women—well, there's Flora. She is a warrior and so much more.

Darkness comes earlier with the rain. We jog the horses along the field margins where rushes hide the line of our passage. A sharp two-note whistle brings our heads up and draws low growls from Shadow and Shade. But the sound has carried across a nearby loch.

"Could be no more than a man calling in his dogs," Cathal says.

Ronan snorts derisively and shakes his head. Flora pulls up the pale dun mare she's riding. Rain beads on her lashes; she blinks it away before she answers: "There's another group on the far side of the loch, and more at the end where we'll have trouble going around them. They're too far away yet for me to have a good sense of how many are there, but it feels...there could be a Grey with them."

We ignore the group along the loch, and use cloud and darkness and rune magic to move us closer to the group at the far end. But Flora gets more tense as we get closer.

"There are three Greys," she says, "and a large group of men. I can't tell if they're soldiers or militia."

"I hate fucking Greys," Lorcan says.

Sean glares at him. "Not helpful, idiot. Why are the Greys here?"

Regardless of the runes, we bring the horses together into a circle to keep our voices low.

"The end of the loch is nearly the island's narrowest point, based on the maps I studied," Flora says. "The altar and the doorway at the Loch of Rebirth are no more than ten miles beyond that, and if we'd crossed the Sound, the likeliest landing site is just there—off to the left of those Greys. There's also a deep sea loch on the opposite side that nearly cuts the island in two, with a river that empties into it from the Loch of Rebirth."

"So from where they are, the Greys can choke off almost every point of access." Niall scrubs a hand over the ash-pale growth of stubble along his chin.

"It only leaves the southeast route, and that's harder through the mountains." Flora bends forward to scratch Eira's neck as the mare stomps her foot impatiently. "With luck, this means Vheara isn't taking any chances because she wasn't able to seal the doorway. If we can battle past whatever she has waiting for us, that might be good news."

Daire gives her one of the grins that never fails to get him what he wants. "We'll need to work on your definition of *good*."

Ronan cuffs the back of his head. "Can we focus, please? Chyr, what do you want to do?"

"I'd say we need to kill the Greys. No point trying to go around them. Whatever is waiting for us at the doorway and the altar, it's close enough that this group can ride in behind us and make the situation worse. Flora, what do you think?"

"Why do you keep asking for her opinion?" Cathal snaps. "She knows nothing."

"She's the Maiden, and she's proven she's damned good at strategy and tactics," Lorcan says.

"Which, Cathal, is more than you've contributed lately," Fergal growls. "So show her some respect."

Cathal pins him with an ice-blue stare. "She really has given you all delusions of power, hasn't she? Picturing yourself wearing a crown, are you, Fergal? You, too, Lorcan?"

"Shut it, all of you." I don't raise my voice, but when I use this tone, the Riders would rather have me shouting. It takes all of my focus to keep my hands from wrapping around Cathal's throat and squeezing him unconscious. "Unless we get past whatever Vheara has waiting for us, Flora won't have a chance to choose anyone, and the rest of you won't be going home."

Cathal is too sure he's right ever to let me think I've backed him down. I smile at him coldly until he nods.

"Flora?" I turn back to her.

The horses stand on long reins, their heads close together and drooping with fatigue. Flora lets her eyes slide around the group, and I suspect she sees what I do. We're all tired and spent. The difference is that the rest of us have endured centuries going into battles of one kind or another. For Flora, this is all new. And she doesn't so much as flinch.

If I hadn't already been certain that I loved her wholly and irrevocably before now, seeing her like this would have clinched it.

"It's too far for me to tell where there are Greys or soldiers beyond that group, but I'd expect them at each of the ports, and maybe another group in the middle before we reach the loch. What if we try to draw this group towards us? Can you create the illusion of sound and figures fleeing? Give them something to chase into an ambush?"

"Not bad," Daire says.

I lean forward in the saddle. "That's you, Cathal. Give them a show—and make it convincing. Niall, lay a wind net to baffle the feel of any magic we or the Greys release. Flora, can you soften the ground enough to sink them to their knees, and then firm it again to hold them in place? That would let us plough through them without wasting a lot of effort we might need later."

Flora nods, and we find a spot between the loch and a copse of trees where we can wait. In my bones, I feel the night waiting with us.

CHAPTER 43
WORTH DYING FOR

CHYR

We tie the horses higher up the slope where the muffling mist will reduce any sound they make. Wet leather creaks as we work, and rain threads down my collar. The smell of peat, soaked horse, and sodden wool curls thickly around us.

Farther down the hill, Flora is waiting behind a tree. I slip in beside her.

"How are you holding up?" I ask.

"Fine," she says, "though Daire might question my definition of that word, too. I'm not sure sanity has ever been my strength."

"Bravery is nothing more than a moment of insane connection to something or someone beyond yourself. I'm here, I'm alive because you're you. Because you have those moments of insanity."

A smile tugs at her lips. It's small and tremulous, then it spreads until every part of her face glows with it. It makes me want to pull her into my arms and tell her all the things it costs me not to say.

I think of that moment in the Sacred Wood when I first saw her, and the moment not long after that when I told her not to help me. Even then, I must have known that I would always choose her over myself.

She has never said she loves me, though that's a hope I hold in my heart. But I know she loves her people and Alba Scoria more. I hope she loves them enough to accept what I have to do.

Daire sets up a perimeter around the trap. Using four stones, he anchors the silence, attention-deflection, and magic-dampening spells from his runes to ensure the soldiers and militiamen who trudge behind the Greys on foot will have no warning before they reach us. Flora draws water from the loch to soak the track, creating deep mud to bog the horses down.

The illusion Cathal has built is perfect, if a little spiteful. He's created near-exact likenesses of both me and Fergal, making it look as though we are whipping our exhausted horses, desperately trying to outrun the Greys. The Greys spur their own mounts to chase the illusion, and he lures them in, keeping the image of us close enough that the Greys can see the fear Cathal's magic is projecting onto our faces as our illusionary selves look back at them across our shoulders. At the same time, Cathal keeps the Greys far enough away that they can't wonder why they don't sense any fear.

I let the Greys run well into the trap we've set, far enough that Flora's mud slows their horses to a walk. Five Greys. No, only four. One of them reins in, checking his speed. Peering around suspiciously.

Sweat mingles with the rain beneath my collar as I hold the signal longer than I should. I wave away a couple of early midges that hover in front of my eyes.

Then the last of the Greys finally rides forward. And I nod to Flora, signalling for her to start.

Flora squeezes the earth around the horses' legs, then leaches the water out of the mud to trap them in place.

Flora's Shadehounds watch me with their silver-ringed eyes, as intent as the other Riders. Then I lower two fingers. *Go.*

We all surge forward, swords out and magic crackling along our skin.

I reach the last Grey who entered. He sends a lance of fire at me, targeted enough to make me throw myself aside. I smother the flame with a burst of air that sends him flying off his horse.

The ground shakes as I stride around the horse to reach him. I barely have time to register that he's an earth-wielder before the mare wrenches free of the ground and rears. Her iron shoe clips me on the shoulder as she rises.

My arm goes numb to my fingertips, and my sword falls from my grasp. The Grey lunges for it. I seize the hilt with a rope of air, and I hurl it, aiming for the Grey's black heart. The blow misses—he's still breathing. But the force was enough to fling him to the ground and pin him to the earth.

Niall gets to the Grey before I can finish him off, and I look around and find that the whole attack is over.

Flora releases the horses and slaps their haunches to send them down the loch in the direction from which we came. I grab one of the Greys' swords while the others start to clean up and toss the bodies in the woods, and I carry the sword back to Flora.

"What's this?" she asks when I offer it to her. "I have my own sword, but I'm better at trapping Greys than stabbing them."

"It's not for them." My mouth is dry now that I actually need to say the words. "Fierceness, you're going to have to choose a Rider."

She stares at me, eyes narrowed, and tips her head.

I'm not sure whether her eyes turned silver when she received the Maiden's crescent moon on her shoulder or if that happened when she received the crowns. I'm not sure what the colour means, but as beautiful as it is, I miss the calm grey that was Flora's, the cool contrast to the fire and moonlight streaks of her hair. She's still too stunning for words, and those eyes look back at me, waiting for me to say something she doesn't already know. To say something that makes sense.

"I'm aware of how much you hate the idea of being trapped, having your choices taken from you," I say. "There's so much I haven't been able to tell you. Things my oaths prevent me from thinking, much less saying. You've guessed most of what's important. Add that to the knowledge that the Compact may protect mortals from being compelled, but that didn't apply before the document was signed."

The oathbands make me pay for those last few sentences, but I don't give a damn at this point. Clenching my teeth against the pain, I force myself to keep going.

"All the oaths I still believe in were made when I was too naïve to understand that the Tirnaeve to which such oaths belonged no longer exists. But those oaths led me to this moment. To you. You are the honour and kindness Siorai used to live by. Protecting you is how I can keep the oaths I thought I was taking—the oaths worth dying for."

"No." She whispers the word.

"Yes. The gods chose you for a reason. The land chose you.

406

And so do I. You have every reason not to trust me, but I hope you do. I hope you can. Because I need you to make me a promise—just like you once made me promise blindly."

Flora's face has gone pale, and she lifts both hands to cup my face. Her skin is cold, and she is trembling. "If it has anything to do with the Grey's sword, I can't. I won't."

I close my eyes and take a breath, then I kiss the palm of one hand and then the other. Threading our fingers together, I hold on to my one spot of warmth and hope.

"I need you to take me as your consort, Fierceness. *Choose me.* Make the sacrifice with me. Win the Crown of Moonlight so you can live. So you can use all your determination and power to remake this broken world into something better.

"You have that in you—the gods know it, and so do I. But I can't ride beside you on this journey.

"Kill me after we make the sacrifice. Unless I'm dead, you'll never be safe from the oaths Chulainn forced me to take. The oaths won't let me go."

"You know I would choose you anyway, don't you?" She looks down at the way our fingers are tangled together. "I chose to let you live, and I chose to make you mine. I will choose you every night for the rest of time because I love you. Even if your oaths kept secrets from me, your actions never did. I could have seen the truth myself if my own prejudice hadn't blinded me. You are not your father. Or your uncle. You're a good man, a true man. Not a perfect one, but you don't have to be. Not for me."

Her words fill my heart with stubborn hope—and my mind with despair. "You still don't understand. I don't know what the oaths my uncle forced on me might make me do. You would never be safe. And if I'm banished to the Gloaming as an oathbreaker and Vheara gets her hands on me, then no one in either world would be safe. We can't take such risks. I'm begging you. Promise me."

Flora's moonlight eyes are so bright that I don't see the tears welling up in them until they spill down her cheeks. She makes a small, choked sound as she shakes her head.

"I can't. I won't make a promise that buries you."

Her hands slip away from mine, and my heart cracks into pieces.

I'd hoped the other Riders would be on the other side of the Veil in Tirnaeve before Flora and I made the sacrifice at the Altar of the Moon. But if she won't promise to kill me, then I'll find another way to die. Oaths be damned. I'll smash my world against the ruins of its lost honour to make sure Flora lives.

CHAPTER 44

THE KNIFE AND THE CROWN

FLORA

M y approach to the Loch of Rebirth and the Altar of
the Moon retraces the last footsteps my ancestors
would have taken. Leaving the ships anchored on
Muilean's western shore, the old Cailleach Queen, dressed in
black, and the Maiden, in a cloak of white, would have ridden
to the loch with an entourage behind them.

When they reached the shore, the Maiden would have
dropped her cloak and clothing and stepped naked into the
loch to bathe. Then, moon-clad and defenceless, she would
have run the moment the doorway opened and the
Anvar'thaine stepped through the Veil to Hunt.

But that is not how we arrive.

The Hunt is long behind us now, and without moonlight,
it's impossible to tell the time. I doubt there are more than a few
hours left before sunrise, when the doorway seals for another
year. Scant hours before I make my sacrifice or die.

It's hard to think of anything except the choice I have to

make. I know only this: Chyr asked me for a promise that I can't give him.

I can't kill him, but even if I choose a different Rider, that doesn't solve the problem. If he keeps his oaths to Chulainn, he breaks his oaths to the Compact. The Gloaming is worse than death.

Looking around at him and the other Riders, I see the same thoughts weighing on all of them. We're all solemn as we push our horses up the last low slope to reach the Loch of Rebirth, dread outweighing any sense of hope to which we might still cling.

Cloaked with Daire's rune of silence and an even more powerful illusion rune that bends the landscape around us and renders us invisible, we don't bother trying to be careful as we approach. Saving time is more important.

Daire's illusion drains magic too fast for him to be able to hold it long, but it gives us a chance to survey the battlefield and make a plan. We crest the rise, and Chyr holds up a hand for us to halt.

My stomach sinks when I see what's waiting for us.

"Six Greys and three dozen redcoats standing out in the open like that? You can bet that's a trap Vheara's set for us," Lorcan says, pulling out his knife to toss and catch it, hilt over tip, over and over with practised menace.

"The Raven bitch must have been playing with us all this time," Daire says, his blond hair dulled and damp beneath the unceasing rain. "Clearly, she knows about the doorway—which means she must have sealed it."

"Not necessarily." Chyr shakes his head. "Take a closer look at those soldiers. That's the Black Knife of Alba insignia: the crossed knives on their sleeves. The Butcher's personal guard."

My breath catches in my throat, and Sean whistles through his teeth.

"Well, now," Sean says. "The bloody Duke of Cumarann himself. Maybe we'll finally have a chance to kill him."

"We'll need to find him first," Daire says.

Chyr's lips twitch in a grim smile. "He won't be with the main group, and he'll be using more of the runes and amulets Vheara's been giving him—just as he did at Culodur. Watch each other's backs. And your own. Don't take anything for granted just because the Butcher's human."

The warning raises the hair at the back of my neck, and I can almost feel a warm breath of air against my skin, as if someone is standing behind me. Shade and Shadow growl, but there's no one there. And then the feeling is gone. The Shadehounds look away.

A steady wind drives bursts of cloud and needles of rain into our faces, and there's no moonlight to show us the wet bog around the loch or the great stone slab of the Altar of the Moon balanced on four black pillars of stone.

We shouldn't see the landscape or the men in the moonless dark, but they've made themselves conspicuous with the purple-hued orbs of magical light that float in the air above them, the Greys' equivalent of the scoutlights the Riders use. The group by the altar is illuminated so clearly that the trap they've set might as well be flashing to capture our attention.

The Butcher must hope we will focus on the threat we can see—and miss the other two groups of Greys and soldiers hidden in the darkness on either side. But I can feel them.

I wrap my arms around my waist, trying to ward off the sudden chill. "There are more of them waiting to ambush us," I say. "Another sixty or seventy men and at least half a dozen Greys split into two groups hidden in the brush and bracken. We'll need to get past one set before we can reach the group by the altar, and the rest are hidden beyond the altar. Then there's a third, smaller group waiting at the far end of the loch."

The Riders glance around at each other. The scent of the bog curls into my nose: the rain-softened citrus of myrtle overpowered by the sweet rot of peat breathing up beneath spring grass. Peat smells of iron, too, as though it's born to be soaked in blood.

"It's a shame you haven't experimented with lightning yet," Lorcan says, giving me a pointed look. "A few good bolts would be convenient now."

"Remind me again if we live through this. I'll be happy to use you for target practice."

Lorcan stares at me, then gives an unexpected grin and shakes his head.

Chyr crosses his arms, watching Lorcan with narrowed eyes. "Let's focus, please. On the bright side, we know what we're up against, and we know it's a trap. That gives us an advantage."

"You could use air," I say. "We have to kill them all without anyone raising an alarm. What if you wrap a rope of air around their necks, then pull the rope tight all at once? You'd still need to finish the Greys off with celestial steel, but at least they'd be held in place and distracted to make that easier."

"None of us has the strength for that much precision magic. Not on this side of the Veil at least." Chyr's brow creases as he thinks. "We'd have to take it in turns, or pool our magic to work together. Ronan, could you use your rune of darksight to guide the rope?"

"You'd need Daire, too," Ronan says. "He'll have to make sure none of the Greys can sense the magic while we work."

Daire's eyes glitter in the darkness as he nods in agreement. "I can do that."

Chyr scrubs a hand over the back of his neck. "Even with that, I don't know how long our power will hold out."

"Here." Niall pulls the spare Veilstone ring from his finger and holds it out to Daire. "Take this."

Daire slips the ring on his finger and stares at it a moment, then lays his palm on top of it in a surprisingly tender gesture. Blinking rapidly, he swallows hard and glares around at the rest of us as if he's daring us to say anything. I turn away and study the group of Greys and soldiers standing by the altar. Their faces are blue and eerie beneath the purple scoutlights.

"Can anyone think of a reason the plan won't work?" I ask.

"Too many to count," Lorcan says. "But I can't think of anything better. Remind me never to make you angry."

"Too late for that, idiot." Ronan's teeth flash white against the bronze skin that almost matches his russet hair. Lifting Rua from around his shoulders, he lets her jump down to the ground.

We tie the horses to stubby rowans that grow nearby, and Lorcan activates a rune, creating an area of silence around them. I wrap my scarf low across my forehead to hide the light from the Crown of Flame.

Chyr, Sean, Niall, Daire, and I walk together, the other Riders following with their swords already drawn. I don't bother arguing when Shade and Shadow pad beside me. They've made it clear they'll do whatever *they* think is best.

The land is beginning to quicken with power. I feel the magic roiling beneath the surface, and four Hallow Keepers appear as we draw closer to the altar. Their too-thin bodies are little more than shadows, their eyes glowing that eerie blue as they turn to me and bow their heads. I touch my fingers to my heart, and they shift to take up positions at each of the altar's four black pillars.

The altar is ready, and the Goddess is waiting. I can feel her attention now.

Power hums around me, shivering across my skin as the

Riders and I skirt the head of the loch, keeping clear of the bog and slipping past the reeds along the outer edges. The corrupted magic seeping from the Greys turns my stomach as we reach the first group and stop a few yards away.

Chyr shifts so that he stands behind me, his big hands splayed wide around my waist. It's a gesture I remember. Without words, it says, "Trust me, Fierceness." It says, "I have you."

"Could you pull the air and feed it to me?" he asks. "If we can combine the strength of your elemental magic with our Siorai precision, we might stand a chance."

"I'll try." Raw power is the one thing I seem to have in plenty.

Closing my eyes, I lean back against Chyr's chest, feeling the strength in his arms and the gentleness in his touch, the steady rise and fall that anchors my breath. I reach for magic in the air around us and twist it into a thin stream of current while Chyr's power coils and shapes it, tightening it into a single, unbroken rope. Almost immediately, I feel Sean and Niall with us, guiding the line while Chyr loops it like an invisible noose around the enemies' necks, one after another, until they are all encircled.

"Now pull," Chyr whispers.

The four of us wrench the rope of air tight and lift it higher above the ground.

Vheara's soldiers and her Greys dangle like men from a hangman's noose, scrabbling at their throats.

I feel their lives snuff out, the familiar ping of loss snapping in my heart. Then only the Greys remain.

Chyr and the Riders stride forward and grimly pierce each heart with celestial steel, and when the Greys die, I feel nothing but relief. Wind brushes my face, as if even the land around me sighs out a breath.

There's no time to pause. We circle around, moving silently and giving a wide berth to the odd purple light that illuminates the enemy beside the altar. The Hallow Keepers standing guard around the altar watch us, but they don't move as we approach. We skirt around them and creep up behind the group of soldiers hidden in the brush at the foot of the hillside beyond. These men are sloppier than the Butcher's personal guard, most of them sitting on the ground half-asleep. Even the Greys that accompany them look bored and listless.

We repeat the trick with the rope. It's harder this time— there are more men, and Chyr and the other Riders can't twist the rope and guide it fast enough to keep the air from dissipating and shredding away as I push it towards them.

I fight to create a slower, more precise stream of air to make it easier for Chyr to manipulate. But that isn't the way my magic wants to be used.

I'm beginning to understand the difference. The Cailleach's magic is a sentient power. It answers when I ask—not when I demand—and it recognises the things I can find in nature. There's nothing natural about twisting air into a weapon. I need Siorai magic for that—and it demands a price.

Needles of glass rake through my veins, clawing at my bones. The pain is sharper the more I force it, and the ember of magic inside me dims quickly because I can't pull magic from outside of myself fast enough to keep it balanced. I don't have a Veilstone to draw from any more.

Searching for a different approach, I try to think of something in nature that could function as a rope, and I almost laugh as I realise I'm wearing the solution across my brow.

Instead of trying to force air into an unnatural shape, I gather it and let it grow the way a vine grows, feeding it to Chyr as a solid shape. His hand tightens at my waist as he senses what I'm doing, and he and the other Riders nudge the vine where it needs to go. We work together until the vine of air is looped loosely around the necks of every Grey and soldier. Then we pull the vine tight, and the Riders fan out to finish the Greys with steel.

Chyr pauses to kiss the top of my head before he runs after the rest of them. "I didn't think you could be any more beautiful to me, but I was wrong."

I reach up to lay a palm across his cheek, memorising the feel of him, the shape, the likeness of those perfect features, and the eyes with endless layers.

"I do love you," I say, because I haven't said it before. I need the words to hold the complex, enormous, and simple truth of what I feel for him.

"Why does that sound like regret?" Chyr asks.

"No regrets, and no apologies." I turn away, choking on sorrow, but I've made my decision—the only decision I can live with making.

When the Riders have killed the last of the Greys, we backtrack to the altar and the group that the Butcher used to bait his trap. There are fewer soldiers, but Chyr signals a halt as we creep closer, and he points out the amulets that the soldiers and Greys are wearing on leather cords around their necks.

The amulets are made of serpentine—brilliant green, veined through with glowing yellow. They're similar to what the soldier back at the Loch Seil camp used to start the signal fire, but these hold three runes each and glow an angry purple.

I tug at Chyr's arm. "They're active—"

"I see them," he whispers.

Still, we have no choice. I grow the vine of air, and Chyr, Sean, and Daire use their magic to direct it around the nearest soldier's neck.

The vine shreds apart like storm-torn clouds. Sean tries

to force it back together, but it drifts away faster than he can hold it.

"Damn it," Daire says. "The amulets are repelling magic."

"In that case, we'll kill them the old-fashioned way," Chyr orders.

The Riders draw their swords again, celestial steel singing in a single voice as it leaves their scabbards. The enemy hasn't seen us yet, but that changes as soon as blood is drawn.

The six Greys in the group swivel towards us, their motion slow and strange. The nearest throws up a palm, pushing out a cone of dark red vapour that reeks of decay and terror. The stench is sharp enough to make my skin crawl as if it's overrun with spiders. My vision blurs, and bile stings my throat.

The mist reaches Niall first. He chokes and screams, staggering to a knee while the red vapour rolls over him and past him. He keeps screaming even as Chyr sends a burst of fire to burn the vapour away.

A female Grey cocks her head, her milk-pale eyes focusing on Chyr with interest. She flicks two fingers, sending fire scorching towards him. He gestures and snuffs the flames.

The Grey counters with another wave of red mist. But this time, it's aimed at me. I react on instinct, throwing up my hand to block it. The crown across my brow sears with heat. Flames burst from me to burn the mist away before it can touch me.

The magic doesn't stop.

Fire rips through my chest, and an inferno pours out from my palm. The mist dries up and vanishes, but the fire doesn't stop. It flashes across every Grey and soldier in its path, flames consuming skin and flesh and crimson uniforms. Then Daire and Niall are in its way, and still it doesn't stop.

Daire throws himself to the ground as the clothes on his back catch fire. Niall is quicker. He puts the fire out with a gust of air, leaving scorched cloth and red flesh along his shoulder.

His eyes meet mine, and I'm too horrified to move. Then I give myself a mental shake and run to help Daire, reaching for his hand to pull him to his feet. He flinches away from me. The smell of singed leather and hair makes my stomach pitch, but I push forward, moving beyond him and Niall and all the Riders who are still wading through the soldiers to reach the Greys. Niall won't meet my eyes as I pass him.

The Greys are damaged, their faces blackened and burned. I push out another wave of fire—push it and continue pushing until their flesh chars and fissures.

"Enough." Chyr catches my arm to get my attention. "Flora, pull back. We can do the rest."

I don't want to stop, but I take a breath and let the flames go out while I watch the Riders check every Grey and every soldier. Ten minutes later, there is nothing but silence and stillness and the stench of burned flesh that has become too heartbreakingly familiar.

The last group of soldiers and Greys is moving towards us now, but they're too far away to pose a danger for the moment. The night has gone quiet. Water laps at the banks of the loch, shushing through the reeds, and peat breathes up its sour-sweet rot beneath our feet. The sky is darker again, the moon vanished behind clouds and mist.

"The moon will set soon," Chyr says. "We're running out of time."

He strides to the loch and stops where the river forms and flows down towards the sea. There's no definite marker, but doorways form in the *betweens* where the Veil is thinnest. Chyr stands between loch and river, between blanket bog and valley fen, between flat and brae, between moor and ring-dyke rock on the cusp between spring and summer.

He thrusts the Sword of the Anvar'thaine into the air.

I hold my breath, expecting something that looks like the Veil in Lannraig's story to appear, for the air to split with strands of light that flicker the way the threads of Tirnaeve's pale gold magic dance within the Veilstone rings.

There's nothing.

My stomach hollows, and my chest aches. Chyr's shoulders slump, but he tries again.

The Riders gather closer around him, arguing with each other, though the answer is clear. Vheara must have remembered the doorway and sealed it, after all. Which makes sense, given the welcome party she had waiting for us here.

The knowledge only strengthens my resolve, and I slip away towards the Altar of the Moon while Chyr and the Riders are still too occupied to stop me.

There's no army coming from Tirnaeve to save us. We're alone, and the nine of us will need to fight Vheara on our own.

And nine is nowhere near enough.

I've seen the strength of the runes the Riders wear and the fire rune on the amulet the soldier used to light the signal beacon. Chyr once said that Vheara was one of the most powerful runesmiths Tirnaeve has ever known. The kind of magic that fuels her power may have changed, but she must still have all her knowledge. I don't know how to counter that.

I'm not a general or tactician. I'm not a Rider. My power is different from theirs—I borrow it; I don't command it, and I don't know how to use it to fight the Raven Queen. As I've already proven, I'd be a danger to both sides on a battlefield. The Riders need the Cailleach's power, but they need someone stronger than I am to wield it.

I reach the altar and move past the Hallow Keepers to stand in darkness at the long end of the pale stone slab. Wind lashes the bracken on the hillside, and the rain has started again, a cold downpour that seeps down my neck.

With a last glance at the Riders, I confirm they're still arguing and occupied, and I remove the scarf that hides my brow. The Crown of Flame reflects in the slick of rain that coats the pale stone surface, fire dancing across the water. It's the first time I've seen the crown—the first time I'm sure beyond doubt that it is real.

Even in the moonless dark, the Altar of the Moon stands out starkly against the hills behind it, a long plank with the crescent moon etched along its centre and a small bowl ground out of the slab near each corner.

Back in the time of the true queens, there would have been four people here to spill their blood into the bowls. The Maiden and the Rider she had chosen would have made the offering to cement the vows that would bind them to each other, to the Great Mother, and to Alba Scoria. But they would also have sworn to sacrifice their lives when the gods and the land decided their time was over.

That was the reason the old Queen and her Consort were there: to finish their time of service. The life of the old Cailleach Queen and her consort had to end to make way for the new Queen's reign.

No one ever knew when or even why it was time for the crown to pass. They knew only that the old Queen would sacrifice herself to ensure that Alba Scoria had whatever leadership it needed for the years that lay ahead.

That's a sacrifice I will happily accept. But I will accept it alone—I and no one else.

The Great Mother watches me—her attention is a weight across my shoulders. I draw my dagger, and the air falls still.

Then something—someone—brushes against my arm.

Instinct screams. Gripping the dagger tighter, I try to whip around, but a fist yanks the hair at the base of my neck and jerks my head back, baring my throat. An arm wraps across my chest, pinning me in place.

I *feel* the arm, but I can't see it.

"Well, now, here's a bit of luck," a male voice says close beside my ear. "The trap I set for the would-be king has caught an extra mouse. Imagine Vheara's gratitude when I bring her head of the Maiden as my crowning achievement."

Pressure slams my back, snatching my breath away. The pain comes later—as sharp as the fiery knives that come from emptying my magic. I look down at my chest, and the tip of a sword has pierced it through.

I fight to free myself, but the man is stronger. The dagger is still in my hand, but I'm pinned too tight.

"That's right. Struggle," the voice says close to my bad ear yet loud enough that I hear it clearly. "You'll make the pain far worse."

"Who are you?"

"Don't you know? Being called the Butcher has a poetic ring to it, I'll admit. I quite enjoy it. Still, I think I'll like Maiden Slayer even more. It evokes so many delightful possibilities."

The name jolts me from the cold shock that grips my body, and fury makes me forget the pain. Every atrocity, every burned village, every dead child fuels my strength.

Dagger held tight, I throw my hips back and use the Butcher's body as leverage to push myself off his sword.

The blade in my chest tears through more flesh as it dislodges. I ignore that and shove magic into the dagger. It transforms into a sword as I turn, but there's no one there. No one I can see. He must be using an amulet or a rune to hide himself, but he's still mortal. He's still there.

I calculate where the Butcher's chest should be from how

it felt as he held me, and I thrust my sword until I feel the blade connect.

There's a gurgle and a hiss of breath. Weight sags against my sword, pulling me to the ground as a body falls. I fight to free myself, to remove my weapon. Blood drips from the blade.

Is the Butcher dead? Or merely wounded?

I reach down, and my fingers connect with hot blood, cloth, and buttons—and a cold stone amulet. I grasp it and yank. The chain it hangs from breaks.

Someone is shouting. Chyr, and others, too. A gust of air slams towards me, but I feel only the edge of it as the Butcher—or one of Vheara's runes—repels it. The Hallow Keepers stagger as it hits them, and even the altar shakes.

Blood bubbles at the corner of the Butcher's mouth as he's suddenly there in front of me. He clutches at his chest with hands etched in runes that glow a sickly, garish purple.

On the ground at my feet, Vheara's mortal general is smaller than I thought he would be. Too slight for all the death and pain he's wrought. He's shorter, younger. His long, powdered wig is knocked askew, revealing an almost feminine face, and his scarlet coat is garish with braid and silver buttons. The remnants of a thick gold chain hang around his neck.

His eyes meet mine—glassy, wide, and shocked. There's no cruelty in them now, just the fear of dying. But I can't stop to consider the weight of that, not yet, and for this death I will refuse the guilt. I'll let him die slowly, but I won't wait to watch him. Killing the Butcher can't unburn the glens or raise the dead, but it is one less abomination for the world to bear.

Shade and Shadow are already tearing at him with their teeth as I turn away.

I take three steps towards the altar before falling to my knees. The blood from my chest has soaked through my bodice, flowing warm and fast. That matters, but I can't stop.

Chyr never stopped.

For one breath, I let myself turn and find him in the darkness, the quiet intensity, the graceful way he moves. The honour and hope that drives him, even though he doesn't see that in himself.

I chose him long before tonight—when I helped him, when I forgave him.

Now I choose him the only way I can. I choose to let him live.

I'm growing cold and weak, and my vision blurs. Still, I force myself to my feet, and I stumble towards the altar.

Everything wavers out of sync—the shouts, the wind, the sound of pounding feet.

Chyr, Ronan, and the others are rushing towards me, but Sean is holding Chyr, yelling something at him.

I lean across the Altar, positioning my body so the blood that drips from my chest falls into the nearest bowl. The stone cavity is already half-filled with rainwater, but it's too late to worry about that now.

"Great Mother, Cailleach," I begin, "I don't know what words I am meant to speak. It's been too long since the last of the true queens died, and the words didn't pass down in our stories. All I can offer you is the truth in my heart. I swear on my last breath that I will be loyal to this land and the people of Alba Scoria, and I promise to serve the gods in any way that is just and honourable.

"I offer my life to you freely, whenever you choose to take it. But Alba Scoria needs a true warrior. Whether that's me or another stronger than I am, your queen will need every Rider fighting at her side if Vheara is to be defeated. And if I fall, you will still need every Rider. I cannot choose a consort if he will have to die to make way for another queen to take my place. With the doorways sealed, Tirnaeve can send no new Riders through to help us.

"Accept my promises and my sacrifice, and let that be

enough. That isn't the law as it was written, as it stood for thousands of years, but it is what we need. What Alba Scoria needs. Let me serve you without a consort."

"No!" Chyr's protest is fierce and raw, cutting through the air. Through me. "Flora, you'll die if you don't take a consort. Choose me, Fierceness. Let me do this for you. *With* you. Choose me. Let me save you."

He reaches for me as if he's drowning, then shakes his head and pulls the dagger from his belt. He slices it across his palm.

Blood wells and thins with rain, and his eyes beg me to let him die.

"Don't." The word scrapes out of me, barely a breath. My lips feel cold and stiff. "Please don't. I'm not refusing you because I don't love you, Chyr. Don't you see? I can't choose you because I do. Because I can't be the one who kills you."

Everything hurts. The ragged pain in his eyes, the burn of torn flesh in my chest. The thought of losing him most of all.

He reaches across the Altar of the Moon to let his blood spill into the consort's cup.

"Stop." The word echoes as I say it, and I realise that both Sean and I have said it simultaneously.

Sean grasps Chyr's wrist and drags him backwards, away from the altar.

Chyr tries to break his hold. "Let go of me, Sean. You'll be banished if you keep me from fulfilling the Compact."

"You can't force her to choose you, you bloody fool," Sean says. "And I can't let her. She can't be the Cailleach Queen."

"You can't break your oaths—"

"Like you, I have other oaths that bind me," Sean snarls, his eyes flashing with fear as well as rage. "Ask your uncle what he forced me to agree to before we left—if you ever have the chance to see him again."

Magic flares somewhere close by. Then a sword sings, and I smell the ironless sweetness of Siorai blood.

Someone steps behind me and catches my waist to hold me up. Magic—healing energy—pours into me, and I look back to find Fergal and Ronan there.

"Hold on, wildcat," Ronan says. "Don't you dare give up."

"That's not what I'm doing."

Sean falls, his large frame thudding as it hits the ground. Niall stands over him, holding a bloody sword.

Chyr straightens and reaches for me.

My eyes close, and I pray as I have never prayed before. Not with words or thoughts. This prayer comes straight from my heart, from the hope I cling to with every stubborn fibre of my being. I pray for the people and the land I love. For the future. For good to win.

And I pray for Chyr, because the way he is looking at me makes me feel like I've betrayed him.

He chose me, though, and now I am choosing him. Just not in the way he wanted. The things we love have to be worth fighting for. Worth any sacrifice.

My vision is leaving, darkness closing in. The force of the land presses down on me, ancient and implacable, as if Alba Scoria itself is asking how I dared to question the way things have always been. But sacrifice is the only language that cannot lie.

Pain flares in my chest, and I cough. Blood spatters across the altar like another offering.

Then more pain bursts across my forehead, much as it did in the bog on the night of the Hunt, but the sensation is cool, not like the searing heat of the Crown of Flame. This feels like the soft chill of moonlight, the sweet refuge of night falling after the killing heat of a summer day.

This, against all odds, is the Cailleach giving me her answer.

The Crown of Moonlight is rest and reawakening. It settles

across my brow, and the pain in my chest ebbs as my flesh knits. Wonder fills me, and a profound sense of peace.

There's peace in acceptance. But there's no joy, no victory.

I pull myself upright and hold out my hand to Chyr as he stares at the Crown in horror. "This isn't what you wanted," I say, "but I meant what I said. Whatever your uncle asked of you—whatever your oaths demand—if we want to defeat Vheara, all of us have to work together. That's our only hope. If your oaths are sentient, tell them that. We win the war first, and then worry about who wears the crown."

Chyr is on his knees, his back bowed and the tendons standing out sharp on his neck as if he's fighting against his oaths with all the strength he has. He looks up at me through pain-glazed eyes, and for the first time, I see no hope in him at all. His oaths, his king, and I have taken everything from him.

"I will love you, whatever happens," he says. "Until my last breath, my last thought, the last beat of my heart. No matter what the oaths will force me to do. I love you in spite of them, and I will fight for you. Remember that."

The plea crushes my heart and breaks me open.

"I—I will," I say. "I know. I'll remember for us both."

He reaches for the hand I'm still holding out to him, his fingers trembling as he tries to make his body obey. Then another spasm wracks him. I move closer, and he shakes his head.

"Stay back," he warns, and though it's still him behind his eyes, there's a glazed darkness rising that makes me wonder how long he can fight the oaths. How long he can fight himself. I want to run to him, to scream until my throat bleeds. Instead, I can only watch while the man I love warns me to keep away.

On the hilltop above us, a column of fire flares suddenly, reaching high into the sky.

A signal beacon.

No, not one. All of them. On ridges and hilltops around the Loch of Rebirth, around all of Muilean, the signal fires leap up in unison, and I release a shuddering sigh.

Long ago, the beacons all burst into flame at once when the Great Mother crowned a Cailleach Queen. That crown will be no less a burden than the oaths that have taken Chyr to his knees.

His eyes stay on me, every part of him clenched against what his oaths demand. My last shred of hope for saving him gutters like a flame. Still, I will hold on to the promise he gave me and keep fighting. For him, for my people, and for this land I love.

Siorai are masters of control, but my love and my magic are free and fierce. However long or short my reign may be, tonight the beacon fires burn for me. I *will* find a way to save us.

THANK YOU

Thank you very much for reading, and I hope you love Flora and Chyr as much as I do! If you enjoyed the story, please consider leaving a review. Even a line or two on Goodreads or your favourite retailer site can help other readers discover the world of Alba Scoria.

Flora and Chyr's story continues in Book Two, releasing March 9, 2027. Pre-orders are available now, and details can be found on the Buy Books page of my website:

https://martinaboone.com/buy-direct-links/

To stay up to date on new book announcements and deals, sign up for my newsletter and get exclusive access to a full five-chapter sample of *The Hollow Crown*.

https://martinaboone.com/newsletter/

THE HOLLOW CROWN

Every night, magic erases her from his mind.
Every day, she makes him fall in love again.

Flora Domhnall claimed the Crown of Moonlight and woke a magic unseen in Alba Scoria for four hundred years. But her coronation didn't end the war—and the immortal warrior she needs at her side is bound by vows carved into his flesh that will force him to kill her if he remembers who she is.

Each morning, he wakes lost to her. Each day, he is drawn back by echoes of a love he cannot name. By evening, tenderness returns. Then she has to let him go again.

The war needs them both. But the love that saves him each day may become the wound neither of them survives.

Glossary,

Pronunciation

&

Terms

Main Characters

Chyr (KHEER)
Siorai warrior, Rider of the Great Hunt, Master of the Anvar'thaine (an-var-THAYN), true name Cóirneach (KOHR-nyakh).

Flora Domhnall (FLOH-ruh DOH-nuhl)
Lady of Dunhaelic (doon-HAY-lik), heir to the High Chief of Clan Domhnall. After the death of her father and brothers, her authority is unrecognised by the Clan Council, and the law prohibiting women from being clan chiefs remains unchanged until and unless it is altered by the Raven Queen.

Lands & Jurisdictions

Alba Scoria (AL-buh SKO-ree-uh)
Land of mortals once ruled by matriarchs chosen by the land and gifted with sovereign magic.

The Compact
Foundational treaty between Tirnaeve and Alba Scoria governing Siorai–mortal interaction, governance, and separation.

The Gloaming (aka the Pit)
The non-magical world between the worlds where immortals are sent for punishment.

Tirnaeve (tir-NAY-veh)
The otherworld of immortal Siorai (Everfolk) beyond the Veil.

DEITIES, IMMORTALS & MAGICAL CREATURES

The Cailleach (KAL-yakh)
The Great Mother, the Moon Mother, Goddess of the Moon, chief deity of Alba Scoria.

Father of Light/Father of Curses
The Great Father, God of the Sun, Lord of Light, chief deity of Tirnaeve.

Shadelings
Shadowy magical creatures of the *betweens*, part of the sovereign magic of Alba Scoria. There are many varieties including Shadehounds, Whisperwraiths, Hallow Keepers, and Twilight Weavers.

Siorai (SHEER-ee)
Magical immortals who reside in the Otherworld of Tirnaeve beyond the Veil. Known to humans in Alba Scoria as Everfolk.

Sovereignty/The Land
Ancient, land-rooted power—the old magic of Alba Scoria. The land magically empowers a worthy candidate, administers tests of loyalty, honour, and sacrifice, and chooses a deserving ruler and caretaker.

Kings, Queens & Generals

The Butcher, General Cumarann (KOO-muh-ran)
The Duke of Cumarann, also known as the Butcher or the Black Knife of Alba. He is the mortal Chief General of the Raven Queen's army, responsible for pursuing the rebels and punishing Vheara's enemies. Known for his cruelty, he makes no distinction between combatants and non-combatants.

The Cailleach Queens (KAL-yakh)
Ancient Domhnall rulers of Alba Scoria selected by the land after proving their worth. To prevent humans from being abused by magical Siorai invaders, the queens made the Compact with the High King of Tirnaeve to seal the doorways between Alba Scoria and the land beyond the Veil.

The High King, Chulainn Solas (KOO-lin SOH-lus)
Immortal ruler of Tirnaeve, the world of the Siorai beyond the Veil. Negotiated the Compact with Nicnevin. Brother of Fionn Solas and uncle of the rebel king.

General Mora (MOH-rah)
Lord Mora, Chief General of the rebel army.

The Maiden
A woman in the magical Domhnall line descended from the Cailleach Queens. The Maiden is marked with a glowing silver crescent on her shoulder when the land chooses her to be tested as a potential new ruler.

Queen Nicnevin (nik-NEV-in)
The Cailleach Queen who ended the human uprisings, agreed to the sealing of the doorways through the Veil between Tirnaeve and Alba Scoria, and signed the Compact to save her people from abuse by Siorai.

The Raven Queen, Vheara (VYAR-uh)
Former Siorai runesmith who was banished to the Gloaming 1,642 years ago by the Anvar'thaine for her crimes against mortals in Alba Scoria. Her abuses led to the Compact. Fourteen months ago, the magic she had stolen and corrupted from other creatures exiled in the Gloaming let her escape to Alba Scoria as a Grey. She murdered the ruling Sun King and now holds the throne. She is fighting a war against the Sun King's heir—the rebel king—who is challenging her for his father's throne.

The Rebel King, Teàrlach Solas (CHAR-lakh SOH-lus)
The Young Pretender, only child of the Sun King, and nephew of High King Chulainn of Tirnaeve. Together with the Riders of the Anvar'thaine who serve as his advisors and companions, he has come from Tirnaeve to battle Vheara—the Raven Queen—and retake his father's throne.

ANIMALS

Ari (AH-ree)
Stallion.

Bramble
Mare.

Eira (AY-rah)
Mare.

Rab (RAB)
Flora's beloved deerhound.

Rua (ROO-uh)
Vixen companion of Ronan.

Shadow and Shade
Male and female Shadehounds, a type of magical Shadeling, who have adopted Flora and become her bodyguards and companions.

Torin (TOH-rin)
Herding dog.

Dunhaelic Household

Ailean (AH-lan)
Loyal elderly headman of one of the Dunhaelic villages.

Catriona (ka-TREE-nuh)
Flora's beloved housekeeper.

Eachann (EH-kh-uhn)
Flora's maternal uncle.

Faolan (FOH-luhn)
Loyal elderly armsmaster.

Iain (EE-yun)
Loyal elderly stableman.

Morag (MOH-rag)
Much-loved cook and household mainstay.

Padraig (PAW-drig)
Former steward who was killed with Flora's father.

Rory (Roo-ree)
Flora's older brother.

Friends & Allies

Camhrain of Locharn (KAV-rin of LOKH-arn)
Chief of a neighbouring clan; supporter of the rebel king.

Donal Domhnall (DOH-nuhl)
Mairi's father.

Leithe Clan (LAY-uh)
Allied clan with territory in Ehrugael.

Mairi Domhnall (MAH-ree)
Young mother who provided food for Flora and Chyr.

Domhnall Clan Branches

Dunhaelic (doon-HAY-lik)
The High Chiefs of the Domhnall Clan who preside over all lesser Domhnall branches. Flora is the sole remaining heir. Her father and older brother supported the Raven Queen before their deaths, but her younger brothers changed sides and died fighting for the rebel king. Flora has advocated neutrality.

Ceapaich (KYAP-ikh)
Branch that lost its chief at Culodur; supporter of the rebel king.

Branch Chief:	Raghnall (RAN-ull)
Heir:	Dughall (DOO-gull)
Steward:	Fergus (FER-gus)

Gleannadail (GLAN-uh-dal)
Branch whose chief has been seized and shipped off by the Butcher's men; supporter of the rebel king.

Branch Chief:	Alasdair (AL-uh-stair)
Heir:	Eonan (OH-nan)
Steward:	Calum (KAL-um)

Gleanngaradh (GLAN-gar-uh)
Branch whose chief is injured and missing after the battle of Culodur; supporter of the rebel king.

Branch Chief:	Iain (EE-yun)
Heir:	Onghas (ONG-us)
Steward:	Tormod (TOR-mod)

Raghnall (RAN-ull)
Branch whose chief is hiding; supporter of the rebel king.

Riders of the Anvar'thaine

The Riders of the Anvar'thaine (an-var-THAYN), the Great Hunt, are elite Siorai warriors who administer justice and hunt and/or banish criminals and oathbreakers (such as the Raven Queen). Each Rider wears oathbands, rings of runes etched into the skin around their biceps, as sentient, magical bindings that enforce the oaths they have taken to Tirnaeve, the Compact, and the Master of the Anvar'thaine. Most Riders also choose to wear power runes etched into various parts of their bodies to enhance specific powers, give them useful skills, and reduce the potential for magical depletion as the result of repetitive tasks.

Cathal (KA-hal)
Wielder of earth magic and skilled with basic runes.

Chyr (KHEER)
Master of the Anvar'thaine, wielder of air magic, fire magic, and magic-sense.

Daire (DAH-reh)
Wielder of water magic.

Fergal (FER-gal)
Wielder of earth magic with light healing abilities.

Lorcan (LOR-kawn)
Wielder of water magic.

Niall (NYE-uhl)
Wielder of air magic.

Oran (OH-rahn)
Wielder of fire magic.

Ronan (ROH-nawn)
Wielder of earth magic with light healing abilities and magic-sense.

Sean (SHAWN)
Wielder of air magic and magic-sense.

Tuirse (TOOR-shuh)
Wielder of fire magic.

ARTIFACTS, LEGENDS & OTHER EVERFOLK

Celestial Iron and Celestial Steel
The gift of death from the Father of Light/Father of Curses to his Siorai children. Celestial iron can be forged into celestial steel, allowing the Anvar'thaine to administer justice and the priests to end eternal suffering.

Crown of Flame
Change in colour of the Crown of Vines, turning it from glowing green into flames of light dancing through the vines and leaves etched into the skin of the Maiden; symbolises the judgement by the Father of Light that she is worthy; the second of three crowns.

Crown of Moonlight
Change in colour of the Crown of Flame, turning it from flames of light to a steady glow of moonlight and renewal; symbolises the sacrifice of the Maiden and the vows of service she is taking in her role as the new Cailleach Queen of Alba Scoria.

Crown of Vines
A glowing crown of green vines and leaves that appears on the brow of the Maiden, a symbol of the Land's coronation and the Maiden's worthiness; the first of the three crowns she will need to become the Cailleach Queen.

Hollow Crown
Crown forged by the runesmiths of the High King of Tirnaeve and worn by the chosen Siorai consort of the Cailleach Queen, a former Rider of the Anvar'thaine.

Lannraig (LAHN-rik)
Child who came too close to the magic of the Veil, lost her eyesight, and became a seer.

Oathbands
Special runes magically etched in rows on the arms of the Anvar'thaine to enforce the oaths they've taken.

Power Runes
Runes magically etched into a Siorai's skin over time, enabling the use of a specific magic at a single touch with minimal cost in magical depletion.

Riadan (REE-uh-dawn)
Daire's sister, a talented runesmith in Tirnaeve.

Sword of the Anvar'thaine (an-var-THAYN)
Magical sword given by the Father of Light to the Master of the Anvar'thaine. Administers one of the tests of Sovereignty and opens specific doorways between worlds.

The Veil
The barrier that separates the Otherworld of Tirnaeve from the mortal realms, including Alba Scoria.

Veilstones
Magical crystals that channel magic from Tirnaeve.

PLACES (IN ORDER OF APPEARANCE)

Dunhaelic (doon-HAY-lik)
The Fortress of the Moon, home of Flora and the High Chiefs of Clan Domhnall since the Sun King murdered the Cailleach Queens and forced the chiefdom to pass through the male line and abandon the former strongholds in the Sacred Isles.

Sacred Wood
Ancient grove with religious and healing significance to the Domhnall Clan, cut through by a military road built by the Sun King to subjugate the Highlands.

Culodur (KOO-luh-dur)
Site of the last battle in the Highland Risings, a major defeat for the rebel king.

Eireen (AY-reen)
Neighbouring mortal realm across the Western Sea.

Galia (GAH-lee-uh)
Neighbouring mortal realm across the Eastern Sea.

Glen Colm (glen KOLM)
Valley with strategic position and summer grazing for Dunhaelic Keep.

Ben Aran (ben AH-ran)
High mountain and strategic retreat near Dunhaelic Keep.

Caelsolas (KAYL-soh-las)
Former capital and residence of the Sun King.

Dunfithic (DOON-FIH-thik)
Current capital and residence of the Raven Queen.

Muilean (MOO-lyen)
Sea island in Alba Scoria once sacred to the Cailleach Queens, site of the Cailleachan on Beltane Eve when a Maiden was tested to become the Queen.

Ehrugael (EH-roo-gail)
Far western territory in the Highlands in Alba Scoria.

Glaschu (GLAS-uh-khoo)
City in the Lowlands that Camhrain of Locharn saved from being sacked by the rebel army.

Aknacaery (AK-nuh-KAY-ree)
Seat of the Camhrain Clan, loyal supporters of the rebel king.

Dun Uilleum (doon OOL-yum)
Stronghold and prison of the Raven Queen in the Great Glen.

Loch Seil (lokh SEEL)
Long loch between the interior Highlands and Ehrugael.

Peathan Pass (PAY-ahn)
Pass between Aknacaery and Ehrugael

Loch Airceig (lokh ERR-kyeg)
Loch leading past Aknacaery towards the Peathan Pass.

Glen Fhionain (glen YO-nin)
Valley in Ehrugael where the rebellion began.

Bhoradail House (VOR-uh-dal)
Manor in Ehrugael near the route around Loch Seil.

Gleannadail (GLAN-uh-dal)
Manor in Ehrugael occupied by the Butcher after the Domhnall branch chief who owned it was taken to Dun Uilleum for supporting the rebel king.

Castle Tchirum (CHEE-rum)
Ruined Domhnall castle near the island of Muilean.

Loch Moadar (lokh MOH-dar)
Large sea loch (inlet) around Castle Tchirum leading to the Sound of Muilean and the sea between Alba Scoria and the neighbouring realm of Eireen.

Altar of the Moon
Ancient ritual stone tied to the Great Mother; locus for vows, blood, and rebirth rites

Loch of Rebirth
Location of the Altar of the Moon and part of the ritual for the testing of the Maiden before she can become the new Cailleach Queen.

ACKNOWLEDGEMENTS

Book ideas can take many years to simmer. I've been fascinated by the history and characters of the Jacobite Risings since middle school, but the spark for *The Crown of Moonlight* goes back to a conversation at a book festival a decade ago. It took that long for me to get over the fear of writing a fantasy— never mind a historical fantasy. I owe so many thanks to the village who helped me pull up my big girl pants and try.

Thank you to everyone who picks up this book and reads. It means everything to be able to share this story with you.

An enormous *thank you* goes to Amy Eversley for her keen editorial eye, to Nora Reed for making sure the UK English was correct, and to Carol, Jaqueline, and Deejah for beta reading.

Endless gratitude to Arsalan Ali for designing a gorgeous cover and the interior graphics, to Irene Adam for the beautiful map, and to Saleem Ahmad for bringing my website back from the dead and truly going above and beyond.

Thank you to Jodi Meadows for input on the early idea and bits and pieces on the way. Her advice is always gold.

As always, more *thank yous* go to my husband, for his patience, my mother for continued support and encouragement, Phinn for giving up long walks on the days I couldn't stop typing, and Izzy and Maya for their helpful cat-edits.

Finally, the biggest thank you of all goes to my daughter, Hailey, who got me out of my book slump by getting me excited about romantic fantasy again, encouraged my odd little book idea, nudged me when I was ready to give up, slogged through the world-building and early draft, and gave me incredible reader notes.

www.ingramcontent.com/pod-product-compliance
Lightning Source LLC
Chambersburg PA
CBHW021120260626
47169CB00005B/1364